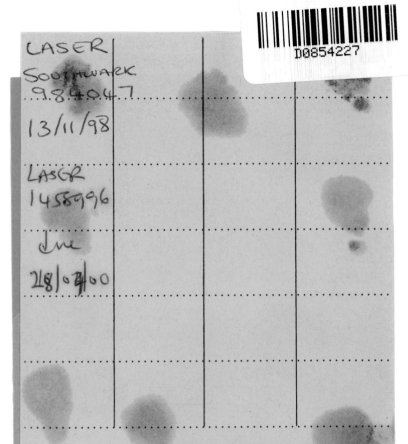

The Final Terror

The Final Terror

James Adams

Michael Joseph
LONDON

100925778

MICHAEL JOSEPH LTD

Published by the Penguin Group
27 Wrights Lane, London W8 5TZ, England
Viking Penguin Inc., 375 Hudson Street, New York, New York 10014, USA
Penguin Books Australia Ltd, Ringwood, Victoria, Australia
Penguin Books Canada Ltd, 10 Alcorn Avenue, Toronto, Ontario, Canada M4V 3B2
Penguin Books (NZ) Ltd, 182–190 Wairau Road, Auckland 10, New Zealand

Penguin Books Ltd, Registered Offices: Harmondsworth, Middlesex, England

First published 1991

Printed in England by Clays Ltd, St Ives plc
Filmset in Monophoto Times $11\frac{1}{2}/13$ pt

A CIP catalogue record for this book is available from the British Library

ISBN 0 7181 3475 3

The moral right of the author has been asserted

The quotations on pages 217 and 218 from *Winnie-the-Pooh* by A. A. Milne are
reprinted by kind permission of the publishers, Methuen Children's Books Ltd, and
Dutton Children's Books, a division of Penguin Books USA Inc. (copyright 1926 by
E. P. Dutton, renewed 1954 by A. A. Milne).

To René

Author's Note

This book is a work of fiction. Names, characters, places and incidents are either the product of my imagination or used fictionally. However, the threat posed by product contamination is real and the likely consequences of a serious terrorist attack using poison have been wargamed in the way described here. Similarly, the tactics used by special forces, the workings of the intelligence communities and the relationship between governments and their spies are closely based on reality, but I have been careful to change a number of methods set out here so that if any criminal or terrorist tried to benefit from ideas outlined in this book, he or she would be unsuccessful.

James Adams
Hampshire, England, 1991

Acknowledgments

A number of people were kind enough to read the manuscript to check it for accuracy. I would like to thank Glyn Volans for sharing his expert knowledge of poisons; Chris gave me an insight into the workings of air-to-air missiles and modern flight systems; Seamus Clarke has extraordinary knowledge about the workings of the financial markets; Oliver Stanley of County NatWest explained how put options work; Robert Pleming helped make the workings of intelligence computers understandable; Harvey and SuEllen Fried shared some fine times in Kansas City; a number of people helped with descriptions of the workings of some aspects of intelligence and I am particularly grateful to Ian, David and Harry; Dave and Mark helped with weapons and tactics; Jack shared his knowledge of Washington; a great man explained the relevance of Pooh; Alistair Stewart was very patient; Geordie Greig and Sally Soames were very encouraging. René was wonderfully supportive. She took the trouble to read every word and I paid attention to what she said.

July 22, 1982

Beirut

IN ARAB TRADITION, The Night of Destiny, Laylat al-Qadr, is the time when all the trees bow down before God at midnight. It is a time when the children make their wishes, knowing that they will be granted. A time, too, for their parents, who have long since ceased to believe, to murmur their own entreaty – just in case. That night, the prayer for peace was common to young and old.

It was three weeks since the Israelis had begun their siege of West Beirut, nearly two months since the first troops moved over the border into Lebanon. For Dr Marwan Nazari the Night of Destiny was just another night. No joyful family reunions this year, no tea and sticky sweetmeats for the children before they sent up their special prayers.

Instead Dr Nazari was where he had spent most of the past three weeks, in the makeshift operating theatre of the Sabra Hospital. Midnight had come and gone with only the fortunate few remembering to make a muttered imprecation to a God who had apparently forgotten them all. The night had been spent like every other in recent weeks, tending the injured and the dying and comforting the relatives of the dead, each action punctuated by the crump and vibration of falling artillery shells.

Nazari bent over the small form of a horribly burned child. By the flickering light of the hurricane lamp – electricity had once again been cut off by the Israelis – Nazari could hardly recognize the shape before him as human. A tug on what had once been a finger and the flesh peeled back up the arm like the skin off a ripe peach.

With a sigh filled with exhaustion and sadness, the doctor

turned from the unconscious form to the nurse by his side. 'Phosphorus. Without transfusions, it's hopeless. He'll be dead within the hour.'

Nazari moved to the next stretcher, this time to treat a young teenage PLO fighter who had been hit by shrapnel. The longer the siege lasted, the more of these RPG kids (so called because of their training in firing rocket-propelled grenades) he was having to treat. There seemed no end to the death and no end to the children, men and women who were prepared to take up arms for the Palestine Liberation Organization against the Israeli invaders.

To Dr Nazari it all seemed almost unbearably pointless. Born in Jaffa and educated at Tel Aviv University, after graduation twenty years earlier he had left Israel for the north. It had all been so clear. He was one of the few of his generation to qualify as a doctor and his skill was prized. He believed passionately in the Palestinian cause and vowed to devote his life to his people. Back then, when the Palestine Liberation Organization was just making its presence felt with hijacking and kidnappings, violence seemed to offer a way forward.

For a doctor, the grenade and the machine-gun were not a serious option, but commitment meant making his home in a refugee camp, the symbol of Palestinian oppression. Dr Nazari lived in Sabra in West Beirut just down the road from the PLO headquarters in Fakhani. Sabra needed him, and his slim figure with the small half-moon gold spectacles perched on the end of his nose was a familiar and welcome sight striding down the narrow alleyways and hidden cul-de-sacs of the camp.

But as his tall frame stooped, his spectacles changed from half-moon to the more conventional full frame and his hair became flecked with grey, so his passion cooled. He supposed that having to deal with the results of failure – the sickness, the malnutrition and even the occasional wounded or dying terrorist – simply sapped his commitment. Killing, he now recognized, would never produce a new Palestine.

It was ironic, he reflected, that a man committed only to peace and making people well should be spending so much time in the middle of war watching so many die.

The moaning wail of the air-raid siren broke across his thoughts. Since the siege began, its chilling ululation had replaced the call of the muezzin to prayer as the signal to break off work. But now the mosque offered no sanctuary from the rockets and bombs of the Israeli air force. Instead, the staff at Sabra took it in turns to hide in the cellars of the café one hundred yards up the road. Tonight, it was Dr Nazari's turn to hide.

Pausing only to gather his wife Lina from the dispensary, Dr Nazari hurried downstairs and out of the hospital entrance. His pace quickened as the urgent call of the siren seemed to get louder and his subconscious raised the memory of the last air raid: the low scream of the jet rising to a crescendo, the instinctive ducking and then almost immediately the roar of the explosions.

Out through the hospital gates now sagging open, their white stucco posts pockmarked with shrapnel, and right into Martyrs Road. Fifty yards to the junction then another left into Chatila Street, past Doukhy's grocery store, now a blackened ruin, to the corner and the Hamda café and the illusion of safety.

Three weeks earlier this journey would have been a pleasant excursion for a coffee, some idle gossip with old Hamda and a return to work with everyone that he passed offering a cheerful greeting. Now the twenty-thousand-strong population of Sabra had been decimated, with only the stubborn, the soldiers and the critically wounded remaining.

Just half a mile from the PLO headquarters, Sabra had been a target not just for precision artillery fire but also for all those near misses by the air force. The result was devastation. Few of the streets remained untouched and few, if any, families had not suffered casualties. In the short journey from hospital to shelter Dr Nazari was shocked to see that there was now not a single building left intact along what had once been a city street bustling with life, laughter and trade.

The doorway of the shelter faced on to the main street to the right of what had once been the Makdadi market, now a gutted husk, bombed and then looted by the hungry camp residents. Two doors further up was Doukhy's, which by some miracle of PLO sponsorship had managed to keep its doors open and some stock on the shelves.

Dr Nazari and Lina hunched down into the darkness against the concrete floor. The cellar was a hundred feet square with a roof too low for the doctor to stand upright. In any event there was nowhere to go and no way of moving. The room was already filled with men, women and children, the light from the occasional hurricane lamp creating surreal shadows in the dust and darkness.

The shelter had become a second home to many of the camp residents and, with the resilience of all war veterans, they had quickly adapted. One group was playing Scrabble, another Trivial Pursuit. A group of small children was being led in songs by their teacher, the words altered specially for the occasion:

> *Dansons la Capucine,*
> *Y a pas de courant chez nous;*
> *Y en a chez la voisine,*
> *Mais ce n'est pas pour nous.*

(Let us dance the capucine, there's no power in our house; there's some at the neighbour's, but there's none for us.)

One hundred and twenty kilometres to the south Uri Dan pushed forward the throttle to engage the afterburner on his F-16A Fighting Falcon and the aircraft began a thirty-degree climb out over the Mediterranean. The single Pratt and Whitney engine developing nearly 25,000 pounds of thrust responded instantly and Dan was pushed into his seat for the sixty seconds it took to reach 6,000 feet, the classic attack altitude for pilots heading north. A twitch of the control column in his right hand brought the fighter around in a right turn to head north along the Lebanese coast.

Flying missions into Lebanon over the past two months had proved an extraordinary experience. One of Israel's elite combat pilots, Dan had trained to attack ground targets in Syria, Egypt or Iraq and for air-to-air combat against modern MiG fighters. That was a pilot's war, where tactics and training are everything, where battles are fought on video screens and missiles make the kill which is marked only by a disappearing blip on the radar screen.

Lebanon was different. The whole war had been fought in

4

an area one hundred kilometres by seventy-five, a distance covered in only five minutes by the F-16. Life had compressed into a series of ten- and fifteen-minute snapshots where the adrenalin rush of take-off and run in to target had been matched by the concentration of effort required to pick out single targets among the city streets viewed from around 2,000 feet at 600 mph. It was, Dan thought to himself, like using a Formula One racing car to go a hundred yards down the street to post a letter.

There had been no air-to-air combat for the Syrians had kept out of the conflict. Instead Dan had found himself flying sortie after sortie against ground targets with only the ineffectual SAM missiles fired by the Palestinians as a threat.

As the war dragged on, Dan found himself questioning the sense of it all. A professional, he revolted against this wasted use of his skills. Then, too, each time he returned from a sortie he saw the results of his work on the television news. This was not the high profile, glamorous world he thought he belonged to, where victory was marked by courage, skill and triumph over a worthy opponent. This was the world of the grunts, the foot soldiers who fight the dirty ground war where cities are targets to be captured and civilians simply 'collateral damage'.

This mission, like so many of the others, was a quick in and out lasting no more than ten minutes. Intelligence had come in overnight from an advanced reconnaissance team that had infiltrated through the PLO lines into west Beirut. The PLO had accessed another of their underground arms dumps hidden inside the refugee camps. The target was inside the Sabra camp, precisely marked by grid co-ordinates that had already been fed into the aircraft's weapons computer and by a detailed description of the target given by the intelligence officer in the pre-mission briefing.

Visual descriptions were only part of the picture, however. The F-16 is designed so that the pilot lies down at an angle of thirty degrees and has to roll the aircraft to see anything of the ground at all. Instruments and computers complement his eyes and the array of buzzers, bleeps and tones from the different electronic warning systems constantly assail his ears.

Dan depended on them to tell him not only his speed, course and height but time to target and the best moment to fire his weapons.

Already, three minutes into the flight, Dan pressed right rudder and used the stick in his right hand to throttle back and bring the fighter on to its new heading towards land and the target. His left hand moved over the weapons control pad while the head-up display unit in front reflected speed, course and time-to-target information.

Suddenly, a shrill and intermittent bleeping sounded through his headphones, indicating a SAM missile had been launched and was on its way. Dan could feel the sudden surge of adrenalin bringing a flush to his cheeks, a heightened sensitivity to his fingertips. The mission computer had been programmed automatically to dispense decoys once incoming missiles had been detected, but instinct and a healthy fear impelled Dan to move his left hand away from the throttle to press the large red button that manually threw out chaff to left and right of his aircraft – cynicism born of experience had reduced his faith in the computer's brainless automation.

The electronic counter-measures automatically began responding to the perceived threat, throwing out a blanket of invisible impulses to confuse any missile guidance system. The chaff began ejecting at three-second intervals to distract the missile's radar guidance system.

Dan moved the control column left and back so that the aircraft began a tight bank to the left leaving the chaff floating down over the ascending missile. As the aircraft began to pull extra g's, his pressure suit automatically inflated around his thighs and stomach to keep the blood from draining to his feet. Looking back over his shoulder Dan watched as the missile sped towards the block of sky where his aircraft had been only seconds earlier. In the telescoped time that is so much a part of air combat it seemed several moments before he knew the decoys had worked and the missile sped harmlessly up through the chaff and into the heavens.

Time to target now thirty seconds. His left hand armed the two Maverick AGM air-to-surface missiles hanging on pylons underneath each wing. The small radar and electro-optical display panel between his knees showed a clear black and white picture of the city ahead. Fifteen seconds and, as the fighter descended, the image became sharper. A twist of the control dial and the image sprang into focus bringing the outlines of the Sabra camp into the frame. A further twist and the image telescoped along the line of the preset co-ordinates.

Five seconds and his eyes flickered rapidly between the radar image between his knees and the head-up display projected on to the cockpit window in front of him through which he could see the distant image of the target area. The television camera in the missile warhead was now relaying a clear picture of the target. A twist of the control column brought the image into the centre of the large cross on the screen. Out of the blur came the distinctive image of a building. Dan's hand did not hesitate. The hovering thumb descended to press the button on the control stick, locking the Maverick's television camera on the target. An instant later, his thumb pressed the FIRE button.

Dan felt the slight shudder through his aircraft as the rocket ignited, blasting free of the launch rails. The image on the screen in front of him flickered then disappeared as the connection between aircraft and missile severed. But Dan's job was done, the missile was locked on to its target, its computer driving it down towards the image that Dan had locked into its memory at more than 2,000 mph.

The instant the first missile left to travel down its invisible tramlines to its target, Dan brought the image of the camera in the second missile to his screen. With a rapid and well-practised movement that perfectly co-ordinated hand, eye and fingers, Dan took a few heartbeats to train, slave and fire the second missile.

In his cockpit Dan pulled gently back on the control column to push-turn the aircraft on its side in a gentle curve over the city as his plane followed the faster missiles to their target. At first his eyes could not define the image detected by the sensitive camera in the missile's nose. Then a group of buildings magnified to become a single building, then a doorway and then simply a double explosion as first one and then the second rocket hit the target.

7

Pulling the control stick back towards him Dan banked the aircraft in a tight turn and brought the Fighting Falcon round on a course south towards home, another mission successfully completed.

In their underground shelter, Dr Nazari, his wife Lina and the thirty others huddled together had no warning of their deaths. A half-heard noise of a jet engine, a millisecond impression of a shattering of the calm cellar air and then nothing.

The two 57-kg shaped explosive charges punched through the cellar door and exploded against the concrete floor. In the confined space the explosives caused instant devastation, first snuffing out the lives of all those sheltering from the war above and then bringing the full weight of the building down to create an instant, mass grave for the doctor and his patients.

Up the street to the right of the ruin of Makdadi's market, the PLO fighters hunched protectively over the rockets, rifles and boxes of ammunition hidden in the cellar of Doukhy's grocery shop. The vibrations from the Mavericks exploding had brought down clouds of dust from the ceiling but no real damage had been done.

The Israelis may have got their intelligence wrong this time but tonight, under cover of darkness, this arms dump would be moved once again. It had been a lucky escape.

July 3, 199-

Sana'a, North Yemen

YASSER ARAFAT WAS late, as usual. The Chairman of the Palestine Liberation Organization had left Bahrain two hours earlier for Sana'a in his Mystère-Falcon 200 executive jet, already behind schedule for the last, critical, meeting of his Gulf tour.

He had come to hate these shuttle trips. Twenty years ago, he had had to use the threat of terrorism on the Arab leaders themselves just to get an audience. Then they had come to understand that he had power and they began to treat him with some respect. Now, the wheel had come around once again.

This trip had been the usual rush: five countries in three days. The last stop had only been added to the agenda yesterday. After he had arrived in Bahrain and had just settled into the guest suite at the Presidential palace, a messenger had arrived requesting an urgent audience. The courier handed over a package. Inside was a handwritten letter from George Habash, leader of the Popular Front for the Liberation of Palestine, requesting a meeting in Sana'a the next day.

'The revolution is faltering,' the letter read. 'You and I both know that something must be done or all that we have worked for will be lost for ever. I have a plan which offers us hope. At last we will get our homeland at a price we can afford. You must come.'

Typical George, Arafat thought to himself. All drama and intrigue. Relations between the two men had been strained for years since Habash broke away from Arafat's Fatah to form the PFLP. However, since the Intifada, they had grown

9

closer, united in their hopes that a strategy of unarmed protest on the West Bank and Gaza could, finally, transform their fortunes.

The messenger was sent off to convey the Chairman's acceptance of the invitation.

The trip so far had underlined the truth of Habash's message. Arafat's sensitive political antennae had detected the changing atmosphere. In a world where the unspoken gesture has more significance than the fulsome words of greeting, Arafat recognized that once again he was a man with a begging bowl and this time he had no guns to hold at the heads of his Arab friends.

He once again cursed his stupidity in not condemning the actions of that madman Saddam Hussein. When the Iraqi president had marched into Kuwait in 1990, Arafat had seen the act not as a threat to the Arab world but as another opportunity for the PLO. He had calculated that, once again, he could portray himself as a mediator, a champion for peace. To do that he had to take the middle ground and the Sauds and all the rest of them had never forgiven him. He had not only miscalculated the Arab reaction but he had completely underestimated the strength of the American response. The result was not Arafat the mediator but Arafat the supporter of the Butcher of Baghdad, Arafat the man who turned against the Arabs who had fed and supported him and his organization for so many years.

He sighed at the memory. It had been a bad mistake, one of the few he had made in walking the tightrope between terrorist and diplomatist. Nothing much had been said once the Iraqi crisis had faded but the little things that meant such a lot in the Arab world were noticeably absent. His calls were not returned, the welcoming committees on the tarmac when his plane touched down were either absent or staffed by low-level functionaries.

At Riyadh, there had been no welcoming committee at the airport, no guard of honour and no sirens to escort him to his meeting with King Fahd. He had had to make do with an interview with the Foreign Minister, who easily promised cash and political support but clearly meant to give neither. It was the same story in Kuwait and the Emirates with the final insult being reserved for the last stop, Bahrain.

Breakfast with the ruler Sheik Issa had gone on and on. Issa was rightly named The Teapot, Arafat laughed to himself, with his almost completely spherical shape and huge nose. The meeting had been worth it, though: another $20 million promised to underwrite the faltering Intifada in Israel. However, that would be the last drop squeezed from the wily old Sheik.

'You must realize, old friend, that I cannot keep pouring money into your dream,' Issa had confided to him. 'For five years now you have been promising us progress and we have seen none.'

'But Highness,' protested Arafat, 'every Western government has recognized the justice of our cause. I have spoken again at the United Nations. The Israelis will be forced to talk to us. We must just be patient and keep up the pressure.'

'This time I will help. But I must say to you that I will need more than your reassurances next time. I – and I tell you here in all honesty that I speak for my neighbours as well – want to see more action, not promises.'

It was not just the implied threat but the choice of messenger that told Arafat he and his organization were becoming bit players on the Middle East political scene. Sheik Issa had never been a serious powerbroker in Arab politics and if he had been chosen to spell out the future then the calculated insult had even more force.

Just past noon, the whine of the jet's turbofan engines changed to a deeper note as the aircraft began its final approach to Sana'a airport. As the plane taxied forward, Arafat pushed aside the hairy pink blanket that accompanied him on all his travels, stood up and moved to the rear of the aircraft, past the ever-present boxes of weapons for use in a last stand should the Israelis ever attack the plane, and into the lavatory. He should look his best for this meeting.

The face staring back at him from the small mirror made a depressing sight. Exercise, he thought to himself, or you'll just become one huge chin. He ran his hand over the greying beard that created his unshaven image. The pictures always gave the impression of a dirty and unkempt man but as so often they lied. He was fastidious, even vain, and grew a

11

beard because time spent shaving was time wasted in a full day. But the streaks of grey and black in his beard always made him look unshaven. It offended his vanity but he was politician enough to realize that it helped his Man-of-the-People image.

Now, he reached into his Adidas sports bag, which reporters always said held a Skorpion sub-machine-gun, and pulled out a small manicure set. With the scissors he carefully tidied the stray hairs from his beard, paying special attention to the moustache where he found the two hairs that had been tickling his nose five minutes earlier. Refreshed by a splash of cold water, he dried his face, took off his black and white headdress revealing a head that was completely bald except for a few tendrils of white hair above his ears. Drawing a freshly laundered keffiyeh from his holdall, he carefully adjusted it on his head, placed a cravat of the same black and white check around his neck and, surveying himself carefully in the mirror, grunted in satisfaction.

The jet drew to a halt outside the light thrown by the airport terminal. As Arafat stepped out of the aircraft, three Mercedes 300 saloons with tinted glass windows drew up. Arafat always travelled in a three-car convoy and chose a different car on each journey to improve his chances of survival should the assassins strike.

This time, he settled in the back seat of the lead car and waited while his bodyguards and aides unloaded equipment from the plane, including the two fax machines which followed him everywhere. They were the equivalent of the American President's Football, the briefcase carried by a Marine which follows a few steps behind the president and contains the alert codes to launch the US nuclear arsenal. With a fax, Arafat boasted he could be in touch with his followers all over the world within minutes.

The thirty-minute drive through the green countryside brought home to Arafat once again the paradoxes of modern Yemeni society. Without oil, a country which centuries ago had ruled one of the world's biggest empires through its dominance of the frankincense trade was forced now to rely on handouts from governments to the east and west.

'This country provides a parable for our own people,'

Arafat commented, turning to Hani al-Hassan, who sat beside him. 'When the Queen of Sheba lived here this was one of the most powerful and civilized countries in the world. They gave us the world's first skyscrapers. They had wonderful art and the most fabulous gardens in the Arab world. And now look at them. A proud people living on their memories. They failed because they refused to adapt and they had nothing to believe in except the past.'

Hassan nodded in agreement. Reinforcement was his role in Arafat's life and, over the years, Hassan – known to other PLO leaders as The Crawler – had become skilled at his job of massaging the Chairman's ego and ensuring his own survival. Officially his title was Chief of Foreign Relations but his real role was confidant and courtier to Arafat.

'You may be right, Old Man,' he replied, using the affectionate title given to Arafat by his close advisers. 'But I trust no one in this country deserted by Allah. They would sell us all if they could see some advantage. Dollars or roubles wouldn't matter to them.'

'That weakness is our strength,' Arafat argued. 'This is the only country outside the Eastern bloc where we can meet with some guarantee of security. This meeting is too important to be compromised.'

The Mercedes drew up at the marble-fronted entrance to the Taj Hotel on the appropriately named Revolution Avenue. Flanking the doorman were two Arabs dressed in shapeless grey suits, stubby Skorpion machine-guns tucked under their arms, walkie-talkies hanging from their hips. As Arafat stepped from the car, one of them brought his radio to his mouth and murmured a few words.

Arafat moved up the steps into the vaulted reception area flanked by his four bodyguards. There was a tremendous bang and an immediate aftershock that vibrated through the hotel floor. Arafat disappeared beneath his bodyguards as he was forced to the floor. The two guards by the door dropped to the ground, the distinctive click of safety catches matching the movement of gun barrels as they searched the street for the expected attack.

But all their questing guns found was the beginnings of one of Yemen's summer rainstorms. As the embarrassed bodyguards picked themselves off Arafat, the rain gathered in intensity so that within seconds visibility was cut to a few feet and the unpaved road became a muddy stream. Arafat was dusting himself down and adjusting his keffiyeh, which had been pushed over one ear by his over-protective body-guards, when George Habash, arms stretched wide in front of him, moved down the stairs to greet him.

Habash was one of the lions of the Palestinian movement. Born in Haifa, he graduated from the American University in Beirut but gave up a career as a doctor to devote his life to the Palestinian cause. He formed the PFLP after the ignominious defeat of the Arabs by the Israelis in the 1967 war. It was Habash above all others who understood the importance of international opinion for the Palestinian cause. He orchestrated the first hijacks and internationalized the cause by drawing terrorists from Japan, Spain and Latin America to fight under his flag. It was Habash who organized the Lod airport massacre in 1972 when twenty-six people were killed and eighty wounded by terrorists from the Japanese Red Army. After that attack he had spelled out his terrorist philosophy: 'Killing one Jew far from the field of battle is more effective than killing a hundred Jews on the field of battle, because it attracts more attention.'

He was a big man, over six feet tall, and his liking for sweets had once ballooned his weight to over fifteen stone. But since a massive stroke in 1980 had nearly killed him, a rigid fat-free diet had peeled the pounds from his frame so that flesh now hung in folds on his face and neck.

As his body shrivelled so had his revolutionary vision. The international Marxist revolution which had once seemed a reality was just a distant memory; the great names of ter-rorism who had bolstered his politics with their guns were mostly dead or in jail; and the dream of a Palestinian home-land that had drawn thousands of young fighters to die for the cause had faded amid the practical pragmatism of today's youth who seemed to prefer the material comforts of America and Saudi Arabia to the privations of the covert world. Even the famous Habash rhetoric that had stirred men to fight to the death had mellowed in the face of experience. Yet Arafat noticed a new spring in the old man's step, the hint of inner tension that revealed a glimpse of the Habash of old.

14

The two men embraced each other, exchanging kisses, as if the touch of lips to cheek would create a new bond between them.

'Welcome, Old Man. Welcome,' said Habash, putting an arm around the Chairman's shoulder. 'Come. I have a surprise for you. A pleasant surprise, I hope.'

At the top of the stairs, Habash drew Arafat down the corridor to the right and stopped before the ornately carved double doors leading to the President Saleh suite. Arafat paused and then, as Habash smiled encouragement and gestured Arafat forward, he pushed open the doors which opened into the room.

Stepping forward, Arafat looked to left and right and then stopped abruptly, turning angrily to Habash. 'What is the meaning of this? This is a trap. You have betrayed me.'

As the tone of the Chairman's voice reached his bodyguards, they moved towards him, hands reaching inside their jackets.

'Wait.' The peremptory note in Habash's voice surprised the bodyguards, who paused, looking to Arafat for guidance. Before Arafat could move Habash spoke again. 'Do nothing, old friend. We are not here to harm you, I promise. We are all unarmed,' Habash reassured him, sweeping his jacket back to reveal an empty shoulder holster.

With a flick of his hand Arafat waved his bodyguards away and turned back to the room. His angry stare confirmed the first, frightening impression: seated at a teak conference table was the aristocracy of Palestinian terrorism. Moderate and militant, politician and gunman had gathered in this one room. Arafat's eyes moved round the room, acknowledging friend and foe alike.

He nodded to Naif Hawatmeh, the Christian Arab leader of the militant Democratic Front for the Liberation of Palestine. Arafat's intelligence network had recently told him that Hawatmeh had been having secret talks with the Israeli left. On his right Majid Mohsin, the leader of Saiqa, the Thunderbolt. Known to friends and enemies alike as The Persian for his love of exotic carpets, Mohsin was dressed in an expensive Armani suit and smoking a thin Havana cigar. His hedonism had always revolted Arafat who saw him as a dilettante using the cause for his own ends.

15

Even Ahmed Jibril, who hadn't spoken to George for fifteen years, had been persuaded to come. As leader of the PFLP-General Command, Jibril had never lost his taste for terror although some of his schemes had recently seemed rather bizarre. Hot air balloons and motorized hang gliders, Arafat laughed to himself.

As far as Arafat could see, the only figure from the movement missing was Abu Nidal, the one terrorist from those early days who had eschewed moderation and become steadily more extreme. Arafat himself had put a price on Nidal's head and sentenced him to death in a PLO show trial. Nidal had responded by trying on a number of occasions to kill the PLO Chairman. Even Habash had balked at bringing Nidal to the party.

The seat at the head of the table had diplomatically been left for the Chairman and he moved across to sit down, beckoning to Hani al-Hassan to draw up a chair next to him. Habash moved to the other end of the table to sit next to a young man Arafat did not recognize.

'OK, you've got me here. Now will someone please explain what this is all about.' Arafat glared around the table to find the person who would risk the Chairman's wrath and speak first.

It was Habash who took up the challenge. 'Chairman, I would first like to apologize for bringing you here at such short notice, but I could think of no way to get you into this room with these people except by a trick.'

'Tricks are for children and we are all adults here,' grunted Arafat. 'But perhaps you can conjure up some coffee.'

The feeble joke raised a few smiles and, relieved that some of the tension had eased, Habash continued. 'The last time most of us met together was in Tunis when we agreed to launch the Intifada. We all hoped it would bring about the revolution for which we have been fighting for so long. And what has happened? After the first months of triumph when the world came to watch the sacrifice our young people made in front of the Israeli tanks and guns, the pot went off the boil. The media became bored, the Israelis increased the pressure and the deaths climbed. The Iraqi invasion of Kuwait played into the Israelis' hands and while the West and the other Arabs moved against Saddam they took the opportunity to strike against our people.'

There were some mutters of disaffection at the recollection of the massacre of the Palestinians on Temple Mount in October 1990 and the free use of guns by the Israelis against the unarmed protesters in the past years.

'May I remind you that as of yesterday 2,850 of our young people have died and thousands have been injured and for what? Nothing.' He glared around the table challenging anyone to take issue with his analysis. Not a voice was raised. 'The Israelis may talk of compromise but they still kill our people. The Americans talk of a new world order but where is our invitation to the peace talks? The Sauds, the Syrians and the rest will join the celebrations claiming a Palestinian state as their victory. But it is we who have that right, we who have sacrificed a lifetime to the cause. They may think they can do a deal without the PLO, but they are wrong. It is our heritage, our future they are discussing, and we must control our own destiny.

'But the Intifada is running out of sacrificial lambs to send to the slaughter. We cannot get the recruits who will die for the cause when they see no progress being made. At the same time, if we arm the Intifada we will lose what little credibility the movement has left. We could turn to terrorism but then Western countries are much better at countering that threat. Anyway some of us have got too old or too soft for that kind of thing.' As if by chance the old warrior's eye fell on Mohsin who flushed angrily and made as if to stand up.

Arafat's voice cracked across the room. 'Enough. We are here not to attack each other but to think of better ways of attacking the Israelis. What you say is painful but true. What do you propose we do about it?'

In answer, Habash put his arm across the shoulder of the young man sitting next to him. 'This is Abu Hassan.'

At the sound of the name there was a stirring of interest around the table and even the most experienced of them leaned forward to get a closer look at the man who sat impassively doodling on a white notepad.

'I see that some of you have heard of him. For those of you who have been asleep for the past two years, Abu Hassan

17

runs the Palestine Fighting Arm and is one of the few of the new generation to have come forward to take the mantle of terrorism from those of us at this table.'

Arafat, too, was curious but was fortunate in facing the man and so did not have to demean himself by leaning forward to study him. Almost alone among today's fedayeen, this man understood the use of terror. His use of high altitude low opening parachutes to land in Tel Aviv and strike deep into the enemy's heart showed imagination and tactical skill. The fact that his two-woman team had managed to kill fifteen Israelis before being killed themselves showed that he could command extraordinary loyalty. A number of other incidents, both in the Middle East and Europe, had secured Hassan's position as leader of the terrorists' favourite force.

Yet even Arafat knew little of the Palestine Fighting Arm. Hassan's security was extraordinary and his source of finances a mystery.

'Comrades.' Habash rapped the table to quell the buzz of conversation. 'I will leave Hassan to explain his scheme to you.'

The young man put down his pencil, laced his fingers together in front of him and leaned forward. His dark brown eyes moved slowly around the table and took in each face as if searching out allies and enemies.

'The purpose of terrorism is to terrorize. All of you know that and all of you in your own ways have done your best to achieve political goals through terrorism. The fact that I am here as a Palestinian to talk to you Palestinians about a future Palestinian state is a tribute to your successes.'

Good, good, thought Habash. A bit of the obvious plus a bit of flattery to keep these sensitive egos happy.

Hassan continued. 'What I would now like to give you is a new definition. The purpose of terrorism is to terrorize those who can influence events. The mistake we have made in the past is to hit targets that in the end don't matter. Attacks at airports, or hijackings of planes and boats, cause individual governments some temporary problems. But people adapt and politicians only respond to each bit of pressure as it is applied. We have all learned that governments are very resilient and we have been unable to keep up the pressure.

'What is needed is something so painful that governments have to dance to our tune. We have to do something that both terrorizes the people and frightens governments in such a way that they have to do what we want.'

He paused to look around and gauge the reaction of his audience. Encouraged by the nods and the apparent lack of any vociferous opposition, he pressed on.

'The only way we can achieve all that is by hitting the Western governments where it really matters. In their pockets. We have to simultaneously terrorize the people and so hurt the business community that the government will be stuck between the rock of the electorate and the hard place of big business. They will have no choice but to agree to our demands.'

Arafat was struck not so much by the words, although they made good sense, but by the way they were delivered. The Chairman had become used to the high-flown rhetoric that tended to mark PLO meetings, the bombastic language that so often disguised fear or inadequacy. Abu Hassan was different. There was none of the exaggerated language, no table-thumping, and the passion was all the clearer for being delivered in such calm, measured tones. Arafat's preliminary assessment was favourable.

'What I propose is this,' Abu Hassan continued. 'Over the next two months, we will use PLO funds to invest in stocks on the New York Exchange. We will invest in Kola Co. and we will also take a position in the commodity market itself. Once the investments are in place, my agents will begin a two-stage poisoning campaign. The first stage will involve poisoning Kola Co. soft drinks in the US and Europe. Once the poison has started to take effect, we will publish our demands.

'The demands will have to be met by a deadline. There will be no negotiation of any kind as there will be no room for compromise.

'I have estimated that the first stage of poisoning will cost the soft drink industry some $5 billion in lost sales. If we plan our attacks carefully and they are spread through a sufficient number of Western countries, there will at the same time be a crisis of confidence in the stock markets worldwide. This has two benefits. First, big business will put pressure on their governments to agree to our demands. Second, we will make a killing in the market.'

Habash interrupted his neighbour. 'Chairman, I took the precaution of taking advice in the financial aspects of the plan and with your permission I would like to ask Ghassan Hussaini to join us.'

Arafat nodded his assent and Habash went to the door, opened it, and called out Hussaini's name. The man who entered looked not like the other terrorists in the room but rather the managing director of a multi-national conglomerate, which is exactly what he was. Dressed in a dark pin-striped Ralph Lauren suit with a Paco Rabanne tie and carrying a Mark Cross leather briefcase, Hussaini looked as if he had stepped straight off Wall Street on his way to lunch at Le Cirque.

Hussaini was in charge of the Palestine National Fund, often known as the PLO Finance Ministry. He controlled assets of $5 billion and an annual income from investments, donations and terrorism of around $1 billion a year. A graduate of Israel's Bir Zeit University, Hussaini had been an investment director with the Arab Bank until he had been headhunted by the PLO.

In three years he had reversed the PLO's annual deficit and devised a new and aggressive investment strategy that had brought in substantial funds. To the men around the table, Hussaini's world was a strange place where profit and loss accounts, traded options and money-market certificates replaced Kalashnikovs and RPGs as the currency of conversation. He was listened to with respect.

'I was asked to look at a scheme to invest our money in such a way as to benefit from a plan to contaminate Kola Co. drinks,' Hussaini began, his precise, dry tones consolidating the air of reality in the meeting. 'In the New York stock market there are a number of ways of buying investments. There are stocks and shares and all kinds of long-term investments that pay interest. But there are also options and it is here we should concentrate our efforts. With options you make an investment by paying a small deposit today gambling that the price will rise or fall by some specific date in the future. You can buy options both in companies and in sectors such as commodities. Normally, options are a crazy gamble but in our case we know that once our campaign starts, the shares in our target companies will collapse. We have eliminated the risk.

'What I propose is this. At present Kola Co. shares stand at around $65. We offer to sell stock in three months' time at $60. We will have no problem getting a contract at that price as the outlook for the market is very healthy at the moment. To commit to the deal we will have to pay a deposit of $1.50 per share. I estimate that if everything goes as we hope, the share price could collapse from $65 to as low as $15. We would then be able to buy the shares at $15 and sell at our preset contract price of $60. I have calculated that an investment of $440 million would give us a profit of just over $13 billion.'

The calm delivery of these astonishing figures made their impact all the more devastating. None of Hussaini's audience had conceived of such sums, let alone been involved in a terrorist operation with such a glittering prize.

'But the Americans will discover what we are doing as soon as we make the investments,' protested Hani al-Hassan.

'Not necessarily,' corrected Hussaini. 'The whole operation will happen quite quickly and as you know we have been investing in America and Europe for many years and have set up companies in Luxembourg, Liechtenstein, the Caymans and Switzerland to handle these transactions. If we spread the money around and invest through different dummy companies with different stockbrokers then it will be months before anyone puts the deals together. By then, it will all be over.'

Taking advantage of the pause in the conversation, Abu Hassan reached underneath the table to produce a black plastic briefcase and withdrew several sheets of paper. He passed them to Habash who took the top copy and then passed it on.

'You will see from the list in front of you that the demands we will make are moderate and reasonable. Indeed, they are broadly in line with what both the Americans and the United Nations have already proposed. That is intentional. If our terrorism is particularly violent and our demands moderate, it will be all the more difficult for governments to resist us.'

Arafat read the list, headed 'Our Demands', printed on a single sheet of white paper:

- A Palestinian state to be established in confederation with Jordan on the West Bank
- The area to be a weapons free zone policed by the United Nations
- In return the Palestinians to recognize Israel's right to exist and agree to abandon all terrorism.

Arafat carefully laid the paper on the table and then, to give himself time to think, reached down to the sports bag beside him and brought out the jar of honey that travelled everywhere with him. He then pulled from his pocket a silver spoon inscribed 'To Abu Amar from Abu Iyad'. Abu Amar was Arafat's nom de guerre and Iyad had been his closest confidant until he was assassinated by the Israelis in 1988. Arafat spooned a large dollop of honey into his mouth, smacked his lips and looked up towards Abu Hassan.

'This is a big gamble you are asking us to take. We are sacrificing an independent Palestinian state and laying down our arms. That is a very high price to pay.'

'But, Chairman, just think if we succeed. We have a homeland, a place for our people.' Abu Hassan leaned forward, both hands now clenched into fists. 'We will have the money to make that homeland rich. In time, who will care about Jordan and its dictator king? We will rule in Amman as well.'

'No.' The single word was shouted down the table by Jibril. 'This is betrayal. We have vowed to destroy the Zionist state and I will not give up our fight to climb into bed with that dwarf from Jordan.'

There was a murmur of support from around the table but Arafat was quick to note that Jibril did not seem to be speaking for the majority. So when the next speaker rose to support him Arafat was ready.

'Jibril is right,' said Abu Abbas, leader of the Palestine

22

Liberation Front, thumping the table with both fists to underline his anger. 'We should fight the Israelis not just with the Intifada in Palestine but with more terror in the world. Our duty is to kill Jews everywhere.'

Arafat stood up and a hush fell on the room. He turned toward Abbas. 'Even if others here have forgotten, I remember the *Achille Lauro*. Your idea of killing Jews was to murder an old American Jew from New York trapped in his wheelchair. I also remember all the empty words shouted by some of those here at the time of the American advance into Saudi Arabia in 1990. We paid heavily for such acts of courage and such brave words,' he added sarcastically.

A master of the theatrical gesture and the carefully timed delivery, Arafat paused, allowing the insult to hit home. He turned back to face his audience.

'That, comrade, is typical of the weakness that has led our movement nowhere in the past twenty years.'

The interruption came from Jibril, normally a natural ally of the hardliners, whose use of the word 'comrade' rather than the more affectionate and conciliatory 'Old Man' or 'Chairman' underlined the philosophical differences that divided the two men.

'You have led our young men to the slaughter of the Intifada and while the widows mourn their children you tell them to be patient, to wait just a little longer.'

Jibril's dark brown eyes seemed to vanish into the fleshy folds of his face as he squinted down the table trying to bring Arafat into focus. He had needed spectacles for the past five years but was too vain to wear them.

'This piece of paper' – he flung the single sheet towards the Chairman – 'is a betrayal of everything we have fought for. The terms are totally unacceptable and will kill what is left of our nation. An unarmed Palestinian state? The Zionists would kill us all. You are asking us to gamble everything on a mission that won't work and even if it does the result should be unacceptable to our people and is certainly unacceptable to me.'

'Ahmed, old friend, you are being too hard and, if I may say so, a little unrealistic.'

The rejoinder came not from Arafat but from his host,

Habash. This discussion, Arafat reflected, was a measure of the movement itself. Jibril the traditionalist was taking a predictable line but Habash, who ten years ago would have marched alongside the hardliner, had become a pragmatist.

'The decision is not so much whether or not we should do this,' Habash continued. 'The real issue is what we should do instead.' Both Abbas and Jibril made to speak and Habash held up his hand to silence them. 'You will tell me that terrorism will work in time. Well, we all saw the effect that the blowing-up of the Pan Am aircraft over Scotland had – an attack organized by you, Ahmed. It achieved nothing because people don't care any more. This plan will kill fewer people but will actually achieve what we want.

'You will tell me that America will turn on Israel in the end. But even after the killings of the Intifada, even after the United States has sided so openly with the Arabs, it has done nothing to force the Zionists to talk to us. And it never will.

'You will even tell me that Israel will realize that compromise is the only answer. But I tell you that is the kind of idealistic nonsense which has got us where we are today, which is nowhere. We must have action if we are going to make progress but it must be action tempered by moderation so that we stand a chance of lining up the Western countries, if not with us, at least against Israel.'

Arafat saw the heads around the table nodding and judged his moment had come. 'The choice is simple: do nothing and our movement will become a small protest group that will probably be no nearer a Palestinian homeland by the end of this century. All of us have given our lives to the cause and we are all facing the failure of our ambitions. It is time to bury our differences and give Abu Hassan the opportunity to give the movement a new momentum. Once we begin there is no chance of any of us denying our involvement and being believed. If we fail, the Americans and the Europeans will desert us for ever and the Israelis will be able to hunt us down. So this will be our final act of terrorism with the Palestinian state as the prize.'

Looking around the table he could see that Habash's allies were clearly with him but the Jibril/Abbas faction remained

unconvinced. Once again, the leaders of the Palestinian movement were in danger of splitting apart. It was time, he
thought, for a bit of compromise.

'Some of you here have seen me as too soft and others say
that I have not been diplomatic enough.' He sighed ex-
pressively, blowing his large lips outward in a typical Arafat
gesture, a kind of Arabic shrug of the shoulders. 'You may
all be right. But today is a time for all of us to come together.
I do not ask for your support, I only ask for your acceptance.
Give Abu Hassan four months for his plan to work. If it
fails we go back to the old ways. If it succeeds we will be
squabbling over which of us becomes Finance Minister of
Palestine.'

It was a classic Arafat compromise. None of his opponents
actually needed to vote with him and those supporting him
did not need to show their hand. The silence around the
table showed that he had bought the time he wanted.

August 6

ALI HASSAN RAMLAWI HAD arrived in Hong Kong two hours earlier from Singapore. The 23-year-old Palestinian was travelling under a different name on a passport supplied by friends in Syrian military intelligence. The passport was clean, its number not registering on any immigration computer.

He had left Tripoli two days earlier on a simple mission to draw money out of a bank account in Hong Kong and then deliver it to a safe deposit box on the railway station at New Delhi. For the highly trained fighter, who was more comfortable with a machine-gun than a bank passbook, more used to an assault course than a comfortable hotel bedroom, the trip was so simple it bordered on the insulting. But he had undertaken it willingly, in part because he thought the mission an opportunity to prove himself to the group and in part because he relished the idea of all the duty-free goods he could pick up during his brief stay in the British colony.

The instructions from his leader had been simple. 'Go to the left-luggage lockers in the lower concourse of the airport. Use this key.' He was handed a small silver key with a black plastic tag and the number 53 painted on it. 'Inside the locker you will find a bank passbook. Take it and go to the main branch of the Hong Kong and Shanghai Bank on Queen's Road and ask to withdraw the $100,000 in US dollars. Then fly on to Delhi and hand over the money.' The leader had paused and in a firmer voice had added, 'You won't see the person but from the start you will be covered just in case anything goes wrong. So don't spend any of the money and don't get seduced by the bright lights.'

The elaborate scheme was all part of the techniques used by any terrorist group to baffle intelligence organizations looking for early signs of a planned attack or of the movement of terrorists from one country to another. Money flows through dummy accounts across international borders and sits waiting to be collected. A courier arrives, withdraws the cash and flies to a third country to finance a terrorist cell. Neither the people receiving the money nor the person picking the cash up have any idea where it came from.

Clutching the red passbook with the bank's black lion crest on the cover, Ali had duly taken a taxi from the airport and been dropped outside the headquarters of the bank. But, trained to kill with machine-gun, pistol or bomb; versed in the rules of safe houses and surveillance, codes and all other branches of clandestine warfare; nothing in his short life had prepared him for this.

Ali had become a terrorist not because he burned with a passion for revenge or a deeply felt political philosophy but simply because his sister had asked him to. Theirs had always been a close relationship in which Annie played the role of the mother he had lost. His mother had died not in an Israeli attack or in the pestilence that was a habitual menace in the camps but in a simple car crash as she was returning from the supermarket. Annie had been the political one, the joiner, the activist. Ali was not by nature a fighter and had no real ambition to be one. He had been happy training alongside his father in the small light engineering shop he ran in Rashidaye.

Then Annie had left 'to stay with friends' in Tunisia. Many people left the camps 'to stay with friends' and nobody ever asked who the friends were or where they lived. She had come back a leaner, harder woman filled with stories of friendship, excitement and opportunities. Killing had not been on the agenda when she first convinced her young brother to join her and her cause. It was more that she was lonely far away from home with the rigorous discipline of the training camp far removed from the rallies and coffee-house politics which had so far made up her experience as an activist.

As ever, Ali was persuaded by Annie and left his home and friends for the Spartan conditions in the Tunisian camp.

Two things quickly brought him to the attention of his trainers: his nascent skills as an engineer which could be turned from soldering broken table legs to designing mines and fragmentation bombs, and his looks. The strong hooked nose, dark eyes and black hair that are the hallmark of the Arab had by an accident of genes passed him by. Instead he looked almost European, with blue eyes and mousy-coloured straight hair framing a Roman nose, which made him into the perfect courier. His Canadian passport had caused no comment as he passed through immigration.

His looks and the tough training in the camp may have apparently turned him into the colourless messenger, but temperament and the overwhelming experience of Hong Kong had, in fact, transformed him into a lonely, terrified and inexperienced youth. To Ali's uncultured mind Hong Kong was an extraordinary place filled with an alien kaleidoscope of noise and colour. Even to the most experienced traveller, Hong Kong is a hybrid city where the sophistication of Europe meets the culture, pride and traditions of the east. Two blocks behind the banking section's soaring monuments to capitalism, Queen's Road, new Hong Kong vanishes into the old where the smell of fried rice replaces car exhaust and the raucous cries of the Chinese hawkers overwhelm the more muted tones of the European businessmen. But Queen's Road not the Chinese quarter was Ali's destination. The taxi passed the gold glass Bank of America building, the blue and grey of the Standard Chartered Bank and pulled up outside the soaring headquarters of the Hong Kong and Shanghai Bank. The building had been designed by the British architect Norman Foster and he had met his brief to produce something revolutionary. From the outside the supporting girders had been joined together to give an impression of wire coathangers piled one on top of the other with acres of reflective glass suspended in between.

Ali walked across the pavement and into the ground floor pedestrian precinct. Following the signs he stepped on to the right-hand escalator and was carried to the first-floor banking hall. The floor of the banking hall was made entirely of glass and Ali stepped tentatively forward to join the queue for the cashiers expecting at any moment to fall through on to the heads of the people walking below.

Standing behind a small round Chinaman who smelled horribly of onions, Ali looked around nervously. He had been unable to spot the cover he had been promised during the drive from the airport and thought he might have more luck in this confined space. But the hall was full of people, a constantly moving mass in which individuals were difficult to pick out, and no one would be stupid enough to stand still and make eye contact as he cast around anxiously.

The queue shuffled slowly forward and, as his time approached, Ali grew increasingly nervous. He had been assured that this would be the easiest part of the whole trip.

'Look, there is nothing to it,' his leader had assured him. 'The bank is used to handing out far larger sums than this. We have never used this account before and there is absolutely no way that anyone can have any suspicions. Just hand in the passbook, ask for the money and you'll be in and out of there in five minutes.'

As always, Ali did exactly as he was told. The smiling Chinese cashier took his red and black book, opened it out at the cover page and slid it into a machine which automatically read its contents. 'This won't take a moment, sir.' The girl smiled reassuringly.

Five floors below, the giant IBM 390 computers registered the information and automatically began a series of pre-programmed checks. In a fraction of a second the computer searched its data banks to find that there was sufficient money in the account, that there had been no similar withdrawals that day and that the signature on the withdrawal slip corresponded with that in the passbook. Then, just before it relayed a flashing green 'OK' sign to the cashier's computer screen, a further specially programmed check was triggered. Two things then happened. First the cashier read a 'Still Processing' signal on her terminal and simultaneously an electronic message was sent from the computer where it merged with the bank's complicated internal security system, then was diverted into the link that connected the bank directly to police headquarters in Armoury Road. From there, it went to a special secure section of the Queen's Road police station just two blocks from the bank.

For the past two weeks, twelve men of the Hong Kong

police Special Duties Unit had been on standby in the Queen's Road police station. The SDU was Hong Kong's equivalent to a US SWAT team or Britain's Special Air Service, by whom they had been trained. Their speciality was hostage rescue and counter-terrorism. Like their foreign counterparts, the SDU kept a low profile and had rarely been seen in the colony. Even their existence was never officially acknowledged, keeping media speculation at maximum and facts to a minimum and therefore leaving tactics and training intact.

Lieutenant Brian Keenan had been briefed to keep his men ready to move at a moment's notice during banking hours until further notice. 'We have received intelligence that terrorists may try to withdraw some money from an account at the Hong Kong and Shanghai Bank branch on Queen's,' his commander had told him. 'A relay has been rigged up so that you will be alerted as soon as a request to take out the cash is made. Your orders are to arrest the people involved as we think they will be able to tell us a great deal. Take no chances and if necessary you are authorized to use force.'

Since then, as so often happened with this kind of work, it had been nothing but boredom and bridge – the SDU holding the record of five consecutive wins in the annual police bridge competition.

Now as the red light began to flash in the holding room on the ground floor of the station, the men moved smoothly into their well-rehearsed routine. Eight of them were already dressed in black fire-resistant coveralls, with webbing belts containing stun grenades, Browning 9 mm automatic pistols, spare magazines and extra rounds for their favoured personal weapon – some chose the Heckler and Koch MP5 machine-gun, others the Remington pump-action shotgun loaded with solid shot for blasting down doors or men, whichever got in the way first. The other four, including Keenan, were casually dressed in civilian clothes. They would go into the bank to confront the terrorists and attempt to arrest them without alarming the other customers.

The entire team carried portable radios with tiny flesh-coloured receivers fitted inside their ears and sensitive throat microphones attached to their jacket collars. A switch to activate the microphones was strapped around each man's right wrist so that a simple squeezing of the palm would allow communication. They could all hear each other and Keenan and his second-in-command could talk to headquarters to receive additional intelligence as they moved towards the target.

Three green Range Rovers were parked twenty yards away from their room and four men piled into each. With sirens silent they drove the two blocks to the bank and pulled up in the identical spot where, ten minutes earlier, Ali had arrived in his taxi. As the eight men in the reserve team moved to cover the entrance and prevent more customers entering the building, Keenan led his four men up the escalator at a run.

For Ali, the easy two-minute wait was turning into five and he was becoming increasingly anxious. The cashier had tried to reassure him that it was only a computer fault which would be swiftly cleared up but his already stretched nerves had begun to scream that this was a trap.

Turning to look back at the escalators, he saw four men suddenly appear one after the other and head at a fast walk in his direction. He had seen in training films at the camp what the Israeli undercover men who worked the West Bank and Gaza looked like and he had been fully briefed on the tactics of groups like the SAS. These men moved with a sense of deadly purpose that instantly marked them as the enemy.

Unarmed and on unknown territory, he turned away from his pursuers and searched frantically for an escape route. As he began to move away from the desk he caught a movement out of the corner of his eye. A woman who had been standing behind him in the queue was reaching into her black shoulder bag. He only had time to take in that she was young, Chinese and with a heavily pockmarked face.

Horrified, he watched as she pivoted, moved into a crouch and drew out a short machine-pistol that she extended in front of her, one hand embracing the trigger and the other gripping the long magazine that extended down towards the floor. He wanted to cry out, to tell her that he was fine, that he did not need her protection, that he did not want to die – anything to stop the clock. He had time to open his mouth to frame the soundless shout but no time for any noise actually to come out.

The four men, who had arrived close together, spread out and in one synchronized movement reached behind their jackets to draw out their Browning pistols.

Before Ali's now terrified gaze, events seemed both to slow down and move at a speed so rapid it was difficult to absorb. As the woman's grip tightened on the trigger, the advancing men shouted the beginnings of a warning and then the first of their bullets struck her in the chest. Her hand convulsively squeezed the trigger even as her body was flung backwards. While still in mid-air, more and more bullets tore into her body, bits of flesh and bone spraying out across the banking hall.

Prompted by the sound rather than the sight before him, Ali's subconscious dragged the image of a calmer time from his childhood when the women used to slap the wet towels against the rocks in his village to wash them as the children played at their feet. With each slap of the towel another bullet found its mark in the woman's body.

The Browning High Power 9 mm semi-automatic pistol is designed to fire its thirteen-round magazine at a rate of forty rounds a minute. The SDU had trained so that they could fire eight times that speed. Each of the four men used half his magazine in what in the confined space of the hall sounded like a continuous roll of fire lasting no more than five seconds.

The deep booming of the Brownings was echoed by the lighter sound of tearing calico as the Uzi, still clutched in the woman's death grip, sprayed in an upward arc through the banking hall. It takes less than a second to fire the full thirty-two rounds from an Uzi but each of the rounds struck a different part of the banking hall as the recoil pushed the lifeless hands of the woman backwards. In a fraction of a second the bullets showed the critical difference between aesthetics and practicality as glass shattered all around the building, spraying thousands of shards down on the panicked customers.

Satisfied that she was no longer a threat the men now turned their full attention to Ali, who had not even completed his search for an escape route before the shooting was over. He saw the leading man open his mouth to shout. Adrenalin rushing through his system like a drug, the panic-stricken Ali reacted entirely by instinct to the death and terror facing him. He continued his turn to the left, with nowhere to go but the urge to escape paramount. Pivoting, his right arm swivelled with his body moving across his chest and inside his jacket which had fanned out with the violence of his movement.

To the SDU men charging towards him the reaction to such a movement was equally instinctive. With one armed terrorist down and another facing them, movement meant danger, and danger could be met with only one response. As Ali's hand reached under his jacket for the weapon that wasn't there, the firing began again.

Ali felt a quick shattering blow in his chest which seemed to lift his body vertically up from the floor. There was no pain, no time for any final thoughts or regrets, just a series of jolts as life itself was pummelled from his slim body. One bullet after another thudded into him. He performed a graceful and macabre pirouette before falling to the floor, the force of the bullets pushing him six feet backwards in a jumble of shattered limbs, leaving a bloody smear on the floor of the once pristine banking hall.

August 9

PUSHING OPEN THE heavy brass door to the Executive Office Building on F Street next to the White House, Bob Gearheart flashed his green-and-white CIA pass at the guard and headed for the elevator. As he pushed the button for the fourth floor, he thought once again about the reasons for his summons to the presence of the Director of Central Intelligence. As a lowly Grade 4 CIA analyst he had never had any direct contact with the DCI and the CIA was generally far too bureaucratic and hierarchical to allow ambitious young men to bypass the orderly chain of command.

The most powerful man in the American intelligence community, the DCI is charged with co-ordinating all US intelligence activity. He – there has never been a she – reports directly to the President. Despite such close contact with the ultimate power, successive DCIs have never shown any ambition of moving into the White House, preferring instead the independence of the building next door. It is as if the proximity of the White House staff might in some way taint the purity of the information to be fed to the President himself.

On the drive into Washington from Langley, Bob was still riding high on the success of the Hong Kong operation which had resulted from intelligence passed from his office. Hong Kong had been a personal triumph and now he was preparing himself to hide his elation behind a modesty he did not feel as the DCI congratulated him personally.

He came out of the elevator on the fourth floor, turned right, walked the fifty feet to the brown oak door, knocked

34

and walked in. The secretary facing him had watched his approach on the television monitor in front of her and as he moved towards her he passed through a body scan that checked him for weapons. She waved him past her to the large green door ahead of him. Once again he knocked and entered.

As soon as he moved into the room, Bob's sensitive political antennae smelled trouble. Directly facing Bob the DCI, Matt Shaw, was framed by a black and white aerial photograph of CIA headquarters at Langley hanging behind his thin body, which was hunched forward over the hands he clasped in front of him on the antique lawyer's desk. Bob knew Shaw as a lawyer by training and a tyrant by nature who was feared by even the most experienced intelligence operators for his exacting standards. Shaw was a by-the-book man drafted in by a President already locked into a bruising battle with a Congress determined to reduce American defence spending even further to cover the ballooning budget deficit. The President was determined that the CIA would not give Congress another club with which to beat the administration following the revelations of bribery and corruption that had emerged from the interrogation of the Panamanian dictator, Manuel Noriega. Shaw intensely disliked anything not done by the increasingly restrictive rules binding all intelligence work. To the veterans at Langley, the Shaw era recalled the dark days of a former DCI, Admiral Stansfield Turner, known as The Butcher for his ruthless pruning of hundreds of CIA agents during the Jimmy Carter Presidency.

Bob knew the DCI only by reputation, from the talk in the canteen and the bars where Agency men and women gathered to gossip and grouch. A good analyst, Bob tended to be cautious about information that he had not checked himself but this time first appearances seemed to confirm the characterization.

For his part Shaw did not even have a reputation to go on. Gearheart was too far down the ladder to have been noticed by the DCI, so Shaw had only five minutes of briefing before the meeting and his lawyer's instincts to assess the young man as he walked the eight paces towards him. The technique that had served him so well as a prosecuting counsel, when his assessment of a witness dictated his tactics, served him equally well now. Hair: blond, short, brushed – good. Eyes: brown, open, direct – good. Beard: none – good. Height: around six feet. No obvious complex. Hands: no nicotine stains, nails trimmed not bitten – good. If he passed the physical tests, Bob failed on the uniform. The DCI took in the sports coat, flannel trousers, penny loafer shoes and Paul Smith tie, all in marked contrast to the dark suits, white button-down shirts, dark shoes and plain ties that were the Langley uniform. Shaw nodded slightly as if receiving confirmation of earlier intelligence.

It was not the DCI's aggressive posture that set the alarm bells jangling in Bob's mind, but the presence of his boss Jim Prentice, the Deputy Director for Operations and, more importantly, of Josh Steinburg, the CIA's legal counsel.

'Bob. Good to meet you. Take a seat.' The conventional platitude was matched by a fleeting handshake as the DCI half stood and reached across his desk. 'I've asked you here today so that we can talk about your CT work. I understand you have had a couple of successes recently. Tell me about them.'

Warily, Bob began an abbreviated explanation of how he had come to specialize in the world of counter-terrorism. This, he suspected, was familiar ground to all the men in this room, particularly as he thought the purple file from personnel sitting in front of Shaw was his own.

'I think we are all interested in just how that information came to reach you, Bob.' The interruption came from Steinburg. As Steinburg finished, the DCI's hands unclasped and he leaned back in his chair, his arms spread wide in a stretch that made him look as if he were subconsciously preparing to embrace Bob's answer.

'Well . . .' Bob began hesitantly. 'It was really a matter of understanding just how they use their banks and getting the relevant information from the bank accounts. Nothing to it once we had the basic information.'

Steinburg leaned forward. 'Sure. But how did you get that information?'

In the past two years Bob had become obsessed with exploring the possibilities of marrying conventional intelligence with the awesome power of the computers run by the National Security Agency. Now, despite the danger of the moment, he found himself unable to resist sharing his knowledge, an enthusiast about to be condemned by his passion.

'You know how we began looking at the movement of cash to try and understand how terrorists paid for their acts and to see if we could stem the flow?'

The heads nodded, familiar with the change in tactics designed to cut off the cash that paid for bombings and assassination rather than simply trying to catch the terrorists after the acts had been committed.

'One of the most visible parts of the money trail is the movement of cash from one bank to another. Every transfer is encrypted by each bank using something called the Trapdoor Technique. Typically, one bank takes two numbers each with sixty digits, multiplies them and then uses the 120-digit number resulting to form the code. The new number is known as the Trapdoor because unless you have the original two numbers it is very difficult to open the door and break the code.

'But we have two advantages over the normal thief. First, the NSA routinely intercepts millions of messages a day and most of the bank transfers are Hoovered up along with more interesting matters. Second, our computers are big enough to crack even the most complex commercial code.'

Bob explained that for the first few months progress had been slow. But then, as other agencies and other countries began to learn of the project, more raw intelligence came across Bob's desk, each piece a signpost to a possible road by which terrorists moved their funds. Two months earlier, a Libyan unit planning attacks on French targets in West Africa had been rolled up after the transfer of cash from a Libyan front company's account in the Cayman Islands to Ghana had been detected.

'Then we picked up the Nidal operation in Hong Kong and it turned into our most successful operation to date. We closed down one of their pipelines and took out a Nidal cell.'

Instead of the rewards he expected from Shaw, it was Steinburg who continued the interrogation. 'Did the banks know what you were doing?'

37

'Not exactly.'

'When you say not exactly what you mean is that they did not. Is that right?' Steinburg's voice rose with the accusation.

'I am sure they knew what was going on and they certainly haven't made any fuss –'

'That is not the issue here, Bob,' interrupted the DCI. 'What you have done is used our computers to access bank accounts in other countries. You have then roamed the world like some kind of latter-day Zorro illegally invading other sovereign nations' rights, interfering with the individual freedoms of the account holders. Have you any idea how that would look if anyone on the Hill got hold of it?'

As the noose tightened around his neck, the cynical motto of the CIA veterans came to mind: 'Punch the computer, punch the time card and beware the Congress.'

Shaw furiously drew an imaginary word picture with his left hand. 'I can see the *Post* now. "CIA invades Hong Kong – by Computer". That single story would set us back years. How can you have been so stupid?'

Stunned by the attack, Bob sat upright, back erect, hands holding on to the wooden arms of the chair. In a tight, controlled voice he addressed all three men, eyes moving from one to the other. He could feel his pores open and the first beads of sweat caused by the heat of anger begin to flush his face and soak his armpits. It was a moment that called for temporizing but the contrast between the euphoria of the past two days with today's attack proved too much of a provocation.

'This is just bullshit.' Bob saw the three men draw back, distancing themselves from him and his assault. But it was too late to change tack. 'You know that I have pulled off one of the best intelligence coups that the Agency has had in months and there are more on the way. I have done nothing that anyone said was illegal, nothing that damaged anyone and nothing that broke any American laws that I am aware of. All I have done is to produce two intelligence successes.'

'Successes that in the end could cost us dear with our friends on the Hill,' Steinburg retorted, his voice tight, his belief in Bob's naïvety quite apparent.

'I'm afraid we simply can't afford that kind of success,'

added the DCI. 'Either we do it legally and properly or we don't do it at all. We uphold the law. We are not the terrorists. We are representatives of the United States government.'

The pomposity of the statement and the unreality of its simple credo stung Bob. He had learned that only the yahoos in the Special Operations Division fitted the clichéd image of the gumshoe spook, but he had also learned that to get anything done in the vast bureaucracy of the CIA required initiative and that sometimes meant bending the rules, many of which were unwritten anyway.

He turned to his boss in an appeal for support. 'Jim, you knew my brief. You knew what I was doing and nobody has told me to hold back, to stop producing the intelligence. I was tasked to make those computers work. For the first time we have done just that and we are going to throw it all away because of some stupid little rule. Every one of our allies would support what we have done.'

'But that is precisely the point,' replied Jim. 'They were not asked for their support and had no opportunity to give it. I am sorry, Bob, but you're on your own on this one.'

As the earthquake gathered force, Bob could almost see the crack that the tremor had produced widening to a chasm beneath his feet. His glance moved towards the DCI and saw nothing but the hard mask of a lawyer waiting to deliver the *coup de grâce* to the defendant damned from his own mouth.

'Bob, I don't deny you have done good work for us but when I took on this job I swore to uphold the law. There is no room at the Agency for people who won't play the game by my rules. I am no Bill Casey and there will be no Norths, Secords and Poindexters as long as I'm DCI.'

He paused, his eyes moving off Bob's face to search the far corner of the room. Having found the inspiration he needed, they returned to meet Bob's gaze. His voice adopted that pompous tone used by bureaucrats when they somehow feel their words are being taken down by the Recorder of the Earth's History for use in some future assessment of the twentieth century and their role in it.

'My remit in this organization has been to tighten up on

the loose cannons, to make it run according to the laws of this country and with due regard to the wishes and concerns of Congress. I am determined to discharge that duty and you are going to be an example to Congress and anyone else in this organization who is tempted to break the rules. I want everyone to be clear that in my book the ends have to be justified by the means.

'I recognize that what you have achieved has made a significant contribution to the counter-terrorist effort. But I want to make it clear to everyone that success achieved outside the law is not success but a failure of the due process. You will be the example to illustrate that important point of principle. As from this afternoon, your security clearance has been withdrawn. You will receive a month's severance pay and your career with the Agency is over.'

Bob stood up as if to reach across the desk to grasp Shaw and shake sense into him. Through his anger, he felt Prentice's hand grab his arm to restrain him.

'This is crazy. I give you an intelligence coup that you can sell to the Hill and our allies as a triumph and you can me! You keep this up and you won't have anybody left except pencil-pushers and kiss-arse guys who will tell you what a great job you're doing as you flush what's left of the Agency down the toilet.'

Anxious to end the embarrassment, Shaw rose and moved out from behind his desk to hustle Bob towards the door. Prentice steered Bob towards the exit. A brief handshake, a nod from Steinburg and Bob found himself standing at the lift with Prentice. In silence the two men descended to the ground floor and stepped out into the sunshine.

'I'm sorry I couldn't do any more for you in there,' Prentice sympathized as the two men stood on the sidewalk. 'I can see why you're pissed. But what Shaw didn't tell you is that the Brits had passed a request via their embassy about unusual communications activity by us in Hong Kong. He was worried that they would push it and find out what you had been doing, so he decided to sacrifice you now rather than be accused of covering up later.'

'Yeah. Well, thanks a lot for your support. Really appreciate it,' Bob replied sarcastically.

'Come on, Bob. Don't be so naïve. The decision was fixed before you went in there and there was nothing I could do. Better to let it ride. When things have calmed down, you'll find you still have me as a friend at the court of King Shaw. Look, right now, this must seem like the end of the world but there are other places that can use your talents.'

He reached inside the breast pocket of his jacket and pulled out a folded sheet of yellow paper.

'I had a word with a friend of mine who heads up the investigations at the Securities and Exchange Commission in New York. I didn't tell him that you had been canned, only that you wanted a change from intelligence work. I said you'd give him a call.'

Bob took the sheet of paper, glanced at it, screwed it up and made to throw it on the sidewalk before changing his mind and putting it in his pocket.

'That was a real lynch mob in there,' Bob said, bitterness now overlaying the anger. 'The noose was already set up and I just had to put my head in it. And I thought you guys fought for what is right. You can take your crumb and feed it to the birds. I want nothing more to do with you, the Agency or that pompous and unprincipled bastard Shaw.'

Prentice sighed in exasperation and put out his hand to grasp Bob's briefly. 'If it works out, get settled in and give me a call. Things could change down here and we may need your skills.'

With a cheery half-wave Jim turned back into the building. Bob walked out of the front entrance, crossed Lafayette Square and walked up 16th Street. On the corner of M Street Bob turned into the short driveway leading to the Jefferson Hotel. As he stepped through the ancient wooden double doors into the marble-floored foyer, Bob recognized the irony of coming to celebrate the end of his intelligence career with his two closest friends in the hotel that Bill Casey, the DCI for much of the Reagan era, had called home for more than three years. Since then, two other DCIs, including Matt Shaw, had used the hotel regularly for discreet meetings. The staff were used to the sight of tall, well-built young men moving through the lobby with bulging armpits, wearing flesh-coloured ear pieces and talking anxiously into tiny buttons in their coat collars. The hotel had absorbed this disconcerting traffic with good grace and the atmosphere of a mid-Atlantic version of an English country house hotel had somehow survived.

As Bob turned off the foyer towards the bar, he saw a hand reach out from the first booth on the left and grab his arm. 'Bob. Great to see you. Grab a seat.'

Before he could accept the invitation, a second pair of hands moved around his waist to be followed immediately by the briefest caress of lips brushing first one cheek and then the other. Holding her in his arms Bob smiled down into the face of Helen Riley, first love, best friend and now wife of his other great friend from university days, Hamid Nazari.

Releasing Helen, Bob turned to grasp Hamid's hand as he took the chair facing them. 'You two are just what a depressed former Agency man needs right now,' he said.

'What do you mean: "former Agency man"?' Hamid asked, puzzled.

'I was just canned by the DCI himself. Apparently they didn't like the way I work. Or rather they felt that the sharks on the Hill might come and take a slice out of the Agency if they found out about my methods. They decided to sacrifice me before the sharks even smelt any blood.' The bitterness had begun to surface in his voice as if speaking about the trauma of the afternoon had brought home to him the reality of his situation.

Helen's hand reached out to press Bob's arm reassuringly. 'Why, that's just terrible. From what little you've talked about, it all seemed to be going so well.'

Bob turned towards Hamid. 'I'm real sorry your help is not going to pay off. In the past few weeks we've just begun to understand the cash network and some of the stuff you have given us looked very promising.'

'Well – a small investment that will produce no dividends,' replied Hamid. 'It's a small matter for me but the loss of your job . . . now that is something we must truly celebrate,' he added with a laugh. Raising his hand, he attracted the attention of the waiter to order a bottle of champagne.

After the drinks arrived Bob raised his glass in a toast: 'To loyal friends.' Their glasses chinked and Bob's head moved back, his Adam's apple bobbing as he swallowed.

The characteristic action made Helen smile. Bob saw it and turned to her. 'I'm glad you can find something funny in all this,' he said, a censorious note in his voice.

'It's not that I'm smiling about,' she protested. 'I was just remembering when we first met and you drank your champagne just like that.' She laughed. 'You didn't quite get it right and the fizz went straight back up your nose. We've all learned a bit since then.'

They had first met during the Eliot House May Ball at Harvard Business School, where graduates and freshmen mingle, the men in black ties and the women in their finest ball gowns. The attraction had been immediate. Looking at him now across the champagne bubbles, Helen found it hard to recall the tall, tanned, fit and apparently shy man she had once loved with such passion. In those halcyon days, everything had seemed so alive. She had believed that the world was there for conquering, that she could make a difference. Above all, she remembered the ardour. She'd cared, really believed in so many things: abortion on demand, the Palestinian cause, women's rights. There was a certainty to the conviction, an absolute belief in the rightness of it all and a clear-eyed knowledge not only that the cause was right but that change was possible.

She sighed. It had all seemed so easy back then.

Bob had looked so romantic in his dinner jacket offset by a lurid bow tie which had a yellow fish swimming from one side of the bow to the other. It was this appealing mixture of the independent and the reserved, the hint of an inner spark that had struck the right chord. Age and experience had toned down her youthful excitement and now she could feel a flush creeping up her neck at the memory of the aggressive way she had pursued him. His reserve had only accentuated her confidence and she'd relished the challenge of drawing him into her social orbit. Now she realized that her initial attraction was as much due to her own insecurities as to her innocent and youthful enthusiasm.

Bob had represented the security she had been searching for since her parents divorced when she was fifteen. Her father had been a pillar of the British establishment, her mother an American who had come to England to work for

43

the London branch of the Bank of America in the corporate finance department. Initially bound by shared interests and a baby daughter, her parents' relationship had prospered only to founder on the cultural divide that developed into the gulf of an approaching middle age. Boredom with each other was matched by the frustrations of a young American mother seeing her friends across the Atlantic pursuing careers while she was housebound by the conservative conventions that dictated she be at home to entertain her husband's tiresome business friends.

The parting was painful with recriminations on both sides. Helen, trapped in the middle, became the shuttlecock batted back and forth between the lawyers squabbling over what they described as legal principles but were actually the tawdry reality of houses, money and materialism.

This uncomfortable background made Helen determined to avoid the pitfalls that had marred her mother's life. She would not become a conventional stay-at-home mother but would make her own way. This apparently simple determination was made more complicated by the insecurities of her teenage years and her relationship with Bob provided the calm she needed in the uncertainties of a freshman year at Harvard. It was also a sexual awakening for them both. Helen, young, innocent and full of fire awoke in Bob passions that had previously lain dormant. As so often happens with first love, lust became confused with romance and depth. What seemed at the time a lasting love that would stand the test of time, children and a career was in fact no more than an important milestone on the road to maturity for them both.

Leaning back in the armchair, Helen brought the cold of the champagne glass against her cheek, rubbing it soothingly along her jawline. Her eyes moved from Bob to Hamid, idly absorbing their friendly chat, content for the moment to be a spectator.

Theirs was a real friendship, one that had stood the test of time and competition and it was she that had been the unwitting catalyst. When Bob had first started seeing her, he had already met Hamid, the two young business students drawn together by a shared delight in going on to the Charles River in the dawn light to scull for an hour before returning to the Weld Boat House for a shower and breakfast.

To Helen, the two men had seemed unlikely companions. Hamid was a Palestinian by birth, his parents having left Lebanon while Beirut was still the Paris of the Middle East, when the casino still worked and Cartier not Kalashnikov was still the symbol of money and power. The Arab-American community in the United States was third in power and influence to the Irish and the Italian, and the Nazari family had been swiftly absorbed and prospered first as bankers in Chicago and then as investment consultants in New York.

Unlike Helen, Hamid came from a close family where arguments and discussion were a normal part of everyday life rather than a symptom of some deeper disease or the first signs of disintegration. Although tall, slim and dark, Hamid had avoided becoming a caricature of the rich Arab all American cartoonists love to hate. He affected no chunky gold medallions or bracelets or designer stubble, preferred a Volkswagen Golf to a Chevrolet Corvette and wore conservative, comfortable clothes free of any designer labels.

Bob's California-surf-boy image contrasted with Hamid's clear Middle Eastern roots. Then, too, Hamid was gregarious, a joker who enjoyed holding the limelight at a party while Bob seemed happy to stay in the background nursing a drink and absorbing the atmosphere. But despite the apparent differences, the two men shared an apartment at Soldiers' Field and became inseparable, swapping course notes, gossip about women and rowing for the Business School eight, Hamid at stroke and Bob at six.

From the moment she had first met Hamid, Helen had known that he was attracted to her. In the instinctive way that women have, she correctly interpreted the furtive glances, the slight hesitancy in his speech when addressing her, the lingering of his touch when he greeted her, as the overt signs of a man on the make. But Hamid made no attempt to press his case, leaving the field clear for Bob. At the time, Helen thought (with a chauvinism that went against her proclaimed beliefs) that she may have fulfilled the Arab ideal with her red hair, creamy-fair complexion and slim figure. She even took some small satisfaction from not wearing a bra to restrain her breasts, knowing that this must have added to Hamid's frustration.

Of the three, politics mattered only for Helen. To her disgust, she supported the Palestinian cause with greater fervour than Hamid while Bob resisted all her encouragements to become involved at all. Hamid argued that he was doing what he could by proving to the world that Palestinians were not just terrorists but could prosper in the most advanced society in the world. Yet he appeared to go through a political awakening after the Israeli invasion of Lebanon in 1982. The massacres at the Sabra and Chatila refugee camps, the siege of Beirut and the destruction of much of that once great city seemed to shake his easy denial of his Palestinian heritage.

Two weeks after the invasion the three of them had been sitting in Café Pamplona, the basement café on the corner of Bow and Arrow streets off Harvard Square. Over dark espresso and thick wedges of chocolate fudge cake they had been talking about the war when Hamid had amazed Helen with an uncharacteristic outburst that revealed sensitivities neither of the others knew existed.

'You talk of atrocities but you don't even begin to understand what is really going on.' Hamid had stabbed the air with his forefinger to underline the statement. 'So a few hundred Palestinians are massacred in Sabra and Chatila and everyone says how terrible it all is. Sure it's terrible but none of you really understand. Those two camps are just an illustration of a problem that has become institutionalized. And it's not just about the Palestinians and the Israelis. It goes much deeper than that.'

Helen had opened her mouth as if to begin a counter-argument but Hamid had talked over her protests.

'No, Helen. Let me finish. Take me. Here we are sitting in this café in the heart of the American dream factory. I'm here because I've got the brains to survive but I'm still an outsider, tolerated but not accepted.'

'Oh, come on, Ham. That's rubbish,' Bob protested with a laugh.

'So let me give you an example, Bob. You just called me Ham. You've called me that almost from the day we met. To you that name is just a handy abbreviation but to a Muslim it's an insult, bearing in mind we are bound by our religion never to eat pork.'

Hamid held up his hand, palm out, to ward off the rebuttals he could see forming on the lips of his two friends.

'Don't get me wrong. You're my friends and I can stand the odd insult. But my point is you have never even thought about the issue before. I may be an American but I am really an Arab-American and to many people here I am actually an Arab. It's a cultural divide I don't think I will ever be able to cross.'

The sobering conversation marked a new maturity in their relationship. Helen had found Hamid's new depth made him more attractive to her, contrasting as it did with the apolitical nature of her relationship with Bob. There had been no magic moment when she had understood that the affair with Bob was going nowhere, rather a gradual decline into mediocrity that crept up on them both.

She knew that it was over when Bob had turned to her for help and she found she could offer none of the lover's succour, only the mild platitudes of friendship. The three of them had been sitting in Hamid's apartment on Sunday October 23, 1983 watching the CBS evening news when the normal reports of fighting in Central America and talk of arms control treaties were interrupted with the first news of a bombing in Beirut. Information was thin but the first reports suggested that the target may have been American forces in Lebanon.

'Will's out there with the Marines,' Bob announced in casual tones that held no hint of the tragedy to come. Hamid switched to CNN and over the next five hours the whole horror unfolded. By the end of the evening, the first pictures had come through showing the devastation of the US Marines barracks, destroyed by a bomb hidden in a truck which had been driven past the unarmed guards by a Muslim fanatic.

The pictures brought to their comfortable student world were of an unimaginable horror. Corpses piled on corpses, arms poking brokenly from rubble, limbs torn from bodies and lying in the dust, even the stark image of a Marine

47

helmet with the strap still in place under a chin that had been severed from a trunk that had vanished in the maelstrom.

Bob had sat through newscast after newscast, his stomach bunched into a tight knot of dread as the terrible story emerged. Hour by hour the death toll mounted until by the end of the day he learned that 241 Marines had been killed and many others wounded. There was no word of exactly who had died but somehow Bob knew that Will, his older brother, friend and mentor, was one of them.

Perhaps because the images had been so stark, perhaps because Will had been his anchor and confidant in the uncertain days of puberty, the images of war brought to the peace of Harvard were a shattering blow to Bob. That night he faced reality, and in his grief found a strength that had never before been tested. Curiously, it was Ham's reaction to the incident that crystallized the anger in him.

'Now you know what my people have been suffering all these years,' Ham had remarked as a particularly brutal camera shot had displayed the tearful image of a live Marine kneeling over the bloody body of a comrade.

'Oh for God's sake, Ham, this is hardly the same. And don't give me all that terrorist and freedom-fighter crap. This was mass murder and those terrorists should be hunted down and destroyed like the animals they are.'

'Well, that's easy for you to say, sitting here in Harvard. But people out there live in a different world. I'm not defending the terrorists, only saying that we need to understand the reasons for such acts.'

Helen had wanted to take Bob's side, moved by the pain he was feeling so clearly. But she couldn't. She found that while she understood and sympathized with his grief, she thought that Hamid was making a perfectly justified point. She slowly began to realize that perhaps it was Hamid and not Bob who was closer to her ideals.

Bob was surprised and disappointed by his friends' liberal arguments and their reaction to the tragedy, but, rather than focus his enmity on her and Hamid, he determined to avenge his dead brother. They remained friends but there was a distance between them. The innocence of their earlier friendship would now always be overshadowed by Will's death.

To Helen, Bob seemed to change, to slough off the West Coast superficiality. He did not become a passionate activist or espouse the causes she and Hamid found in common, rather he too gained in depth, the serious side of his character developing to give his personality a direction and strength he had previously lacked.

Bob's anger had quickly turned to frustration, first when the US pulled its forces out of Beirut giving victory to the terrorists and then when his government appeared impotent. There were no retaliatory raids, no isolated assassinations, although he kept reading in the press that the government knew precisely who was responsible and even where they lived.

There was no immediate outlet for Bob's frustration but his anger festered and his determination to avenge his brother's death remained. Yet the task seemed so vast that he did not know where to begin.

Like every other university Harvard is a target for the recruiters from the intelligence agencies. Unlike in Britain where all recruiting is done through the old-boy network, the CIA and other agencies publicly drum up business on campuses around America. Bob attended one such visit from the CIA recruiting team. There was little talk of covert action, assassinations or destabilization but a great deal about career prospects, job security and the importance of intelligence to the United States. The pitch was reasonable but Bob saw behind the recruiting façade an opportunity that could offer both a competitive environment and a channel for his pent-up frustrations over Will's wasted death.

Shortly afterwards, Hamid abandoned plans to go to Wall Street to seek his fortune and instead elected to join the Arab Bank in New York.

The Bank had been founded before World War II in what was then Palestine. When the Palestinian exodus began in 1948, the Bank lost its three branches in Haifa, Jerusalem and Jaffa to the Israelis but, alone among Palestinian banks, the Arab Bank made sure its depositors got their money back. Neither the Palestinians nor the PLO forgot this loyalty.

The Bank's founder, Abdulhameed Shoman, had died in

1973 and his son Abdul-Majeed took over as chairman. Backed by Arab oil money, the Arab Bank rose to become one of the largest in the world, with assets of over $10 billion and branches all over the globe. Before becoming chairman of the Bank, Abdul-Majeed Shoman had been chairman of the Palestine National Fund, the economic arm of the PLO. This close link between an international banking institution and the PLO was of benefit to both sides. The Arab Bank became advisor to the PLO's legitimate investment arm. As such it was a natural home for the newly politicized Hamid.

'I must do something for my people,' he told Helen one evening as she finished telling him of her troubles with Bob. 'The least I can do is use my training to give the Palestinian people the money they need to work. Who knows, maybe one day they will have a country of their own and I can help build an economy.'

This was a new, mature Hamid who had built on the awareness that came out of 1982. Helen saw in his espousal of a fashionable cause, romance; in the possibility of living in the Middle East, adventure.

Hamid and Helen moved to New York and Bob to Washington. For some time, he had little contact with his former friends. He heard that Hamid and Helen had married and that Hamid had been posted first to the headquarters of the Arab Bank in Amman and then to Tunis. Eventually, three years later, Helen had written to say that she was pregnant and that she wanted Bob to be the child's godfather 'as you were the one that brought us together'. Visits to New York followed and gradually the triangular relationship found a new equilibrium. Hamid and Bob found they had interests in common once Bob began working on the financial resources of terrorists. Hamid proved a useful source. At the heart of the bank that managed many terrorist accounts, he was perfectly placed to supply valuable intelligence.

'Palestine is still my goal,' he told Bob, 'but I can be of real value to the cause working in the international community. The banks need my dollars, the businesses need my people. And for every bomb that goes off, there is a reluctance to deal with the Palestinians as human beings. Terrorists are so unsophisticated, they can't see beyond the bombs and the bullets.'

50

Bob was not going to argue with a source and as the months moved into years, their relationship gradually changed so that what they now had in common was terrorism where once they had the shared loves, fears and ambitions of regular friendship. Helen knew that she continued to provide a common bond in the triangle but now, looking at the two men, she realized that her role as catalyst had become marginalized as both of them had found a new level at which their relationship worked, one of expediency rather than friendship. Each found a reason for using the other.

It was information from Hamid that had given Bob his recent coup in Hong Kong.

If both Hamid and Bob had prospered over the years, Helen knew that time had not been kind to her. New York had been the adventure she wanted but the moves to Amman and Tunis had been less successful. Once away from the civilizing influence of America, Hamid's veneer of Western sophistication quickly wore off. The conventional suits were replaced by the uniform of the Middle East, a long flowing white jellaba.

The customs of the region meant that she was forced to stay in the background. No longer did she sit alongside Hamid, voicing her opinions which were listened to with respect. Either she served at table or stayed in another room with the other men's wives with whom she had nothing in common. The birth of her son, which should have helped restore the marriage, only served to drive the wedge deeper. Hamid insisted he be called Abdullah rather than the Richard she wanted after her English godfather. But she had held on to her heritage and had brought Abdullah up to speak English and to understand the principles of an American way of life.

Where once Helen saw excitement she now saw only boredom. In her lonely world her letters and occasional visits to see Bob were cathartic and he had come to represent a kind of safe haven where the world as she once knew it remained normal. Above all, she saw herself repeating the experience of her mother, the very thing she had been determined to avoid as she set out for Harvard.

The trip to Washington was Helen's first visit abroad for

three months and she had hoped that Bob would be the perfect antidote to her depression. Looking at him across the table, though, she saw that now was not the time to talk of her problems but a moment when she could provide him with support.

'Well, what are you going to do?' she asked.

'I haven't had time to think about it. I have an offer of something at the Securities and Exchange Commission in New York and I might look at that. Or I might just bum around for a few weeks while I think about things. Perhaps this is the opportunity I needed to kick my life into a new direction. I really don't know.'

Hamid leaned across the table, raising his glass of champagne ahead of him. 'A toast. To Bob Gearheart. A man with a great future. Whatever it holds his friends will be there to help him in his hour of need.'

Their glasses came together and there was a pause broken only by the sounds of swallowing. Bob put his glass back on the table and glanced at his watch. 'Christ. I'm late,' he exclaimed. 'I've promised to meet the love of my life for dinner tonight and I've got to get going.' He paused. 'Why don't you both join us? It would be wonderful. I've found this great Italian restaurant called Obelisk up near Dupont Circle. We can smother my sorrows in pasta.'

'We'd love to but we're committed elsewhere,' Hamid replied. 'Who's the lucky girl?'

'Mary Arkin. Fashion photographer. Works for *Vogue*, *Vanity Fair*, that kind of thing. Perhaps you've seen her work?' he asked Helen. She shook her head. 'Oh well, you must make sure you leave a bit more time next time and we'll all get together.'

A kiss, a handshake and he was gone.

August 12

Bonn

ROUTINE IS THE TERRORIST'S friend. The opening of the front door, the fifteen paces to the car parked in the driveway, the firing of the ignition is a pattern for the car bomber to exploit. The relaxing walk home from work through the leafy park with the pause to admire the small bonsai garden is an invitation to the assassin's bullet. Even the pause every third day to pick up the bouquet for the mistress is an invitation for the patient watcher with murder in mind.

Potential targets are warned, of course. Vigilance and an ever-changing routine are supposed to become part of day-to-day life. At the beginning, the advice is always heeded but then vigilance itself becomes routine and mistakes are made.

That morning Hans-Joachim Wirtz died because he had forgotten that all the professional terrorist needs is one fixed point in an otherwise varied day.

The day he had become Deputy Justice Minister, the security men from the Schutzpolizei had come to interview him, first at his house in the village of Oberwinter south of Bonn and then in his office in the government complex at Steigenberger just outside the old part of Bonn. The dour, tough Schupo captain was not interested in the Minister's explanation of why changes in routine were difficult, perhaps impossible, only that they had to be made.

'You are a target,' he had bluntly warned the Minister. 'From now on, the terrorists may be watching everything you do and if you do any one thing regularly that is when they will strike. So vary everything – the time you leave home, your route to work, the time and place you eat lunch, the time you set off home in the evening. Everything.'

The harsh warnings had been followed by the arrival at his house the next day of a black Mercedes 300SE car complete with chauffeur. The driver, Johann, was also from Schupo and showed Wirtz around the armoured car, pointing out the firing ports concealed in the doors, the tear-gas vents hidden in the bumpers and the Heckler and Koch MP5 sub-machine-guns concealed on spring clips under the front dashboard and beneath the front seats. The demonstration was both frightening and reassuring.

For the first few weeks Wirtz had been under observation, the watchers had noted that he followed the instructions they knew he had been given. But as time and the pressure of work took their toll and the immediacy of the warnings faded into the background, the watchers saw that he gradually adopted a routine that to the casual observer was erratic, but to their expert eyes had a distinct pattern.

He always left home after seven o'clock and before eight o'clock in the morning and returned – at his wife's insistence – by seven in the evening unless they were both going to an official function. Johann had three routes for getting from home through the village to the main road. After that, the Koblenz-Bonn highway, running along the banks of the Rhine, was the only practical way to get into town.

That morning the trap had been carefully laid, five minutes outside the Steigenberger complex, just south of the American military base near Königswinter.

Since shortly after the Second World War, residents of Bonn and its suburbs had become used to the sight of American soldiers wearing their distinctive green and brown camouflage and helmets resembling an upturned fruitbowl. As with any army, there are lawbreakers and the military police, too, had become part of the scenery with their white helmets, red and white armbands and heavy truncheons.

The two patrols patiently waiting by the side of the main road were as much a part of the routine of Bonn life as the local police and their presence caused not a flicker of concern to the law-abiding citizens heading to work that clear, sunny morning.

An observant citizen might have thought it slightly unusual that a woman appeared to be in charge of the first patrol. But then, in that stolid and complacent Germanic style, he would probably have dismissed it as just another crazy American idea that a woman should command a military police unit.

In fact, no women officers command military police squads in Germany and the commander of this particular unit was in fact Inge Becker, the 32-year-old leader of the Bonn cell of the Rote Armee Fraktion, Germany's leading terrorist organization.

Inge Becker's cell of terrorists killed in the name of the Martyrs of May 10. Their names and faces were known to the police and adorned wanted posters around the country, but they had been well trained at PFLP camps in the Beka'a Valley and the most experienced of them had survived. Today it was a battle-hardened group that waited for the Deputy Justice Minister to drive to work.

'Hunter 1 to Hunter 2.' The short message from the watcher at the junction of the main road leading from Oberwinter on to the Bonn road ended with a low murmur of static.

Inge picked up the microphone from the dashboard of the Volkswagen camper van. 'Hunter 2 receiving.'

'Check one.'

The signal that the quarry was following his predicted route and had now turned towards them caused a small stir of anticipation in the two men sitting inside the van. Dressed, like her, in the US Army uniforms they had stolen six months earlier in a raid on a base near Frankfurt, they were carrying army-issue M-16 rifles. What were not standard issue were the fragmentation grenades hanging from the webbing at their waists and the Russian-issue rocket-propelled grenade launcher lying on the floor behind Inge.

Once again, she stroked the transmit switch of the microphone. 'Hunter 3. Do you copy? Three minutes.'

'Hunter 3. Three minutes.'

As soon as the message ended, the clock began to count down and the two teams moved with well-rehearsed precision. Hunter 3, in a Volkswagen bus identical to Inge's, moved out from the turn-off by the banks of the Rhine a mile further up the road. Emergency blue light flashing, it eased into the outside lane where already single-line traffic was being channelled to avoid the construction work on the right. The driver of the bus immediately slowed to ten miles an hour and the German rush-hour commuters dutifully slowed down and fell in behind.

Two minutes later the black Mercedes of the Deputy Justice Minister sped past. Inge tapped the driver on his shoulder and the van moved out in the wake of the Mercedes, accelerating rapidly to fall in two cars behind. As the signs warning of construction ahead came into sight, Inge pressed the transmit button of the microphone. 'Stop.'

At the command Hunter 3 immediately braked and slewed his van diagonally across the road blocking the lane. Jumping out of the side away from the oncoming traffic, the two terrorists unslung their weapons and waited.

At the back of the now stationary line of traffic, the Mercedes braked and drew to a halt. The Volkswagen, too, pulled up and Inge reached behind her seat to pick up the RPG while the driver slid open the sunroof. Resting the three-foot-long launcher on the floor between her knees, she tore open the small cardboard box containing the rocket and, lifting it out, pushed the narrow end into the barrel of the RPG. She waited until she heard the click as the rocket locked into place, cocked the weapon and then pulled the small safety pin out of the rocket tip.

Swiftly she stood up on the seat, drew her upper body outside the van and pulled the rocket after her. Two cars and fifty feet away she had a clear view of the back of the Mercedes, the silver-grey hair of her target clearly visible through the back window. She saw an arm move as he appeared to emphasize some point to his driver.

She brought the telescopic sight up to her eye and immediately the head of the Justice Minister came into focus. His driver must have noticed something in his rear-view mirror for Wirtz suddenly turned round and stared back at her, the picture she had stared at for so long during the briefings for this mission abruptly brought into stark and human relief.

To Wirtz, the bulbous head of the rocket must have seemed huge, terrifying. The clear prospect of his own death gave him an unexpected and unwelcome feeling of impotence. Inge welcomed the shock she saw race across his face, enjoyed the terror she saw draw his mouth back open in a last shout. She savoured the final seconds when his lungs screamed forth the first chord of a plea for mercy. Although she heard nothing, Inge could clearly read the movement of the lips and knew that Wirtz was hoping she would hear the shouted 'No', as if that single word could stay the execution.

Her finger took up the first and then the second pressure on the trigger. Watching through the sight she felt the punch as the percussion cap fired the rocket and propelled it out of the barrel. Fifteen feet from the van the rocket appeared to pause as the stabilizing fins appeared at the back and with an explosion of flame the missile fired and shot towards the car. A millisecond later there was a burst of flame and then the shock wave of the explosion rocked the van.

Already Inge was reaching down to pull up the second rocket being handed to her. Only after she had completed the loading process did she look at her target. It was as she had expected. The boot of the car had been blown off but the armour had protected both the fuel tank and the back of the rear seat. The car and its occupants had survived. The armoured glass in the rear window had held together and Inge could see that Wirtz had been thrown forward by the blast and knocked unconscious. His head lay at a slight angle against the front seat, his face looking off to one side as if admiring the view of the river. Only the protruding tongue, half bitten through with blood dripping off its end, showed that it was not the view but his death that he was quietly contemplating.

Screwing the sight into her eye once again, Inge brought the rear of the car into view. This time the rocket ran straight into the boot and the armour, weakened by the first blast, shattered under the impact. The explosion seemed to lift the whole car off the ground before the force blew out first the windows and then the roof. Inside, the two men were torn apart. Only fractured images – of a bloody arm flying towards the river, two legs still strangely joined together without hips apparently jumping into the air to land sprawling by the side of the road – registered with Inge.

Before the echoes of the explosion had died away, Inge had moved back inside the car. The driver leapt out, pushed open the van's sliding door and reached in to place a metal ramp from the car to the road. Inge stripped off the US uniform to reveal the supple black leathers so fashionable among German motorcycle enthusiasts. She straddled the Yamaha XT500 motorcycle, turned on the electric start and with a slight twitch of the throttle moved it down the ramp. The driver boarded the pillion and put his arms around her. Moving at speed outside the stationary traffic, she clicked the bike up through the gears. By the time she passed the remains of the Mercedes she was travelling at fifty mph and looking ahead to her comrades at the road block. She did not even glance at what was left of the Deputy Justice Minister.

For the Martyrs of May 10, security was the obsession that had kept them alive. The killers who had destroyed the Deputy Justice Minister and his bodyguard left the scene and headed into the safety of Bonn. Once inside the city they split up, the three men heading for the flat they had rented three weeks before in Poppelsdorfer Allee, the student quarter in the northern suburbs. Unknown to the rest of the group, Inge too lived there in a house rented with some of the cash taken in a post-office robbery earlier in the year. Poppelsdorfer Allee was an unusual combination of apartments and two- and three-storey villas built at the turn of the century. Inge had hired the top floor of one villa, telling her landlady who lived on the two other floors that she was an investment banker posted to the city for six months from Frankfurt.

Parking her XT500 by the side of the road, she moved across the pavement, reaching inside the pocket of her leather trousers for the keys to the front door. As she moved up the three steps and paused to insert the key, she heard a car door slam behind her, then the sound of hurrying footsteps. Her right hand continued the movement towards the door while her left reached inside the open flap of her leather jacket to touch the butt of the Browning 9 mm pistol that rested against her right breast.

Before she had time to draw the weapon, a hand firmly gripped her left arm just above the wrist. She turned, gripping the keys in her right hand in her fist and bringing her arm around to thrust the improvised dagger into the eyes of her assailant. As her head moved, she felt and then saw a dark head come over her shoulder and suddenly lips met hers. His other arm moved around her body to hold her right arm. Pinioned, her eyes opened wide and she recognized the black curly hair and tanned face of Abu Hassan.

Relaxing into his arms she returned the kiss. Her tongue moved out between her open lips to dart around the outline of his mouth and then reach deeper inside. It was an instant response, a signal to him of her excitement and her need for more.

This urgency combined with the lingering smell of cordite told Hassan that Inge had been on a mission. When they had first met, trained and made love together in the heat of the Beka'a Valley, he had found that Inge was only truly liberated after a kill.

From the start, they had both recognized that their individual commitments to their beliefs would always transcend their personal feelings for each other. They had parted and come together infrequently since then. Terrorism is a lonely business and theirs was a relationship based on need and convenience. Each remained useful to the other, Hassan because of his links to arms supplies in the Middle East and Inge because of her access to a network of safe houses in Europe and as a source of false papers to carry terrorists freely around the Common Market.

'Hassan, you are just what I need right now. Come.' Inge took his arm, opened the door and led him up the stairs to the door of the apartment. Shutting the door behind her, she leaned back against it and drew him close. One hand moved underneath his jacket to rest in the middle of his back, pulling his chest towards her breasts, while the other gripped his hair, forcing his mouth on to hers. Their tongues danced together, thrusting and caressing. Panting, they drew apart and paused, then Inge reached forward and began to unbutton Hassan's shirt. He knew that she needed to control him, to dominate his body, to reassert her position as woman and lover.

She removed his jacket and shirt and ran her lips over his chest, her tongue wrapping around his chest hairs, drawing them between her teeth so that he almost cried out with pain. Her lips moved down following the path of her hands to his trousers. Belt and zip fell before her questing hands which slid inside his pants, embracing his penis.

She fell to her knees and drew the head of his cock between her lips. Both hands moved behind him to pull his buttocks hard into her face. Feeling him harden in her mouth, the swelling head filling her cheeks, excited Inge. She felt her nipples harden and her vagina swell and moisten in anticipation of the entry to come.

Hassan had one hand against the wall of the passage to prevent himself falling backwards, the other in Inge's short dark hair pulling her towards him, as if trying to drive himself through her bobbing head.

Inge slowly released his penis and looked up at him, the picture of eroticism. Her lips were swollen and wet; her leather jacket fell open so that he saw the swell of her breasts and the brown outline of her nipples. It had always amazed – and excited – him, he thought inconsequentially, how small her nipples were normally and how huge they became during sex, expanding outwards so that they thrust forward pointedly marking her passion.

She interrupted his reverie, pulling him down to the carpeted hallway and helping him out of his trousers and pants. Standing up again, she unzipped her leather jacket and shrugged it off. He watched from below as her hands ran over her breasts, fingers pausing to pull hard on her own nipples. She let out a small moan of excitement. Leaving one hand on her left breast, her right hand popped open the top snap of her trousers and in quick succession the rest followed, exposing the dark, matted mass of her pubic hair. Her hand moved inside and Hassan watched as one finger moved inside her vagina while another rolled over her clitoris. In the past Inge had masturbated to a climax while Hassan watched but this time she wanted more.

She stepped out of her leather trousers and squatted over Hassan whose erect penis was pointing up towards her. With one hand she guided him to the opening clearly visible through her glistening pubic hair and with a sigh took his length inside her. Leaning forward, her breasts brushed his face and he eagerly took first one and then the other nipple into his mouth, tugging and biting each in turn. Her hips took up the rhythm of his mouth and as he moved from one breast to the other so his penis thrust inside and then out almost to the edges of her vagina.

His hands moved behind her to grip her buttocks and one finger moved inside the cleft to first rest and then move slowly inside her anus. She tensed slightly and then relaxed, groaning and pushing back against his hand to open herself even more.

Uncontrolled now, the two moved faster; Inge sat upright to draw his penis even deeper inside her, a hand moving to a breast, the other, forefinger extended, moved to touch her clitoris. Both hands became a blur as she rushed towards her climax. Moaning then shouting, Hassan felt her anus open wide to absorb his finger at the same time as her vagina seemed to expand and take his penis in another inch. Roused by her passion, he could feel his balls tightening, the head of his penis growing as he approached his climax.

With a scream drawn from the depths of her soul, Inge stepped over the line of passion into orgasm, thrusting herself down hard on Hassan's penis as she felt him spurt into her. She swivelled her hips to milk every last drop from him, holding him tightly as the spasms in her stomach calmed.

She moved forward so that she was lying on his chest, her sweat mingling with his. 'That was wonderful,' she murmured into his ear. 'You always had perfect timing. Today was the best timing of all.'

'You're too kind,' he replied, laughing. 'What business have you been doing today that has made you so excited? Is that cordite I can smell on you?'

'We took out that pig Wirtz this morning.' She pushed herself up from his chest so that she was looking straight into his eyes. 'You should have seen it. Perfectly planned and went like a dream. He was blown to pieces just down the road from the American base and they had no time to do anything. That bastard deserved to die. Just as I fired he knew he was finished. One more for us and one less for the oppressors.'

These days, Hassan thought, such simple revolutionary fervour, which he had once found so attractive, was rather childish. He was too intelligent and too experienced to believe that real change was possible by a few simple acts of terrorism. They had not worked in the past and there was no reason to suppose things would change. But he was not about to undermine Inge's confidence in her pursuit of the elusive revolutionary dream.

Idly running a hand over one breast, he broached the purpose of his visit. 'I have come to you for help,' he began.

She turned lazily towards him, waiting for him to continue.

'We are about to start an operation which could end in triumph for us all. The leadership have at last understood that we have to do something or we will end up like the Basques or the Irish terrorists, an irrelevant annoyance with no chance of achieving political power. I for one am not prepared to give up so easily. For once, everyone from Arafat down has agreed to sign on for one last try.'

Inge's hand moved across his chest, her fingers lightly curling in and out of his chest hair. The gesture was more absent-minded than affectionate. She was fully alert now, the languid post-sex femininity replaced by the attentive terrorist. 'So, what can I do to help?' she asked.

'The plan calls for a number of products in America and Europe to be poisoned. It would be difficult for our people to do that as we have problems moving around, particularly in the United States. I want you to find the people to plant the poison and I need your advice about the right kind of poison to use. We need something that kills painfully and for which there is no known antidote.'

'The people should not be a problem but I will have to think about the poison and let you know,' Inge replied. 'This sounds like a high-profile mission and I may lose some of my best men. What's in it for me?'

'Well, I could remind you of the training your group has received, the weapons we have sent you and play on your conscience . . .' As he paused, she began to move back and he felt her fingers tighten on his chest. His hand moved so that his palm faced her in a calming motion. 'But I know you need more than that,' he chuckled. 'So, what I propose is that you commit the resources to this mission and provided your people do what is needed I guarantee you a payment of $5 million. I will also open up a channel to Damascus so that you can get a regular supply of arms. Win or lose, your group will become one of the richest and best-armed terrorist teams in Europe.'

It was a glittering prize that he dangled before Inge. She showed no hesitation in accepting.

August 14

ABU HASSAN ALWAYS GOT a perverse feeling of satisfaction from walking down Abd Al-Wahab street in the Jebel Weibdeh suburb of Amman. It was the interplay between fantasy and reality, deception and truth, that gave him such pleasure. Now he was just another Arab businessman dressed in an ordinary grey suit, briefcase in hand, walking through the banking district of Jordan's capital city. The cultured veneer was so thin that three hundred yards away from where he walked lay the main thoroughfare of King Faisal Street and the vast marble, concrete and glass headquarters of the Arab Bank, a symbol of the modern Jordan that the Palestinians' old enemy, King Hussein, had helped create.

But here in this anonymous side street was a different world, the world of the real Arab and, above all, the sanctuary for Abu Hassan and others like him.

Reaching the door of number 24, Abu Hassan entered, pushing aside the long beaded curtain that screened the doorway. He looked around as he moved into the gloom, dark eyes flicking to left and right, checking, assessing. His brain registered the familiar routine. To his left two secretaries busily punched the keys of ancient IBM electric typewriters. Behind them, the wall was dominated by a poster of an exceptionally pretty Arab girl with the caption 'There Will Be a Tomorrow'. Along the wall facing Abu Hassan was a row of bookshelves packed with dry tomes covering such arcane subjects as Arab Monetary Integration and Documents of the Non-Aligned Countries. To his right there was another desk where a young man sat reading a newspaper, a curl of smoke rising from his cigarette to be snatched by the whirling ceiling fan and shared with the two women.

The public purpose of the room was proclaimed by a banner that stretched along the wall above an iron barred gate that faced Abu Hassan. The banner described the office in green and gold as the home of the 'Palestinian Friendship Society' with the subtitle 'Working Together For Our Future'.

There were five of these offices spread around the Middle East. Each of them pandered to the widely held Arab view of the Palestinian movement as a largely ineffectual idealistic group with a few terrorists running around the periphery. This office merely confirmed the prejudices of the authorities and was left alone.

As Abu Hassan stepped forward into the room, Ghassan Hussaini rose from a worn, stuffed armchair to the left of the guard's desk and moved forward, hand outstretched. 'My friend, how good to see you again.' He smiled, revealing the even white teeth that came from expensive American dental work.

Abu Hassan accepted the offered hand and true to Arab custom drew the smaller man towards him and briefly touched his lips to the air next to either cheek. Both men considered the Arab practice old fashioned and vaguely distasteful so instead of their lips touching either cheek they leaned forward making a 'mwah' noise that expressed the intention if not the act.

His ambivalence about the tradition reflected Abu Hassan's thinking about Hussaini himself. Hussaini's whole background was in banking, accountancy and money. He understood perfectly the power that wealth could bring and had shown the leadership how to exploit this both to increase their assets and expand their influence. Under his stewardship, assets of the PLO had increased by seventy-five per cent. More importantly, the return on capital invested had risen from 7.5 per cent to just over twenty per cent, a return that was the envy of many international conglomerates. But, as Hussaini was fond of telling friends, 'Terrorists don't pay taxes.'

Yet Abu Hassan felt that Hussaini was so absorbed in his role as the Arab banker that it was difficult to believe he had any faith in the terrorism which had to play its part in the national struggle. However, while his skills were needed Abu Hassan had resolved to do his best to encourage the banker and conceal his reservations.

'I'm glad you could make it,' Abu Hassan replied. 'I got in last night and came round to see how your people were getting on. It seems you've already made a lot of progress in setting up the operation.'

Smiling gently, Abu Hassan pulled out his wallet from the inside pocket of his suit, walked up to the metal grille and pushed a laminated card into the slot in the wall. The red button above the slot changed to green, he pulled the gate towards him and the two men moved up the steep flight of stairs.

At the top was another door. Looking up into the lens of the security camera that had watched his progress, Abu Hassan pressed the button in the wall. With a hiss of air, the seals around the door opened and the door swung back.

The familiar sight revealed to Abu Hassan as he stepped through the gap had never ceased to impress. To left and right a single long room opened out to cover the top floor of this building and the one next door. The whole room was around forty feet long by twenty wide. The far wall was covered with a single line of light blue metal filing cabinets, each with a transparent glass top half with two computer reels visible which moved to a rhythm dictated by one of the two dozen terminals that occupied all the remaining space. There was a hushed, almost reverential, air to the place broken by the background hum of the air conditioning and the rapid stroking of keyboards as one of the white-jacketed operators entered new data.

Like Hussaini himself, many of the fifteen men and women in the room had been trained in the United States, some at the Massachusetts Institute of Technology, and it was hardly surprising that the computers were IBMs, exactly the same as those used by the American intelligence agencies who tried to track the activities of the Palestine National Fund.

'So, how are we doing in setting up the buys?' Abu Hassan asked.

Hussaini moved across to one of the terminals, sat down

66

and began to tap the keyboard using the two-fingered hunt-and-peck style of the proficient amateur typist. 'I have given the operation the codename Hayat,' he said, his tongue slightly protruding from the right-hand side of his mouth as he concentrated on the sequence of commands needed to access the relevant files. 'To get into the file you then have to type the numerals 1684.'

Abu Hassan was too young to have experienced the early days of the PLO but he had read his history and understood the flattery that, typically, Hussaini was using to ingratiate himself with the Chairman. Hayat was a reference to the magazine that Arafat helped produce in 1958 called *Filastinuna: Nida Al Hayat* (*Our Palestine: The Call of Life*). The numbers were those of the Post Office Box that readers were invited to write to to make contact with the leaders of the nascent Palestinian movement. If this all worked, then 'Life' would take on a new meaning, he reflected.

Behind him, he heard the hiss of the door and turned to see the huge form of Arafat's personal bodyguard, known as The Knuckle for the size of his enormous fist, duck through the doorway. He was followed immediately by the Chairman himself who appeared tiny against the looming forms surrounding him.

Unlike the Sana'a conference, Arafat was dressed for his surroundings in a well-tailored green safari suit. The creases of both jacket and trousers were sharp and the silver buckle at his belt shone. As he moved into the cool of the room, Arafat reached up and pulled his red and white keffiyeh from his head. He dabbed the sweat from his neck and then rubbed his bald head vigorously, making it look shiny and polished.

'Ghassan told me you would be here today and I thought this would be an opportunity to check on progress. I understand the money has been found and we have started buying,' Arafat said, leaning forward over Hussaini's shoulder.

All three men stared at the screen as Hussaini entered the code numbers. The flashing green cursor disappeared for a moment and then the heading 'Operation Hayat' scrolled across the screen and under the sub-heading Funds and Purchases lists of figures unfolded.

'The left-hand column sets out what we have available.' Hussaini pointed at it. 'The middle column shows where those funds are held. PA means Panama, LX for Luxembourg, CI for the Cayman Islands and so on. The right-hand column shows how much we have allocated to the scheme.' He pressed another key and the figures changed. 'This takes us into the Cayman Islands accounts and you can see that we currently have $150 million invested through eight different accounts, three with banks and five with local corporations. Each of these accounts will be used as vehicles to invest in Kola Co. The pattern is the same wherever we have investments. In all there will be over a hundred different accounts buying options from all over the world. We started buying two weeks ago and everything should be in place in another week.'

'Has there been any reaction from the markets, any sign that what we are doing has been picked up?' asked Arafat.

'Not so far and there is no reason why there should be,' replied Hussaini. Abu Hassan detected both condescension and pride in his voice as he continued. 'You have to remember we have been doing this kind of thing for years now. It's all perfectly routine and I am sure the Americans have no idea of the extent of our network. Even if they did, it would be impossible for them to track the money in the time they have available. As far as I am concerned after next week you can get on with your terrorism.'

Arafat turned away from the screen to Abu Hassan. 'Ghassan seems to have done his part. Have you got your people in place?'

'We seem to have the agreement of some of our friends in Europe that they will do the poisoning for us. Their leader has access to the poison and their people should be ready very soon.'

'And your timetable for the terrorism?' Arafat asked.

'It depends a little on just when we can get our people in place in the different countries. But I am hoping the poisoning will begin in the second week of September, around a month from now.'

At heart, Arafat was a great romantic. He loved the flowing extravagances of Arabic poetry and he could still shed tears on command. Leadership of the Palestinians had allowed him to indulge in the grand gestures for which he had become well known. With such a small audience, there was no opportunity for anything too magnificent but Abu Hassan detected the beginnings of an Arafat inspiration as the Chairman moved between his two comrades and embraced them both with an arm around their shoulders.

'The last years have been a hard struggle for us all,' he said. 'I can tell you honestly that at times I have begun to despair that we would ever win our rightful heritage. But now, here, I see that everything is possible. With your skills in the market, Ghassan, and your brilliance in the field, Abu Hassan, I am confident that this time we will win.' He looked up, as if seeing suddenly a distant, wonderful vision. 'Imagine, two months from now we may all have realized our dream. Palestinians will be living in Palestine once again. My people will have a home.'

Abu Hassan noticed a tear form in the corner of Arafat's left eye to trickle down the side of his nose before vanishing in the wisps of his grey moustache. He found the sight faintly ridiculous. He felt no sentiment about the forthcoming operation, just a certainty of its success.

August 16

THE CROISSANTS WERE perfect: the crisp, buttery outer layer giving way to a softer centre mercifully free of any of that chewy uncooked dough that anywhere else but in France can ruin a good breakfast. A large spoonful of blackcurrant jam followed by a generous swallow of rich dark coffee and Ghassan Hussaini dabbed at the corner of his mouth with a starched pink napkin. He sat back with a contented sigh.

'My friend,' he said, turning to his companion sitting on his left. 'It was so good of you to meet me at such short notice. I hope the journey was not too inconvenient for you.'

Hirsh Kronstein smiled, acknowledging the social nicety, but did not bother to reply. This was always Ghassan's way. A gentle ramble around the course before the point of the conversation was eventually reached. People always said that such a gambit was the Arab tradition but Kronstein preferred to believe that it was Hussaini's method of trying to establish control of the conversation. Still, it was a pleasant enough way to do business and Kronstein was happy to wait.

He had received the single three-word code via the telephone number cut-out registered to a tailor in London regularly used by Hussaini. The message it contained was a summons to this rendezvous and Kronstein had cleared his diary and caught the first available flight from Tel Aviv.

The two men had first met at a conference in Cairo of the Arab Monetary Fund. Kronstein, then calling himself Richard Ogden, had attended as an observer on behalf of the World Bank in Washington. He had struck up an apparently casual conversation with Hussaini, then a rising star in the Palestine National Fund. Kronstein had explained that the World Bank was very interested in any developments in banking in the Middle East and in particular was keen to keep in touch with the Palestinian economy.

It was only later that the two men had begun to be more open with each other. Neither ever talked about Kronstein's real employer, which Hussaini rightly assumed was the Israeli intelligence organization, the Mossad. Neither ever mentioned the word spying but instead had established a *modus vivendi*; both were realists and recognized that each had a use to the other, limited by expediency and mistrust. Within those boundaries, theirs was a useful relationship where, in the intricacies of Palestinian politics, Hussaini could weave complex plots with the aid of the Israelis and Kronstein could gather titbits of intelligence that put the final part of a jigsaw in place for the analysts back home.

They made unlikely conspirators. Hussaini, the product of three generations of Palestinian business acumen, came from a wealthy family. Educated in Palestine and the United States, he was as comfortable in London and New York as in Bahrain or Riyadh. Kronstein was one of a growing number of South African Jews who had left the country of their birth in protest against the apartheid government in Pretoria.

He had arrived in Israel – leaving behind a promising career as a university lecturer, a pleasant house in Sandton outside Johannesburg and a couple of black servants – in time to be immediately drafted to fight in the 1973 war, first in the paratroops and then, once his knowledge of languages was known, into intelligence where he stayed. He now had a small flat in Tel Aviv where it was a struggle to survive but, within his limits, he was happy, living a life he believed in for a country he loved.

In looks, too, the men were in marked contrast: Hussaini every inch the tall, slim, elegant businessman with middle-aged good looks that were almost Italian; Hirsh short, squat even, with broad shoulders and a strong, hard, tanned face completed by the prominent nose of his race. His single distinguishing characteristic was his walk which signalled his whole character: he moved like a boxer powering out of his corner at the beginning of a round with short bouncy strides, head tucked into the shoulders and thrusting forward, every movement indicating strength and energy.

The two men were sharing breakfast on the balcony of Hussaini's suite at the Crillon. Staying at such luxurious hotels, a giant step away from the Palestinian refugees whose money he was spending, was one of the benefits of being head of the Palestine National Fund. A love of luxury, however, had not diminished his commitment to the cause.

Kronstein watched Hussaini drain his second cup of coffee, put down his cup and lift an arm to embrace the view of the Place de la Concorde clearly visible from their second-floor balcony.

'I always ask for this suite in this hotel. I can look out from this room and see the history that has made France what it is today.' He pointed straight ahead. 'The obelisk from Luxor – 3,000 years old and as much a part of my history as yours or the French. But aside from the view, I also like the idea of you and me meeting next to the American Embassy, so close that they would never think of looking for us. Out here the noise of the traffic should help disguise our conversation!'

Kronstein laughed dutifully at the jibe against the Americans whose magnificent embassy also faced the Place.

'This view was made possible by a nation with education, money and a sense of tradition. But above all, the French had somewhere to build, somewhere to call their own. You see, Hirsh, today we have so many of these things: money, education, traditions, some of the finest architects and accountants in the world, but we have become squatters on the rump of the world. Everything we have counts for nothing in the end because we do not have a homeland.'

Kronstein poured them both another cup of coffee, added cream to his own and then stared out over the Place, watching the French go through their daily gladiatorial perfomance known as the *heures de pointe*. This was the familiar ritual. It always seemed to Hirsh that the Palestinian had to establish his credentials to himself before he could get on with the betrayal. Hirsh simply tuned out and waited for the meat of the meeting.

Hussaini chuckled. 'My dear Hirsh. I can see that already you are bored with the ramblings of this old fanatic. But there is a purpose to my chatter. I have given my life to making sure that when we get our nation, as we surely will, there will be enough cash to run the country. We have investments everywhere and that money is now sufficient for our needs. But we have agreed a plan that is going to place it all at risk; a plan that not only involves committing a substantial amount of our liquid reserves but will also set the status of the moderates in the Palestinian movement back to the dark days of the 1970s.'

At Hussaini's words, Kronstein's eyes lost their distracted look and fixed themselves squarely on the Palestinian's face. Two small furrows appeared between his dark eyebrows, an indication that, behind the bland mask, he was concentrating fiercely.

'Sometime over the next few months, terrorists in Europe will begin killing people all over the Western world by poisoning food. I don't know how many will die but it will be enough to cause panic. We reckon that the stock markets around the world will collapse, which will play into our hands as we are already investing heavily in the stocks of those companies that will suffer, gambling that their price will go through the floor and we will be able to sell short in advance of the fall –'

'But that's crazy,' Kronstein interrupted. 'You can never keep an operation on that scale secret. Once it is discovered your investments will be frozen and the terrorists caught. And where will that leave you and your peaceful Chairman?'

'That's precisely the point. My people are charged with handling the money side of things and that new man Abu Hassan is responsible for the terrorism. He's convinced all the old men that it has a very good chance of success and they see it as an opportunity for one last throw, a massive gamble and winner takes all. But what they don't seem to understand is that instead of gaining a state we're likely to lose everything just at the time when the tide is turning in our favour. Your government is being driven into the ground by the Intifada and they're losing support everywhere. It may take another few years but in the end they will be forced to negotiate. In the meantime, I can make the PLO richer than most Third World countries so that when we get a state, the money will be there to pay for it.

'This way we risk everything on an operation that is being run only to satisfy the vanity of the Chairman and all the other old leaders who want a last shot at victory before they die. It's madness and it is up to you to stop it.'

Kronstein leaned forward and laid a hand reassuringly on Ghassan's arm. 'Of course we will do everything we can. But what I need from you is names, dates, places. Everything you know.'

'You ask too much, my friend. Only a handful of people know about this plan; any leaks and all those close to Arafat will be suspect. The mood of the militants is such that they will shoot first and ask questions later and I have no wish to have a bullet aimed in my direction. Anyway, I don't know Abu Hassan's real identity and he has told us nothing about the terrorists and exactly what they plan to do. Even the money side of things is not sorted out yet, so you already have what I know.'

Kronstein watched the banker dab delicately at the edge of his mouth with a napkin and wanted to reach across the table and put his hands around that scrawny neck and squeeze until coffee, croissants and then information came pouring out of the self-satisfied mouth. He hated the way the Palestinian dribbled out the information knowing that Hirsh was powerless to force him to give more. He suspected that the banker actually got a perverse satisfaction from being able to keep a Jew hanging on every word, jumping to every summons. He knew he had to swallow the frustration, smile encouragingly and hope for more next time, but he determined on one more try.

'Why don't we set up another meeting for a week from now and then we can discuss what we have found out and you can pass on anything from your end.'

But Hussaini had done enough to satisfy his limited conscience. 'Security is already tight and as the operation develops all of us who are involved will be closely watched. I'm afraid there will be no chance of getting away to meet you and even being in contact with you would be too risky. I'm sorry, my friend. You have all the information you are going to get.'

74

Tel Aviv

A knock on the door, a muttered 'Come' and Kronstein entered the room deep inside the headquarters of the Mossad.

'Well, Hirsh. Welcome. Come in. Sit down. I hope you had a good trip.' Isser Sachar shook Kronstein's hand and gestured towards one of the canvas chairs while he slumped back into his comfortable armchair to rest his back.

Kronstein was pleased to detect the note of warmth in Sachar's voice, a clear sign that this man, who in so many ways had become a father to the younger agent, was in one of his milder moods. A call from Kronstein that morning had alerted Sachar that an urgent meeting was needed. It was now late and darkness had fallen over Israel's largest city.

The headquarters of the Mossad lies in Tel Aviv, just outside the city centre near the museum. The seven-storey cream-coloured building on Shaul Hamelech street, distinguished only by the jungle of antennae and satellite dishes on its roof, blends perfectly in a city that seems to have gone out of its way to produce some of the dullest architecture in the world. All government buildings in Israel are austere; the soaring Jewish spirit allowed to speak only through memorials to the past: ancient temples or more recent structures dedicated to the memory of those Jews killed by the Nazis or victims of later wars. In one of his increasingly frequent moods of gloomy introspection, Sachar, who had trained as an architect, had recently remarked to Hirsh that its buildings symbolized Israel itself. 'We Israelis think that life is far too serious a business to be trivialized by its visible environment,' he philosophized. 'We seem to insist on surrounding our people with the cold reminders of this harsh world. We seem to have accepted that only death deserves reverence as a constant reminder that the later life will contrast gloriously with the impurities of an earthly existence.'

Kronstein had thought it appropriate then that Sachar's office was in keeping with a man who saw all the darkest side of Israel's fight for survival. Hidden inside the grey building, the only window looked out on to a central courtyard where a few sparse shrubs struggled to reach for what little sun and water filtered through. His office was dominated by a functional grey metal desk surrounded by uncomfortable steel chairs with canvas seats. This rather austere scene was Sachar's choice. He disliked meetings and particularly disliked his junior officials' habit of taking up his time with interminable reports and bureaucratic distractions. So he made the chairs as uncomfortable as possible to encourage everyone to keep the meetings short. The tactic seemed to work.

There were two exceptions to relieve the brutality of the furnishings. The first was a modern, high-backed leather armchair which Isser had ordered especially from Sweden. The second was a large and now fading oil portrait of his wife Nurith. Both were a legacy of a car bomb planted by the side of the Jerusalem-Tel Aviv highway in 1967 when he was a young and enthusiastic immigrant to Israel from his native Soviet Union. The bomb planted by Palestinian terrorists had gone off just as his car entered the first of the tight bends that wind down towards the main road to Tel Aviv. Nurith, who was driving, took the brunt of the blast. The nails that had been added to the bomb had sprayed into the car in a deadly hail of flightless darts that almost severed her head from her neck. As Isser desperately tried to staunch the flow of blood, the car had left the road to crash in the scrub twenty feet below.

Sachar's legacy of the incident was a scar down the left-hand side of his face that pulsed a purple colour when he was angry and a back that was a constant source of pain, which was why he had made a small concession to luxury with the modern chair. But there were deeper, hidden scars too. With the death of his wife, Sachar's ambition to make a career as an architect had died also. While still racked with grief, he had tried to find out just why the authorities had allowed the terrorists to penetrate so far into Israel. He got no satisfactory answers but friends told him that despite the propaganda, Israel was sorely lacking in sources inside the terrorist groups and relied instead on a heavy security screen at the border to prevent terrorists infiltrating the country.

Three months later, the 1967 Arab-Israeli war began. It

was a devastating victory for the Israelis but they paid a heavy price. Sachar had determined to do what he could to improve Israel's intelligence capability and joined the Mossad where his imagination and orderly mind led to swift progress through the ranks. Six years later, after his career had been well grounded in the Mossad, the intelligence community was taken totally by surprise when the Egyptians launched a surprise attack across the Suez Canal. In the recriminations that followed a whole tier in the Mossad's structure was swept away to make room for a new generation of younger, less complacent men, among them Isser Sachar.

He was the first of the new breed of Israeli intelligence to be appointed head of the Mossad, the first leader who could not trace his history back to the demise of Palestine. But even without the backing of any legendary exploits of that time, few could criticize Sachar's record. It was he who had orchestrated the smuggling of an Iraqi MiG-25 from Iraq to Israel in 1975, had established Operation Exodus in 1978 to smuggle more than 10,000 Falasha Jews out of Ethiopia and had spirited the nuclear spy Mordechai Vanunu from Britain to Israel for trial in 1987.

It was an impressive professional record, but in one of those cruel and subtle examples of black humour so beloved of the Israelis, Sachar was known to his colleagues as Isser the Big. Where the original Isser Hirel, one of the founders of Israeli intelligence, had been a physical giant, his namesake was short with an unusually large head on which perched, like the spreading wings of some prehistoric bird, a pair of huge ears. It was these ears that had first made him the butt of schoolboy jokes and gave him the nickname Big Ears which later his intelligence colleagues changed to Isser the Big, an inside joke understood by few.

It was during a tour of the front during the 1973 war that Sachar had first come across Kronstein, then a recent and enthusiastic immigrant from South Africa. At first it was the languages that had impressed Sachar. As a European South African, Hirsh spoke English fluently without the guttural intonations common among Afrikaners or the nasal whine that so many Israelis speaking English have. In addition, Hirsh's academic background showed an interest in analysis,

77

a requirement for all intelligence agents. Plucked from the obscurity of the paratroopers, Hirsh found himself, as a Mossad man, one of the elite, able to make a singular contribution, which contrasted with the collective mindlessness of the ordinary soldier. Sachar took Hirsh's idealism and channelled it for his own purposes. Hirsh welcomed the older man's encouragement and returned his support with a fervent loyalty that had led to Hirsh's rise through the organization along with his mentor.

But while Hirsh's early idealism had been tempered by the fire of experience, he had noticed that the commitment that had driven Sachar to rise to such heights was beginning to die. In the early days, Sachar had explained that Israel would stand above the world, a shining example of what convictions matched with the high moral standards of a nation decimated by that most immoral of men, Adolf Hitler, could achieve. At the beginning, he reflected, it had appeared like the dream was going to work. Certainly there had been a war, but then the Jews were used to fighting for everything and the battle for their new nation was the most important of all. But despite the problems, they really had made the desert bloom, built cities and brought everything from Jaffa oranges to avocados to the world.

Sachar himself traced the change in Israel's fortunes to the rise of the Palestinians. When their enemy was solely their Arab neighbours, there was a simplicity, almost a purity about the fortunes of war. But terrorism that could strike the infirm and the young, the rich and the poor, without discrimination, anywhere in the world, was a different threat that required a very different response.

It was as if his fine and principled country had slowly been dragged down to the sewers that were the natural home of the vermin who joined the terrorist ranks. He, too, had played his part – a part always justified by the need to ensure his nation's survival. The assassinations: Ali Hassan Salameh, the organizer of the Munich Olympic massacre; Abu Iyad, Arafat's master planner. He had helped his country develop that most terrifying of weapons, the nuclear bomb, by smuggling a supply of enriched uranium from Belgium to the Dimona reactor in the Negev. And always there were the mistrust and the betrayals where friends had to be treated as enemies and enemies be given no quarter in what he had come to view as a fight to the death. The trouble was he was no longer sure whose death it was that would mark an end to the struggle. Arafat's? Israel's? Perhaps only his own would close the particular chapter that concerned him.

The weight, the sheer unceasing effort of it all had worn him down. Older now, his tired body was matched by a mind wearied by the intrigue, made cynical by the endless compromises of friends and principles and his country that had become an essential part of his job. To Hirsh it all seemed so unutterably sad.

One step removed from the decision making, Kronstein had retained vestiges of innocence and idealism as Sachar's had crumbled beneath the weight of responsibility. Sachar saw in his younger protégé himself at that age and he liked having Kronstein around to remind him of how it used to be.

'I'm sorry you've had to wait around until all hours but I thought you'd better hear my news straight away,' Kronstein said.

Sachar made a casual wave with his right hand which Hirsh took as a signal to go on.

'I have just returned from a meeting with Essex,' he continued, using Hussaini's codename which had been coughed up by the computer when it was having a run on English place names. 'I'm afraid he had some bad news. He says that the PLO have united behind a plan put up by Abu Hassan to poison food in Europe and the States. They reckon that the poisoning will cause panic and the politicians will be boxed in by pressure from the public and international business. At the same time, they are buying into the stock market, gambling on a massive fall once the poisoning begins. When the market collapses they expect to make millions, maybe billions.'

'They did that once before, you know,' said Sachar. 'Back in the seventies, Habash's lot injected mercury into a crate of Jaffa oranges. No one died or was even injured and they only hit one crate but it was enough. The market in our best product fell by fifty per cent. It took five years before we won it back.' He paused and then continued in a slower, more thoughtful voice, as if speaking to himself. 'That man Abu Hassan is smart enough. He'll kill enough people to panic the business community and hit them in their pockets. Once that happens political allegiances will go out the window and they'll rush to be the first to get their governments to agree to whatever the terrorists want.' He looked up at Hirsh. 'Did Essex say what their demands will be?'

'No. He would give me only the barest details. As usual that slick bastard is covering his back. He passed on the fact of the plot, which he fears will destroy the credibility of the Palestinian movement, but he said that the knowledge is so closely held that if he leaked all the details then they would finger him as the source. We can assume the demands will include the usual: a Palestinian homeland and an insistence that the PLO run it.

'As for timing, we'll have to reckon on it happening soon. They know we have our sources and are bound to get wind of something as big as this so they'll want to get on with it. The longer they wait, the more likely the whole thing will be blown, so my bet is sometime in the next few weeks, maybe even this month. You should call an emergency meeting of the Va'adat and the Prime Minister should be told at once.'

The Va'adat was the Va'adat Rashei ha-Sherutim, the Committee of the Heads of the Intelligence Services, which meets in the Mossad building every week.

There was a pause. Sachar's fast and politically attuned mind had already moved several steps forward in what was undoubtedly going to be a long and complex game. As always, the calculation was more difficult than it at first appeared. A summons to his colleagues, a meeting with the Prime Minister, all meant revelations, a baring of the Mossad file so that defences could be raised, allies warned and action taken.

Of course that was the right thing to do. Or was it? The PLO could be about to dig themselves a deep pit and with some assistance Sachar might be able to put some sharp poisoned sticks in the bottom and encourage Arafat and his friends to fall on them. If he said nothing then the attacks would take place and the PLO would be exposed for the terrorists they are. There would be casualties, but already the Intifada had cost them more than 2,000 dead. The Israelis had suffered fewer direct losses but their national will was steadily draining away. This could be the one incident that could turn the tide – all that was required was that he do nothing. Mind made up, he turned to Kronstein.

'We will do nothing. The PLO have made their plans and Essex is right. It is a trap they have set for themselves which could well destroy their organization.'

Kronstein sat forward in his chair as if about to bound out of it. He was appalled at the implications of Sachar's statement. 'You can't just do nothing' – the anger shortening his vowels to reveal a trace of his South African heritage – 'we have information that could be vital in stopping this attack. It's information we should share so that the Americans, the British and the rest can join the hunt. At the very least they should be alerted. If we don't do this and it ever gets out we will lose the few friends we have left.'

Kronstein could see in the tightening of Sachar's mouth, in the fixed, hard look in his eyes, that he had lost the argument.

'No.' The single word was an abrupt counterpoint to Kronstein's pleas. With the old bomb scar pulsing a deep blue down the side of his face, Sachar could barely control his voice. 'You talk of duty. Well, my duty is not to the Americans or the British or the French. They would betray us at the first opportunity and have done so often enough in the past. My duty is to my country, to Israel. This plan of Arafat's will play into our hands. The PLO will be discredited and at one stroke we will regain all the ground we have lost in the past few years. We do and say nothing and Israel survives. I am quite clear where my duty lies and that is to ensure the survival of our country.

'Only you and I know of this plan so far, so there is no chance of the information leaking, which makes this less of a gamble. Once again, my dear Hirsh, I and your country are relying on you.'

Appalled, Kronstein could feel himself being embraced into a web of conspiracy. Torn between loyalty to his mentor, to his country and to his conscience, he said nothing.

August 21

THE DROP OF LIQUID EMERGED slowly, like a tear drawn from the corner of an eye at the remembrance of a single, sad, passing moment. It swelled, was poised briefly and then fell to shatter on the clear glass table, the hundreds of tiny droplets scattering on the surface.

All eyes in the room followed the drop's brief flight.

'That is what we will use. A few drops like that will kill enough people to sow panic across Europe and America.'

As she spoke, Inge Becker removed her thumb from the plunger on the syringe and laid the needle down on the table. Looking up, she faced her hushed audience and continued.

'In each of these packets,' – she paused to indicate a small pile of sachets filled with a fine white powder lying on the table in front of her – 'is a product called thallium nitrate. It is one of the most powerful poisons around today. It is lethal and there is no antidote. All you have to do is mix it with water, fill a syringe and inject it into the product you have selected.

'The Iraqis used this against some of their enemies in Britain a couple of years ago. They sprinkled the thallium on peanuts in their target's house. Unfortunately, the family dog ate the peanuts and died. We will not make such a stupid mistake.'

She noted with approval the few nervous chuckles that greeted this anecdote. Inge knew that each of the people in the room was to a degree frightened of her. She knew, too, that this fear ensured that each of the Martyrs of May 10 would follow her faithfully, partly out of the fear she actively encouraged and partly for their own individual motives. In

82

some cases they had joined the Martyrs out of excitement, others had joined because they were politically committed while a few had come to be with friends and lovers. All were now bonded to her through the shared experience of terrorism and the fear of retribution from Inge at the first hint of weakness or betrayal.

She had summoned each of them over the previous two days. In every case, a telephone call to their flats, houses, squats or, in one case, the family home, had been brief.

They had come alone or as couples, some with bottles of wine, others with chocolates to help maintain the fiction of a simple social evening. The flat, two blocks from the railway station in Bad Godesberg, was a perfect safe house. Situated about three miles south of Bonn, Bad Godesberg is close enough to be almost a suburb but far enough away so that its wealthy inhabitants could happily justify its identity as one of the most prosperous towns in Germany. Most of the residents either worked in a government department in Bonn or were part of that city's 5,000-strong diplomatic community.

The May 10 safe house was on Heidelberger Strasse, one of many such streets leading off the main highway running along the banks of the river Rhine. Large turn-of-the-century houses lined both sides of the street with Mercedes and BMW cars emphasizing the wealth of the residents inside. A few of the houses remained intact but many, like number 39, had been subdivided into apartments.

Like all good terrorist organizations, the May 10 group was carefully subdivided into cells, each with a different responsibility. There were cells responsible for weapons and explosives, one for safe houses, another for reconnaissance and yet another for the act of terrorism itself. No member of one cell knew the identity of others in a different cell and only Inge had a clear idea of the organization's real strength. But recent losses had led to a blurring of the distinctions between the different cells.

The Red Army Faction had been founded in 1967 by Andreas Baader, Ulrike Meinhof and Gudrun Ensslin. In a series of particularly ruthless attacks in West Germany in the early 1970s, the RAF had been one of the leading members of the terrorist international, co-operating with groups in France and the Middle East to attack anyone and anything that represented capitalism or an obstruction to their ideal of establishing a Palestinian state in Israel and communist governments in Europe.

The founder members of the movement had been captured in 1972 and, after attempts to release them from jail had failed, they all committed suicide in 1976 and 1977. The movement, however, did not die with them; their legacy had been handed on to a new generation of terrorists that had learned from the mistakes of the past, that was better armed and trained and made up for its small numbers by a fervent commitment to its cause.

Inge Becker had been a child when Baader and Meinhof had first begun killing. But she was in her first year at Munich university in May 1976 when Ulrike Meinhof tore up her towel, made a rope from the strands and hanged herself from the bars of her cell in Stammheim prison.

Inge's father was a successful industrialist in the city, the director of the Krupp steel works. He had encouraged his daughter to gain a science degree with which she could face the new world emerging in the latter half of the twentieth century. The tours around the vast steel works holding tightly to her father's hand and staring in awe at the vast vats of molten steel, hearing the sizzle as they poured out to make bars, ingots and sheets, the workers almost incandescent in the reflection from the yellow-red pool of fire, had made a strong and violent impression. But initially it was not to the sharp end of the business that she was drawn but to the clinical decorum of the chemical laboratory. It was here she felt that the real power lay, where the chemists made their magic on which the rest of the vast factory depended.

She showed a clear talent for science and a fascination for the combination of intellectual precision and laboratory imagination required in experimental chemistry. It seemed perfectly logical that she should study chemistry at university.

Like thousands of other students from such a protected middle-class background Inge was a child suddenly thrust into the heart of a world uncertainly straddling the divide between adolescence and maturity. Those first weeks were an agony of loneliness and insecurity. She was still carrying the fat that had first emerged three years earlier but she was tall for her age with long, dark curly hair, of which she was quietly proud among all the blondes that were common at the university. Her most expressive features were her mouth and eyes. Her lips were full and in those days smiled easily to reveal strong even white teeth. Her dark brown eyes were peaked by strong eyebrows, reflecting her strong character.

Her background had not prepared her for the revolutionary ferment at the heart of German university life. A late developer both physically and mentally, her sexual and intellectual insecurities made her pliant material for the faculty seducers.

Her course included obligatory tuition on post-war German politics and her professor was Helmut Croissant, brother of Klaus, the left-wing lawyer who had defended many of the revolutionaries. With long blond hair fashionably cascading over broad shoulders, bright blue eyes and the kind of Aryan good looks that stared out of posters extolling the glories of the Third Reich, Helmut at first seemed as if he would be more at home in the fields of Saxony than campaigning for violent change in German society. But his conviction was certain, his rhetoric powerful and the spell he cast over the young Inge total.

Swept away by the power of the man and the excitement his cause represented, Inge moved swiftly through sexual and political initiation. She embraced first the man and then the cause he espoused. Her association with him gave her access to the inner councils of the radical chic, known to the Germans as Schicke Linke, where the talk was of change, hope and revolution with violence a necessary and exciting part of the agenda. The radical journal *Konkret* and not the traditional *Frankfurter Allgemeine* became her staple reading, the Bonn government the oppressive enemy and her parents symbols of a middle class she learned to despise and swore to destroy in the name of revolution.

Her long hair, once the source of such pride, was cut spikily close to her head, the plain dresses exchanged for the uniform of jeans and sweatshirt complete with radical slogan. As her political convictions sharpened, so her puppy fat fell away to leave a slim, confident and beautiful woman whose hardened body was in tune with her new mind.

Although others had marked her earlier, she noted May 15, 1976 as the day she became a committed terrorist. That day Inge was among 4,000 mourners who gathered at the funeral of Ulrike Meinhof in the Protestant cemetery of the Church of the Holy Trinity in the Mariendorf district of West Berlin. The cold wind and grey overcast day set the tone for the sombre occasion but the rain sprinkling on the crowd did nothing to dampen their emotion.

The thousands, nearly all young people in their late teens or early twenties, had gathered to pay their last respects to someone who had, to Inge, become an icon, whose haunting picture hung on the walls of student rooms and police stations all over Germany; to one a symbol of hope, to the other a manifestation of incomprehensible evil. The poster showed her standing against a brick wall, hands on top of her head, hair crudely cut short, dressed in the ugly prison uniform, with her fierce and uncompromising stare shouting defiance at the prison camera.

The funeral had been a sad affair, but what Inge remembered most was the hope and the unity. So many people had come all with one common political belief and all united in their grief. The emotion and the power were like a drug, the oneness of thought like a spiritual conversion and Inge emerged from that day a faithful believer.

Her solid beliefs gave her the courage to carry out the bombings and the killings that ensured her a place at the tables of the inner councils of the RAF. Her first killing, that terrifying moment between pulling the trigger and seeing the knowledge of death appear on the face of the victim, that horrible flat sound like a rolling pin slapping wet pastry, had all been submerged beneath so many other, more recent, acts of violence.

Her choice of the name for her group, the Martyrs of May 10, was her way of ensuring the date of Ulrike Meinhof's suicide lived on. The group's rigid cell structure had come in response to the police successes against Germany's Baader-Meinhof and later the Red Army Faction. The police had managed to build up very detailed profiles of the type of person who was joining terrorist groups – they were mostly aged between eighteen and twenty-five, had a university education and came from comfortable middle-class backgrounds. This in turn had allowed the police to target particular sections of the West German population and to build up millions of dossiers on the police computer at Wiesbaden. When the police managed to capture one of the terrorists, he or she usually knew the identity of several other members of the group, the location of safe houses and where cash and weapons were stored. So each arrest was a potentially devastating blow and accounted for the poor performance of the terrorists in the 1980s.

But now things were very different. A new, smarter breed of terrorist had emerged. The recruits came from all sections of society and the May 10 organization included in its ranks a printer, a university professor, a pimp, a smattering of students (but they were only used as couriers as Inge considered them unreliable) and several members of Germany's immigrant underclass.

Each of the team had their speciality: Norbert, a self-employed carpenter, travelled around the country looking for work and scouting likely rural locations for the group to hide out; Ali, a Turkish immigrant, one of the despised labourers on whom the successful German economy now depended, had unique access to a sub-stratum of society where even the police had few connections. The pick of the cell was Gabriele, who, like her angelic namesake, appeared on the surface an adoring and adorable ordinary middle-class girl. A qualified librarian, Gabriele still lived in Bonn, the city of her birth, with her parents. She had never joined a demonstration, never fired a gun and certainly done nothing to attract the attention of the ever-watchful police computer. A friendship with an RAF member had been abruptly cut off when he had died in a police ambush. Gabriele had created a memory of the man that gave him martyrdom and herself a constant state of mourning for someone she had never truly been allowed to love. Inge had focused this passion for the dead into an active hatred of the establishment, had recruited Gabriele and turned her into the perfect undercover agent.

It had been demure little Gabriele, dressed in her sensible skirt, pale blouse and slightly unfashionable coat, who had replied to the advertisement in the *Generalanzeiger*, the main

Bonn daily newspaper. Three weeks before, she had gone in person to be interviewed by the house agent and explained that she was the personal secretary of Herr Reichard Schinschke, the head of a small US firm of consultants based in New York who were advising American companies about the prospects of doing business in Europe. She explained that a new contract with Standard Oil meant that he needed a base in Bonn and this apartment sounded ideal. References and three months' rent in advance (the first courtesy of Petra the printer and the second thanks to a bank robbery a year earlier in Hamburg) had sealed the deal. Since then, the apartment had remained unoccupied, one of six located around Bonn that May 10 kept just in case.

Inge looked around the room at the people she had chosen to be her instruments. There were ten in all, exactly twice the normal number for a single terrorist attack. There were risks in this as one caught could compromise the rest but she had no choice if the countries were to be hit simultaneously and the campaign sustained. To minimize that risk, she had decided to keep the orders vague, allowing each unit as much flexibility as possible. That way no one, including herself, would know the precise targets.

'I will handle this end of the operation. You will go to the United States, France, Britain, Italy, Belgium and Spain to carry out your mission. I have arranged papers for each of you courtesy of our friends in Ireland.' She held up ten green Irish passports, from a batch of thirty that had been sold to the IRA by a sympathizer who worked in the consular section of the Irish Embassy in London. He was still in place and, as far as the IRA knew, the loss of the passports had not been discovered, nor would their numbers ring any bells on the immigration computers in the different countries.

The documents had come expensive: Inge had passed on to her IRA contact the latest bomb triggers that they had developed and successfully tested against Dr Alfred Herrhausen at the beginning of December 1989. The head of the Deutsche Bank had been driving to work in Bad Homburg in his armoured Mercedes with bodyguards in cars ahead and behind him. Immediately after the first car passed the killing zone, a light beam had been switched on. As the second car drove through the beam, the bomb hidden by the side of the road was detonated. It destroyed the car, killing Germany's most powerful banker and his three bodyguards.

This weapon marked a major step forward in terrorism and the IRA, which until then had been limited to radio-controlled detonators, put out feelers to see if they could get some. Inge had been happy to oblige once the Catholic terrorists had agreed her price.

'I have here $10,000 for each of you which should give you enough cash to set up your identities. Everything must be clean. Nothing stolen and no amateurish forgeries. There'll be more money for you just before you go.

'Once inside your country's borders, the exact target is up to you. There are only two restrictions. The first poisoning must not take place before the third week in September and the target must be any soft drink produced by Kola Co.'

'But what exactly are we supposed to do?' The question came from Hans Krocher, the male half of the best assassination team in the May 10 group. As always he sat next to his wife Brigitte; to the casual observer they would look like a perfectly ordinary middle-class couple, the man dressed in well-cut corduroy trousers, blue and white striped shirt and a fashionable blouson leather jacket, the woman in a simple red and grey checked dress with a high rounded collar and a tight black belt with a silver buckle drawn in above her hips to emphasize her excellent figure.

It was only the faces that gave any indication of the real people lurking beneath the comfortable façade – particularly Hans. He had an easy smile, which showed even teeth that had begun to yellow from the incessant smoking of Gauloises; a strong chin, slightly sunken cheeks and grey-black hair cut short completed the picture of a good-looking, middle-aged man, a designer perhaps, or even someone moderately successful in advertising. This sensitive image was upset by the eyes, one grey and the other brown, a combination which in some could be interesting – even attractive – but in him appeared only sinister. The ready smile never seemed to stretch beyond the crinkle lines around the nose, the eyes remaining flat and empty. Their steady gaze was both unsettling and intimidating. The air of menace was underlined by his voice which he never raised in anger but which carried all the authority he ever needed.

Even among their friends their ruthlessness was legendary. Their first kill had set the tone. Willi Stroessner was sitting in his patrol car one Tuesday evening having a quiet cigarette, blowing the smoke out of the open window. He had been approached by Brigitte who stooped at the car window to ask for directions. As he leaned out to answer, her hand moved swiftly in a quick right to left movement, the old-fashioned open razor cutting quickly through the main artery and the soft underflesh of his throat. His head flopped backwards in a ghastly grin as blood pumped out of the car window.

Three things emerged from that first killing. The two terrorists had their first guns, which made the next one much easier. In the death of the policeman they discovered a new excitement. And Hans, in describing with relish the policeman's death, mimicked how his throat had opened up in a bloody yawn – and from then on Brigitte had been known to the others as The Yawner, a name given in both fear and respect.

Their country was to be America. Neither had been there before but it was an assignment they accepted with relish. The symbol of imperialism, the country that had provided a focus for their youthful political extremism with its oppressive and adventurist policies in Central America and the Caribbean, America was the perfect target. But, above all, it was the challenge. The US was the soft underbelly, the bloated and fatted calf sitting self-satisfied and vulnerable. No terrorist group had yet accepted the challenge of breaching those seemingly open defences and The Yawner and her husband thought they not only deserved the opportunity but would make the best use of it.

Inge picked up the can in front of her and held its top towards the group. Bringing the syringe up with her right hand, she gently inserted the thin needle in the join between the ring top and the can itself.

'All of these cans use a minute seal to bond the ring pull to the can itself,' she explained. 'In the older cans with the ring that you can pull completely off, you have to find that join and gently push it in. The needle is fine enough not to depressurize the can in the short time this operation takes, particularly if you make sure the can is cold.

'Inject the poison. Then, before you withdraw the needle, put the can down and with your other hand take a pin and a small dot of superglue so that as the needle comes out you cover the hole with the glue.'

She paused and followed her own instructions precisely. Inge then picked the can up.

'As you can see, not a mark. Remember. You need the old-fashioned kind of ring top. The newer ones which have a pull top that remains attached to the can were supposed to have been introduced to stop people polluting the environment with the metal tops. In fact, the manufacturers were concerned at stopping precisely what we plan to do and with the new design it is much more difficult to get a needle in. Fortunately for us Kola Co. was one of those companies that ignored the advice of their security people and were not prepared to invest in the new canning machines so the door is still open.

'So, first order of business is to buy the cans at a local store, take them to your hotel and inject them with poison. The next problem is getting the cans back on the shelf. Fortunately for us, all supermarket security is designed to stop people taking things out of stores, not putting stuff back on the shelves. The simplest way is to take a shopping bag, put in your cans and walk back into the store. When you find the right shelves, simply put the cans back where you found them. Even if the cameras see what is happening it will look as if you have changed your mind about a purchase and there should be no problem.

'Then along comes Mrs Housewife. She buys your can, pays for it, takes it home to her family and a few days later the dying begins.'

Inge looked carefully at her audience to assess their reactions, to detect a sign of hesitation, the dropping of eyes, the flush to cheeks that might indicate weakness, the first telltale signs of betrayal. She was pleased to see only enthusiasm.

August 22

Tarhunah, Libya

IN QUICK SUCCESSION, HE drew three deep breaths, raised the Remington 870 pump-action shotgun and fired four rounds. Each time his finger squeezed the trigger, the Brenniker solid-shot round left the barrel at 400 metres per second. At 500 feet the two-ounce ball would hardly have burst through a paper bag. At four feet the effect was devastating.

His left hand moving in a pumping blur, he aimed each shot carefully to take out the hinges of the door, which literally blew apart under the impact, tearing a six-inch round hole where the hinges had been. The force of the shots propelled the left-hand side of the door inwards, the pressure forcing the lock on the right-hand side to give way and drive the door into the room.

Throwing the shotgun to one side, the man drew his Ingram MAC 10 sub-machine-gun from his waist holster and in one single fluid movement stepped through the doorway, rolled to the left, then back on to his feet. He came up into a crouch, eyes searching the gloom for friend and foe.

'Watch, wait, move,' he intoned to himself again and again, recalling his instructor's litany for survival. Already he could feel the adrenalin surging through his body, making him feel strong, powerful. This was dangerous, he knew; over-confidence would be fatal. Survival depended on his ability to combine his highly honed skills with an instinct that might give him that vital fraction of a second which in his business marked the difference between success and death.

Moving forward in short darting steps like a crab on its first foray after sunset, he scuttled further into the room, the gun in his hand following the movement of his eyes, its barrel questing, sniffing for a target.

From behind the shadowy outline of a couch near the left-hand wall, a figure sprang up. The gunman fired once and then again. The suppressor on the barrel deadened the sound so that all that was heard in the room was the click of the bolt chambering a new round. To the gunman the loudest sound in the room was now his heartbeat which had suddenly kicked into overdrive and felt like it was beating an exit up his chest, heading for his mouth.

The target disintegrated as the soft-nosed bullets found their mark.

Adrenalin pumping now, his soft rubber-soled boots making no sound on the wooden floor, his black-clad form the merest shadow, he moved towards the couch, the source of the first attack, instinct telling him that the next threat would emerge elsewhere.

A bright beam of white light burst from the other side of the room pinning him in its glare. He feinted left and rolled right, back the way he had come, firing two bursts of two shots each at either side of the light hoping to catch the person holding it. But the light continued to move, probing the darkness, seeking his new cover. Again he fired, this time at the light itself and with a crack the glass protecting the bulb shattered and then the bulb itself went with a loud explosion leaving an orange glow to remind him of where it had been.

A brief pause to regain some of his night sight and then up and moving forward in quick bursts looking for the next target.

To his left, from the side of a bookcase, a figure burst out. He pivoted, gun hand moving up to the aim, hand and eye co-ordinating the instant, deadly, response. His finger took the first pressure on the trigger. Then his eye registered the hands moving out and up and the brain responded to the change in the threat. This one was no threat, an innocent bystander or a released hostage.

He moved deeper into the gloom, his eyes fixed ahead so that his sharper peripheral vision would pick up any movement. Two shapes left and right. A pivot at the hips, fire twice, turn and fire twice again. Both figures disappeared.

A final rush and he was at the table, his arm reaching out to sweep the figure of the woman hostage to the floor, his body moving to cover her, pistol extended to sweep the room. With only bodies behind, his eyes tried to pierce the gloom ahead knowing that there may be one target still alive but unsure of his location.

The soft, almost caressing coldness of a gun barrel touched the back of his neck. He stiffened.

'Drop it,' a harsh voice ordered.

His gun clattered to the wooden floor.

'You should have checked behind the couch,' the voice chuckled. 'Just because there was one man there didn't mean there wasn't another. You're getting too complacent. You can stand up now.'

The gunman did as ordered, edging away from the woman and drawing his knees up into his body. As he felt his toes find a grip, he pivoted, his left arm driving his captor's gun hand out and away from his body. His right moved into the small of his back to pull out a tiny .22 pistol. As he stood upright his gun hand came forward so that the little barrel was placed in the centre of his captor's forehead.

'No, my friend. It is you who is getting complacent. Just because the rules say one gun, you should not have assumed that I would obey them.'

The exercise over, the two men moved forward leaving the cardboard cut-out of the woman lying lifeless on the floor.

Leaning forward, Abu Nidal pressed the button that stopped the video, freezing the frame on the 64-inch television screen in front of him. Then he leaned back in his chair and turned to his companion.

'Well, my friend, you survived that test, although I have received yet another complaint from the instructors that you refuse to obey the rules.'

'Rules are for the bureaucrats that make them,' replied Said Rosan. 'My job is to survive against the odds and I do that very well.'

Such a flippant response to any form of criticism from Nidal would normally have earned a stern rebuke at the very least and on a bad day severe punishment. But Nidal only chuckled tolerantly.

'You are sometimes too confident. The time will come when that over-confidence will kill you. But I have something that will test just how good you really are. This time I am going to trust you to carry out the most important mission of your career. We have two targets, America and Arafat, the country that has stood against us in our fight with the Zionists and the man who has betrayed the revolution. Succeed in this, my friend, and the revolution will be ours once again.'

Between these two men there was no real need for the fervent inspirational rhetoric that gave the young fedayeen the courage they needed. Rosan was too experienced to be moved by such simple stimuli and Nidal too embittered a terrorist leader to believe in the sentiments any longer.

Abu Nidal did not look like the world's most wanted terrorist. Sitting in a black leather armchair in the large white sitting room of his comfortable villa fifty miles southeast of Tripoli, he looked and acted the role of the comfortable middle-aged middle-class businessman that he should by rights have become.

The air-conditioned villa was furnished in the stark style popular in Europe ten years earlier. Moulded aluminium, leather and teak were the common threads with only the gold taps in the bathroom, the garish red and gold carpet in the sitting room and the AK-47 by the front door suggesting that this might be the home of an Arab. Lest he be thought uncivilized, Nidal had decorated the walls of his villa with his magnificent collection of coloured tiles from the Mamluk dynasty which had ruled Syria and Palestine in the fourteenth and fifteenth centuries. Over the years, his collection had grown to be one of the finest in the world and was a constant reminder to him of his heritage and what his struggle was all about.

That Abu Nidal should reflect this reverence for old and new and should fit so effortlessly into this comfortable lifestyle was hardly surprising. Born in Jaffa in 1937 and christened Sabri Al-Banna, he was the youngest son of his father's eighth wife. Unlike many others who were to gravitate towards the Palestinian movement in the years to come, Al-Banna's family had earned their wealth from the citrus orchards they owned and lived in great comfort in a three-storey villa overlooking the sea. Sabri was educated privately at the Catholic mission school in Jaffa until his father died and responsibility for his education then fell on his more devout elder brothers. He was taken away from the mission and sent to a Muslim school in Jerusalem where he was driven by the family chauffeur each day.

When Israel was founded, the family fortunes plummeted. They were forced to abandon their house, the orchards were confiscated and for a year they shuttled from one refugee camp to another. Although this must have had a searing effect on the young Al-Banna, who was then in his early teens, he showed no sign of political activism. It was only later, after a period at school in Jordan, when he went to Cairo to study engineering at university (like his later mentor Yasser Arafat), that the young radical appeared.

He dabbled in Palestinian politics, then in its infancy, and as the PLO emerged from the heated debates in Cairo cafés, so Sabri came to prominence. It was fashionable in those days to adopt a *nom de guerre* and Sabri became Abu Nidal, the Father of the Struggle, which gave an early clue to his self-perception and the role he was to make his own in the years to come.

At first Nidal was an administrator, a recruiter of men rather than a terrorist. But 1967 changed all that. During that year he returned to visit the family estates in Jaffa. He found that the orchards were now run by Jewish immigrants and the house that held so many happy memories from his childhood had become the Tel Aviv district military court-house where Jewish justice was dispensed. To Nidal this was a living symbol of the immorality of the Israeli state. He was later to frame a photograph of the house and show it to recruits as an explanation and justification for his militancy.

Three months later, the Israelis thrashed the Arab nations in a war where Palestinians like Nidal recognized for the first time that they could not depend on their Arab allies to win anything – certainly not their homeland.

Nidal was one of the first members of the PLO to be sent to China and North Korea for training in guerrilla tactics and Marxist-Maoist theory. The lessons he learned were never forgotten and the few months spent in the communist countries hardened his nascent militancy into a rigid political philosophy. Long after the Maoist revolution had been discredited, he was fond of quoting his mentor's inspiration that 'political power grows out of the barrel of a gun'.

As a base theory this may have suited the young and idealistic Nidal but the stubbornness he had exhibited as early as childhood made him unable to adapt to changing circumstances in adult life. His friendship with Arafat and his coterie soured as the PLO grew from a purely terrorist organization to a more sophisticated political movement where contacts with Western nations were encouraged and even secret discussions with the Israelis not considered unthinkable.

Through all this Nidal kept to his fundamental Maoist line, that guerrilla warfare has three basic stages: a preliminary process of preparation, a stage that establishes the movement and expands its control over a wide area, and finally the emergence of the guerrilla force as a regular army capable of taking on the government forces and defeating them.

Nidal saw himself as keeping the flame of active terrorism alive, but as youth moved into middle age and finally into old age, he had become increasingly bitter about his inability to expand the revolution beyond the level it had reached twenty years earlier. He chose to blame this failure not on his lack of political sophistication but on what he saw as the betrayal of the revolution by all those others who had started on the road together many years ago.

Keeping the revolution pure had been a costly business. The men under his command had committed many of the most terrible terrorist acts in more than twenty countries and killed over 300 people. A Nidal attack was characterized by its extreme violence and the utter dedication of the men and women who carried it out. His ruthlessness appeared to attract in turn a particular type of devotion. A message found on the body of one of the terrorists involved in the attacks at Rome and Vienna airports in 1985, when eighteen innocent civilians were killed and sixty injured, read: 'As you have violated our land, our honour, our people, we will hit you everywhere, even your children, so that you should feel the sorrow of our children. The tears that we have shed will be washed away by your blood.'

Now Nidal was almost alone, surrounded by the few who remained true to his political purity. He had become one of the most hated figures in the Palestinian movement. Arafat found his extremism embarrassing and had put a price on his head, while the Israelis and other Western nations devoted great efforts to tracking him down. He was the rabid animal that everyone wanted to see shot.

The years of isolation, of living on the outside, had taken their toll. His close-cropped curly dark hair was now streaked with white, his body had slowed, no longer fit, and his chain-smoking had produced a racking cough and constricted arteries that struggled to meet the demands of an already weak heart. Open heart surgery had reminded him that however good his security, like everyone else, his own body would in the end produce the ultimate betrayal.

His physical vulnerability made him determined to make the most of what time was left to him. Against his doctor's advice he continued to smoke the Rothman's King Size cigarettes he had specially imported from Cyprus and indulge his fondness for fettucine. The result was a fat and unfit terrorist but his physical infirmity in no way weakened his control over his followers.

A sense of time running out had made an already obsessed man even more paranoid. He had not spoken on the telephone for years fearing the kind of remote control bomb that had killed several Palestinians in the 1970s. And in the past two months Rosan had noticed that his master had plumbed new depths of paranoia. As the thought came to mind, the door opened and Nidal's chef, a small, plump butterball of a man, who had arrived from Italy a year earlier, entered. He was reported to receive a fabulous sum paid into a Swiss bank account to swallow his fear and prepare the gourmet feasts that appealed to Nidal's jaded palate.

The chef set out plates, knives and forks and with a flourish produced an enormous pile of tagliatelle con prosciutto. The chef beckoned his assistant forward and indicated the steaming food. With a gesture of faint distaste, the man tentatively dug a fork into the pile and popped a mouthful of the pasta into his mouth.

Nidal watched this performance with intense interest. Like a latter-day Roman emperor, he had started to employ this personal taster as a deterrent to any would-be poisoner. As the man chewed and swallowed with no apparent adverse effects, Nidal dismissed him and the chef with a wave and began to ladle the food on to his own plate.

In the past, purity of action was the requirement of membership of the Nidal group. Today purity of thought was demanded also. This was a difficult thing to satisfy as no member of his group knew from one day to the next exactly what their leader required. His behaviour had become increasingly unpredictable. At first his targets were exclusively Jewish, then as relations with other Palestinians soured they expanded to include members of the PLO. Then he targeted the British because they imprisoned two of his followers after their attempted assassination of the Israeli ambassador in London in 1982. Finally he had turned on his own followers and orchestrated a massive purge.

In one night 200 of his followers in Libya had been killed in what he described as a 'purifying' of the organization. It had been a terrible bloodletting with men, women and children dying as they slept, stabbed and shot.

The organizer of this had been Nidal's heir apparent and current favourite, Said Rosan.

The two men had first met when, five years earlier, Rosan had knocked on the door of Nidal's villa in Baghdad. He had approached the leader of the world's most feared terrorist organization because he felt that Nidal might provide an outlet for his frustrations. Then twenty-four, Rosan had spent the previous three years in the camp for Palestinian fedayeen, twelve miles south of Sana'a in North Yemen.

Like many of his generation Rosan had joined Fatah to fight the Zionists. He had undergone the basic training, the endless belly-crawls through the dust under the barbed wire, which apparently simulated the Israeli border; the leaping through the burning ring of fire to test courage; the interminable discussions of guerrilla theory that never seemed to be put into practice. He had seen the twelve men and women who had joined with him gradually reduce in numbers until there was only him left. They had been sent out in their ones and twos on missions into Israel and all had fallen crawling under barbed wire that was laced with infrared detection systems they hadn't been warned about or been killed because they used tactics that the Israelis had countered long ago.

Rosan's determination to fight was undiminished but he placed a high enough value on his life to want to make sure it was not wasted on some stupid scheme that had no chance of success. He had no wish for his obituary to be made into a childish piece of propaganda creating a martyr out of yet another failure of planning and execution.

So he had trekked north to Baghdad to meet the man who, alone among the Palestinians, appeared to know that terrorism meant terror and not a pussy-footing mixture of politics, bureaucracy and compromise.

He found a ready home in Nidal's organization and found, too, that what he had learned about guerrilla warfare from his instructors in South Yemen had not begun to touch his potential. He found that he thrived on the challenge of working underground and – to his surprise – that he was one of the few to whom killing meant very little. A knife slicing through flesh, the pressure of a rifle stock in his shoulder, the slap of a bullet hitting muscle were merely part of a clinical whole where death was the goal and the challenge the clean execution of the task.

Nidal had many killers but what drew Rosan to his attention was not his ruthlessness – there were many his equal in that area – but his instinctive understanding of a problem and his ability to think out a solution. He was both planner and executioner, an unusual combination that ensured his swift rise through the ranks of the organization.

He found that Nidal was the one man who had the vision and the dedication to understand that force won guerrilla wars and that acts of terrorism were the perfect example of this philosophy. Rosan was fond of explaining to the new recruits that until the PLO started hijacking aircraft and killing Jews in the late 1960s nobody had ever heard of the Palestinians or cared about their fight for a homeland. 'In five years everybody knew who we were and what we wanted,' he would tell the students. 'Then what happened? The leadership, headed by the traitor Arafat, lost their nerve, they became old men led by the Old Man himself. Instead of attacking while the enemy was on the run, they decided to retreat and seek to negotiate.'

He would then pause and, with a loud hawking noise, produce a round gobbet of phlegm to spit on the sandy floor in front of his students.

'Diplomacy,' he would shout, drawing out each syllable as if to underline the depth of the betrayal. 'Diplomacy got us nowhere. The Palestinians became like the goatherd on the hills above Jaffa whose goats are stolen by the Jews, the fighter who lays down his arms just as the enemy begins to put his hands in the air. We alone carry the flame for Palestine. We are the true believers. It is we who will win the victory for our people.'

It was all good stirring stuff that would have the young recruits from the camps in Lebanon, Jordan and Tunisia raising their right arms in the clenched fist of solidarity.

From the moment Rosan had joined Nidal, the terrorist leader had taken the raw intelligence that lay unawakened in the young man and cultivated it for his own purpose. So Rosan had learned not simply how to kill but how to survive in a wider world. He was taught the basic rules of a modern society: how to use a credit card, book an airline ticket, write a cheque and move around within Europe. Above all, he was taught languages. First English, then enough French and German to get by, and finally enough Farsi so that outside Iranian territory he could pass in disguise as one of the Hezbollah fanatics. Nidal believed in brushing his trail and he intended that Rosan would have all the tools to do a good job.

A number of simple tasks as a courier were followed by three missions where he acted as cell co-ordinator; first for an attack in Britain in 1982 when the Israeli ambassador, Shlomo Argov, had been shot and badly injured – an attack that had provoked Israel's invasion of Lebanon that year. The following year he activated a cell in Greece that attacked the Glyfada Hotel in Athens where a delegation of handicapped Britons were staying. Two were killed and nine wounded. Then, just after Christmas 1985, Rosan had orchestrated the attack on the El Al counters at Rome and

Vienna airports, where eighteen passengers were killed and sixty wounded, along with three of the four terrorists.

In each case, Rosan had remained the man in the shadows, the contact who had activated the sleepers with the right code words spoken quietly down the telephone. He had directed the team to their arms dump, watched over them from a distance and given them the target. Even in the investigations that followed he appeared on nobody's file. No interrogation – and the ones in Athens had been particularly brutal – produced his name or description for the simple reason that he had never met any of the terrorists who carried out the attacks.

When Nidal was expelled from Baghdad after the Americans applied pressure on the Iraqi government, Rosan sat alongside Nidal as their small convoy left the villa for Damascus that dark and rainy night. It was Rosan who established the new headquarters in Libya, Rosan who persuaded the Colonel to supply their new training centre and Rosan who became the expert at devising new methods of penetrating the buildings and dummy aircraft that were carefully hidden from the probing satellites.

Unlike Arafat, who cultivated a man-of-the-people image, Nidal was always carefully turned out with pressed trousers and a freshly laundered shirt. He insisted on the same standards from his men and so that morning Rosan was wearing light brown cotton slacks and a short-sleeved light green Lacoste shirt. Both men were drinking strong, dark Arabic coffee from tiny white porcelain cups.

'Said, my friend,' Nidal continued, pausing to take a noisy slurp from his cup, 'you are the best of my men, the one I trust above all others.'

Rosan briefly ducked his head in acknowledgment of the compliment while waiting to hear the details of the mission.

'I have heard that Arafat and his henchmen are planning an operation. I hear too that all the old men have come together for this, that they hope for one last throw to give them the power that all their negotiations, all their politics, have failed to produce. It was inevitable that they would turn back to my way but even now they have refused to invite me to join them. They've even given the operation to Abu Hassan, who seems to think he's the new me.'

Nidal coughed to clear his throat and spat into a brass spittoon on his left, as if to signify his disgust for the betrayers of the revolution. His voice rose.

'But I have prospered all these years without them and they will now learn that it is *they* who need *me*. I do not have the details of the operation except that the target is America, so I want to make sure that we strike at the heart of the Zionist network. We will make the fat capitalists in Washington sit up and pay attention.'

'My father,' Said began respectfully, 'you know I am here to do as you command. But what will attacking Washington achieve against the traitor Arafat?'

Nidal bared his teeth in a brief, wolfish grin. 'Whoever does an attack in America it will be blamed on the PLO, especially when I claim responsibility for it in the traitor's name. That will make it difficult for them to pretend they are the peacemongers they claim to be. Then, too, I think that if the traitor hasn't invited me to take part in his plan, whatever it may be, I will wreck it for him.

'Once you have completed your mission, the Americans will launch one of their great inquiries to find out what went wrong. They will blame each other and everyone else. But they will also improve security and Arafat will find it impossible to do whatever it is he is planning.'

Rosan sat back in his chair and gave a slow nod of appreciation and understanding at the subtlety of Nidal's thinking. 'So, what do you want me to do?' he asked.

'I have been searching for the right target and I have found it,' Nidal replied.

He reached down to the floor and picked up a copy of the *Washington Post*. He spread it out on the glass-topped table in front of him.

'You remember the courier we lost in Hong Kong?' Rosan nodded. 'We have lost people before during operations. The Zionists have taken some and others have died during an attack. But this one was different. It was the first time that someone has got through our security to set a trap for us.

Until now, I did not know how it had been done but now I think I have found the answer.'

He indicated a story on the front page. Rosan picked up the newspaper and took in the headline. 'CIA Official Fired – Computers Used to Invade Foreign Bank Accounts'. The story described how an Agency official, Bob Gearheart, had been dismissed by the DCI after it was learned he had been using the CIA's computers to look at foreign bank accounts in an attempt to track terrorist funds. The tone of the story suggested to Rosan that it had been leaked by the CIA itself in an effort to pre-empt any criticism by Congress, to demonstrate that it was moving swiftly to stop any illegality.

'It seems the Americans have found a way of looking into our bank accounts and following the money as we move it around,' said Nidal. 'A clever idea and one that could do us a lot of damage in the future. It's typical of them to fire the man who did it because of some stupid rules. But the key is in the last paragraph.'

Rosan read: 'Intelligence officials say that Gearheart is now working for the Securities and Exchange Commission in Washington. The SEC confirmed last night that Gearheart started working there a week ago but Gearheart himself could not be reached for comment.'

'So what has all that got to do with me?' asked Rosan.

'The American intelligence and counter-terrorist community always look outside their own borders. But they have changed the rules of the game and I think we should too. As you know, it has always been my policy to attack those who attack me and I am not prepared to make an exception in this case. In fact, aside from teaching the Americans a lesson, there is an opportunity here to exploit this for other purposes. The Americans have grown soft. They seem to think they are immune from attack in their home base. I want us to show them that they are wrong and at the same time make them pay for Hong Kong.

'A successful operation in the United States will put the Americans into overdrive. As usual, they will find excuses for their failures and shut all the stable doors long after you have bolted. The increased security should stir the whole place up so that whatever Arafat's got planned it will either become impossible or his operation will be stopped. You are the stick that I am going to push into the American wasp's nest.

'I want you to go to Washington, find this Robert Gearheart and kill him.'

August 28

New York

THE BUILDING FACING BOB across the narrow sidewalk was a seven-storey dwarf alongside the giants patrolling on either side. But then the Corinthian columns and sculptures representing commerce lining its door hardly lent themselves to the smoked glass and marble that is today's Wall Street chic. Bob walked up the steps and into the lobby. Ahead of him was the city's most magnificent monument to Mammon, the trading floor of the Exchange. One hundred and eighty feet high, the vast atrium contained the hundreds of people whose lives revolved around the fortunes of the market reflected on the giant screens lining the walls. The cavern also echoed with a background noise that to Bob sounded like the ebb and flow of waves crashing on the shore of Chesapeake Bay during a storm. But there was no charm in this sound, merely an overlay of tension underlined by the occasional shrill exclamation as a fortune was won or lost.

As he stopped at the security desk to the left of the front entrance, a tall, dark-suited black man put down his copy of *Forbes Magazine* on the glass-topped table in front of him, got up and moved towards him, hand outstretched.

'Hi. I'm Frank Abrams, head of the Enforcement Division in New York. You must be Bob Gearheart. I thought you might welcome an escort through the maze.'

Bob took the proffered hand and returned the brief and firm handshake. He looked Abrams over with interest. His new colleagues in Washington had told him that the man was a legend in the SEC. He looked what he was: a tough ex-cop. Bob had always read that cops looked like cops and he now thought it must be true. Abrams was short, the top of his head coming up to Bob's nose, which must have made him around five feet six. He looked shorter, the body apparently compressed by the large stomach swelling over the tightly cinched belt. The black hair had receded from the centre of his head leaving a bald dome surrounded by two greying wings. At that instant of meeting, it had been the brief moment between eye contact and the first greeting that had betrayed his background. The slight hesitation, the piercing examination, the checking of the mental computer, all suggested the wary experience of law enforcement.

According to the office gossip in Washington, Abrams had moved from the West Coast to New York in pursuit of a now forgotten love affair and joined the SEC in the days when investigations were few and regulations largely ignored. But Abrams had embraced the computer revolution and used the new resources to give the SEC some much-needed muscle.

Twenty years spent exposing all the schemes that clever men could devise to try and squeeze that extra piece of profit from the system had left Abrams with a sceptical view of Wall Street and those who made their living there. While hardly a socialist, Abrams despised most of the people with whom he was forced to rub shoulders every day, disliking their forced optimism, their constant manipulation of the innocent and, above all, their obsession with money.

'Follow me,' he said to Bob, turning in the direction of the elevators. 'You are about to enter the soul of the new machine, the centre of the enforcement universe.'

As they walked, Frank, all thrusting nervous energy, filled Bob in on the background of the city and Wall Street in particular.

'To understand this place and the people who work on the Street, you need to go back to 1653 when Peter Stuyvesant – who was city governor back then – ordered the construction of a wall of thick wooden planks between the Hudson and East Rivers to act as a barrier against marauding Indians.' He laughed gently. 'This may have been the first known example of the New Yorkers' dislike of rules and the men who make them. Neither the Indians nor the New Yorkers co-operated with the governor's plans. The Indians regularly broke through the wall and the locals saw an opportunity to either make or save a buck so they stole the wood to heat their homes or to use in building new houses.'

They reached the elevators and stepping inside, Abrams pressed the button for the third floor.

'Then the English arrived in the seventeenth century, tore the wall down and redeveloped the area as a business centre,' Frank continued. 'But the street on which the wall had once stood continued to be called Wall Street. Over the next century, Wall Street gradually emerged as the financial centre of New York, the urban sprawl moving the focus of the administration and residential areas uptown towards Central Park.

'As you probably saw when you arrived here, unlike many of the streets in this fine city, Wall Street has never recovered from its heritage and has hardly been redeveloped, so we poor moles hidden by the skyscrapers hardly ever see the sun. That may explain why the people here think of themselves as separate from the real world. Certainly, many of them are still stealing the wood from the wall, stretching, bending and twisting all the rules wherever they can.

'They've even invented their own language. Optimists are known as bulls, pessimists as bears. Barefoot pilgrims (customers) and elephants (institutional investors) can buy pinstriped pork bellies (stock market index futures) or a jellyroll spread (a mix of options). And that's where we come in. To protect the innocent world from these foreign barbarians, the citizens invented the Securities and Exchange Commission to act as their first line of defence. It's our job to patrol the street, to make sure the pilgrims don't get taken by the scalpers and gunslingers.'

Frank laughed at the baffled look on Bob's face and steered him out of the elevator. Turning left, the two men walked down a beige-painted corridor with plain brown doors stretching into the distance on either side.

There had been no time for depression or self-recrimination since Bob's dismissal from the CIA. The day following his ignominious firing, Bob's anger had been quickly cooled by the reality of bills to be paid and a living to be made. He simply could not afford to maintain the high moral ground of a man wronged. Jim Prentice had been as good as his word and Bob had started work immediately in the Enforcement Division of the SEC at their headquarters at 450 Fifth Street NW, in Washington, DC.

For the first few days he had been shown a new and strange world. Although Harvard had given him the business background, Bob had no real experience of the world of commerce. At the CIA his total attention had been given to the subterranean world of terrorism where analysis, intuition and supposition combine to try and turn a tiny gem of information into real hard intelligence on which others can act. At the SEC there was no shortage of information, as every company and every deal in every company had to be registered and recorded in full bureaucratic detail, but the critical difference was that for the SEC to act there needed to be proof that would stand up in a court of law that someone somewhere had done something wrong. At the Agency, hunches were enough to get action and legal proof a rare luxury.

Since Black Monday in October 1987 the SEC had played an increased role in monitoring the activities of the US exchanges. Black Monday, when markets around the world had collapsed, had in part been caused by automatic computer selling artificially driving down prices. Since then, the SEC had been at the forefront of both devising new computer programmes to prevent a re-occurrence of the disaster and using those same computers to detect more effectively attempts to manipulate the markets. Four days of briefings in Washington had convinced Bob that his expertise might actually be of use in his new job. The trip to New York was supposed to be the final brick in the education wall.

Halfway down the corridor, Abrams went through a doorway on which was marked in plain black letters 'Stock Watch'. Inside was a room around twenty-five feet square. Lining the walls in little cubicles with half-wall divisions were about fifty computer terminals, the green letters on the black screens adding splashes of colour to an otherwise drab room.

'I thought it best we meet here, as this is where most of our investigations begin,' Abrams explained, his right hand gesturing to encompass the room. 'This floor is actually run by the Stock Exchange. They have a system called Stock Watch and all the computers that you see here link up with ours so that they can monitor the transactions and detect anything unusual.

'You know how brokers are always painting this wonderful picture for their clients?' Abrams asked. Bob, recalling his own past failures in the market, nodded. 'Well, there was this girl who got married three times but each time she got divorced on the grounds that the marriage was never consummated and she remained a virgin. The first time she married an old guy and he couldn't get it up any longer. Then she married a gay and he wouldn't do it. Finally she married a stockbroker and all he did was sit on the edge of the bed and tell her how great everything was going to be.'

As Bob burst out laughing, Abrams steered him to the left-hand corner of the room and the coffee machine. Feeding in two quarters, Abrams pushed the buttons and after a few seconds handed Bob his cup. The two men sipped and as one made that grimace, half disgust at the taste, half pain at the heat, that marks the office coffee-drinker the world over. Abrams turned back to the room and the rows of computers.

'What this does is pick up any attempt to turn that rosy word picture into hard cash illegally. Stock Watch uses Quotron software and Tandem computers that analyse trading patterns and send out an alarm when an unusual trade is detected.'

'But there are millions of trades each day,' protested Bob. 'How can the system sift through all that and decide on which is the questionable deal?'

'What we've done is design a complex algorithm that has about eighteen inbuilt parameters, including the price range of the stock and how frequently it's traded. Then if there's a blip the computer flags it and one of the staff here can bring the details on to one of these screens.'

Abrams went on to explain that if the Stock Exchange finds something that looks suspicious, it can order all brokers who have traded in the stock to hand over the 'blue sheets' or trading records that give the names, addresses, social security numbers and other information on every customer that has done a trade. The Exchange information is then fed into the SEC's own computer system known as ASAM for Automated Search and Match.

'That little baby has transformed our lives. Investigations

that took six months we can do in half a day or less. Half a million people have their names in ASAM, mostly without their knowledge. What we have tried to do is list every corporate executive above a certain level, every investment banker, broker or accountant who may deal with a public company and every employee of every company that is a member of the Exchange. With each name we include as much detail as possible – wife's maiden name, club memberships, college and employment history. Then say, for example, Cyrus Sleaze, the chairman of XYZ company, knows a deal is in the wind and there is a sudden fall in the stock. We can track the deals made before the announcement and the computer tells us that Hiram Hincklehoffer is the main seller. It also tells us that he and Cyrus Sleaze both went to Harvard together and, bingo, we have the beginnings of a case.'

'But the market is more than just New York,' Bob pointed out. 'There's the exchanges in Chicago, the Pacific and then London, Tokyo, Paris and Hong Kong. From what you say, all I have to do is get out of here, trade offshore in US stocks and there's nothing we can do.'

'In this country it's fine,' Abrams replied. 'Chicago tells us what is happening when it happens but the difficulty with the other exchanges is that they don't have ASAM. It costs a lot, there are lobby groups who complain about invasion of privacy and some of the Board members can't see the value of the system. So, sometimes we think we see a pattern but we can't follow it up because the data isn't available.

'It's rather like getting murdered in the Big Apple. If it doesn't fit a profile within twenty-four hours and if there aren't strong leads in forty-eight hours then the case is dropped. It's like that with us. The computer allows a more efficient investigation but it also makes sure that a lot of interesting stuff slips under the wire.'

'What about overseas?'

'Huh,' Abrams grunted, his disgust clear. 'They all seem to think that regulation is a dirty word and that the Yanks have gone overboard as usual. The Brits are doing some interesting stuff but we get nothing from the French, Swiss or Japanese unless we can show it's drug money. Then they may help . . .'

'So,' Bob interrupted, 'if I read you right, the perfect criminal buys and sells in London or Tokyo on a stock that is traded in New York and, provided he keeps his business small, you guys would have little chance of tracking him down.'

'Yep, that's about the size of it. But that's why we need people like you around. To help us cut through all that crap and get some answers.'

'Yeah, well, I'll do my best. But this is all pretty different from my last job.'

The show over, the two men moved back towards the door, crumpling their plastic cups and throwing them into a bin on the way. A handshake, a promise to keep in touch and, thanking Abrams for the tour, Bob moved back towards the elevator. The trip had been interesting, he reflected. Abrams was a guy he could work with. But, despite the technology, he was surprised to find that the meeting had left him depressed. It was the similarity between the SEC and the Agency, he decided. Too much bureaucracy, too little co-operation between different agencies and once again the bad guys had the initiative.

Bob set off for his dinner date with Hamid. Just before Bob had left DC, Hamid had called from Paris to say that he was on his way over and could they meet? Bob had agreed to a rendezvous that evening in New York, welcoming the opportunity to combine a trip at government expense with a little personal pleasure. The Arab had been doing business in the financial district as well so Bob had taken his advice and reserved a table at Harry's in Hanover Square which Hamid had described as 'a favourite Wall Street watering hole'.

Pushing open the doors to the Stock Exchange, Bob stepped out only to stop in amazement as he took in the sight below. From his vantage point just above the throng, Bob could only stare astonished at the scene. The towering buildings had plunged the Street into premature darkness. Through the gloom a surging mass of people tried to make their way with dim flashes of white shirt beneath the uniform dark suit providing the only brief glimpses of light.

Taking a deep breath Bob stepped into the sea and was

immediately swept along with the tide of humanity, all of which appeared to be going in different directions, determination of effort matched only by the rudeness of execution.

Three blocks later Bob squeezed out of the main stream and popped breathless into Hanover Square and the refuge of Harry's Bar. Pushing through the gloom of the dark wood-lined bar, Bob made his way to the restaurant at the rear to find that Hamid was already sitting with Helen at the table.

'Welcome Bob, great to see you.' Hamid reached out and embraced Bob in an effusive hug.

Bob turned to Helen and holding her by the upper arms kissed her affectionately on both cheeks. Standing back he was shocked to notice how tired she looked. The lustre that normally gave her skin the glow of health was dulled; her eyes, which always seemed to engage his with her enthusiasm for life, appeared withdrawn, frightened even. They only briefly touched his before sliding away, as if nervous of revealing too much of herself.

'God, this place is a nightmare,' Bob said, beckoning for a waiter. 'I don't know how you bankers can stand it.'

'Even for us it can all get a bit much sometimes,' Hamid replied as one of the many Wall Street hustlers crushed into the bar pushed past, four drinks precariously captured between the fingers of both hands. 'And this is one of those times.'

Bob heard the underlying exhaustion in Hamid's voice, fatigue that was reflected in the deep lines around his friend's eyes and mouth. The normally urbane banker seemed a little frayed around the edges, he thought. Maybe whatever he's got is infecting Helen.

As if hearing the unspoken question, Hamid continued, 'Since we met in DC I have been doing nothing but travelling. I was in Paris on Monday, Tokyo Tuesday and now here today. Tomorrow morning I'm off to Amman and then back to Tunis for the end of the week. The Bank has been looking at its investment strategy and they have asked me to come up with some ideas. As always they think up these things today and want the answers yesterday.'

'Have you been working the same schedule?' Bob asked Helen. Before she had time to reply, Hamid answered for her. Bob noticed a quick frown of annoyance flit across Helen's brow.

'Helen flew into New York to join me today and we head out to Amman together. She always likes New York and it gives her an opportunity to see her folks before we leave tomorrow. Anyway, Amman is a bit more civilized than Tunis and she has been lacking civilization recently. Haven't you, my love?'

This last remark was addressed to a Helen whose eyes were focused not on the men but on her drink. She did not reply to Hamid's overture and he quickly rushed on, crossing the embarrassing gap with accomplished ease.

'Look, before we get too locked in here, I have got to eat and run. I have a meeting across town with some clients which I can't cancel so I'll have to leave you two to look after each other for the evening. I hope that's OK with you, Bob?'

'Sure, that'll be a pleasure,' Bob replied immediately with a swift glance at Helen for confirmation. There was no indication that she had heard the exchange but Bob, unwilling to force the issue, simply took silence for agreement.

'Great,' Hamid said, hand flicking into the air to summon a waiter. 'Let's order and then you can tell me how you are finding your new job.'

There was little choice at Harry's Bar, one of the many such bars in America all named after the Venice original, which was all marble, glass and velvet with barmen in tailored jackets making exotic drinks, mercifully free of the umbrella and vegetation that their American counterparts seemed to consider so fashionable. But the New York Harry's Bar was nothing like its quiet, elegant Italian counterpart. Brash, unsophisticated and raucous, it was the archetypal New York bar even down to the limited, though excellent, menu of steaks, salads and fries.

'So how are you finding life away from the cloisters of the intelligence world?' Hamid asked.

Fresh from his briefing from Abrams, Bob enthused about the SEC and the systems available for tracking down the crooks.

'It's not that different from what I've been doing except

that we cast the net much wider and I'm only interested in finding criminals and not just terrorists.'

'But don't you find the two overlap?' said Hamid. 'After all, you know better than most that a hell of a lot of terrorists are pretty successful entrepreneurs and they must use the markets like everyone else. And where you have crooks and cash they are hardly going to invest in ITT and watch their money grow. More likely they quietly shuffle their millions from one offshore account to another using dummy companies to front their investments and you'd never pick it up. Provided of course none of your wonderful computers detects a pattern and sends you a warning.

'In fact, there's been a lot of movement in the Bank's funds in the past week or so. Big sums are being moved around and I am not sure where they are going or why.'

Temporarily reverting to his former persona, Bob asked Hamid how much was involved.

'A lot. In the last ten days around $150 million has moved through the Arab Bank and the strange thing is I am being cut out of the loop. I have made some discreet inquiries at the Bank using my own contacts and I have got nowhere. As far as I can gather, it's all being handled by my deputy, George Bakr, and he refuses to tell me what's going on. He claims it's some kind of security matter and any questions I put to Amman just don't get answered.'

A questioning, rather self-absorbed note entered his voice.

'I have been trying to think what it could be and the most logical explanation I can come up with is that the Intifada is simply costing a lot of money and they have decided to draw on some funds to pay for some new initiative or other. I shouldn't think it's anything for you to worry about in either your old or new job. No terrorist action can cost that kind of money and I doubt any of the cash has come into this city. You haven't picked up anything on your net, have you?'

Bob digested what Hamid had said, assessing the possibilities and wondering if he could recall seeing anything on the daily summaries that could account for such a movement. Then he laughed ruefully.

'Thanks for the information. I don't do that stuff any

more. Anyway, from what you say, the action must have started around when I was leaving and it certainly doesn't ring any bells with me.'

'Well, either it's just some internal paper shuffling for a particularly sensitive client or else it really is nothing. Whatever, if you hear anything could you give me a call?'

'Yeah, sure,' Bob replied. 'Mind you, the way life is, either you or CNN will hear about it long before I do. But if I pick up anything, I'll let you know.'

Hamid glanced at his gold Patek Philippe watch then, dabbing at the corners of his mouth with his linen napkin, rose from the table. 'God, I'm late already.' He reached over to kiss Helen on the cheek and then grip Bob's hand in a brief gesture of farewell. 'I've got to go. Sorry to eat and run. I'll catch up with you both later.'

Hamid's departure left not just a physical gap – Bob and Helen were sitting at either end of the rectangular table – but without Hamid's conversation, there was an embarrassing and flat silence. To break the impasse, Bob moved up to take Hamid's seat and tried to engage Helen's attention.

'You seem to be very preoccupied this evening. Do you want to do the five?'

A hint of a smile flitted across Helen's face at the memory of the relationship game they had once played. When Bob left California, the five questions were all the rage, the key to breaking down the emotional barriers and forming a stable and lasting relationship. On regular occasions each partner had to ask the other five key questions: Is there anything you want to tell me? Is there anything you don't want to tell me? Is there anything you want to be forgiven for? Is there anything you want to be acknowledged for? Is there anything you are withholding? At first Helen had dismissed the questions as California bullshit but they had eventually become a regular feature of their relationship, a way for them both to talk openly about the most painful issues.

Then, it had been she who asked the questions and Bob who was the reluctant responder. Now the positions were reversed.

'I have nothing to tell you except that I am totally miserable. There's nothing I don't want to tell you. Maybe I would like to be forgiven for making such a mess of every-thing and I haven't done much to be acknowledged for recently and what you see shows that I'm not withholding much of interest.'

Bob was touched that Helen remembered their game but was distressed by her clear depression, so different from the self-confident person he used to know. He tried to reassure her.

'Look, Helen, that's crazy. You've got a life most other women, or men for that matter, would envy. Beautiful home; waited on hand and foot; successful husband; jet-set life. What more can there be?'

Helen answered, but not directly. 'When I was a child I used to have one of those horrible dreams. It terrified me. You probably had something similar.'

'Yeah, I was always being chased by this huge tiger with enormous jaws and falling over a cliff. What was yours?'

'I would be chased down this long, shapeless tunnel. I never really knew whether it was inside or out or even what it was made of. I just knew it was a tunnel and every few yards long thin ropes, or bits of jungle, would reach out to wrap themselves around my legs, arms and body.

'I would fight free and run on but the things would grab hold more often and I knew I was losing my strength and would eventually be smothered. Then suddenly out of the dark I could see a lake in the distance, glistening soft and white in the moonlight. I knew with complete certainty that the lake was sanctuary and I'd push on. At the bank of the lake I dived in and, for a few seconds, the water felt wonder-ful, all warm and comfortable. Then it would start to move and I was fighting again, struggling against the current. I was being gripped so tightly that the life was being squeezed out of me and I knew that I was going to die.

'Then, looking towards the centre, I could see a deep, dark tunnel opening up and feel my body being sucked into the vortex. Just before I vanished altogether, I would wake up, the image so clear that I would be panting and terrified. Sanctuary always lay in my mother's bed down the corridor.'

'Yeah, I used to do the same,' Bob sympathized. 'I'm sure my mother used to get really fed up with me crawling in next to her hugging my security blanket. But I haven't had that dream for years.'

'Neither had I. Then, a few weeks ago, it started again. This time my mother's not there and Hamid's been away such a lot, there's been no one to turn to.'

Bob watched as her eyes filled with tears. He felt momentarily helpless, realizing that the divide between them now was such that he did not know the right words of comfort or even understand the reasons for her unhappiness. Instinctively, his hand reached out to touch hers, his palm covering the knuckles of her left hand.

'I don't want to pry but we've known each other long enough for you to tell me what's the matter. Revisiting childhood nightmares one moment and crying the next is hardly the happy Helen I once knew. It doesn't take a genius to figure out that there's something wrong between Hamid and you. Do you want to talk about it?'

Bob met Helen's gaze before her eyes slid swiftly away from his face. She seemed at once frightened to meet his questions and nervous of what her answers might reveal.

'I tell you what,' a note of false enthusiasm entering her voice, 'why don't we get away from all these Wall Street suits and go somewhere fun for a nightcap?'

'Great idea. Follow me.' Bob paid the bill and they left the restaurant arm in arm.

They took a cab to the Café des Artistes, on West 67th Street. The bar was the perfect antidote to Helen's depression. A popular nightspot, it was packed with New York revellers, their jaunty mood matched by the Howard Chandler Christy nude murals lining the burnished wood walls.

Bob forced his way through the crush, pulling Helen after him. The crowd of people produced an enforced intimacy between them that neither had experienced since their days as boy- and girlfriend. Helen's breast pressed against Bob's arm had sent shivers of excitement down his arm. He could even on occasion feel the hardness of her nipple against his bare flesh. The noise, too, conspired on their behalf. To talk at all they were obliged to shout into each other's ear like lovers in a crowded train seeking the privacy to whisper erotic promises.

Bob bought them both Old Fashioneds and pushed back to squeeze into two seats next to a group of men and women celebrating a birthday. Their party was so filled with raucous good humour that Bob felt his spirits lift.

'Now *this* is New York,' he said into Helen's ear, turning to one side to hear her reply.

'I'd forgotten that there were places like this.'

Bob could hear the pleasure in her voice and relaxed, satisfied that he had produced a solution to her depression.

'I miss all this, you know,' she continued. 'The people, the freedom, the excitement. It's what life is all about, not being stuck in the back of beyond with nothing to do and no one to talk to.'

Her admission that she may have made a mistake produced a small worm of satisfaction in Bob who recalled the depression he had been put through after she and Hamid had gone off together.

'But you were going to change the world and Hamid was the man who was going to help you do it.' The words were undercut with a laugh but they reminded Helen yet again of what might have been.

'Sure. Tell me how different the world is today than when I left Harvard,' she replied, the bitterness of failed ideals acid in her voice. She shrugged as if to dismiss her concerns. 'Anyway, that's enough of me. How's things with you? Work seems good but how are things going personally? Are you still seeing that photographer – what was her name? Mary?'

'Yeah, we still see each other but not enough really to make it work. She's always flying off someplace and when she's around I'm not. I can't really see us surviving . . .'

The words had come easily but their content surprised Bob. His relationship with Mary had been proceeding in an agreeable if undemanding way. Now, prompted by Helen, he found himself expressing reservations which his subconscious had clearly been feeling for some time. Had the new-found intimacy with his former lover brought to the fore long dormant feelings for Helen? His aspirations had fed off her failure, his optimism off her depression. Certainly, looking at her now in the soft romantic light of the café, it was possible to imagine that they were back where it had all begun.

September 12

Antwerp

ANTWERP HAS ALWAYS BEEN a centre for smuggling. In the latter part of the twentieth century the goods may have changed from cigarettes to guns and drugs but the essential character of the city remains. On the banks of the River Schelde, Antwerp provides access to a network of canals and roads that lead south to France, east to Germany and north to the Netherlands. In the sixties, the Belgian Connection had been as important to terrorists as the French Connection to drug smugglers. To the despair of their European colleagues the Belgian authorities had shown little interest in prosecuting terrorists operating on their territory. There appears to have been an unwritten rule that provided the terrorists did not hit Belgian targets then they could, within reason, come and go as they pleased.

The result of this *laissez-faire* attitude is that Antwerp is today the single most important city for the illegal import of weapons from the Middle East and Africa, the place where terrorists on the run from neighbouring countries can find sanctuary. In the 1980s Pierre Carette, known as The Printer, fled France and rented a flat in the Antwerp suburb of Wommelgem; Natalie Delon, one of the founders of Action Directe, also ended up in the city along with a number of fellow travellers from the Red Brigade in Italy.

But the terrorists pushed their luck. In 1984, Pierre Carette helped form a new terrorist group called the Cellules Communistes Combattantes which attacked Nato targets in Belgium and stole guns from the local police. Belgium at last realized that deals with terrorists were unreliable at best and a crackdown was ordered. In four years the CCC was put out of business and most of its members put in jail.

While this may have reduced terrorism, the reputation of Antwerp as the criminal entrepôt of Europe remained. Terrorists may no longer use the city as a base, but still travel there to meet the arms merchants and to get the documents they all need to survive.

The one major legacy that Pierre Carette left behind was a forging network that had became pre-eminent in Europe. When Carette went to jail his mantle was passed to Julie Ketel, at one time Carette's girlfriend and now owner of a small printing shop specializing in high-class engraving for wedding and party invitations for the city's social elite. Her shop was just behind the St Pauluskerk church between Kwartzusterstrasse and Vleeshouwersstrasse at 153 Appelmansstraat, above the Boerenbrood patisserie.

As Hans and Brigitte climbed the steep wooden stairs running up the side of the shop, Hans fingered the new credit cards that had arrived two days earlier at the Bonn safe house. The greed of the banks had made life so easy for them. They had even given him a $3,000 credit limit, more than enough for the trip ahead.

Hans had met his wife when they were both turning twenty and living in Berlin. He had arrived from the East and was a resident in West Berlin while Brigitte had arrived from the small town of Völklingen in the heart of Southern Germany's Saarland. As she had grown from nervous child to attractive teenager, the narrow confines of her home town had become stifling and she had wanted new, richer horizons. Her parents, simple folk who loved their quiet community, had little understanding of her claustrophobia but wanted her to do what she wanted. With grave reservations they had agreed to her going to Berlin's Free University.

The city was all that Brigitte had hoped: cosmopolitan, stimulating and with an undercurrent of sensuality, even depravity, that she found intensely exciting. When she first arrived as an innocent southerner she was overwhelmed by the opportunities. Her tiny allowance from her parents was swiftly swallowed up and she desperately needed a student grant from the Berlin Land. To qualify she needed to marry

121

and Hans seemed the perfect candidate. They were both studying sociology and had shared a few late-night drinks and earnest discussions about the future of Germany. He had already formed his revolutionary views and Brigitte found the vision he laid before her exciting, worlds away from her home town where tradition dictated birth, marriage, family and death all within the same stable community. Hans offered the possibility of real change which she could help bring about. Even the idea of violence had its appeal.

Initially it was a marriage of convenience and the sex had started almost as a 'why not?' by-product of the registry office ceremony. But they had found in each other the perfect partners, and in the sex they first found in each other the violence that had been waiting for the right stimulation. Both found the excitement of a beating, the thrill of the rope released hidden passions, crossing the fine line between control and helplessness, dominance and dependence.

Just when politics, passion and violence merged into terrorism, they could not remember. Certainly politics was their justification for the killing, but a psychiatrist might argue that they were driven by other instincts. Politics was the excuse.

Julie greeted the couple like old friends who had stopped in for a coffee and one of the pastries from downstairs. Sitting in her small office, the terrorists discussed their requirements while Julie made notes in small spidery writing in a yellow spiral notebook.

'So, two passports in the name of Taylor with your own photographs.' It was more of a statement than a question and Hans merely nodded and reached into his inside pocket. 'You should be able to work with these,' he said, handing over two green Irish passports.

Julie idly flicked through the pages of one of the passports. 'Unfortunately for you, the Irish changed the design recently so that they are acceptable for the EEC and that's caused me all kinds of problems. First, I have to match the signature of their official.' She opened the front page and pointed to the scrawled S. O'Connor that ran across the bottom. 'Then, unlike most other passports, you don't actually sign the document. You put two signatures on the application form and one is torn off, put on the page and then covered in laminate. Also, as you can see, the Irish have their passports in Irish, French and English. All this makes the job much more complicated so it puts up the price.'

Like so much in terrorism, the nature of the forging business had changed over the years. A reliable false identity requires two things: cash and a clean passport, the most important of all international documents. Artists in the past had simply created documents to order, keeping stocks of paper, ink and stamps with files filled with the signatures of clerks whose handwriting appeared in passports. But today's forger has to be as much a master of the technology as the world of inks and paper.

When passing through immigration in any major Western country, the passport control officers have two checking systems. The first is a manual check against a large book, updated weekly, into which are entered the names of all those on any kind of wanted list. The second is computer-based. The immigration official enters the name of the passport holder, the passport number and the nationality. The computer then searches its database for any flags attached to that passport or name by immigration if they've been alerted by an intelligence service that a particular passport is in circulation or that an alias is favoured by a certain terrorist. The two or three questions the immigration officer asks the passenger are meaningless and are designed to catch the unwary, sweating amateur who rarely falls into the immigration net.

Those two systems have remained virtually unchanged for twenty years and have been left behind by the stolen passport racket which has developed into a multi-million-pound international industry.

Each one of the hundreds of thousands of passports that disappear each year is used to provide a false identity and until recently the usual method of doctoring them was simple. The picture would be removed and a replacement photograph inserted. The picture is then covered with a plastic film and heat sealed. Many countries also require the bearer to sign over the photograph so that the signature runs on to the page of the passport itself. When a false picture is used the signature is carefully forged so that it marries up with the old writing.

As there is no common method of recording a stolen passport and no routine exchange of stolen passport details between countries a doctored passport stolen in Canada will be valid in London or Sydney and one stolen in Amsterdam will work at immigration control in Los Angeles.

Passport control is a very unsophisticated system, full of holes which the terrorist community has learned to exploit. All efforts to produce some common passport standard have failed. There are no special inks that will show up under ultraviolet light, no hidden strips of foil that will show up on metal detectors, no clever designs that are difficult for the forger to imitate. But in the last two years, Western countries have invested in a new system called a Video Spectral Comparator that detects these forgeries. Using a sophisticated infrared imaging system the machine scans the writing in a passport and is able to detect differences in ink. If two different inks have been used to produce the same writing or the same ink has been used at a different time, the machine produces a television picture showing the inks in contrasting shades of white on a black background.

Corruption was now the key to a safe passage through the border checkpoints. A bribe to a clerk in an embassy in Abu Dhabi or London and passport blanks could transfer from the Embassy safe to the terrorists. Abu Nidal's men were still travelling on a batch of fifty Moroccan passports bought from an interior ministry official in Rabat and Iranian terrorists had managed to suborn a frustrated clerk at the West German embassy in Bahrain.

Julie looked up at Hans and Brigitte. 'The going rate for one of these is $8,000. But for the sake of revolutionary solidarity I'll give you them both for $14,000.'

There are plenty of Julies in the terrorist underground, skilled workers who have grown rich on the back of failed revolutions. Julie's skill had served Hans and Brigitte well and getting into the United States had proved ridiculously easy. They had passed through immigration in New York and then picked up a flight to Kansas City.

They had arrived in Kansas City on Eastern Airlines Flight

162 on Monday afternoon. Police like stereotypes; therefore terrorists live in rented apartments in low rent areas frequented by drug addicts and criminals. So, following a standard terrorist maxim that the more expensive the place, be it hotel, apartment or house, the less likely the police are to check it, they went to the Ritz Carlton Hotel, overlooking the Country Club Plaza. They justified the $180 a night expense as a secure solution to the problem of finding somewhere to stay.

Once inside the fortress, moving around was astonishingly easy. The Visa card and international driving licence had satisfied the Hertz counter at the airport and they had spent a comfortable night at the Ritz Carlton before setting out for the grocery store.

The Plaza is Kansas City's answer to those who say the residents live in a hick town. It was also their way of dealing with a congenital Midwestern inferiority complex. The Plaza was one of the first shopping centres to be built in the United States and in its day was a showcase. It came complete with fountains and fancy tilework to underline the Spanish theme, which had been chosen as part of the city's attempt to demonstrate its cosmopolitan heritage. Of course, Spaniards and Kansans made strange bedfellows but despite this handicap the Plaza had prospered and expanded to include the ubiquitous Macy's, Saks and Ralph Lauren.

Two blocks from Ward Parkway, which marks the eastern boundary of the Plaza, stands the shopping centre's main grocery store, Muehlebach's – a typical American Goliath. It was to be the first stop for Hans and Brigitte Krocher on their short poisoning tour of the United States.

Pushing their trolley before them, Hans and Brigitte had made the circuit of the shopping aisles taking items at random from the shelves so that their trolley was bulky, anonymous. Only the soft drinks aisle was a firm destination. Hans selected a dozen of the blue and white cans from the shelf, wheeled his trolley to the check-out, paid and walked back to the hotel room.

With the cans spread out in a tidy row on the table Hans prepared the poison solution. The white thallium powder was stored in a small pink and white box of Lancôme face powder. Brigitte fetched a glass of water from the bathroom as Hans prepared the syringe. Screwing in the thin needle, he carefully drew 200 millilitres of fluid into the body of the syringe while Brigitte measured out a flat teaspoon of powder into another glass. Hans squeezed the plunger of the syringe so the water squirted in a thin stream into the powder. A vigorous stir and the thallium was quickly absorbed into the water, which turned into a thin milky consistency.

With the deadly mixture back in the syringe, Hans picked up the first can. The group had practised the technique of contamination on dozens of cans back in Bonn. They had found that the manufacturers had left a small space of air between the liquid and the top of the can, sufficient to inject a further twenty-five millilitres and still leave enough air to allow the can to expand or contract in the heat. Further experimentation taught them that a few hours cooling in the fridge reduced the pressure of the carbon dioxide so the loss of gas when the can was punctured was reduced to a minimum.

Hans carefully inserted the needle along the line of the join between the ring top and the body of the cold can and pushed. There was an almost imperceptible hiss as the pressure seal was broken. A delicate push on the plunger and Hans injected the precise measure of poison. As he pulled out the needle, Brigitte moved forward and placed a pinpoint dab of superglue on to the tiny hole left in the can. Picking up a hairdryer from the floor, Hans turned it on and directed the hot air at the tiny spot. Within thirty seconds all trace of the tampering had vanished.

Fifteen minutes later, their work was complete. Carrying their deadly cargo in the same brown bag they had been given by the store earlier that morning, the couple walked out on to Wornall Road, turned left, crossed over Brush Creek and were back in the Plaza. To the other shoppers it appeared that they had simply changed their minds about buying the Kola Co. drinks as they placed them carefully back on the shelf. To avoid leaving without buying anything and to indulge her sweet tooth, Brigitte picked up two Hershey Bars and a pack of M & Ms and walked with them to the check-out.

As Brigitte walked towards the exit, Hans put his hand on her arm, holding her back. 'Wait, let's watch.'

Hans picked up a copy of the *National Inquirer* and flicked through the pages, his eyes passing over the stories of ghosts and sex scandals of the stars, his focus entirely on the shelves fifteen feet away. Two women passed. The third shopper reached to pull out the cans that a few minutes earlier Hans had placed so innocently back on the shelves. Hans felt a small glow of satisfaction. It was not, he reflected, the same as watching a victim comprehend that death was imminent. But even so, he was warmed by the secret knowledge he shared with Brigitte, the realization that the shopper in front of him would shortly die. And as the apparently happy couple sauntered out of the store, he reflected on how easy it had all been. There was none of the stomach-tightening tension that marks the beginning of an assassination; none of the post-adrenalin-rush depression that follows a robbery; none of the heart-stopping anxiety as a detonator is attached to the explosive and the timer activated. This had been a simple trip to the shops. Yet the results would be more devastating than any bombing or assassination Hans and Brigitte had ever carried out.

Two hours later they had picked up a TWA flight to St Louis with an overnight stop before they planned to move on. There were another eight stops to make before they could fly home.

September 14

Washington, DC

ALL SAID ROSAN'S TRAINING had been designed to instil confidence. The house assaults, the fitness tests, the staff planning and the intelligence gathering produced a young man finely honed to do his master's bidding and do it well enough to survive and carry out the next mission.

But for a man who had survived and prospered in the shadows, America was different: a vast, brutal power whose image had been formed in Rosan's mind from watching the videos of *Rambo*, Chuck Norris and *Miami Vice* that were popular in the camp cinema, and the financier and armourer of the hated Zionists. Thus the United States was both the oppressor and the seducer, the country responsible for the camp he had been born in and the Levis he loved to wear, for the existence of the Zionists he hated and those gorgeous blonde women he desired from afar. It had produced an ambivalence in him which in part accounted for his nervousness before the mission.

The prospect of striking at the heart of America excited both the trained killer, who exulted in the challenge, and the materialist, who relished the prospect of seeing the reality of the movies and the advertisements. But the fear of the unknown, the imagined threats, the pervasive police state produced a sense of danger the like of which he had never experienced before. He had found in the stillness of the quiet desert nights a slight knotting of his flat stomach that told him this one would be different.

Rosan had travelled from Tripoli to Malta on a Moroccan passport and then flown to Amman in Jordan where he switched identities to become a Jordanian dealer in carpets travelling on a genuine Jordanian passport courtesy of one of the many Palestinian sympathizers who worked in the Interior Ministry in Amman.

On the flight from Amman to Frankfurt, Rosan reflected on the last seven days. The week had been an intense indoctrination into the alien world of the United States. His tutor had been Frank Terpil, the one American Nidal and his sponsor, Colonel Gadaffi, had been able to turn to for advice over the past fifteen years. Terpil had once been a CIA man who by his own account had been a master of clandestine warfare, an expert in ciphers, silent killing and operating undercover in hostile territory. In fact, while he might have looked the part (he was around 15½ stone, over six feet tall with huge hands that could lift a case of AK-47 ammunition with practised ease) he had never been anything other than a clerk for the CIA. He had joined the Agency in 1965 and had served first as a courier and then as a communications expert in America and India.

Always a man with his eye on the main chance, Terpil had seen in India an opportunity to make a fortune. He had first smuggled jewels out of the country in the diplomatic bag and then traded in currency on the black market in neighbouring Afghanistan. The serious covert guys in the Agency are expected to show some entrepreneurial flair but for a low-level operator like Terpil such behaviour was unacceptable. He was recalled and dismissed.

He had offered his services to Gadaffi when the newly arrived dictator was anxious to consolidate his power and export his revolution around the world. Terpil seemed to provide exactly the kind of expertise he wanted. But now Terpil had virtually outlived his usefulness. His contacts in the underworld had long dried up. His experience of the arms business was years out of date. In the mid-1970s, he had smuggled a cargo of C4 plastic explosives into Libya from Texas labelled 'drilling mud'. Now, no self-respecting terrorist would use anything so crude that could be detected with ease by dogs and electronic sniffers alike. Instead, they all wanted Semtex, the Czech-made explosive that was odourless, malleable and virtually undetectable. Ostracized by the expatriate community in Libya, hunted by the Americans and the Israelis and of little use to the new generation of terrorists, he spent time alone in his villa watching *I Love Lucy* and *The Flintstones* on satellite television and keeping in touch with America via CNN.

Rosan found that Terpil shared his perception of America as the hunter and they as the hunted. Being on the run and living in a subterranean world had become second nature to them both. Now Rosan was required to emerge like a mole blinking into the sunlight – and not only emerge but exist and thrive alongside all those other animals on the surface.

'Remember,' Terpil cautioned him, 'America is an open society and people will tell you things because you ask and they want to help. The more you try and achieve things by the back door the more people begin to suspect something is wrong. You want to know someone's address and telephone number, ring up information. You want to know where someone is working and when he is likely to be there, ring the office switchboard and ask.'

Rosan had nodded enthusiastically as Terpil passed on this sound advice but training and logic told him that this was madness. Ask for information and you are dead, he had always been taught. Come into the sun and the sniper will blow your brains out. His world was the night and his weapon was the knife. He did not understand this new place where people were helpful and not automatically suspicious of questions.

At Frankfurt, Rosan was booked on the Pan Am flight to Washington, DC via London. He had made the reservation against his own instincts but with Terpil's strong encouragement.

'Look,' he had been told, 'ever since the Pan Am 103 was blown up, the Americans have said security is better, that terrorists are being watched, that it would be impossible to get a bomb on board a plane now. Well, yeah, maybe. The 103 bomb was put on board in Frankfurt and for sure they have done things to tighten security there. But they'll be responding to what happened, not what might happen. They think they are looking for terrorists and bombs but actually what all those security guards are looking for is bombs. They have been trained to look for terrorists but none of them actually believe that any terrorist is going to try and board an aircraft in Frankfurt. You'll be asked questions when you go to check in. But remember they're routine for them and they expect nothing but the normal answers that you give them.' Terpil had leaned forward to slap one of his huge hands across Rosan's shoulders. 'So relax, kid, it's going to be just fine.'

And indeed Terpil had been right. Standing in line at Frankfurt security, he had been amazed to see that the guards looked just like him. Mostly in their twenties, many looked as if they came from the Middle East. If he had been in charge of security, he would have thought both the guards and himself might have fitted the computer profile of a terrorist. And while all were wearing impressive uniforms and carrying official-looking clipboards, the questions they asked each passenger were identical and the answers they received almost identical.

His baggage had been examined and his small roll of Afghan carpets had been opened but otherwise the checks were routine, no different in fact from any other flight he had taken.

After the ten-hour flight, he had disembarked at Dulles into a bus that had taken him to the terminal. A short walk down a winding stair and he was in the queue for immigration. Fifteen minutes later he was facing the blue-shirted official. Looking at him, Rosan could not help a feeling of superiority swell inside him to overcome his fear. The official must have been four stone overweight and wore thick spectacles that made him look like an owl. Just another bureaucrat, he thought. The knowledge of his secret mission, knowledge this man would never share, boosted his confidence.

The immigration official spoke and Rosan's confidence suddenly vanished as he leaned forward, unable to understand what he was saying. A momentary flash of panic, swiftly controlled, and then the official repeated the question more slowly, the Spanish accent now subsumed by the English he had been expecting.

'The purpose of your visit?' the official asked, the routine of the question disguising its purpose. The nervous, the garrulous, the smuggler and the illegal immigrant were all supposed to find the formality of the interrogation frightening, but now that the action had started, Rosan was calm, his answers coming out smoothly, but not so fast as to sound rehearsed.

'I'm on business. Selling carpets from Afghanistan.'

'Have you been to visit us before?'

'No, sir. This is the first time.'

'And how long will you be staying?'

'Two weeks or a month. It depends how the business goes.'

Rosan saw that the passport had passed inspection and the official was now consulting his computer and the large ledger to find out if either the name or the passport triggered any memory in the database. A check in the computer, a flick through the ledger, a stamp and an illegible scribble on the white immigration card and he was through.

Customs admired his carpets and asked him how business was doing now that the war was over. He went into a long explanation of how his family had supported the Mujahedeen and were now helping them find their feet again.

After a thirty-minute cab ride to downtown DC he checked in at the Capital Hilton at 16th and K, three blocks from the White House. In his suite on the fourth floor, he unlocked the fridge, poured himself a miniature Jack Daniel's and lay back on the bed, sipping his drink and reflecting how easy it had been to get inside the belly of the beast.

September 15

New York

FRANK ABRAMS HAD JUST TAKEN a large bite out of the jam doughnut he'd bought at The Friendly Fattie on the way to work when the phone rang. Wiping a smear of red strawberry jam from his chin with a napkin, Abrams reached out for the phone and, cradling it into his neck, tried a firm 'Good morning' which came out as a doughnut-filtered grunt.

'HiFrankhowarya.' The voice at the other end produced a single word which came down the line in the deep nasal whine which New Yorkers claimed as a mark of distinction but which Abrams, a West Coast exile, found simply offensive.

'Hi, Marty, what can I do for you this morning?' The caller was a familiar weekly irritant. Marty Liebowitz was the chief investigator of Harrington Stockguard Inc., a firm that kept a watchful eye on movements in stocks of major public companies. They were the first line of defence for companies that might be a target of a dawn raid, or where a predator was buying stock in preparation for a Saturday Night Special – an overnight takeover bid.

The two men had met at a conference in Chicago on corporate security. Marty, a small rumple-suited fast-talking Jewish wise guy from the Upper East Side, had introduced himself to Abrams as 'a man you should be doing business with'.

Abrams was unconvinced, even when he learned that as well as being chief investigator, Marty was also the owner of Harringtons. 'Hey, what do you expect,' the little man had explained. 'I'm working among Wasps who like to do

133

business with each other or nice Jewish boys who have an inferiority complex and wish they were Wasps. Harrington Schmarrington. Who cares as long as it brings in business?'

Since that fateful meeting fifteen months earlier Marty had telephoned Abrams each week without fail, ostensibly for a gossip but in fact to pick the SEC man's brains for any tidbit he could feed back to his clients. It was a two-way trade though, as Marty occasionally picked up trends and unexpected movements that the computers hadn't noticed but which were currency on the Street.

In his characteristic rapid-fire speech Marty spewed out the mixture of fact, rumour, half-truth, salacious gossip and downright lies that Abrams had come to expect. Abrams looked on him as a pig snuffling for the truffles of information that he might pick up in exchange for the gossip he passed on. So far, Abrams was satisfied that the traffic had mostly been going his way.

'The Street's piranhas are gathering around the corpse of Honywood,' Marty began, referring to a stock that had recently gone into Chapter 11 to avoid bankruptcy. 'I hear that Bear Sterns have a toehold purchase in Woolpack and they may be planning a blitzkrieg tender offer,' which Abrams interpreted as a move by the bankers acting on behalf of an unnamed client to buy stock in the clothing company before making a formal bid. He made a short note on the legal pad in front of him. 'Roman have devised a lollipop as a shark-repellent against Pickens.' This one merited another note as it suggested that Roman, a multinational quoted in New York, were about to produce an attractive share scheme to undermine a bid by the corporate raider T. Boone Pickens.

Afterwards Abrams would not be able to say why his antennae twitched as Marty reached his last item, but his subconscious had his hand moving across before he had consciously processed the information and decided that it just might be of some interest.

'There's a funny rumour going around that there's been some heavy buying in puts in Kola Co. I've looked at it and can't get a handle on it and I wondered if you had heard anything?'

In 1975 the American Stock Exchange had added options to its trading possibilities following a trend set by Chicago two years earlier. A put option is the right to sell a stock at some time in the future at a lower price than is being quoted at the time of the deal. By taking a put, the investor is gambling that the price will fall while the opposite of a put, a call, is made when the gamble is on the price rising.

'What's strange about this one is that the strikes are being done around sixty dollars, which means someone is gambling on a hell of a fall.'

While Marty continued to speculate, Abrams quickly tapped the keyboard to his left bringing the latest stock prices to the screen. He saw that Kola Co. were currently standing at sixty-five dollars. So, if Marty was right, the investor was gambling on a near ten per cent fall at a time when all the pundits were reckoning on a steady increase over the next three months.

'News to me, Marty,' Abrams replied in an offhand manner. The slightest suggestion of interest and Marty would have caused a major SEC investigation into Kola Co. before he had had time to finish his doughnut. 'But if you hear anything else give me a call.'

Reviewing his pencilled notes after Marty had left him in peace, Abrams found his curiosity was still piqued by the Kola Co. information. He resolved to put it in his weekly report down to Washington.

September 17

Kansas City

KANSAS CITY WAS ONCE A frontier town, the pre-
serve of cattle barons bringing their beef along the
Chisholm Trail to the railyards for shipping back east.
With the development at the turn of the century of refriger-
ated freight cars and a proper road network, Kansas City
became a Midwest backwater. But the city always had a
strong bedrock of prosperity from the farmers who turned
the Midwest into one enormous wheat field.

In the 1960s when Joyce Hall was looking for somewhere
to base her growing greeting cards business she settled on
Kansas City. It was a perfect marriage. The city welcomed
the business that Hallmark Cards brought and was proud of
its association with a conservative – some might say saccharin
– product that was familiar to millions of Americans. Hallmark became part of the life of the city, replacing the cattle
barons of a century earlier as the area's largest single employer.

In the way of American corporations, the company took
its responsibilities to the community seriously, sponsoring a
show of Norman Rockwell illustrations at the Kansas City
museum one year and a series of concerts by the Boston
Pops Orchestra another. They were proud of their company
and proud of Kansas City and the feeling was matched by its
6,000 employees, their families and local people alike.

Each of the projects that the company sponsored was
carefully calculated to enhance their image in the community
as a traditional, conservative, caring company. In keeping
with those goals, fifteen years earlier the directors had
decided that each division in the company should hold a

summer picnic for the employees and their families. It had begun as a simple affair with a barbecue, canned sodas and a softball game. But as with all such things in America, where the competitive spirit is a tribal badge of honour, it had grown so that today, while the barbecues remained, the picnic had expanded to include frisbee competitions, a softball league, and a professional magician going through his routine for the children.

Kathy Freed, assistant packer in the Valentine card division, loved the summer picnic. For her, the day was exactly what the company had hoped when it was first launched: a happy affair where workers and their families joined the extended Hallmark family for a day of simple pleasure that bound old and young to the company's blue and white flag.

Kathy knew that the day would bring the kind of riches she looked forward to from one year to the next. She lived with her three children on Grand at 25th in Prairie Village, a small suburb of Kansas City on the Kansas side of the Kansas/Missouri line. Two hundred years ago, Prairie Village was a tiny settlement next to Shawnee Mission, one of the last outposts of the once great Shawnee tribe that had roamed the Midwest. Today Prairie Village is just another working-class suburb with white-painted tracked homes, each complete with a picket fence and small patch of yard, a model of conformity in a town that truly believes in an orderly approach to life.

Most of her neighbours on Grand Road were friends from Hallmark and many of them would be going to the picnic at Loose Park, a ten-minute drive from the house.

Today Kathy was expected to produce drinks, crackers and hot dogs for the barbecue. But she was also expected to produce the now famous Kathy Freed Key Lime Pie. Kathy used a legendary recipe that by family tradition had been passed from her grandmother who got it from her mother who had brought it out from the east at the turn of the century. In fact her mother had found the recipe in an old copy of the *Kansas City Star* when Kathy herself had been a child suspicious of all new food. The fictitious story had helped ease the passage from plate to stomach.

All Friday evening she had been baking so that her three

children, nine-year-old Mary, six-year-old Joseph and the five-year-old baby of the family, little Pete, could not only eat their fill but share the fruits of her labours with their friends. These family occasions had taken on a new importance in the last two years since her husband Dave had left to go and live with a woman from the greetings card division. The picnic was a welcome time for the family to be together, time when the difficult moments were set aside and the four of them were united in fun.

By the time the family had packed the picnic into the Ford Pinto, gathered the picnic blankets, the folding chairs for Mom and her friends, the Walkman for Mary, the new kite for Joe and the hairy flannel blanket that Pete still liked to suck on during moments of great excitement (of which plenty were expected this afternoon), most of the other picnickers had already arrived at Loose Park.

The park covered fifty-three acres in the centre of the city so the Hallmark contingent took up only a tiny fraction near the running track; their domain clearly marked by the 25-foot banner suspended over the barbecue which read 'Eat Your Hearts Out Valentines'.

Two hours later they had all done just that. Gorged, Kathy lay back in the armchair snatching a few minutes in the sunshine before taking little Pete to watch the magician.

Idly, she looked over to her left, a smile turning to a frown of concern as she took in Pete lying thumb entwined in his beloved blanket sucking gently in a half-sleep. She could see beads of sweat standing out on his smooth and lightly tanned forehead, sweat that had already soaked into the roots of his blond hair.

Kathy placed the palm of her hand on Pete's forehead, only to draw it back sharply with an exclamation of surprise. 'My God, he's on fire,' she muttered to herself, looking around for someone to confirm her diagnosis. Spotting Maria Ortega walking by she called out, 'Maria, come over here. Take a look at Petey, something's the matter.'

As Maria moved in her direction, she felt a tugging on her right sleeve and turned to see Joe standing next to her.

'Mom,' he began in that half-whine that children adopt when they are about to pass on bad news, 'I feel real sick. I have a pain right here,' indicating his stomach.

Hardly had he finished speaking than he turned away and retched, first a dry heave and then quickly half a dozen spasms, each one faster than the other, spewing out vomit in a yellow-brown stream on to the green grass. So violent was the motion that he dropped to his knees and Kathy saw to her horror on his forehead, too, sweat had sprung out actually to drip into the pool of vomit by his knees.

Hardly had the first spasms passed before Joe began jerking forward from the waist as his body tried once again to reject the poison. This time there were no hot dogs, chips or Kola to smooth the motion. A series of rending retches came from his mouth with only a thin stream of mucus to show for the effort.

Kathy had reached out both arms to embrace and comfort her boy when she heard a high-pitched scream from her left. Looking over she saw to her horror that little Pete was arched off the ground balanced on the back of his head and the heels of his feet, stretching his little body into the shape of a taut bow. As the rictus took hold and the pain enveloped his body, his lips were drawn back from his teeth in a horrible parody of a child's funny face. From his mouth came now only a mewing whimper. For a full thirty seconds, while Kathy and Maria froze, paralysed with the horror, Pete held his body convulsed, then with a groan it unbowed and flopped to the ground. But there was to be no respite. As soon as his tiny frame was straight once more, his head flicked to one side and his mouth spewed out a deep puddle of vomit. Weakened by the trauma, the boy had no strength to lift his head and it was only a choking gurgle that gave life back to Kathy.

With a cry that held within it all the defensive sympathy of a mother for her wounded child and the beginnings of a plea for help, Kathy leaned over and with her left arm tenderly moved Pete's head away from the suffocating vomit. She found herself muttering soothing noises of reassurance as her right hand moved over to mop the soaking brow of her youngest child. As her fingers touched his forehead she felt another spasm pass through his body and again a high, keening wail was forced from Pete's mouth, cut off once again as his body arched. In a quick reflex action, Kathy pushed out her arm to try and force her son's body back on to the ground but the convulsion was so powerful that even his tiny frame proved too strong for her.

'My God, my God. Somebody help me. Please somebody. Help. Help me.' The words came out in an unformed rush. The screams had halted the picnic. Games had stopped and people stilled as if by a camera's freezing eye as they searched for the source of the chilling sound. Then, swiftly, they moved as one to the huddled group of Kathy and her two children, prompted like all crowds in part by sympathy and in part by curiosity.

By the time the picnickers had gathered around them, both children had lost consciousness, lying pathetically alongside their vomit, only the occasional tremor passing through their bodies as a small indication of the life struggling within.

Washington, DC

The hookers had made the most extraordinary impression on Said Rosan. He had had his share of women. Indeed, while Nidal was happy to welcome women into the revolutionary ranks, he retained much of the Arab chauvinism and promiscuity was accepted, even encouraged, among the women.

The Tripoli camp also had access to the Praetorian Guard who looked after the Colonel. Always the attention seeker, Gadaffi had surrounded himself with women bodyguards all of whom were both attractive and loyal. Well trained in the martial arts, they also tended to be fitter and leaner than the average Arab woman and so appealed more to Rosan's taste. But they were still dark, many of them with the large hips and lips that are a characteristic of North African women.

In a spirited role reversal, the women would appear once or twice a month in gangs of twelve or fifteen, driving the forty miles from their barracks to arrive after sunset, armed with the latest imports; a Michael Jackson cassette one week, a video featuring Burt Reynolds the next. These women were nearly all unsophisticated Libyan peasants with tastes created from what little exposure they had to Western culture. This produced some extraordinary sights with the women donning make-up and clothes under their more formal Islamic chadors that could equally have suited the painted lady at the circus. But to Nidal's fedayeen they were bounty indeed and no time was wasted on criticizing fashion or facials. After the brief formality of a dance or movie, the real purpose of the evening would begin. The women would select their young fighter and slide out of the communal hall to find a quiet part of the camp or an unoccupied bed for some frantic coupling. This was not love. There was no tenderness, no mouthing of endearments, but simply raw sex, a physical act as meaningful as going to the bathroom or brushing teeth.

In his previous travels, Rosan had always worked to a tight schedule where appointments had to be kept and people met. This time he was on his own and the hookers had been a serious distraction. The first night he had ventured from his hotel and come across a glittering array of talent outside his door. Tall, slim, apparently young women dressed in tiny shorts or minute mini skirts paraded along the sidewalk and offered themselves. It was a wonderful and alluring sight.

Like birds of paradise, each girl wore brightly coloured plumage to stand out in the crowd. One white girl wearing a blue sequined mini skirt and open red blouse that clearly revealed the large, milky white breasts underneath had approached him.

'Hiya, honey,' she had begun. 'Wanna show a girl a good time?' Her routine and stunningly unoriginal opening gambit washed over Rosan who was overwhelmed at being propositioned by what to his eyes was a vision of loveliness lifted straight from the pages of the magazines that had been passed hand to hand in the camps.

In a daze he had allowed the girl ('My name's Paula, what's yours, honey?') to put her arm through his, the touch of her breast on his arm sending shivers of excitement through his body. He had taken her straight back to his hotel, past the disapproving eyes of the doorman and up to his room. The idea of making love with a white woman had so overwhelmed him that the brevity and simplicity of the

141

act itself had in retrospect taken on a kind of mystical quality. Where Paula saw just another john, Rosan saw a vision who embraced him with her mouth, drew him gently between her legs and brought him to a shuddering orgasm moments later. Even the sordid moment where money changed hands was for the contented Rosan simply a time for him to be munificent to someone who had brought him pleasure.

He was not so seduced by it all that he forgot his mission, but Terpil had proved right. It was too easy to find out where the target lived. He had simply dialled 411, asked information for the number of Robert Gearheart. They had supplied the number and followed it up with the address he requested.

A visit to Hertz at 16th and L and a few minutes later he drove away in an anonymous red Ford. He followed the direction provided by the helpful girl behind the counter and three minutes later he was parked outside Bob Gearheart's house. A quick check on the letter boxes in the entrance way to the house confirmed that he was at the right place.

Rosan reckoned there was no need to wait outside all day while Gearheart was at work. He need simply return in the late afternoon and sit waiting for the people in the building to return from work. He planned to enter the apartment where the target lived in the early hours of the morning, kill him and then make his escape. If all went well he would have flown out of Washington on the first shuttle to New York and then caught the morning British Airways flight to London.

The night of the 15th he had counted ten people entering the house, six men and four women. He had drawn a picture of the building and as each person entered and a light went on so he wrote a description of the person next to the room. He gave each of the men names. The one with the spiky hair and spectacles was The Scientist, the one with the half-grown black and grey beard he called Arafat and another who had a prominent dimple in his chin he had named Kirk after Kirk Douglas, whom he had seen often in the Western movie *Vera Cruz*, one of Nidal's favourites.

The following morning, Rosan was outside the house again watching the residents go to work. This time he managed to place three of the men and all four women.

142

By the end of the second night he had placed all the original ten and added another two to his list who were also located by the following morning. But he still did not know which of the men was his target.

During the day he visited Mario's florist's around the corner from the hotel and ordered a dozen roses to be delivered to Bob Gearheart's address. Payment of an extra twenty dollars produced the guarantee that the flowers would be delivered at precisely seven o'clock that evening.

At the appointed time, Rosan was parked across the road with a clear view of the front door of the house. Just after seven the florist's delivery boy pedalled his bicycle to the house, propped it against the lamppost and went up the front steps. He searched the postboxes and pressed the Gearheart button. Watching carefully, Rosan could see no lights change in the house but a few moments later the door opened and a man leaned forward to receive the flowers.

Ah, it's Kirk, thought Rosan with a small, satisfied smile. He looks surprised. Wait until he reads the message. Someone is in for an even bigger surprise. At that moment, Bob had opened the little white envelope and was staring puzzled at the card which had written on it: 'Please Forgive Me.'

September 19

Kansas City

TWO DAYS OF hospital vigil had taken their toll. Kathy's contented, slightly overweight middle-aged body had both shrunk and aged. Weeping had made her eyes bloodshot and lack of sleep had driven them deep into her skull so that she had that look of utter exhaustion more commonly found on mountaineers who have just reached the peak or marathon runners passing the finishing line than on a greetings card worker. But it was her hands that really betrayed her. Her fingers moved constantly, playing with each other one moment, moving in a nervous flicker to touch her unkempt hair another, then stretching forward lightly to stroke the cheek of one or other of her sons who lay on either side of her.

The children had arrived at St Luke's Hospital within thirty minutes of the first convulsion two days earlier. Both had been rushed into emergency and from there into Ward B10 where they had been isolated from the other patients. The room reminded Kathy of the control room at work, where computers printed, dried, folded and stacked millions of cards for distribution around the nation. Only the machinery here would not produce any joy for Kathy or anyone else.

Both children were connected to the paraphernalia that modern medicine demands to diagnose life or impending death in a patient and prevent a doctor suffering a malpractice suit. For two days Kathy had looked at each machine in turn as if their mute signals might give her some clue to the progress of her children. For two days she had understood nothing except that before her eyes her two sons were dying.

144

They had entered the hospital unconscious and neither had opened his eyes since. Drugs had controlled the contractions and quietened their small bodies but drugs could not disguise the disintegration. Pete's thick fair curls – oh, how well she remembered running her hands through them as he fell asleep – had first become lank and lifeless. Then earlier that day they had started to fall out in great tufts to lie on the pillow like the clippings from a poodle parlour. It had been horrible. Her anguished questions to the doctor had merely produced some unpronounceable Latin name in diagnosis that meant nothing to her and, evidently, little to him either.

Now, as she looked tenderly at the little boy, he was almost unrecognizable as the son she had known and loved only forty-eight hours earlier. His head was completely hairless, even the eyebrows had disappeared. His body now lay completely still, the drips feeding panaceas to calm the stomach and control the retching. The only thing the drugs had not controlled and the only sign of life in either of the boys was an intermittent twitching of the eyelids. When it happened it was as if both were trying desperately to wink in some dreadful parody of a children's game. On one occasion the spasms had been so bad that Joe's eyelid had flicked open and a sightless eye had briefly fixed Kathy in its gaze.

But in the past few hours even that tiny sign of life had ceased, leaving only the machines to record the faint pulse, the shallow movement of lungs.

Kathy knew but had refused to admit to herself that her sons were dying. The hushed tones of the doctors, the overwhelming kindness of the nurses, the mouthed but meaningless platitudes had all confirmed that medicine had failed. But despite the urging of the medical staff, she was determined to stay with her boys until the end, as if by the sheer force of her mother love she could will them well.

Her hand reached out to grip Pete's tiny fist, to embrace it, a poor substitute for the hugs she used to give him. There was no answering pressure.

Suddenly, the largest of the machines standing against the opposite wall began to emit a single high-pitched tone which was faintly echoed down the passage. The sound of hurrying

145

footsteps was followed by a rush of people into the room hauling behind them a trolley piled high with equipment. Kathy was pushed aside and stood, fist to mouth, against the wall as the bedclothes were stripped back and Pete's pale naked body exposed. With cries of encouragement that seemed so out of place in this room, doctors and nurses piled around the body injecting, pummelling and pulling. Five, ten minutes and their efforts lost their urgent energy and she knew it was over.

Numb, Kathy moved to the bed, knelt, rested her head on Pete's naked breast and wept.

Beirut

Harry Cartwright hated Beirut, every smelly, rat-infested, terrifying, lunatic inch of it. After two years at the front line of reporting he had had enough.

He had arrived to run the Reuters bureau in the city at a time when the Syrians appeared to be introducing some kind of order into the chaos of a country gone mad. He had seen the job as a chance to make good, to convince the honchos back in London that he could handle the most difficult jobs with the best of them. But this was not the Iran-Iraq war, Chad, South Africa or even El Salvador. This was Lebanon, a country in nothing but name. He had begun the assignment with a confidence born of experience and a certainty that this was a country like any other with a constant fund of stories to keep London happy and the rest of the world interested.

He had swiftly discovered that after the first few files – the colour on the young kids fighting for the different groups, the beach life that continued amid the chaos, the resilience of the locals – it became an incomprehensible jungle where the minutiae of politics baffled even the residents and was of no interest to the outside world.

As the story settled at a level where killings would rate a paragraph and a massacre a few hundred words, disillusionment had set in. Cartwright wanted out because professionally the job was going nowhere. Personally he wanted out because he was sick of living in a constant state of fear.

When he had first arrived he had taken an apartment around the corner from the Commodore Hotel, the sanctuary in West Beirut for journalists and spies for more than twenty years. But that first apartment had been made uninhabitable by an artillery bombardment that had blasted most of his block (he never learned who had actually been doing the firing that day). He had moved twice since then but that instability had been the least of the pressures.

A two-mile journey around the city could involve being stopped at three static checkpoints manned by any one of the different warring factions in the city. The guards would be heavily armed – the AK-47 was part of the uniform and a bandoleer of magazines an essential part of the macho image. The difficulty he had found with these checks was that he never really knew where he stood that day, at that minute, in the political equation. One day he had been held for ten hours by the Syrians who wanted to teach the PLO down the road, whom he was going to see, just who controlled the neighbourhood. Another day his car was confiscated because the local militia commander needed some transport.

That lawlessness extended to a vast sub-culture of local bands, many of whom were simple criminals. These groups roamed the streets, stopping people and cars at will. Death had become such an accepted part of everyday life in Lebanon that each barrier across the road, each youth in a camouflage uniform standing with hand upraised could be the first sign of the end.

There were no police to appeal to, no court that would punish the guilty and protect the innocent. It was anarchy and it was terrifying.

Harry had lost count of the times when his heart had seemed to stop and his armpits pour with the sweat of panic. He had had nightmares for months now about being trapped inside one of the coffins that he knew had been used to transport some of the Western hostages around the city. He knew that the fear was beginning to control his life and it was time to leave.

It had become his habit to walk the ten minutes from his apartment to the Commodore to have an early morning

147

espresso and pick up on the daily gossip. It was a routine and he knew that he should vary it but he had figured that by now everyone knew him and where he lived so if they wanted to take him they could pick their moment.

The stroll took him out of his apartment block up towards Hamra Street and then a left turn along the busy highway towards the hotel. He had just made the turning when he heard the squeal of brakes, a sound he had always dreaded. This morning, like all the other times, it made his pulse race, his heart pump in his chest. The moment of panic usually passed quickly when the car engine raced again as the driver overcame the temporary obstacle.

This time, the car drew into the kerb and then halted a few feet ahead of him. He thought of running but dismissed the option as his mind swiftly raced on to imagine the feeling of the bullets entering his back, pushing him face down into the cracked pavement.

The rear door of the battered Mercedes opened and Harry saw first the long barrel of a machine-gun and then the green and brown of a camouflage cap as a man ducked his head to get out of the car. He stood in front of Harry, gun pointed at his stomach, finger on the trigger.

'Get in, Mr Cartwright,' the man ordered, the machine-gun gesturing to his left. Harry had imagined this moment many times, how he would fight off his attacker, turn and run. He always visualized the elegance of his escape and telling the story of his luck to colleagues in the bar that night. But his craven behaviour on the day disgusted him. He stepped meekly forward and slid across the seat in the back to be sandwiched between two militiamen. The car accelerated away from the kerb to rejoin the traffic heading west.

'What the hell do you guys want? Who are you? Where are we going? You can't do this, I'm a journalist.'

As he heard his babble, Harry recognized the fear in his voice and knew that his captors would hear it too. He stopped talking and waited.

The man sitting in the front seat turned and leaned an arm over the seat. Harry noted that he wore no uniform but a Western suit. Unlike most of the militia in Beirut there was no designer stubble, no sign of the weapons that were part of so many residents' daily dress.

'Relax, Mr Cartwright. It is precisely because you are a journalist that we have asked you to take this little journey with us. We have a message we would like you to deliver for us.'

The tone of the cultured American accent and the pacific nature of the message all helped to reassure Harry. The man reached inside his suit and produced a cream-coloured envelope which he passed back.

'This is for you. Inside is a message from Abu Hassan, a message that we want you to transmit to the rest of the world. The price of your freedom today will be your assurance that you will have this filed by lunchtime.'

This was not a time to worry about negotiating with terrorists, Harry reflected.

'Sure, that should be no problem,' he replied. 'But you'd better let me off soon as I'll have to get back to the office.'

The man in front made a cutting motion to the driver and, with another squeal of brakes, the car pulled in to the side of the road. The back door opened, the gunmen got out and Harry swiftly followed.

'I hope we can do business in the future, Mr Cartwright,' the American voice called from the front seat.

'Don't count on it,' he shouted to the retreating back of the Mercedes, his courage recovered now that he was free.

Standing on the street, he turned the envelope over in his hand. There were no markings. He tore the flap and extracted the two sheets of A4 which had been carefully stapled together.

'In the name of the oppressed Palestinian people,' he read, 'we, the Palestine Fighting Arm, claim responsibility for the deaths from food poisoning that have occurred in the United States, France, Great Britain, Germany, Italy, Spain and Belgium.'

The first paragraph was enough for Harry. He started to run, eyes scanning the street for a taxi, the professional reporter once more taking over.

'Great story. Great story,' he chanted as he ran. 'But why couldn't those bastards just have telephoned.'

Washington, DC

It was supposed to have been the perfect, romantic evening. On the way back from work at the SEC headquarters at 450 Fifth Street near Pennsylvania Avenue, Bob had stopped first at Brad's Liquor on the corner of 13th and H and then at Suzanne's Delicatessen to buy fresh pasta and two enormous slices of homemade lemon tart. Bob had the bachelor's slovenly habit of buying pre-cooked food whenever possible which, combined with a preference for Suzanne's rather than Stouffer's, produced a steady drain on his finances.

As he walked home through the pleasant heat of the Washington fall, he reflected how his firing from the Agency had produced some unexpected benefits. When he had first moved to DC, he'd opted to rent downtown and commute out to Langley rather than become one of the thousands who chose to live in one of the characterless dormitory suburbs on the periphery of the nation's capital.

Now he was within a twenty-minute walk of the SEC. Unlike New York, walking in Washington was not an ordeal marred by muggers and carbon monoxide poisoning. The press may have billed it as the murder capital of America but the crime was mostly confined to the black ghettos east of the Capitol. Muggers knew better than to step off their own turf into the heavily patrolled and well-defended Wasp heartland.

So, each day Bob took to walking to and from work, enjoying the wide-open streets; the fresh air either preparing him for the day ahead or restoring him after ten hours spent in what was grandly described as an 'office' but which was, in fact, a cubicle in a floor filled with similar three-sided boxes in the SEC's open-plan headquarters.

He was beginning to understand his work although to date there had been none of the buzz, none of the feeling that you could change history, could influence the course of nations by thinking creatively. Instead he had discovered that the SEC was a vast bureaucracy where the end game was satisfying the Hill that its $150 million budget was justified.

If work was passable, the home front was less satisfactory. The solace provided by Mary on that first night after his firing had been the climax of their relationship to date. She had left the next day on an assignment to Colorado for a shoot for *Vanity Fair* and he had been absorbed in learning about his new work. They had met twice in the two weeks since her return and Bob thought he detected in Mary a cooling.

He had tracked back the problems with their relationship to his meeting with Helen a month earlier. He had thought about the evening often but failed to analyse why it still intruded to the extent that it was interfering in his affair with Mary. In any event, the result had been a shadow cast over the relationship. His solution, common to many bachelors, was to get Mary on to his territory for a long, gentle evening where problems, imagined and real, could be thrashed out to his satisfaction. Hence the dinner.

His apartment was two blocks from Suzanne's at 14th and P. A two-bedroom apartment in a turn-of-the-century block, he had inherited it from another bachelor at Langley who had married and moved out to the burbs. Like many such places in DC, there was a simple entrance off the main street with no security. Even his front door had only a standard mortise and no alarms. If this had been New York, he reflected as he balanced groceries in one hand and front door key in the other, there would have been a uniformed guard to get past, an elevator guard and triple locks on all the doors with video cameras eyeing the corridors.

Putting the groceries down on the kitchen counter, Bob unpacked the pasta, turned on the gas and put a pan filled with water on the hob for the pasta. As it started to heat, he took some ham and mushrooms from the fridge and began chopping them up for the cream sauce. He turned on the TV that perched on top of the fridge. The picture immediately brought up an ad for Coca Cola. Idly watching the foot-stomping ad and mouthing the words of the background song Bob waited for the moment when the camera caught the movement of the girl as she crossed her legs in front of her boyfriend and there was a brief and almost missed flash of her underwear. Then the image cleared and the sombre features of Bernard Shaw, CNN's veteran black anchorman appeared.

'CNN has learned that a terrorist organization called the

Palestine Fighting Arm has claimed responsibility for a wave of food poisoning that has so far killed seventy-five people in seven Western countries. So far twenty-five people have died across the United States. The latest victim, five-year-old Peter Freed, died in hospital in Kansas City earlier today.'

The cameras cut to a still photograph of young Peter, fresh-faced, blond and innocent.

'The terrorists, who delivered their message this morning in Beirut, say that they have poisoned soda made by Kola Co. in seven Western countries. Unless their demands for a Palestinian state are met within the next two weeks, they say another campaign of poisoning will begin against a new range of products.

'The State Department said today that the PFA was a previously unknown terrorist group. Until now the poisoning cases were being treated as an unfortunate if extraordinary coincidence. Now the US government has promised to co-ordinate the international investigation to see if people are dying from natural causes or because of terrorism.

'A spokesman at Kola Co. contacted at their headquarters in Detroit, Michigan had no comment on the PFA claims.'

As Shaw's face faded to be replaced by an ad for a new washing powder, two things happened at once. Steam from the boiling water began to cloud the kitchen and the telephone rang. He stretched along the kitchen counter and cradled the phone between shoulder and neck while his left hand reached back to lift the pan from the stove.

'Bob, hi. It's Jim Prentice.'

Bob paused. He had not heard from his former Agency colleague since he had been banished to the obscurity of the Stock Exchange. He had enough experience of the intelligence world to know that calls like this did not come without purpose so there was caution in his voice as he replied.

'Jim. I haven't heard from you in a long while. How's things?'

'Pretty good. Pretty good.'

Bob thought he detected nervousness in Prentice, perhaps even a hint of embarrassment. There was a slight hesitation before his former colleague got down to the purpose of his call.

'Have you caught the news yet?'

'Sure, I was just watching CNN. That's one smart move those guys have made,' Bob replied.

'Yeah, right.' In those two words Bob heard tension, frustration, anger even. 'This one has really got our balls in the wringer. We need your help.'

Bob felt a flush of anger rising to his face and was grateful for the telephone line that kept him invisible from Prentice. Controlling his emotion Bob probed for more information.

'I'm out of all that stuff, remember? You guys decided I was the loose cannon on the intelligence deck and I was canned. I've got a new job, a new life. I can't see what use I can be to you now.'

Prentice's voice took on a reassuring tone, the sort of deep-timbred voice American executives seem to practise daily in front of the mirror to project confidence and honesty.

'I can understand that you feel sore about that and you know that wasn't my decision. All I know is that we have a major crisis and I need the best people around. Take it from me, Bob, I do need you and I need you right now.'

Despite his reservations, Bob could feel the familiar stirrings, the undercurrent of excitement that ran through so much of his work at the Agency. It was something he had missed.

Prentice pressed him. 'We have a meeting going on at State right now and I want you over here. Come to the C Street Entrance and there'll be one of my people waiting to take you up.'

Bob had made up his mind. There was now no hesitation. 'I'll be right over.'

Pausing only to grab a sweater (experience told him this could go on long into the night), Bob headed for the door. As he touched the latch, the bell rang and he opened the door before Mary's arm had returned to her side.

'Hi, honey,' he welcomed her, bringing his lips down to meet hers fleetingly. 'I'm afraid something has come up and I'm needed down at State. I don't know how long I'll be but make yourself at home and save some lemon tart for me.'

Before Mary even had time to frame a reply, Bob had

turned and headed down the stairs taking the steps two and three at a time. She was still poised on the threshold of the apartment as she heard the front door slam.

It was a short cab ride from 14th Street to the C Street Entrance to the State Department. The cab dropped Bob off underneath the canopy that shielded State's important overseas visitors from rain and sun. He paid the driver and walked through the glass double doors and approached the security desk.

The lack of intelligence among the security guards at State was legendary. Usually getting a pass was a ten- or fifteen-minute operation while forms were filled and questions answered. But this time the word must have come down from on high, an indication of the level of the crisis.

As soon as Bob gave his name to the desk, the female guard looked to her left and gave a signal to a tall, slim black man standing just the other side of the bomb detection equipment. He moved forward and with a polite 'Mr Gearheart? Would you follow me please?' they moved off towards the bank of elevators.

All the elevators at State are programmed to stop at the first floor so there was a minimal wait before the two men got out at the seventh floor where the Operations Center is located.

There were no fancy screens hidden behind fake wooden walls showing the readiness state of US nuclear forces and no huge television screens relaying the satellite pictures from the Middle East or Africa. Instead, Bob was disappointed to note that it was a simple, functional committee room. The only things that set it apart from any other executive suite in any corporation were the banks of secure phones, all of which seemed to be ringing as he came through the door.

'Bob. Good of you to get here so quickly.' Jim Prentice moved away from the table and grasped Bob's hand in a quick, firm handshake. 'I called a TWIG on this so we are busy rounding up the usual suspects,' Jim continued, turning to address the whole room.

In the confusing world of Washington fastspeak, as soon as a group is formed, a decision taken, a new policy decided, it is generally given a handy acronym, and counter-terrorism is no exception. To those not inside the system it is a foreign language and even to those in the know it can be difficult to follow. TWIG actually referred to the Terrorist Incident Working Group which was set up in the early Reagan years to co-ordinate a US government response to an incident. Members included representatives from CIA, the Defence Intelligence Agency, State, the FBI, the National Security Council, the Pentagon and the National Security Agency. A meeting could be called by any member and additional people could be co-opted on to the Group such as a representative from the Federal Aviation Administration in the event of a hijack. The difficulty with the group was that the initials TIWG did not easily compress into an understandable acronym so some Washington wit had translated it into TWIG, 'the right name for a tiny branch far from the tree of government' as one cynic put it.

'I've asked Bob to join us because he may be able to give us some help on tracking the guys involved.' Prentice drew Bob into the room. 'He knows the money side of the house and has done outstanding work on tracking the flow of funds between terrorist groups. If there is any intelligence around, I hope Bob will be able to put it together for us.'

'Let me introduce you,' Prentice went on, his arm moving to the left to point in turn at the six people sitting round the table.

'Frank Dearth from State.' Bob had heard of Dearth, an appointee who had survived from the Shultz era. He had a reputation as a 'hunt 'em, find 'em, kill 'em' counter-terrorist activist who had been held in check by cooler heads. Dearth was known in the terrorism world as Jaws, a reflection of his predatory inclinations and the expensive gold bridgework he had had done which had produced a ridge of gold running along the outside of his top teeth. It was said he had the most expensive smile in Washington.

'I think you know Ambassador Rule from OCT.' Bob had briefed the ambassador in his capacity as head of the Office for Combating Terrorism. Harry Rule had asked some tough questions, backing up his public image as a no-bullshit guy in a job where an ability to play the political game was practically a prerequisite. In fact, Rule had been brought back from Ghana to take up his new post at a time when the administration wanted to downplay terrorism and devote more resources to the fight against drugs. Rule had argued effectively that the two were so closely connected that the fight had to be maintained on both fronts.

'Harry Macklowicz from DIA, Doug Frink from the Bureau, Sue Alexander from NSC, Sy Koch from NSA and I asked Joe Hathaway from the Food and Drug Administration to sit in.'

Bob nodded at the others and moved to the vacant chair while Prentice took his place next to Dearth at the top of the rectangular table.

As this was Dearth's territory, it was he who chaired the meeting and he took up the briefing.

'Well, lady and gentlemen,' he began. 'It looks like we have a real ball-breaker, a ten Domino at least.'

Beirut, Tripoli, the hostages, Panama had all helped make crisis management not exactly routine but certainly a regular feature of successive administrations. Among the few involved with TWIGs or any of the other elite teams that handled such events, a scale of measurement of such affairs had been devised. These were based not on some arcane government system for point scoring. Instead, the crisis managers had discovered that only the Domino pizza company could deliver at all hours to the different government buildings. Frequently crisis management meant that people worked, ate and slept in one office, sometimes for days at a time, and the severity of the crisis was judged by the number of empty pizza boxes that accumulated over the days. If Dearth estimated a ten Domino, they all knew they were in for a long haul. On the evening of January 15, 1991, the night the United Nations deadline for Iraq to leave Kuwait expired, the White House ordered fifty-five pizzas from Domino's, up from its average of five, and the Pentagon, which usually orders three pizzas a night, ordered 101.

Dearth picked up a thin sheaf of papers next to him. 'Some of you may have seen CNN earlier. They got the story from the same place as we did. Reuters filed the text of the communiqué two hours ago and this is the text.'

He took off the top copy and passed the rest on. As the diminishing pile circulated around the table Bob thought back over the past few years and how often it was that the first State or Langley knew about a kidnapping or a bombing was from the media. If the public ever knew, he thought to himself, how much the spooks owe to the *New York Times* and the wire agencies, they'd demand a saving in their tax dollars.

He picked up his copy of the Reuters file and read it slowly, his respect for the terrorists growing with each paragraph.

In the name of the oppressed Palestinian people, [it began], we, the Palestine Fighting Arm, claim responsibility for the deaths from food poisoning that have occurred in the United States, France, Great Britain, Germany, Italy, Spain and Belgium.

We regret the deaths of the innocent but many innocent Palestinians have also died at the hands of the Zionists and their allies.

Until now we have only poisoned the products of the American company Kola Co., a company we chose as a symbol of American imperialism.

Our comrades are already in place ready to poison again if our fair and reasonable demands are not met.

These demands are:

1. A conference will be convened in Geneva and chaired jointly by the United States and the Soviet Union. This conference will have delegates from Jordan, Israel and the Palestine Liberation Organization as representatives of the Palestinian people.

2. The conference will begin on October 5 and will last no more than one week. It will agree:

a. the establishment of a Palestinian state on the West Bank in confederation with Jordan.

b. to establish a demilitarized zone running for five miles on either side of the Jordan river. This will be policed by a multinational force, the composition of which is to be agreed. The force will exclude any Israeli, Jordanian or Palestinian forces.

c. that for a period of five years the new government of Palestine will not allow its people to bear arms.

d. that the PLO will recognize the right of Israel to exist.

157

We believe that it is in the interests of the world that these just demands are met. If they are not met before October 5 another campaign of poisoning will begin against a new group of products.

There will be no further contact.

It was Dearth who opened the discussion.

'So, what do we have? Do we buy this claim on the poisoning? Is it really some Palestinian group? We need answers and we need them fast. The White House have already been on the horn and they expect something from me within the hour.'

Turning to Prentice, he was clearly waiting for Jim to open with the CIA's offering.

'Well, we can't answer that at this stage,' Jim replied defensively. 'Just before this meeting I checked Flashboard and there is nothing that suggests any imminent terrorist activity in the Middle East.'

Prentice was referring to the special computer programme that had been set up some years before so that intelligence gathered by one agency could be accessed by another. In theory, this should have improved the sharing of valuable information, but in the cut-throat world of competing agencies, he who has information has power and so there was still a reluctance to share the best intelligence. The fact that Prentice had turned up nothing on Flashboard did not mean that there was nothing there, merely that nothing had been shared.

'We have picked up nothing unusual from any of our assets in the area and the Israelis have sent no flags up saying something was being planned. As for the claims, we are looking at that and should have something hard later today.'

There was a dismissive grunt from Dearth and he was just about to follow up with a caustic comment when Hathaway, the FDA's expert, spoke up. A small, round-faced man whose eyes looked enormous behind thick pebble glasses, he peered anxiously around the table, clearly uncomfortable to be in such company. A small, pink tongue flicked out to moisten his thin lips.

'I think I may be able to help,' he began tentatively. 'You

will recall that one of the attacks was in Kansas City.' There were affirmative nods around the table. 'Well, the hospital had initially been treating it as a simple case of food poisoning although the symptoms, vomiting, diarrhoea, convulsions and hair loss were most unusual. But one of the doctors at the hospital had recently been doing some work in Guyana in South America. While he was there there was an epidemic among people who had been working cutting sugar cane. More than 200 people died and this doctor said they had exactly the same symptoms as the children who died in Kansas City.'

'So what the hell caused it?' asked Dearth.

'The government had suffered a plague of rats in the sugar-cane fields and decided to get rid of them by putting down a poison called thallium. This had got on to the cane which the workers used to chew during their breaks. Apparently it takes only a tiny amount of this stuff to kill. It has been banned in this country for twenty years and is almost never used as an insecticide in the West.'

Hathaway paused, took off his glasses and peered myopically round the table.

'We took some blood from the dead kids and sent it down to the Center for Infectious Diseases in Atlanta. We briefed them to check for thallium and the answer came back this morning. It was thallium. The problem is that there is no known antidote. Sometimes a dose of something called Prussian Blue can work but its effect is spasmodic. Basically once the poison is in the body there's nothing much to be done . . .'

Prentice interrupted. 'But could they have done it? Infecting a can of soda is a tough job. That means they had somebody in the factories in each of the countries. Surely that's not possible?'

'I'm afraid it's much simpler than that. I checked with our people in the product contamination division up in New York. They tell me that there's not a single product on the market today that can't be poisoned by someone determined enough. I asked them how they would set about putting thallium in the soda. The preferred method would be to do it on the production line where most contamination takes place,

159

but that would hardly work in this case given that each country affected has its own canning plant. So they have either placed a concentrated derivative on the lip of the can that can be absorbed on drinking or they have injected it using a fine laboratory needle. It would take a few seconds and would be completely undetectable.'

'So I think we have to accept that they have done what they say,' said Dearth with a heavy sigh. 'Next question: who are these guys. Jim, Sy, you got any views about that?'

'The PFA has been around a couple of years but their operations have been pretty limited so far. In fact, we have tended to think they are an offshoot of one of the bigger groups, the PFLP-GC perhaps or the DFLP. Their leader Abu Hassan is a bit of a mystery man. No pics, no voice print. We're not even sure where he is based,' Jim said. 'This kind of sophistication though puts it into another dimension. The old guys in the Palestinian movement seem to have run out of ideas recently and it's Nidal and the Iranians who have shown more imagination and the capability to do something like this. Abu Nidal has used fifteen different names that we know of to claim responsibility for terrorist attacks. It could be the Iranians, Nidal, or it could be Abu Hassan operating on his own.

'My inclination is that it isn't Iranian as they'd be unlikely to commit the considerable resources this has required to win something for the Palestinians who are little more than a convenient political label for them.

'As for Nidal, I just don't know. The demands don't sound like him. He's a fanatic, a madman who likes nothing more than to spoil everybody else's party. Yet here he is playing mainstream Palestinian politics and fairly moderate politics at that. I say no to Nidal as well, but I don't have a smoking gun to point at anyone else either. What about you, Sy?'

The National Security Agency had become the all-seeing all-knowing intelligence source. For the past twenty years the world of COMINT (Communications Intelligence) and SIGINT (Signals Intelligence) had been the rising star of the intelligence community. By comparison the HUMINT (Human Intelligence) world was in decline. The days of the traditional James Bond agent who by feats of daring, diplomacy and debauchery brought home the vital information appeared to be virtually over. The all-seeing all-knowing image wasn't true, of course, but the NSA carefully nurtured it at their Fort Meade headquarters so that the generous funding continued. When it came to Congressional budget cutbacks they were last on the list.

If the NSA was not the God they allowed their supporters to claim, interception of military signals and telephone conversations has become a science where computers and satellites make it possible to Hoover up thousands of conversations every day for later analysis. This kind of work is invariably on the leading edge of technology and so, from its birth in 1952, the NSA could hide success and failure behind an all-embracing blanket of secrecy. To others in the covert world, the NSA's obsession with hiding everything and revealing only the minutest amounts of information and then only under pressure had given rise to various derogatory titles such as No Such Agency, No Secrets About or, more commonly, Never Say Anything – a no-doubt apocryphal story had it the latter was coined by Bill Casey after a particular acrimonious meeting to discuss Soviet involvement in terrorism. 'That's all those bastards down at Meade ever have to tell me,' he was reported as saying.

So it was with a certain lack of enthusiasm that the meeting turned towards Sy Koch. True to NSA form, he pursed his lips, looked pensive, ticked an imaginary box on the yellow pad in front of him and then looked up at Dearth.

'We've had a preliminary look at the traffic and we see no sign of anything at this stage.' He paused and Dearth leaned forward expectantly. 'Of course, we have now begun to trawl back through the database to see if there is anything we have missed. But it will take at least a week to come up with a definitive answer.'

Harry Rule interrupted what appeared to be the beginnings of a long statement about nothing very much.

'Look, this is not getting us anywhere and in less than thirty minutes Frank and I have to be heading for the White House. Right now we have to answer three things.

'First, is it possible to poison people in this way. The FDA say yes to that.

161

'Second, do we know who they are? The Agency and the NSA both say No and I assume DIA concurs?' Harry Macklowicz nodded.

'Third, do we know why now and why Kola Co.? It seems extraordinary to me that a terrorist group should commit an act of such barbarity in the name of the Palestinians when Arafat and all his henchmen have been arguing for a diplomatic solution for years now. Yet this operation smacks of a big organization and plenty of resources which in turn suggests some kind of central control.'

He turned towards Bob. 'You're the guy who's best placed of all of us to know if an operation could be put together without us knowing. Have you seen anything to suggest something was about to go down?'

Bob had been listening to the exchange and reflecting that these inter-agency meetings always seemed to turn into a pissing contest with the nation the loser. The CIA trying to score off DIA and both of them ganging up on the NSA with the Feebies hating the covert boys and the politicos like Dearth just looking for opportunities to turn the crisis to their own advantage. His firing from the CIA still hurt and his attendance at the meeting was strictly voluntary. With no allegiance to any of the factions, he felt a new and heady freedom.

'Well, as I have been unable to see any of the traffic for the last month or so I can't give you the complete picture,' he began, underlining his new-found amateur status. 'But these operations usually take from three to six months to set up and this one would have had to be underwritten by somebody with plenty of cash –'

Sue Alexander interrupted. A Middle East expert, she had been brought on to the NSC because of her work at the Bureau of Intelligence and Research in the State Department, where she had specialized in the Middle East and specifically Libya.

'What about Gadaffi? He got a bloody nose in Chad and the Sudan and he has been promising retribution.'

'Well, Gadaffi always talks a good game but this kind of operation would be very out of character,' Bob replied. 'Just think it through. It's an international operation running

162

across Europe and into the States. That suggests good long-term planning and co-ordination, two things that are not the Colonel's strong suits. Then this must have cost big bucks to set up and whoever is doing it must be calling in plenty of favours for safe houses and documents. Again that doesn't sound like Gadaffi. He's short of cash and in recent years has had to pay his own people to do his dirty work. I'd write him out.

'But I'd like to pick up on something the Ambassador was saying. There are two curious aspects about this business. This is a classic hostage-taking situation except the terrorists are holding the public of several nations as hostages. They have clear political objectives but if they are going to set up a new state then they'll have to fund it, yet there's no mention of money. By my reckoning the PLO currently have assets of around $5 billion and an annual income of over $1 billion. Even if they disband their military wing that's still small change if they are going to get their new state off the ground. So, who's picking up the tab?

'Second, why target Kola Co.? They have been very specific about that. Yet they could have simply hit a number of different products, oranges in Italy, chocolate in Britain and frozen pizzas here. But they chose one company for all countries and have been careful to name them. That's going to play hell with the stock.'

A white-shirted aide came into the room and placed a single sheet of paper in front of Dearth. He glanced at it and then looked at Bob. 'It already has. The company have just announced they are recalling all their products worldwide while they review their packaging. In Tokyo their stock has fallen from sixty-five dollars to sixty. When the markets open in London in the morning I expect it will fall through the floor. Anyone holding that stock is going to take a pounding.'

Since the beginning of the meeting, something to do with Kola Co. had been floating on the edge of Bob's subconscious. He was sure he had heard or read something about them in the past few days. A deal, a trade, something. Now Dearth's words triggered the memory.

'Jim, could you fix me up with a phone. I need to call New York.'

Bob moved to a corner of the room to make his call. Two minutes later he had reached Frank Abrams at home. Abrams confirmed that he had sent a message to Washington the previous week reporting a higher than usual number of trades in put options in Kola Co.

'Look, Frank, forgive my ignorance here. But if someone had bought these options knowing the price was going to go down they would make a killing. Right?'

'Yeah, that's true,' Abrams replied in a thoughtful voice filled with scepticism. 'But the whole point of puts is that they are a gamble. The stock could go either way.'

'Not if you've rigged the bet by contaminating the product so that it kills people all over the world. Then you know you're on a winner.'

Bob hung up the phone and turned back to the room. The sheer vision of the scheme was almost beyond his comprehension. It was beyond any doomsday scenario anyone in the room had ever conceived.

'Lady and gentlemen,' he began, the formality of his tone getting their instant attention. 'I now have the answer to why there was no demand for cash – and you're not going to like it.'

The White House Situation Room has entered the mythology as a centre of high-technology excellence. From here the President is expected to fight his wars, release the missiles and guide the nation's destiny in times of adversity. A common description has the President and his advisers sitting on a raised platform with the full extent of America's military power, both conventional and nuclear, arrayed below them. Along one wall are liquid crystal displays that show maps of the world. One of the operators at the banks of computers ranged below the President can change the display to show the location of Russian missile silos or the US Sixth Fleet.

However, the White House is an old building and much of the technology in it is old as well. If it ever came to a shooting war, the first thing the President would do would be to get as far away from the Situation Room as possible. In the event of a nuclear strike on Washington, both the White House and the Situation Room would become simply a large hole in the ground. The President and his advisers would either take off in one of the flying command posts, codenamed Nightwatch, or head north to Pennsylvania. Thirty minutes by helicopter from the White House is the Alternate Military Command Center, built deep inside Raven Rock in the Catoctin Mountains, a spur of the Appalachians. This is where the President would stand a reasonable chance of survival in a nuclear war.

However, despite its limitations, in a town where so much is gauged not on substance but on form – the placing of the guests at dinner, the location of the table at Maison Blanche – the Situation Room had become something of a symbol for successive Presidents. It was a way of the President telling his closest advisers that This One Was Serious. Of course, when he did call a meeting for the Situation Room, there was an undignified scramble to Be There, with each of the politically ambitious men and women who make up the White House entourage unwilling to give up their place in the sun.

When Bob entered the room underneath the West Wing of the White House with Frank Dearth and Harry Rule, he assumed they were the last to arrive. The small (it couldn't have been more than twenty feet by twenty-five feet) and windowless room was filled with people, some sitting around the oval oak table in the centre, the remainder standing protectively behind the senior officials to whom they owed the most allegiance.

At the head of the table sat President George Bush, his silver-framed spectacles glinting in the reflection of the ceiling lights as he looked up to scan the new arrivals. Bob's gaze moved round the room registering the faces he knew: Cheney at Defence; his old nemesis the DCI, Matthew Shaw; James Baker, the Secretary of State; John Sununu, the White House Chief of Staff; the FBI director, Bruce Hoffman; and the erect, imposing figure of Colin Powell, the chairman of the Joint Chiefs.

There was an air of calm urgency in the room. Each of the places at the table had a telephone which gave off a delicate and discreet purr for an incoming call, the noise pitched sufficiently low not to disturb the flow of conversation.

Looking round, Bob was disappointed to note that there was no evidence of the fabled state-of-the-art high-technology equipment. It was all surprisingly dull, a windowless board-room.

It was Dearth who had insisted that Bob accompany him to the White House. At State it had been issued as an order which Bob had obeyed without question; it was only in the car on the way to the White House that he got an explanation.

'This meeting is going to be a zoo and all the animals will be sharing the same cage. I want to toss them a bit of meat and I'm afraid you're all I've got.'

The President slapped the table with his hand and the hum of conversation in the room instantly stilled. Bob noted the reaction of those present and was surprised. For years the President had stood in the shadow of the charismatic Ronald Reagan, the master of the staged interview and the rehearsed one-liner. He had appeared then as a man of little substance whose grey personality would disappear beneath the politics of the Presidency. In fact, once standing on his own he had flourished. Loyal and self-effacing as a second in command, the Iraqi crisis had allowed him to emerge as a decisive leader. Then he had demonstrated all the qualities of command. He was firm, aggressive where necessary, listened to his advisers and took clear decisions. Now it was evident that he had the respect of the other men in the room and they listened carefully to pick up the direction of the President's thinking.

'I have heard CNN and I have read a preliminary report from the NSC,' he began. 'I understand that we should take this terrorist threat seriously and that it is possible to poison people in the way they claim. What I want to know from the people in this room is what we are going to do about it.'

He paused and began to tick off his fingers.

'We need to know who these terrorists are, where they are based, how they got into this country, what our allies know, what our military options are and what we should be doing politically.' Turning to the DCI sitting on his left, he said, 'Matt, why don't you begin?'

'Well, Mr President,' the DCI began tentatively. 'We have been unsighted on this one. State picked up no diplomatic signals that we are aware of and our Mossad friends seem to know nothing either. We are currently evaluating the situation and should know more in another twenty-four hours.'

Recalling his own discomfort of a month ago when this same man had shot his intelligence career down in flames, Bob gained some satisfaction in watching the DCI squirm. Everyone in this room understood the way the political game was played and the 'twenty-four hours' excuse just didn't begin to play. At face value it was a delaying tactic but in practical terms it was an admission of defeat. No experienced infighter was going to let the opportunity of embarrassing the Agency pass and Dearth was the first to jump in.

'Mr President, I just can't allow Matt to get away with that. We at State have been telling the Agency since the early summer that the Palestinians were up to something. That's what our diplomats tell us but it's up to the DCI's agents to put the intelligence together.'

Fifteen-love, thought Bob, seeing heads nod around the table at Dearth's fast volley.

It was a skilful finesse by State. If Dearth looked hard enough there would certainly be some suitable carefully phrased telegram from Amman or Tel Aviv that would have been copied to Langley that would indeed have raised some warning signals. 'Under certain circumstances . . . it is possible that . . . indications could be taken to mean.' Something like that which diplomats the world over use to secure their careers and ensure that when it all goes wrong they have a well-built, -lined and -insulated escape tunnel already prepared.

Seeing the way the discussion was already beginning to disintegrate into the usual faction fighting and turf battles, the President interrupted.

'Gentlemen, this is not an inter-agency pissing match. I have no interest in what should or might have happened, only in what we know and what can be done about it. Let's all keep our contributions to seeking solutions and not scoring cheap points off each other. As Commerce is on one side here perhaps we can get a view about the effect this will have on the markets.'

He turned to Charlie Stoll, the Secretary of Commerce. One of the Bechtel mafia who had come to prominence in the Reagan years, Charlie Stoll had made his reputation by marketing Bechtel in the Middle East. He had been persuaded to join the Bush administration and because of his background he had been a firm – some would say too firm – advocate of new trade agreements coupled with a relaxation of high-technology exports to the Eastern bloc. He had become a controversial figure. Unusually for a salesman, he had a slight stammer which both hampered his speechmaking and made him run consonants together so that words sometimes came out in a rush. This had led right-wing commentators and columnists to refer to him simply as 'SSS' for Stoll, Soft on Soviets, a cruel play on his speech impediment and his politics. But Stoll was tough and his lean, permanently tanned face with the large Dunhill designer spectacles a familiar sight at international conferences and at hearings on the Hill. Even those who disagreed with his political views respected his knowledge of the international scene so his comments that night were listened to with care.

'Wwwwell,' he began, speech, as usual, uncertain. But his message could not have been more stark: 'This is the most serious threat to the American economy since the '87 crash. In fact, the effects may be even more serious.'

The majority of those around the table were either politicians or intelligence experts and the world of commerce was strictly peripheral to their normal experience. The DCI, still smarting from his lack of knowledge, tried to play down Stoll's assessment.

'Isn't that a bit stark, Charlie?' he asked. 'What we have here is a blackmail threat and not some crisis in confidence in the dollar or some bankrupt bank.'

'Mr President,' Stoll continued, dismissing the interruption. 'I have taken some preliminary soundings with the Fed, the New York Stock Exchange and with my colleagues in Commerce and there is no doubt that things are very serious indeed.

'First let me give you a little bit of history. Product contamination has never been seriously used by terrorists but it has been a growing criminal problem. In Japan a gentleman called The Man With Twenty-one Faces has been waging a blackmail campaign against candy manufacturers for the past four years. He has poisoned candies in a number of shops using a technique similar to this gang.

'In five years nobody has died. Indeed, nobody has even eaten any of the poisoned candies. Yet five companies have gone bankrupt, 50,000 workers in the industry have been made redundant and the Japanese government have introduced subsidies to keep the whole industry alive. The Japanese police have launched the biggest manhunt in their history involving thousands of house-to-house searches and the result has been no arrests, public humiliation and the collapse of the candy market.'

His audience had listened with rapt attention. Scepticism had been replaced by a growing awareness that here might be the beginnings of a problem that none of them had experienced before, a crisis whose dimensions Stoll was only beginning to draw. Taking off his spectacles, he squeezed the bridge of his nose between finger and thumb, a characteristic gesture that friends knew as a clear sign of inner tension.

'OK, that's the foreign experience. Now let's move closer to home. In 1984 Johnson & Johnson had three packs of Tylenol poisoned. One person died. There were no other injuries. The company withdrew all stocks of the product and they lost around $250 million. That attack and the publicity it generated provoked 800 copycat attacks which cost the industry as a whole some $3 billion in lost sales over the next eighteen months. We took some steps to deal with that problem by establishing a new product contamination unit at the FDA and introducing new legislation that made the penalties for such crimes much tougher. Until today, the situation was manageable.

'Now we come to this attack. So far, seventy-five people have died and it seems likely the number of deaths will rise above that figure. We already know that Kola Co. is recalling all its stocks worldwide. In a brief conversation I had with the company before coming here I understand that will cost them in the order of $1 billion.'

The President leaned forward, his mouth still chewing pensively on the stem of his spectacles. 'That's all very fine, Charlie. But I still don't get the feeling that here we're talking about some major disaster. This isn't a new Black Monday.

And even if it was I thought we'd introduced new systems that stopped the kind of panic selling that caused all the problems back then.'

Stoll responded with the growing impatience of the expert who sees the problem and its consequences with the utmost clarity but is having difficulty communicating his vision to others less informed.

'With respect, Mr President, you don't seem to understand the seriousness of what we face here.' He began to tick off points on the fingers of his left hand. 'You have the financial loss of the company itself. That is going to hit the stock very badly, and remember that the stock is one of the benchmarks by which the performance of the Dow is measured and is also one of the one hundred in the Financial Times index in London.

'On top of that you have the loss of public confidence in the company. The New York Exchange tell me that they expect the stock to open tomorrow morning sharply down and if the deaths go on it could fall by as much as fifty per cent. Unless we are able to provide some reassurance, the effect on the market as a whole, given the general nature of the threat, is incalculable. You are certainly looking at a major fall and the market may take the view that we are facing a prolonged period of instability and that could have a very serious effect on public confidence. Tomorrow the Dow could be off 200 points and there will be similar falls in London and Tokyo.

'Unless we are seen to be doing something, it is my belief we could face the most serious loss of confidence that the business community has seen since the '87 crash and this one could be much worse. I'm sorry to be so depressing but that's how I see it.'

'OK, gentlemen, so now we know what we face. But we still don't know who is behind this or what we can do about it. The people who did this presumably came in from abroad working to a careful schedule. What have the FBI got on any of this? Any sign of known people coming in or contacts between foreign terrorists and people resident here?'

The President's question was directed at the FBI director, Bruce Hoffman, but he like the rest of his colleagues had no information to offer.

'We are running through the records right now. We have gone back a month to work through the database but the task is enormous. During that period two million people came into the US. We are looking for names or passports that indicate a pattern but frankly without more information we have little or no chance of success –'

'So,' the President interrupted, 'if I understand the position thus far, we believe the terrorists could have done what they claim; we believe we may be on the brink of financial disaster; we have no idea who the terrorists are or how they got into this country. As we don't know who they are there is no possibility of taking military action although I assume we are ready to go if the need arises?'

The question was addressed to General Powell. The first black to head America's armed forces, Powell was a tough general who had survived all the latent prejudices of the American military to rise to the top backed by a powerful intellect and an almost intuitive understanding of Pentagon politics. In the aftermath of the US invasion of Panama in 1990, it had been Powell who fielded the press and in an almost impossibly hostile environment had actually won plaudits for his no-nonsense style. The skill he had shown in Panama was honed during the Iraqi affair that had seen the first real testing of America's will and military might since the Vietnam war. Powell had pulled together the military to fight and win as a single force. He was as direct now as he had been then.

'We have alerted Delta down at Bragg and the Seals at Little Neck. ISA are also ready to go. But until we know where and what the nature of the target is, there is no point in doing anything else. They can be on their way within the hour once we have something concrete for them to do.'

Delta, the Seals and ISA were the cutting edge of American special forces. Delta Force had been formed in 1977 as the 1st Special Operations Detachment – Delta, based at Fort Bragg. In peacetime they trained for a wide range of counter-terrorism missions including rescuing hostages from aircraft, houses and in hostile territory. Although superbly trained, Delta had suffered from over-management by the military bureaucracy and their first overseas deployment, an attempt to rescue the American hostages held by Iranian Revolutionary Guards in 1980, had ended in disaster. Poor planning, faulty equipment and untrained helicopter pilots combined with an unwieldy command structure almost guaranteed failure. Two helicopters collided at the desert rendezvous setting off fires that ignited stores and other aircraft. Totally compromised, the mission was abandoned and Delta retreated to the recriminations and humiliations of a Washington looking for scapegoats. Since that inauspicious start, Delta had been looking for The Big One, the operation that would restore their image among the conventional military, who still viewed them as a bunch of cowboys.

The Sea Air Land Teams (Seals) belonged to the Navy and had evolved a similar but sea-going role to Delta. Their wartime mission was advanced reconnaissance and sabotage, often behind enemy lines. But they had developed a potent counter-terrorist capability. The Seals had been involved in the capture of the terrorists who had hijacked the Italian cruise liner *Achille Lauro*. But that success had been marred by other failures such as the invasion of Grenada when the majority of their missions went badly wrong and the invasion of Panama when faulty intelligence led to high casualties.

The Intelligence Support Activity, ISA, had been formed after the abortive rescue mission to Iran. During the planning for that operation, the military had realized that the intelligence community's dependence on computers meant that they had very few experienced agents who could be sent into the field to gather information. An ad hoc group was formed and sent into Iran where it did a very good job. Since then the ISA had become part of the military command structure, reporting directly to the Assistant Secretary for Special Operations and Low Intensity Conflict in the Pentagon. They had produced outstanding intelligence on the hostages being held in Beirut and on the Sandinistas in Nicaragua.

These three different groups would be deployed to deal with the terrorists if and when they were identified. Until then, there was just the waiting.

'I'm afraid, Mr President, that I have no good news for you on the political front either.' A calculating infighter, Frank Dearth had kept his peace, waiting until the others

172

had had their say. He had decided that now was the moment to toss the animals his piece of meat. 'The demands of the terrorists are little different from those we have been pressing the Israelis to accept for the past few years. In fact, their very moderation is going to give us some serious problems. We can hardly say that these demands are unreasonable when they are the same as our own and our usual stand of not negotiating with terrorists is difficult to sustain as well. After all, we can hardly negotiate about their demands, merely the way in which they are being forced on us. In fact, whoever has organized this has judged it brilliantly.'

The President cut in. 'Before you get too carried away in your admiration, Frank, I assume you're not advocating surrender and, even if you were, that's not in our gift since it's the Israelis who have to sit down with the PLO and not us. What are they saying?'

'Well. So far they say they know nothing about this attack and have simply repeated to me their standard formula of not negotiating with terrorists. In fact, this afternoon I had a pretty uncomfortable conversation with their ambassador. He basically told me that this was all our fault for encouraging the PLO by suggesting there might be a negotiated settlement to their claims. He also told me that this proves what he had been telling me all along, that the PLO are terrorists and that there can be no negotiating with terrorists.'

'That's just so much horseshit and they know it,' said the President. 'Before this meeting, I had my people alert a number of heads of state that I might want to speak with them. I suggest that the Prime Minister of Israel jumps to the top of my list.'

Bush picked up the red secure phone with his right hand and muttered into it. Bob had read that the President had first done this kind of personal diplomacy during the Iraq crisis, telephoning every head of state from President Gorbachev to a surprised President Saleh of North Yemen. This top-level contact had cut through the bureaucratic morass and helped bring the alliance together and hold it intact over the months. Since then, Bush had seen himself as the pre-eminent US ambassador, believing that the personal touch, one President to another, was often very effective.

He flicked a switch on the phone and the call was automatically relayed to speakers around the walls of the room. There were a few clicks and then the nasal tones of an Israeli voice came on the line.

'Hello.' No introduction, no politeness, just the flat statement.

'This is George Bush. Is the Prime Minister available?'

There was a brief pause while computers scrambled then unscrambled the voice at either end. Then the distinctive tones of the Israeli Prime Minister came on the phone.

'Mr President. Good evening to you. And how are you today?'

Bush clearly had no time for the social niceties and plunged straight ahead. 'Mr Prime Minister. I am sure you will have seen the reports of the terrorist attacks in Europe and in my country and the claims of responsibility by a group calling itself the Palestine Fighting Arm.'

'Yes. We had heard this report. Indeed we were just discussing it when you called. I have Isser Sachar of the Ha-Mossad here with me now.'

'And are you able to help us at all, Mr Prime Minister? Do you have any information on the PFA or their leader Abu Hassan?'

'Well, Mr President, I have to say that these attacks do not come as a surprise to us. We have warned you often enough that your encouragement of the Palestinians, your support for the Intifada and your continued criticism of my country has done nothing but increase the expectations – wrongly I may say – that the Palestinians will soon get their state. You can hardly come running to us when the trail of powder you yourselves have laid is suddenly set on fire.'

Bush's pencil began to beat a silent tattoo on the pad in front of him.

'Mr Prime Minister, I would just like to remind you that when President Saddam Hussein of Iraq invaded Kuwait it was I who ordered United States troops into the Gulf. I called you then and said that I was taking that action to defend your country as much as I was doing it to defend Western economic interests. You were happy to accept my help then and I am now in a position of asking you for help.

This is not a time to exchange insults but an opportunity to remember where each other's real friends really are. Could I ask you again – what do you know about the PFA and Abu Hassan?'

'I have spoken to Isser Sachar about this and he tells me we have no knowledge of this operation. Abu Hassan we know because he has taken some action against us, but until now we never thought him a leader of any consequence. Of course, you are welcome to any information we have. Our files are at your disposal. In the meantime, we are investigating further and if we discover anything we will be in touch.'

'Mr Prime Minister, I am grateful for your co-operation. Thank you and good evening.'

Replacing the phone on its cradle, the President addressed his audience. 'Well, they're being their usual co-operative selves. Opening their files indeed.' He smiled sarcastically. 'They're probably making one up right now.'

The failure of Mossad had underlined Dearth's clear advantage at the meeting and he was quick to press it home.

'But we do have one line of investigation which I think it might be worth following up.'

He leaned back in his chair and beckoned Bob forward. Bob had been leaning against the wall watching the interplay between the different Presidential advisers. He had been struck by how average the people around the table appeared to be, how ordinary. There was no MIT and Harvard brilliance shining through here, just a bunch of guys talking about the issues and scoring points off each other. It was hard to believe that in this room was gathered America's finest. Each of them had been given mortality and humanity by proximity. The President and his affairs of state had been reduced to an ordinary, even banal, level.

Even so, when he felt Dearth's hand on his arm, Bob's heart suddenly began thumping in his chest and he could feel little prickles on his palm as the nervous sweat broke through.

'This is Bob Gearheart,' Dearth said. 'He used to be with the Agency and has been working for a while with the SEC. Some of you may recall an incident a few months ago in Hong Kong where some terrorists were shot in a bank while picking up some cash. That was Bob's doing. He did it by following the money trail left by some of Abu Nidal's henchmen and he knows more about the financing side of terrorism than anyone around. I asked him along today as he has some interesting thoughts on the current problem which I thought you might like to hear. Bob?'

In a surprisingly steady voice Bob told the meeting what he knew about the buying of the put options, the money to be made and the apparent use of the markets to make a financial killing.

'It may all be nothing but I think it is worth investigating just who has been buying these puts and where the money has come from.'

There was a dismissive grunt from in front of him as Matt Shaw sat forward in his chair. Pointing an unlit cigar at Bob, Shaw turned to the President.

'This guy is obsessed with money and I canned him from the Agency because he doesn't understand that we have laws in this country that we all have to live with. If we let him loose, we are packing all sorts of trouble and I personally won't be responsible for the consequences. If we believe any of this – which I don't – then we should take his knowledge and put some people we trust on to the case.'

The President immediately stepped in. 'I hear what you say, Matt, but I don't think this is a time to sit on our legal asses. Bob, I think that's an interesting idea and you should run with it. Take whatever you need from any of the agencies and follow that money trail. I want to know who has been buying into Kola Co. and why.

'From the rest of you I need some answers. Let's meet here again this time tomorrow to see what we have. In the meantime, no leaks, no statements. Nothing. I'll be handling the media personally and my line is the only line. Understood?'

You never really get used to the waiting. Rosan remembered when he first ran errands in the camp. In the Arab way he would be kept waiting, squatting in the dust outside the entrance to one safe house or another. How impatient he used to become. Five minutes seemed like an hour and an hour a lifetime. Then the fedayeen had piled on the agony. He had been expected to lie in a tiny scrape in a hillside for hours and then days keeping an 'Israeli' target under observation, with only dried fruit and the occasional sip of water for sustenance and a plastic bag to contain his excreta. The fact that it was an exercise made it all the more difficult but after a while, five minutes passed without notice and hours were tolerable. Even days became part of a discipline whose value he understood.

He had been parked outside the house on 14th Street for five hours when Bob appeared on the other side of the road, took the steps two at a time, unlocked the front door and disappeared inside. Rosan tracked Gearheart's progress by the pattern of lights going on and off in the house. Finally he saw him enter his own apartment. The light in the bedroom came on for only a short time and then the house was in darkness once more.

Rosan's enjoyable tour of the city had been rudely interrupted earlier that day when the first reports of the poisoning attacks and the claims for responsibility had been broadcast. He had immediately realized that this was the attack that Abu Nidal had referred to, the secret PLO operation from which he had been excluded. While admiring the daring of the plan, Rosan realized that any further delay could fatally compromise his own mission. America's guard would be up and any Arab would automatically be suspect, making travel difficult and escape risky.

He had resolved to attack that night, take the early morning flight to New York and then the first international connection out of the United States.

Foreigners believe that buying a gun in the United States is just like buying sweets in any other country. That is not so. Even American gun dealers need the purchaser to provide an American driving licence or other form of identification as well as proof of residence. Of course, there is a huge illegal arms market but Rosan calculated that a covert approach in a city where he had no contacts was as likely to result in his arrest by an undercover cop as the successful purchase of a gun. In any event, he wanted a swift murder that raised no alarm and would give him time to make good his escape. He decided a knife was the perfect silent killer.

It had all been remarkably easy. He had taken a cab to Georgetown Park, a smart shopping mall in Washington's smartest suburb, and walked around until he found a knife shop. Inside there was every conceivable weapon, from throwing knives in embossed leather sheaths to knives disguised as pens, to gutting knives for fishermen. He had selected two knives, the first with a thin five-inch blade and a plain horn handle. 'Perfect for skinning the toughest buck,' the salesman had proudly explained. The second was a smaller knife, ostensibly for gutting trout. He had also bought a sharpening stone and a roll of tape.

For two hours that afternoon in the privacy of his hotel room he had honed each blade. Rosan always found the gentle rhythm of the blade moving back and forth against the stone strangely calming, a soft caressing movement that soothed and distanced the knife and its owner from the brutal act for which it was being prepared.

Before leaving the hotel he had taken off his jacket and rolled up the sleeve of his shirt, exposing his left forearm. He held the sheath flat against the arm and strapped it in place using the tape. The blade fitted snugly inside the sheath so that a quick movement with his right hand inside his left sleeve would unclip the knife and draw it from its hiding place. The smaller knife went underneath his right sock so that it lay vertically along the Achilles tendon. It was Rosan's experience that even the most comprehensive search by trained security personnel rarely troubled with the inside of the wrists or the backs of the ankles. There was always the lazy assumption that the terrorist or the criminal would do the obvious and carry a gun in a shoulder holster or at the waist. If stopped and searched, he was confident that his secret weapons would remain undiscovered.

For these waiting times, the hours, sometimes days, that marked the void between preparation and action, he had devised a personal fantasy that took him away from the confinement of his uncomfortable world. It was always the same, the very familiarity of it producing a feeling of comfort and security, a knowledge that there was another, better, place far away from his present discomfort.

The dream was part fact and part fantasy and took him

178

back to his childhood in Lebanon. It was a time he now recalled like a multi-sense picture album. A turn of the page could produce old Jamal standing on the corner outside his bakery, his apron covered in flour and the aroma of baking bread wafting down the street. Further on he would walk past Père Ignatius, the ancient Catholic priest whose church always smelled of incense and whose presence seemed to the fanciful child to be the harbinger of death, so frequently was he seen heading the funeral cortège through the town. But the journey's goal was the sea: vast, rich in mystery and filled with possibilities of romance and adventure. The smell of the sea began to fill his nostrils a mile or so from the beach. He would pause and sniff deeply, drawing in that peculiar mixture of salt and rotting fish that is so much a part of the Mediterranean. It seemed to the young Said that the ocean and its partners, the fishermen, represented all the hope and challenge that life had to offer. The water itself was at times dark, wild and impenetrable, at others smooth, warm and embracing. The men who sailed away each day, their little boats burdened with nets piled high, were the true adventurers, heading off to places he could only imagine. Even now he could remember the days spent sitting on the beach watching the unchanging patterns unfold, imagining his part in it.

He stirred, looked at the luminous dial of his watch and realized that two hours had passed, enough time for his target to have fallen asleep. Silently unscrewing the light bulb from the courtesy light, he opened the car door and stepped out into the night.

Bob had returned to his flat exhausted. The meeting in the Situation Room had broken up with the President personally ordering him to follow the only lead they appeared to have. 'You have my full authority to use whatever resources you require to follow this through,' he had told Bob. It was a heady edict for a man who until that evening had been considered a pariah by his own intelligence service. He was now back in the fold with backing even Matt Shaw would be unable to withstand.

When he arrived back at 14th Street, he had wearily

climbed the stairs and, to his surprise, seen a note lying on the floor in the hallway in Mary's distinctive, looping hand. 'Take me. I'm yours,' was all it said. He had smiled ruefully. At any other time he would have moved rapidly down the corridor leaving clothes in his wake, ready and willing to accept her offer. But this time he had simply tiptoed down the passage, taken his clothes off outside the bedroom and crept inside to slide into bed next to her warm body. Still asleep, she had turned wrapping an arm around his chest and drawing a leg over his thighs. Embraced, he had fallen asleep.

There have been many refinements in lock-picking since the nineteenth-century cat burglar and his bent wires. The heart of the locksmith's art are two strong pieces of metal, one to turn the tumblers and the other to force round the central plug of the lock. The most common method of picking locks is known as The Tucker System, after its inventor, W. M. Tucker, a South Carolina locksmith who published his monograph *Super Systems for Picking Pin Tumbler Locks* in 1956. The Tucker System calls for a simple four-inch-long strip of steel spring with a slight curve at one end. This is inserted into the top of the keyhole and delicately raked back and forth to force the tumblers to spring back into their grooves. At the same time, another L-shaped strip of metal made from a clock spring is inserted in the bottom of the keyhole. This keeps the tension on the lock and as the last tumblers fall into place, a twist of the wrist opens the lock. It sounds and is simple but requires a sensitive touch and a great deal of practice.

Lock-picking was one of the skills that Said had perfected in the training camp and he put it to good use this evening. Two minutes with the second of six picks he carried in a small leather pouch and Rosan was inside heading for Gearheart's front door. Rosan knew that no city house is ever truly dark, with moonlight being helped by streetlights, passing cars and the reflection from nearby buildings. For those with the patience to sit and wait, enough night sight can be acquired to see to walk around objects in an apparently darkened room. Using a flashlight not only ruins the night sight but makes discovery much more likely and is never used by the serious professional who, instead, would use infrared lights and special glasses. Without these, Rosan had to compromise with a small pencil flashlight over which he had taped some red paper.

The front door to the Gearheart apartment was more complex. Drawing the torch from a side pocket, Rosan turned it on and holding it between his teeth peered at the two locks facing him, both of which were eerily illuminated by the red cowl on the light. The top lock was a double action Chubb and the lower an Ingersoll. Both required the use of two different Greig picks, one to probe and hold the first line of levers and the second to reach past the first and force open the next line of defence.

Inside, Rosan was faced with a dimly outlined hallway. Fingertips lightly touching the wall, Rosan crabbed his way along the passage, each foot stretching ahead of the other like a ballet dancer to touch a sensitized toe down first, feeling delicately for any hint of give in the floor that might break the silence with an alarming creak. The room he wanted was, he knew, two windows along and so he passed the first door and paused at the second to draw his knife from inside the sheath strapped to his left arm.

The first finger of his right hand stroked the blade, a brief and nervous gesture of reassurance. His left hand reached out for the doorhandle and turned it gently. Easing the door open he looked into the gloom. It was a warm night and Gearheart had left the window open to allow the breeze to cool the room.

The moon cast both light and shadow into the room so that Rosan could see quite clearly the shape of cupboards, a chair and a tall mirror along the right-hand wall. In shadow to his left lay the bed where he could make out not one bump but two.

A woman, Rosan thought. Rapidly his mind computed the options. Leave and try again. No. Too risky and every day of delay improved the chances of his discovery. Turn on the light and identify his target, kill him and leave. No, too risky. Light meant warning and warning meant danger. Hit first body, one deep disabling throat cut, and hit the second body, again at the throat. A ten-second attack. Yes, yes, yes.

Killing with a knife was always the most intimate death.

This was no remote long-range snipe where distance softens the humanity to little more than another three-dimensional target. The knife brought reality; killer and victim united in one last embrace where, like the closest of lovers, each quiver, each spasm was transmitted from one to the other.

The neck is the most vulnerable part of the body to an attack with a knife. Blades can be blunted or turned by a rib cage or breastbone and even a knife plunged up to the brain from under the chin – a favourite method of assassination among the Chinese gangs – is uncertain. But the neck is soft, the main artery is exposed and if the shock doesn't kill, the loss of blood certainly will. Rosan had practised the single left to right movement on corpses supplied by the Colonel so that there was both confidence and artistry in the stroke. The first moment always reminded him of that first cut into a honeydew melon when the smell of the fruit enters the nostrils to arouse the senses, the moment when what once seemed so firm is laid bare as weak and vulnerable.

Two long strides and his left hand reaches out, drawing back the covers, fist into the hair pulling back the head. Rosan briefly registered that this was not a man's skin, giving new urgency to the attack. Right hand loops over and the blade drives down towards the exposed neck.

The knife pierced her neck just below her left ear, ran in about three inches and then with a single firm stroke Rosan drew the blade across the width of the neck. As the knife went in, there was a gush of warm blood against his hand. He felt the woman thrust up from the bed, her legs trying to kick him away but instead only thrashing inside the restraint of the sheets.

Halfway through the cut, Rosan's knife sliced through the girl's windpipe and the silence of the killing was disturbed by a deep gurgling as air mingled with the blood escaping from her body.

As the knife completed its brutal passage, Rosan felt a slackening in his hand as the flesh that held the head on to the rest of her body parted leaving only the spinal cord to hold the two together. There was a limpness in her body now; time was draining her body of blood and life.

*

182

The moment of waking can be gentle, snuffly and warm or sudden, sharp and strange. However it happens there is always that half-moment between sleeping and dreaming when the awake world tries to drag the dream from fantasy into reality. Bob had been dreaming of waffles – a favourite dish – piled high on the plate and had begun to pour the hot syrup when his nostrils detected that the syrup smelled terrible, a smell so bad that some deep, primordial instinct filled his mind with a feeling of dread, bordering on terror.

He woke, suddenly, to hear the gurgle of air expelling from Mary's lungs and the syrup turning to a flood of hot, warm blood pumping across his naked body.

An instant of horror, a briefly glimpsed outline of a dark, looming shadow leaning over the bed, a rush of adrenalin and he was pushing away from the threat to the edge of the bed and then over to fall in a pile of sheets on the floor. A moment of absolute panic as the sheets tangled his legs, holding him to the floor; then he was free, his only conscious thought one of escape, of running, of buying time and space to think, to absorb the unimaginable.

As Bob stood up, the shadowy form separated from Mary, whose body was still now, not even a twitch of her legs to show that life had ever flowed through her. The dark figure moved around towards Bob, silent, menacing, a brief glint of moonlight from the window signalling the knife in his hand.

'For God's sake . . .' The words tumbled out, not expecting an explanation, not a supplication but an admission of fear and an instinctive questioning of something unthinkable.

Like most men, Bob had imagined confronting this kind of situation. A burglar or a rapist would be met with calm and controlled force. A kick in the balls, two fingers to the eyes and the attacker would be disabled. A modest quote for next day's paper; with an unassuming smile he would acknowledge the plaudits of family and friends. Now facing reality, he was briefly disappointed to note the tremor in his voice, the complete lack of any coherent thought and the extraordinary vulnerability of being naked, his manhood open to a casual cut of the knife. Everything had been subsumed by the fear, the gut-wrenching, sickening fear that paralysed his mind and froze his body.

The attacker began to move around the bed using a

smooth, flowing walk. It was the left to right movement of the knife that broke the spell. Somehow Bob's subconscious recognized the preliminary moves of a blade searching for a home, a weapon sniffing out the perfect spot in his body. In his panic he could actually feel the first slice of the blade against his flesh, the moment when the vulnerable became victim. The very thought brought the bile rising in his throat, but atavism, some long-dormant instinct, propelled his body before his mind had begun to form the thought of escape.

He leaped on to the bed just as his assailant came crabbing around the far end. A single giant stride and he was across the width of the bed and leaping for the floor, the door and safety. As his left foot landed on the floor, his right caught in the rumpled sheet causing him to stumble then fall against the wall by the door, the impact forcing the breath from his lungs. His attacker, more cautious and experienced, moved in for the kill. Bob pushed himself to his feet using the wall for leverage and thrust for the door once again. He knew that he was too slow, that his brain was incapable of driving limbs and muscles fast enough to escape the knife. But then his arm, then his head, then a leg were through the gap and heading for the illusory safety of the hallway.

A flame, bright, sharp, and agony flared in his left side followed by a drenching warm flood down his side, and he knew that he had failed. There was no pain, only the knowledge of hurt, of injury, possible death. The momentum kept his body moving through the door, only inches ahead of a second thrusting slice from the knife. Then he was in the passage driving for the front door, the stairs, the street and space; help was there, even police.

Two steps into the passage and Bob knew that death was inevitable. But the instinct to fight remained strong. There was an anger now, a memory of Mary's horribly mutilated corpse, and adrenalin-fed resentment – even fury – at this invasion of his life and his body. Into his mind came a single word: weapon. But where? The hallway was bare except for pictures and a table. Without looking behind him, his hand reached up and flicked a picture from the wall which landed with a crash. He grabbed for the edge of the hall table. With a heave of the wrist he tried to pull it away from the wall into the path of his attacker. It was a near-fatal mistake.

The pause had been just what his assailant needed. Instinct, a rush of breath on the air and Bob knew it was too late. A moment to half turn and meet the attack and he felt a deep burning as the knife sank into his side.

Human flesh is very unpredictable. A knife blade can sink into the body and be cleanly drawn out with no resistance. Or, under slightly different circumstances, the layers of fat and tissue can react like a clam seizing the intruder in a grip so tight that it is extremely difficult to withdraw the blade.

Bob's turning movement dragged the knife around to the left as it sank into his body and when the killer came to draw it out for a second strike it was stuck fast. Still turning, Bob's fist came up in a round, flat punch against his enemy's head. It was a desperate, badly timed blow but it stopped him, broke the momentum of the attack.

Twisting around so that he was facing the intruder, the knife still hanging from his side, Bob's hands came up in front of his face, a classic boxer's defence from the days when he used to spar in the ring. But those were times when there were rules and people played by them.

There was a brief pause while the two men confronted each other. The one panting, frightened, blood oozing down one leg in a steady flow. The other still silent, breathing heavily but calm and determined.

While Bob was still trying to think of a distraction, a deception, anything to buy time, his attacker's right leg flicked out, the toe turning in at the last moment so that the arch of his foot struck Bob just below where the knife was hanging from his body. The stab of agony was unlike anything he had felt before: abrupt, sharp and instant. It seemed to invade every part of him, overwhelming him so that he sank towards the floor with a groan. But he fell forward, some last instinct for preservation pushing him towards his attacker's legs. The force of his fall drove his shoulders into his assailant's thighs and Bob's hands encircled the legs pushing them back towards the floor.

As the killer fell he pushed his hands out behind him to

break his fall while Bob's arms were forced down towards the man's ankles.

Horizontal, the killer began to twist and turn trying to lever his body up from the floor, his hands scrabbling to reach something. Bob was forced to hang on to his ankles in desperation, knowing that once the killer got free he would be lost, without the strength to force himself to his feet once more.

This was a fight that could only have one victor. Bob could feel his strength draining away with his blood, oozing out across the floor of his apartment. He would black out soon, he knew, and then his supine body would be at the mercy of his assailant. A fleeting memory of the horrible noise of Mary dying spurred him on. His right hand reached behind him, groping for the shaft of the knife in his side. His violent struggles had loosened the grip of his body on the blade – or perhaps he had the strength born of despair. He pulled and pulled again and with a disgusting rending, sucking sound the knife came free in his hand.

There was no hesitation now. His hand stabbed upwards into the flesh of his attacker's thigh. There was a howl of pain and Bob felt his hand flood with blood. Like a mountaineer using a piton as a lever to move up a rock face, Bob used the shaft of the knife to draw himself up his assailant's thrashing body. Then with his left hand embracing the thigh, he drew the blade out and stabbed again, this time deep into the stomach wall. Holding tight, head buried in the crotch of his attacker, he stabbed again and then again, moving the blade back and forth across the body lying above him.

Blood was now spraying out above him, hot, sticky and blinding. He could not believe that one body could produce so much liquid and still be struggling.

For Said Rosan the world had compressed into tiny circles of acute pain. The first stab of the knife had been shocking in its suddenness, the cut of the blade the first time anyone had actually managed to draw his blood. He had been so confident, so positive that this one young American would be an easy victim that defeat had never been an issue, his death a total certainty. Now he struggled, though he knew his life was draining out of him with each cut. He continued to resist because that is what he had been trained to do, but as the seconds passed his efforts began to lack conviction. It was as if he could actually feel his body getting smaller, like a deflating balloon as the blood spurted from his wounds. With each pump of his weakening heart the blood fountained out; his heart, that source of such passion and power, his final betrayer.

Then it seemed to Rosan the pain was actually reducing, fading into the background. He could smell again old Jamal's bakery, the incense of Père Ignatius and the first, welcoming, scent of the sea.

September 20

New York

The poisoning first appeared in Kansas City three days ago. Since then, in the United States, deaths have been reported in St Louis, Atlantic City, Chicago, New York, Los Angeles and Atlanta. To date, 56 people have died. A further 72 people are in hospital. Of those infected, none have responded to treatment and we expect a 100 per cent fatality rate.

The FDA has received reports from Britain, France, Italy and Germany that the poison has appeared in Kola Co. products there also. Reported deaths so far number 58 but we expect that number to rise considerably in the next few days.

The poison has been identified by the Center for Infectious Diseases at Atlanta as thallium, a product more usually associated with rat poison. There is no known antidote.

At this stage, the poison only appears to affect Kola Co. products. But we are unable to advise that other soft drinks have not been poisoned or even that other foodstuffs may not be affected.

We expect this to be the worst crisis in confidence among consumers that this country has ever seen. Already, rumours are driving the market. In the past two days, the FDA has received 3,000 calls from members of the public reporting suspected poison in 260 different products. Poison has been found in 13 of these products but we believe these are copycat poisonings and have not been carried out by the terrorists.

If the experience of the Tylenol case is repeated, we expect the number of false alarms and copycat poisonings to rise to such levels that the FDA will be unable to respond.

Christ Almighty, Frank Abrams thought, that's really going to reassure folks. Nice to know the friendly FDA is as encouraging as usual.

The message he had been reading had been written by

officials at the Division of Emergency and Epidemiological Operations at the Food and Drug Administration for distribution around the various computer networks linking different government agencies. The FDA had led the campaign to educate manufacturers about the dangers of food poisoning, a campaign met by widespread indifference in the face of a natural conflict between the regulators who wanted to make all packaging tamper-proof and the producers who wanted to make all products easily accessible to the consumer.

The conversation with Bob the previous evening suggested that he might have one of the keys to the riddle of the killings. The excitement in Bob's voice when he had talked about the buying of Kola Co. stock suggested that there might be a clear link between the purchase of the put options and the terrorist attacks. Frank Abrams was ambitious and ambition recognizes opportunity. He had turned the scheme over in his mind that night and determined to join the hunt.

As a relatively new member of the computer-literate society, the first thing Abrams always did on sitting down at his desk was to log on to his computer terminal to pick up messages and catch up on any overnight traffic. The SEC was one of the twenty or so government agencies that had been integrated into a new information system known as SMART or System Message and Retrieval. SMART linked different agencies so that they could share routine information. But in a crisis like this, a special file could be set up so that all the relevant facts could be poured into one pot. SMART also linked into the intelligence agencies' Flashboard system, which included more highly classified data.

SMART was a stunning improvement on the old method of memos and photocopies that took days to distribute. This way, Abrams could log on to the file codenamed 'Snow' (another humourless joke from the faceless people who made up the names, Abrams thought. Despite there being no link between Coca Cola and Kola Co., the operators had made the connection Kola Co. = Coca Cola = Coke = Cocaine = Snow).

Lighting the fifth cigarette of the day from his pack of Salem Lights, Abrams inhaled deeply, reflecting on what he had read. Terrorism was the province of the Feebies and the spooks but this one might, just might, fall into his patch. The organization that cracked this one could write its own ticket and the man who orchestrated the coup could take his pick of the plums hanging from the government tree. Action decided, he stubbed out his cigarette and began to summon his staff.

'You all know about the poisoning of Kola Co. products,' he began, addressing the ten people crammed into his tiny office. 'Some of you will have read the Snow file on SMART this morning. For those of you who haven't I recommend you do. The FDA are running real scared on this one. Their butts are hanging over the fire and they can already feel the flames. Well, it's not my job to save their. asses, but there is a chance – just a chance – that all of you sitting here may have the key to the problem.'

There was a stirring in his audience, a flicker of excitement among his team whose usual remit was far removed from the headlines.

'There has been some surprise down among the experts in DC that there has been no cash demand from the terrorists. However, one of my people told me the other day that there had been an unusual number of put buys in Kola Co. stock recently. Now, if you were a real smart terrorist with access to plenty of cash and you knew what your outfit was planning a few months from now, what would you do?' He pressed on, answering his own rhetorical question. 'What you would do is buy puts in a company knowing that your terrorism would cause the stock to collapse.

'We know, or at least I think we know that there has been a lot of movement in Kola Co. puts in the past few months. We also know for a fact that Kola Co. products have been poisoned by terrorists. What you guys have to do is give me the link between the assumption and the fact. And I want it yesterday or sooner.'

Over the next few hours, Frank sat at his terminal, the spider at the centre of his information web. Every time a drop of information hit one of the sensitive strands on the outer edge of the web, it was transmitted to him via the fibre optics of the computer links. He loved this stuff. As a cop, information-gathering was such a visible business. You got out on the street, knocked on doors, flashed the badge and got either insults, information or, more likely, a mixture of the two. But this was intelligence by remote control. This was real power, the power of the seeker over the sought. He could find out so much without leaving the sanctuary of his office.

By mid-afternoon, he could scroll through the file which listed every single blue sheet transaction that had taken place in Kola Co. shares in the past four months. The ASAM computer system sifted out the transactions below $100,000 and then looked through the balance for any evidence of a common thread. There had been 300 transactions each involving sums of no more than $2 million and no less than $250,000.

At each touch of the Execute key on the computer, he moved from one file to the next. Each file was entered in the same way with the name of the company, the type of transaction, the cost of the deal, the date the bargain was struck and the date it was due to be completed. After reading through fifteen blue sheets, Abrams began to see the beginnings of a pattern. After twenty he was certain.

He reached for the telephone and dialled a local number. The call was answered on the third ring by a man who simply responded with a 'Yes?'

'Jeff. It's Frank. Could we meet? Fifteen minutes for a dog.'

Exactly fifteen minutes later, Frank was standing in front of Big Al's Burger Stand ('New York's Finest') taking his first bite of a chilli dog with everything when Jeff came around the corner. After a brief handshake the two men began what two ex-cops do the world over: a little bit of horse-trading. No law that Congress passes can undercut the private network that cuts through so much of the legal crap to get the job done. Cop talks to cop, spy to spy, even lawyer to lawyer. Cards are marked, debts called in, information handed over.

Jeff and Frank went back a long way to shared patrols in the Santa Monica PD. Their patch had taken in the fringes of the drug culture in Venice and the stars further up the coast in the other direction. Both had had their problems and had learned the street lesson: to make arrests, you deal. Frank had escaped to the SEC and Jeff to the Drug

Enforcement Administration and the two men found that in their new careers they frequently had common cause.

'I'm working on the Kola Co. poisoning and thought you might be of help.'

Jeff looked surprised. 'What for? That's not your patch. Have you been seconded off to the Feebies?'

'No. But it looks like there may be a money link to the operation, which is where I come in. We've been looking at the records of stock buys in Kola Co. and there seems to be a pattern. Each of the deals within a certain spread have come from offshore. They're all front companies doing the buys and I haven't got the time to go through the lawyers even if I could show any kind of case, which I can't.'

'Are you saying you think this whole thing is some kind of drug scam?' Jeff asked.

'It's definitely terrorist. But I know you guys have done a lot to uncover the laundering network used by the drug boys. We both know that drugs and terrorism often mix and the terrorists have learned a lot from the Colombians' and the Mexicans' laundering operations. So I was wondering if you could give me a name and a lever to get behind the fronts.'

Jeff took a huge, final swallow of his hot dog, chewed and belched gently. It gave him the time he needed to weigh Frank's information and structure his answer.

'That's a pretty general request into a very sensitive area, Frank. Any people we have that can open the offshore doors are Alpha sources. You do anything to burn them and it'll be my neck in the noose.'

'Look, I don't need much and not in every country. So far, we know buys have been done from Panama, the Bahamas, the Caymans, Turks and Caicos and a few from Switzerland and Luxembourg.'

'Well, you can forget the last two. Those Europeans never tell us anything unless they get a handwritten kiss-ass letter from the President himself. Even then it takes months and they give you shit.'

'Yeah, I know all that. So I thought that maybe if you had anyone offshore then maybe I could use a bit of leverage and get the name of the people behind the fronts. I'm sure it must be a common hand doing the buying and if I can get that name then we'll be able to get some idea of who is doing all this.'

Jeff nodded thoughtfully. 'I'll tell you what I'll do. I'll go back to the office, talk to a couple of people and see what we have. No promises. But there may be one or two people who might be able to help.'

Two hours later, Abrams was back in his office when Jeff rang.

'I've had a look into that matter we were discussing earlier today,' he began cautiously, with the intelligence agent's awareness of bugged lines. 'I think we may be able to help. The two names you need are a woman called Fran Rafferty, an accountant in the Caymans, and Joe Garcia, a lawyer in the Turks. Those two were both implicated in work we have been doing and we decided to let them run. We thought they might be useful down the road and now we'll find out if we were right. They know we know and they know they would have to pay sometime. Mention my name and say you're calling in the marker.'

After scribbling down the telephone numbers Frank rang the woman first. The number he had was clearly a direct line as a strong female voice immediately identified herself as Fran Rafferty.

Abrams had learned early in his career that a successful squeeze was not achieved with finesse but with brutality. He lowered his voice to make it deeper, more menacing.

'Ms Rafferty, I'm calling on behalf of Jeff Drayton whom I believe you know.'

There was a distinct, sharp intake of breath and the cautious 'Perhaps' emerged reluctantly a moment later.

'He asked me to pass on his regards and to tell you that this call is the one you have been expecting that is calling in the favour he paid you.'

Abrams' left hand drummed four beats of his fingers on the desk while the voice absorbed the words.

'I see. And what exactly is it you want, Mr . . .?'

Frank did not answer the unspoken request for identification. He wanted no tapes of this call to end up with some Congressional committee.

'I'm interested in a couple of transactions that have come

193

out of the Caymans in the last few months.' He read over the company names and the dates of the put options buys. 'What I need to know is who provided the funding through the front and who ordered the buys. All I need is a name but I need it now.'

'Look, Mr Noname. We are half an hour from close of business here and even if I were able to help I don't know whether I have enough time to do so.'

'That's not good enough, Ms Rafferty.' Abrams allowed both anger and determination to enter his voice. 'I'm not in some piss-ant little game here. I'm calling you because you can get the answers. And I'm calling you because Jeff suggested that you would help. He also made very clear to me what would happen if I told him you were unable to help. And I can assure you, Ms Rafferty, it was not a fun prospect.'

Having made what she evidently felt was the right degree of protest to maintain her self-respect, the woman had agreed to see what she could do and promised to call later that night. The call to the Turks and Caicos went along similar, predictable lines. Clearly, the inroads the DEA had made into the drug-laundering operations had left its scars.

September 21

Washington, DC

I T HAD BECOME A LIVING nightmare. It was not the moment when Bob had turned killer that haunted him but the immediate aftermath. He had dragged himself back along the passage to the bedroom, hoping that the brief glimpse of Mary had played him false, that somehow her wide smile would be there to welcome him as usual. But her bloody body was still and lifeless on the bed. There were no signs of a desperate struggle for life, a fight to draw a final shuddering breath. There was just that terrible, dark yawn, the gaping flesh that separated her beautiful face from the rest of her body which was now surrounded by a dark pool of drying blood.

Reaction had then begun to set in. His body was gripped by shivers of horror and he stood shaking. Imagination replaced instinct and he thought of the knife entering first Mary and then himself. His stomach convulsed and he vomited violently, spewing his revulsion across the floor.

The effort had drained the last of his energy and he'd realized that he had to reach a telephone before he passed out.

For a CIA operative like Bob, an administrator rather than an action man, there are no fallback positions in times of trouble, no secret numbers to call when things go wrong, no 'laundrymen' waiting for the call to come and take away the dead bodies, sweep the carpet and wash the blood from the wall. A man like Bob does what every other citizen does: he calls the cops.

But Washington is a city that lives, eats and breathes information. For the men and women who come to work in government, information is the currency with which they buy and sell careers, status and power. For the media who leech off the administration, information is the path to fame and the unique glory, even worship, that is accorded the successful American journalist. This thirst for information in a city that has more secrets than most has led to the development of an extraordinary network of leakers, buggers and sources. These range from officials betraying their colleagues in the hope of stepping on their fallen bodies to climb further up the ladder, to the genuinely concerned, to the clerk or cop who wants to make a little extra on the side. In other countries – indeed in other cities in America – such people might be considered spies, traitors or criminals. In Washington they are just folks.

So, when Bob had picked up the phone on the evening of the attack and dialled 911 for help, he may have thought he was just ringing the police. He was in fact indirectly dialling into the Washington information network. By the time the ambulance had arrived at 14th Street, two minutes after the first police car, the advance guard of the Washington press corps in the shape of a Channel 9 television crew had also rolled up.

On a slow news night, the sight of Bob being taken out of the apartment on a stretcher to be followed shortly afterwards by Mary in a body bag, made good news the next morning. It took a further four hours for the press to discover the CIA connection and the newspaper libraries to deliver the clips of the story of Bob's firing the previous month. These elements combined to elevate Bob from a Metro story to a major item and for two days his fate had been a matter of national concern.

From his sanctuary in the Bethesda Naval Hospital in Maryland, Bob had been spared the ravages of the media pack in full cry. Instead he had bled mentally and physically. For the past forty-eight hours he had been reliving those few minutes, thinking again and again of how much more he could have done to save Mary. There was no thought now of how sterile their relationship had been. She had become a saintly figure, forever laughing and forever loving. A person whose life had been snatched away because of his stupidity.

Aside from the mental anguish, he had been physically exhausted. The loss of blood combined with the trauma of the fight had left him drained and in almost constant pain. His side had been stitched and bandaged but he could still feel that first horrible moment when his flesh parted to let the knife enter his body. The sensation was still so real and his imagination so active that he was reluctant to move in case the stitches parted and he would feel that awful moment of vulnerability once again.

His first visitor had been Prentice, bringing with him sympathy and news. To Bob, swathed in bandages and tied to drips, the words of quiet understanding for his loss seemed to have more form than substance. After all, Prentice had never met Mary. Bob almost shrugged the kindness off, eager to chew on the meat of the meeting.

'We found nothing on the killer's body to say who he was or where he was from,' began Prentice. 'Some cash, a few receipts, stuff like that. We are checking it and running his prints and mug through our system and checking overseas. There's no news on that yet. But we did find a note on him. He'd clearly intended to leave it on your body.'

Prentice handed Bob a single sheet of paper with three lines of writing in the centre.

'This is a copy of the sheet, which was about half this size,' explained Prentice. 'We've sent that off for analysis to see if we can trace the origin and the handwriting.'

Bob read the note with a feeling close to what he imagined someone else might experience reading their own obituary. The message was clear and simple.

This man died because he interfered with the destiny of the Palestinian people. Let his death be a warning to all those who work against the legitimate struggle of the Palestinians to remove the Zionist invaders and re-establish a Palestinian State in the West Bank and Gaza.

It was signed simply 'Abu Hassan'.

Bob looked up at Prentice in amazement. 'For Christ's sake, what have I ever done to this guy? Why me? Nobody's ever heard of me. The SEC is hardly the place where terrorists track their targets!'

Prentice shrugged. 'That's the funny thing. We still know very little about him. He is a man with no face, no real name and no base that we have been able to discover so far. If he really is behind the poisoning then attacking you seems nuts. Unless of course you know something you don't know you know. Or they think you know something that you actually don't know.'

Prentice picked up the remote control for the television and pressed a button.

'Trouble is we could chase our tails for ever down that road. We need more information before we can come to any kind of judgment.'

The picture on the screen cleared to show Charles Bierbauer, CNN's White House correspondent.

'The President's due to give a press conference anytime now. I thought you'd like to see where we'd got to since you were attacked. The answer is not very far but I'm sure the President will dress it up differently.'

As he finished speaking, the cameras moved away from the correspondent to focus on the lectern with its eagle motif on the front. Bob watched as the President emerged from behind the blue curtains to the left and strode to the podium.

'I thought I would take this opportunity to share with you some of the information we now have available regarding the terrorist attacks that have taken place in America and Europe in the past few days,' he began. 'To date these attacks have occurred in six countries including our own. One hundred and twenty five people have died from drinking cans of Kola Co. soft drinks which have been poisoned by these terrorists. In the United States all cans that may have been infected have now been withdrawn from sale so the risk to the public here is now considerably reduced.

'These attacks mark a new level of depravity. The terrorists have chosen not only to murder innocent men, women and children but to attack the very foundations of our democratic societies.

'The demands which the terrorists are making are unacceptable. As you know, it is United States policy not to negotiate with terrorists and I see no reason to change that policy now. We are in consultation with our allies and a great deal of information has already emerged regarding the terrorists. I am confident that they will be brought to justice. Until that happens, I would ask you, my fellow Americans, to be strong in the face of these cowardly attacks and to show these criminals that the United States will not surrender to terrorism.'

The President looked up from his notes and as soon as he uttered the two words 'Any questions?' the press conference was reduced to its usual posturing as the reporters vied for their moment on camera. Prentice pressed the button and the President disappeared from the screen.

'A carefully crafted piece of nothing,' Prentice said dismissively. 'Which just about sums up where we are on this one. The Israelis have come up with zip, we have no serious leads and, despite what he said' – he jerked a thumb at the television – 'we have no chance of catching them given that we don't even know who they are or where they are operating from . . .'

Prentice was surprised when Bob interrupted, his voice low and hard.

'Well, isn't it about time you guys got your shit together and did something about this? Two days ago the honchos in the Situation Room were going on about how we had to sort this out. Shaw even told me how essential I was to the hunt and, sucker that I am, I was flattered enough to believe him. And what happens? I get attacked by some mad terrorist, my girlfriend gets killed and you people get nowhere. Mary died because we didn't take this seriously enough. Isn't it about time that we did?'

'Oh, come on, Bob. That's ridiculous,' Prentice protested. 'There's no way you could have done anything more than you did. You could hardly have expected to be attacked in your home. No terrorist has ever done anything in this city before. You weren't to know that you were going to be the exception.'

'That's as maybe. But I know and you know that if I had been more engaged, we could have picked up the signs earlier. I'm getting out of here tomorrow and I will be on the job full time from now on. The money is why I was brought in and the money is the key. If we can just find out where the cash came from, then we'll at least have a starting point. I'm going to find these bastards who did all this' – his hand swept across bandages and bruises – 'and make them pay.'

Prentice was startled to see how the last forty-eight hours had changed Bob. A good analyst needs the skills of a tracker to lead him to the prey. Now Bob had shown that as well as being a capable hunter, he was a killer too. For all his reassurances to Bob, Prentice hoped that he would remain angry and bitter. With those two emotions driving him, Bob could use to good effect the killer instinct he had so clearly demonstrated in the attack.

After Prentice had left, Bob had spent a stressed night, torn between the pain of his wounds, which had now reduced to an annoying background ache, and the frustration of an active mind confined to worrying at the same problem over and over again. The frustration had been aggravated by a call he had received from Frank Abrams that morning. Although the two men had only met twice, they had developed an instant rapport, an understanding that they were fighting the same battles with the same values.

'I'm sorry I've not got through before,' Frank began apologetically, 'but the hospital said you were too sick to take calls. Christ, Bob, from the news it sounds like it was a bloodbath in there. What the hell is going on? Are you OK? Who did it? Is it anything to do with our investigation?'

The questions tumbled out faster than Bob could field the answers. 'Wait a minute, Frank. One thing at a time,' he replied. 'First, I'm OK and they expect to let me out of here later today, which is about two days longer than I wanted. Second, they've not identified the man yet but there could be a link with what we are doing. It makes no sense to me and until they work that one out, life's going to be a little difficult. They're worried about another attack so I guess I'm going to be surrounded by goons with bulging armpits for a while.

'The good news is the President has given me the authority to follow the money trail on the contamination case. So what have you got for me?'

'Well, there is just one little thing that might be of some help . . .'

Bob, hearing the undertone of satisfaction in Frank's

voice, interrupted. 'Look, cut out the crap, Frank. You're talking to a sick man here who needs something to help his recovery. What have you got?'

'Well, first I got my guys to run the put purchases through our computers. They narrowed down the deals to around 300 and most of those came from offshore. It took a bit of time getting the other exchanges to pull the same information but I think we've now got a pretty clear picture of around 220 buys in Kola Co. puts with the investment totalling nearly $300 million.'

'Jesus Christ,' Bob exclaimed. 'This must be the biggest terrorist operation of all time. But who the hell is doing it?'

'Well, I then had a word with a friend of mind in the DEA to see if we could apply some squeeze offshore to find out any more. He gave me a couple of names and I had a quiet word with them to call in some favours.'

He paused, drawing out the suspense.

'In both cases, they named the Arab Bank. Specifically, their branch in Tunis made the buys.'

In his excitement Bob sat up in bed and felt a stab of pain in his side. With a groan he lay back down again. Frank made noises of concern down the phone.

'No, it's nothing. I'm just excited about the news. That's fantastic. Have you had anything from the other exchanges overseas?'

'Nothing so far but both the Brits and the Japs will come up with something in due course. Their terrorist laws are tougher than ours and they should be able to force some answers. But, whatever we do, we'll never get the whole story, given that some of the deals were done from Switzerland. And in other places offshore, we just don't have the squeeze.'

There was a short silence while Bob thought through the implications of Frank's information. There was elation at the news that it was the Arab Bank. He had Hamid in there as a source and was sure that given the amount of people who had died so far and the seriousness of the problem, he would help find the person doing the buying. But the second problem was the put options themselves. With around 200 buys the money involved must be enormous.

'Have you worked out just how much the guys with the puts stand to make from this?' he asked.

'I've done some back-of-the-envelope stuff. I reckon, with an investment of around $300 million and with, at this stage, the stock off around fifteen per cent, they could make $10 billion, maybe more. The markets are in chaos at the moment, so only God knows, really.'

Bob whistled. 'This is unbelievable. We've got to suspend the shares and stop them cashing in the puts.'

'It's not as easy as that. If we suspend the shares or give the terrorists any idea that we know what they are up to then the poisoning could start again immediately. And the next round could be much worse. Neither the markets nor the country could stand another dose like the last time.

'You've got no idea just how bad this thing is getting. The word on the Street is that several of the major players on the Big Board are suffering badly. The bankers are certainly nervous and the little guys are really getting screwed. Some of the smaller food companies are technically bankrupt and the bad vibes are spreading out of the sector and across the whole market. The President went on TV last night to reassure us ordinary folks but privately he's giving us all hell. Trouble is everyone has questions and I haven't heard too many answers.

'This whole thing has been very carefully thought through and I think we have to sit it out until we've identified the main man and taken him out. Otherwise we stand a good chance of driving the terrorists deeper underground and losing all the leads we've got.'

Seeing a solution to the investigation and then having it snatched away infuriated Bob but he saw the sense of Frank's argument.

'OK, I'll buy that. You keep on tracking the money so that when we've got the mysterious Abu Hassan we can also move on all the dummy companies and roll them up as well. I've got a source in the Arab Bank and I'll tap him to see if he can help. I'll get on to that just as soon as I'm out of here.'

The conversation ended with Frank promising to keep Bob posted on developments. Bob lay back on his pillows thinking that already the investigation was showing signs of greater progress than he could ever have expected. He began to sort out the order of business, beginning with early contact with Hamid.

The phone rang. To his surprise it was security downstairs announcing a Helen Nazari. A few moments later, there was a knock on the door and Bob watched as a tray appeared in the doorway followed by the smiling face of Helen.

Bob jerked upright in bed and immediately fell back, hand pressed to his side.

Helen put the tray down on the chair by the door and moved to his side, lines of concern drawn across her forehead.

'Bob. Thank God. I'd heard you were at death's door.' Helen put both hands round his right forearm and held him tight. 'In the papers it sounded so terrible.'

'What a great surprise this is,' Bob replied, a grin breaking through the solemnity of the past two days. 'I'm in pretty good shape all things considered.'

'I was so sorry about Mary. It must have been awful.' A look of concern swept across Helen's face as she saw Bob's smile fade at the reminder of his loss.

'Yeah, I've thought a lot about that. Seeing her like that was ... Remembering ...' His throat constricted as the memory of Mary's macabre death grin flashed into his mind. Helen reached out and touched his arm.

'I know it sounds trite but time really does heal. The memory of it all will fade.'

'I'm sure that's true but right now I'm sick of being in pain, and full of guilt that I didn't do more to save her. It's been tough learning that I'm not the man I thought I was. Hardly the brave protector I always imagined myself.'

'You're being too tough on yourself, Bob. You're hardly James Bond. You're not trained to deal with this kind of thing. I'm sure you did everything you could.'

'What I'd like to do is find out who was responsible and make them pay. Instead I'm just stuck here waiting for the docs to set me free.' He glanced briefly outside to remind himself of another life and then shrugged in resignation. His hand reached out to cover hers which still lay along his arm. 'You're the first bit of good news I've had since I got here. I

203

thought you would be back in Tunis with all this covered up from people like me.' His hand gestured towards her elegant beige suit.

'I was down staying with my mother and heard the news so I caught the first plane up here to see how you are. It was quite a tussle getting in with the press camped on the doorstep and enough guards to stop an army.'

This was a Helen transformed from dinner three weeks ago. Gone was the repression, the withdrawn, haunted look that had so shocked him when they had met at Harry's Bar. This was the old Helen, the woman whose laugh had filled his heart, whose zest for life had inspired him. The transformation was extraordinary.

As if reading his thoughts, she laughed and explained that after they had parted in New York, she and Ham had a long discussion.

'Being with you helped focus my feelings and I realized that I needed some time to think. The conversation was something of an uphill struggle as Ham didn't agree and wanted me to come back with him.' She sighed. 'We eventually agreed that I would go and stay at home for a week or two to get some rest. I was just about to head back to Tunis when I heard about you.'

Her hands, which had been clasped together on her knees, parted and she rubbed her palms along her thighs as if dusting off that particular memory.

'But tell me about you. When will you be out of here? Is there anything badly wrong or are all these bandages just doctors' insecurities?'

'Oh, I'm in pretty good shape really. A few stitches round the back. A cut here and there. It's a bit sore to move but the doctors say that'll wear off in a few days.'

'We seem destined to play doctor and nurse to each other, don't we?' Helen said ruefully. 'Last time I was the one laid low and you were the welcome shoulder to cry on. Now it's the other way round. It's been a long time since I've had that kind of equality in a relationship.'

Helen sat back in her chair and folded her arms across her chest. As Bob remembered that the gesture was always a clear signal that Helen was about to say something she thought might cause offence, she spoke again.

'I remember back at Harvard you were always the one who stood against the rest of us. We were anti-war, you were pro-government; we were going out to change the world, you thought you could work within it. I thought you were a traitor to your generation when you joined the CIA and I remember you gave me a long speech about duty which I thought really pathetic.'

She paused, her eyes reflecting not his own half-embarrassed, half-angry smile, but her own deeper, more introspective thoughts.

'Maybe I haven't changed the world and I certainly am not the "naïve and romantic fool" you once described me as, but at least I can see my faults now. I know where I went wrong and I've grown up. It may not be my place to lecture you, but I'm sure this attack was pure chance, an accident that could happen to anyone. If you were still at the Agency this sort of thing could be a natural hazard of your job. You must be really glad you've quit all that.'

Bob looked surprised. 'Of course, you haven't heard. When this poisoning started they asked me to come back and see if I could do anything to help. I agreed, so it may be that the attack was connected with the terrorism after all. But if they've won this round, I've got a little something that just could make their life difficult in round two.'

Taking up the hand that was lying on the bed, Helen gripped Bob's fingers in both her hands. 'Now who's the naïve fool? Can't you see that everybody is taking advantage of you? You're being screwed by these people you've given your life to. They don't care about Mary, they don't care that she's dead – except for the inconvenience of it all. And they certainly don't care about you. Get out of it all. Chuck it all in before it's too late. Wait and they'll simply stitch you up. They'll sacrifice you as a pawn in some complicated game that you don't understand and probably don't even know about.'

The analyst in Bob heard and understood the logic of Helen's argument. But the emotion generated in the past two days smothered his natural caution.

'Thanks for the advice but I think you're way off about the Agency. Sure I was fired, but then I had pushed the legal boundaries out too far and got caught. I'd probably do the same thing again, but that doesn't make it right. As for being used by my colleagues, sure that happens, but their sympathy over Mary is genuine enough.

'Anyway, this poisoning business is the first real chance I've had really to use the technology I've developed, to see if the money chain is as important as I've always said. Even if you're right, there's no way I'd leave it now, just when everything is starting to come together.'

Recognizing that revisiting an old argument was doing little for the atmosphere between them, Bob tried to shift the focus away from himself. His hand reached out to touch Helen's arm in a tentative gesture. 'That's enough of me. I'm much more concerned about you. It's been obvious, even if you won't admit it to yourself, that you have been getting more miserable with each passing day. You're an American living in a foreign country in a foreign house with a foreigner.'

Helen made faint sounds of protest.

'Come on, you know that's right. Both you and Hamid are friends of mine and I should be able to tell you both what I think. And I think you married a Harvard graduate to find out you had really married an Arab banker. And I also think you made a mistake and it's time you admitted it to yourself.'

There was a brief pause as if Helen was thinking the matter over. 'That's easy for you to say. You've never been married and have no idea what it means. You don't have children and I have Abdullah. Life may not have turned out the way I'd hoped, but then most relationships go through a rough patch and I'm prepared to work at this and come out the other side.

'My parents' divorce made me miserable for years. I'm not prepared to put Abdullah through that ordeal, nor am I prepared to betray my husband. Anyway, it's Abdullah's birthday in a couple of weeks and I have to get back to get things organized.'

Bob sighed, recognizing the futility of further argument. His thoughts returned to the hunt. 'You know this business about the money?' She nodded. 'Well, there may be some kind of link with the Arab Bank. I haven't tracked it down yet but perhaps you could mention to Hamid that I need to talk to him about it.'

A nurse came into the room and warned Helen that it was time for her to leave. She leaned forward and kissed Bob on the mouth. 'Actually, Bob, you can tell him yourself. Ham is flying in in a couple of days. He's got business in New York and then we're flying out together. He's going on somewhere else and I'm going home.'

Bob moved his upper body forward from the pillows, grimacing with pain as the stitches in his side stretched across the knife wound. 'No. You don't understand. This is urgent, really urgent. The terrorists' deadline runs out in fourteen days and every moment is vital. Tell Ham that I have to see him. See if you can get him to fly down here from New York. The forensic people are still working over the apartment so the Agency are putting me up at the Jefferson and he can get me there.'

Helen made soothing noises of reassurance as the nurse ushered her out of the room.

Langley

In the last 24 hours the number of deaths from thallium poisoning has risen to 65. A further 23 people are in hospital and these, too, are expected to die. There is no prospect of an antidote being discovered in the time frame available.

The number of calls reporting suspected poisoning has risen from 3,000 to 10,000 in 24 hours. Poisoning has been investigated in 457 cases. Thallium has been confirmed in 72. Ground glass has been found in 34; faeces in 2; cyanide derivatives in 21; metal items, from nails to wire, in 15; and the remainder were false alarms. At this stage, only the thallium appears to be terrorist related. The balance of the attacks comes from individuals and groups exploiting the current crisis for blackmail or other purposes.

We have reports from food manufacturers, the police and even churches that the public are beginning to panic. Preliminary reports suggest that sales in food stores are down 15 per cent across the nation.

The situation will continue to deteriorate as the thallium continues to claim victims.

'Jesus. Who is this guy?' Bob asked Prentice. 'Mr Optimist USA?'

'These messages have been getting more depressing by the hour,' replied Prentice. 'I rang the FDA a couple of hours ago to ask them to tone it down a little. I spoke to some little prick up in New York who said that they had been predicting all this ever since the Tylenol case; that the stores and the manufacturers had ignored their advice. Now it had happened I was asking for restraint from them.' He laughed ruefully. 'He basically told me to go fuck myself and I guess I can understand his point of view. But if the FDA keeps predicting the end of the world and they're right in saying the panic will spread, then the Hill and the White House are going to want solutions and right now we don't have any.'

Bob had left hospital two hours earlier, the pills supplied by the doctors allowing him to step across the road to the Agency car with hardly a twinge. The body's natural instincts ensured that when he bent over to get into the car, he did so slowly, favouring the stitches that still remained in his side. But, considering the short time that had elapsed between the attack and his leaving the hospital, he had been surprised how well he felt. He had read somewhere that people who had open heart surgery were made to totter a few steps the day after the operation. If he could manage this, there was no reason why other miracles were not possible also.

The Agency driver had made the 25-minute journey in smooth silence. The 219-acre site of the CIA headquarters above the Potomac River nine miles from Washington always reminded Bob of a college campus: low, modern buildings with walkways through the woods and people strolling among the flowers and the lawns. The jackets and ties – CIA uniform since Allen Dulles' days – jarred with the collegiate atmosphere as did the concrete and Georgian marble of the main seven-storey building that dominated the landscape.

As the car drew up in front of the portico, Bob's eyes ran over the much-quoted verse etched into the marble: 'And ye

208

shall know the truth and the truth shall make you free.' The quote from John had always struck him as pretentious nonsense, particularly for an intelligence agency where truth was a goal rarely reached and an ideal often compromised.

Prentice had moved forward to greet him as the car drew up. 'I thought I'd better be around to help you through all the security crap,' he said. 'I'm afraid it's going to take a bit of time to get your pass restored and your clearances reactivated. In the meantime I or one of the other guys in your section will have to bring you in and out.'

'Jim, I may have some news.' Bob had debated what to do about the Arab Bank information, wondering whether to keep quiet, to investigate it on his own. It was his information and he had the sources. But he had got canned for being too independent last time so he had decided to share what he knew.

'That's great,' Prentice replied. 'We've been following your money idea but have nothing so far. In fact, the community has come up with zip.' He guided Bob towards the first of the security checks. 'Let's wait until we're inside.'

The two men had gone through the different security checks and the X-ray detectors and then walked past the travel office, first aid, the credit union and the insurance claims office to the bank of elevators in the centre of the corridor. As Bob stood waiting he looked to his left and saw the stern, faintly smiling face of Matt Shaw staring down from the wall. To his left was William Webster and, on into the distance, a gallery of all the DCIs since Donovan.

The two men got out on the third floor and walked along the vinyl-floored corridor to stop at the bright yellow door of room 57. (Some years ago the CIA's behavioural scientists had argued for bright colours to relieve the monotony of the institutional grey walls and drab floors. The changes hadn't worked.)

Stepping into the room, Bob had walked around to each terminal, muttering greetings to the men and women who formed part of his team. The greetings were effusive, welcoming. He was not naïve enough to believe that it was just because of him, it was more because of what he represented. This crisis was the analyst's dream, an opportunity which, if exploited properly, could mean a step up for each of them.

The final desk, which looked out over the others, was his. He had sat down and logged on; first he brought up the SMART data and then crossed into Flashboard. Scrolling through the Flashboard data on the crisis confirmed the gloomy interpretation from the FDA and from Prentice. Files from CIA and DIA stations in the Middle East and Europe, analysis from State and the FBI, highlights of intercepts from the NSA detailed the breadth and comprehensive nature of the hunt. But they made depressing reading.

'All this' – Bob gestured to the screen – 'tells us that everyone is working on the problem but not much else.'

'Everyone is working with the same handicap,' Prentice agreed. 'We've got the assets to attack the task but we don't know what the task is. We have no name, no place, no people, no knowledge of how this was set up. Nothing. So it's down to you. What's this lead you say you've got?'

Bob explained about Abrams and his search of the blue sheets which had led him to the squeeze play in the two offshore centres. 'At this stage, it's hardly definitive but at least it's something,' he concluded.

'Who needs definitive,' Prentice exclaimed. 'At least we've got something to feed into the system. I'll put the details on Flashboard and make sure the NSA start to trawl back to see if they've got anything in the database. Your people can work with this guy Abrams to firm up the information. When can you meet with your guy in the bank?'

Bob explained that Hamid was travelling and would not be in the States for a couple of days.

'That's great,' Prentice responded. 'But what we need right now are leads, something to attack. Above all, what we need are people. Names, a face for us to follow, something that will set the computers going. Is there nothing you have, nobody you've come across in the past who helped move cash for these guys?'

Bob continued idly to scroll through the Flashboard files as his mind wandered back and forth over the past few days. 'Look, this may mean nothing,' he began tentatively. 'The last time I met with Hamid he mentioned that one of his staff, the deputy at his branch of the bank – Bakr I think he said his name was – had been behaving strangely recently;

keeping things from him, stuff like that. Maybe you could get our people out there to get some material on the guy.'

'Sure, I'll get on to it right away,' Prentice agreed. There was a pause as they both digested the plans and mulled over any other options.

Prentice snapped his thumb and forefinger together. 'I just remembered. There's a meeting in London tomorrow to review progress. One of those interminable co-ordinating groups that always sprout up on occasions like this. They're usually a bust but this one has some high-level commitment given the nature of the crisis and the idea is to pool the information we have gathered independently and then agree a common way forward. The Brits are chairing it and fielding their top team. All the Europeans will be there and I think the Israelis are sending someone in.

'Until now, I thought we were just going to have to sit there and listen. Now we've actually got something to say. I was down for it but why don't you go? You can brief them on what you know and believe and we can show those guys that even if they know nothing, we're getting on top of the problem.'

'But don't you think I should stay here to keep things moving?' Bob asked.

'No. I'll take care of all that. Anyway, it'll be a short trip. You and those goons you've got in tow can catch the British Airways from Dulles that gets you to London early tomorrow. After the meeting you can catch the afternoon Pan Am back and you'll be in DC in time for dinner.'

Action combined with the chance to work at the heart of the hunt was, as Prentice knew it would be, a seductive idea.

September 22

London

THE PRIVATE DINING ROOM of the Director-General of the British Security Service, otherwise known as MI5, lies on the fifth floor of their headquarters in Gower Street in London next to the vast Victorian railway station of King's Cross.

MI5 is responsible for counter-espionage and counter-terrorism. Befitting its undercover role, the building is non-descript, even drab. Constructed in the early 1960s, it betrays its origins with a flat grey edifice of concrete and steel without a single relieving architectural feature to suggest form rather than function.

But unlike its counterparts in Washington, Paris or Tel Aviv, the building and its workers are totally integrated into the life of Britain's capital. There are no defences against the photographer who chooses to wait across the road; faded lace curtains cover the ground-floor plate-glass windows.

Inside the glass doors, an ancient and unarmed doorman fills in passes for casual visitors or scans the laminated security cards of those coming to work. It seems a remarkably relaxed system except for the hidden cameras that record every movement, the shutters that lock at the touch of a button and the lifts that can be sealed to prevent an intruder making any progress inside the building.

Bob had been met by June Manston, the Director-General's secretary, and escorted into the lift facing the security doors. Glancing around, he reflected how surprised he always was that the British appeared so like their caricatures. He was never sure, though, whether the Brits played up to their image and disguised their true feelings or whether they really

212

were the clichés that the novelists and cartoonists suggested. He suspected the former and that behind the open faces, the bonhomie and the upper-class accents they were all secretly laughing at him – and all other foreigners, for that matter.

Idly looking around the lift during the short journey to the fifth floor, he thought that MI5 certainly fitted the image, even down to the DG's secretary. June could have been modelled on Miss Moneypenny: late forties, greying hair clipped neatly behind the ears, restrained Jaeger skirt, cream blouse and cashmere sweater with a single line of pearls at the throat. No ring on her finger, either, although Bob reflected there was unlikely to be a James Bond for her to love from afar, just a lonely devotion to her profession.

Bob's stomach rumbled angrily, a noisy protest at his own refusal to eat the revolting food offered by the airline on the way over. A glance at the restaurant menu on the wall next to him was not encouraging. A chef's salad was a small gesture towards health (as was the gym in the basement) but the effect was rather spoiled by the mention of plum duff – some horrible and impenetrable British dessert, Bob imagined. Perhaps it had been named after Sir Antony Duff, an earlier DG, and his memorial was to be eaten daily by his former staff.

Out of the lift and thirty paces along the corridor past plain brown doors, the DG's office with his two secretaries guarding the door and the Deputy DG's office and they stopped before a door labelled simply Dining Room.

Like the rest of the building, the furnishings were sixties Scandinavian modern with plain cream walls, light teak furniture and a darker reproduction oak dining table. There were no portraits to Britain's previous spymasters, no homilies to encourage the troops, no hint anywhere that this room or even this building was anything other than home to a small and moderately prosperous company. The only suggestion of Britain's Imperial past was a Victorian watercolour on the wall facing the windows which showed the Houses of Parliament at sunset. If this had been Langley, Bob thought, there would have been a plaque underneath with some trite inscription such as 'Lest we Forget'. But, even without the reminder, their mission was clear: to maintain democracy.

The British were hosts because uniquely among the Europeans they maintained a large worldwide network of intelligence posts based in countries that were part of their Imperial past, such as China, Cyprus and much of Africa. In intelligence, information is power and an extensive network had given Britain an authority in the covert world that far exceeded the country's economic or political influence.

Today, British intelligence is divided into three main areas. The Security Service is more commonly known as MI5 for Military Intelligence 5, the number of their original room in the War Office. MI5 is also known as 'Box' after its postal address of PO Box 500 although these days it has a new Box number, 752. MI5 is responsible for counter-espionage and counter-terrorism in the United Kingdom. The Secret Intelligence Service, or SIS, is responsible to the Foreign Secretary, and runs Britain's intelligence-gathering overseas. The largest of the three, with some 9,000 employees, is the Government Communications Headquarters based at Cheltenham, which is responsible for all electronic eavesdropping and codebreaking.

'Bob. So pleased that you could make it.' Gearheart turned and saw the DG, John Runner, advancing towards him, hand outstretched. 'And how are things over at Langley? Still fighting off the more aggressive advances of your new Director, I hope,' he added with a smile. It was a typically subtle Runner opening, indicating both an open hospitality and a knowledge of Bob's recent problems with the DCI.

'I was very sorry to hear about your loss and pleased that you have recovered so well.' Bob coughed deprecatingly to cover the embarrassment of his personal grief being known to this man and at the sympathy he showed.

The two men had first met when Gearheart was in London and Runner was head of the branch of the security service responsible for all counter-terrorism. Although separated by many years of experience, they found they shared a common creative approach to the difficulties of combating terrorism. Runner was able to share his knowledge of dealing with the IRA and in particular undermining their financial resources. Bob could pass on his ideas about using the US legislation known as RICO, which had been designed to deal with corruption and the Mafia.

They had worked closely during Operation Free Will, an undercover mission to prevent the IRA buying some of the Stinger missiles that had emerged on the black market from Afghanistan. The two men had organized a plot where the IRA men operating in Paris had believed they were buying a Stinger launcher and four missiles for $1.5 million. The missiles were clever but useless fakes and the IRA had lost their money. It was the kind of operation Runner enjoyed: completely secret, successful and a psychological and financial blow to the enemy.

Runner had been promoted to the DG's chair two years earlier, the first time a man from G Branch had been given precedence over K branch who handle counter-espionage. Runner's promotion reflected a change in emphasis within MI5 following the arrival of Gorbachev and *glasnost* in the Soviet Union.

Bob had always found that British intelligence, like almost everything else in the country, broke down into clear divisions of class. The men from the Secret Intelligence Service, also known as MI6, were still Eton and Oxbridge, privately educated languid men who thought enthusiasm a bore and prefaced too many remarks with words like 'frightfully' and 'awfully'. He felt that the SIS, which insisted on only taking graduates who had passed the Foreign Office entrance examination, had failed to move with the times.

The Security Service was an altogether rougher crowd. They welcomed people from all walks of life and actually encouraged contact with the outside world. A revolution had begun with the appointment of Sir Antony Duff as DG in the late 1970s. He had swept away much of the dead wood, firing some of those senior officials who were still fighting the Cold War and assiduously searched for reds under their beds each night. In their place came a new breed, men and women who had experience outside the closed world of intelligence and who could bring a fresh eye to problems.

'I will not have this organization run by people who have no idea what goes on in the outside world,' he had told the heads of department over a memorable inaugural lunch. 'The world is changing and if we are to do our job we must change too. The Soviet threat is dying while terrorism is on the increase and we must reflect this. I do not believe that any of you understand how a terrorist thinks, who joins a terrorist organization or why, and how we should set about dealing with the threat. I want new blood brought in and I want the Service to be reorganized to encourage young people with ideas.'

This heresy had not been well received, but Duff had persevered. He had toured every department, talking individually to each member of staff, seeking opinions and exchanging views. A newsletter was started to inform the staff about what was happening in different departments so that one week a success against the Soviet embassy might be trumpeted and the next the reasons for firing two homosexuals explained. Each week, he would meet with the section heads in his private dining room for lunch to review progress (an occasion known throughout the building as Director's Buns). Against considerable internal opposition the changes were pushed through and a new regime began.

It was at one Director's Buns that Duff had allowed his frustration with their conservative approach to intelligence to erupt. A tall, elegant man, Duff had been brought into British intelligence after he had retired from a successful diplomatic career. He was a personal appointment of the former Prime Minister, Margaret Thatcher, which was surprising given their completely different politics. Duff was a sceptical, even cynical intellectual whose inclination might be to vote Labour, or at least Liberal. But he shared with Mrs Thatcher a dislike of conventions and the latter admired his quick mind and enjoyed his sardonic wit.

It was three months after his appointment that Duff had addressed the Directors.

'The trouble with this organization is that you all suffer from the Pooh Syndrome,' he told them. The men at the table, though used to his elliptical remarks, had no idea what he meant. But a lifetime in intelligence had taught each of them that pretence of knowledge was often as valuable as knowledge itself, provided the bluff was not detected. So they all sat looking wise and waited for Duff to continue.

'I am sure you all remember Winnie-the-Pooh.' There were nods from around the table and even one or two smiles at

216

the fond recollection of childhood stories about the Teddy bear. 'I am equally sure that you also remember how we are introduced to Pooh.' He paused, looked at the ceiling and then dredged up from his prodigious memory the opening lines of A. A. Milne's book. '"Here is Edward Bear, coming downstairs now, bump, bump, bump, on the back of his head, behind Christopher Robin. It is, as far as he knows, the only way of coming downstairs, but sometimes he feels that there really is another way, if only he could stop bumping for a moment and think of it. And then he feels that perhaps there isn't."'

Another pause to allow his audience to digest and analyse the childish prose.

'What we are in this organization is Pooh. We have all got used to doing certain things in certain ways and while we may feel that there could be ways to improve what we do our heads keep bumping on the stairs and we have no time to think of the solutions. We have allowed the Pooh Syndrome to overtake our lives. In future I want you to be more like Christopher Robin and control your own lives and less like Pooh with the bumps on your head distracting you from improving things around here.'

There were nods of agreement as each of the directors signed up to this new management incentive. Several thought the old fool was nuts but none were prepared to say anything or step out of line and thus jeopardize their careers.

That afternoon, the story of Director's Buns and the Pooh Syndrome had spread from the fifth floor all the way to the Registry – known as the Salt Mines – where shifts of girls input data to the blare of rock music from BBC Radio 1. And it took only forty-eight hours for the office wit, Simon Wrestall from F Branch, to take the Pooh Syndrome and develop a new intelligence language.

Contrary to the popular image, spies are in fact very unimaginative about how they see themselves and their colleagues. Until Wrestall did his stuff, there were no nicknames, no 'insiders'' language. The CIA was called the CIA or, occasionally, the Agency; the Surveillance teams were known as Statics or Mobiles depending on their role; SIS was known simply as that or '6', while the Security Service generally referred to itself as 'Box' or 'The Service'.

The novelist John le Carré had invented a different language in which the Americans were called the Cousins and the surveillance team Watchers. Although an invention, some real spies had taken up his nomenclature but it was always second hand and had none of that insiders' spice so beloved of the intelligence world.

So that Tuesday lunchtime, Simon Wrestall, a 35-year-old assistant director, whose practical jokes and irreverence were renowned, did in reality for Box and British Intelligence what le Carré had only managed in fiction.

'Our leader believes that we all suffer from the Pooh Syndrome,' he began. 'I think this was unusually prescient of him. As a careful student of Milne, I am able to reveal to you that the Pooh stories were not mere children's stories. They were in fact carefully coded – the Nostradamus of the intelligence world – and it is I who have cracked the code.

'Who was Pooh's greatest friend? Why, Piglet of course, an appropriate name for our colleagues across the river,' referring to SIS whose headquarters was south of the Thames on Westminster Bridge Road. 'It makes sense for the leader of the Piglets to be called "P" rather than "C" and, given the present incumbent, it seems a just sobriquet.' There were laughs at this, all of them being familiar with the current head of SIS, a small bespectacled man whose habit of tightly puckering his lips before speaking gave his round face a decidedly porcine look.

'In the words of the great Pooh himself, where there are Bees there is usually honey. I am sure you all remember the little poem Pooh recited as he climbed the tree to the hive:

> It's a very funny thought that, if Bears were Bees,
> They'd build their nests at the *bottom* of trees.
> And that being so (if the Bees were Bears),
> We shouldn't have to climb up all these stairs.

Clearly this was a reference to our friends from Dzherzhinsky Square. The KGB are the bees and the honey is the intelligence we are all after.'

His analysis had been greeted with appreciative laughter from his colleagues, and what had begun as a simple jape soon gained wider currency. Incipient sycophancy meant that

218

Duff soon learned of the expansion of his little illustration and professed himself amused. So the inner circle adopted the words. Then the ripples from this pebble in the intelligence pond widened so that those in the know along with those who hoped they were in the know and others who wanted to be in the know started using the latest slang. Today, the KGB is always referred to as The Bees, intelligence as honey, the Director of the Security Service as Pooh or Pooh-Bah, and to members of Box the SIS will for ever be known as Piglets with 'P' at the head.

John Runner straddled the divide between new and old. A former colonial officer, he had seen service in Kenya during the Mau Mau rebellion of the 1950s and after independence had returned to Britain where his experience in guerrilla warfare had been put to use in the fight against the IRA. He had seen his share of action in the field, the clandestine meetings on the border with the Irish Republic, the hurried telephone calls, the sickening lurch of the stomach when you know an agent has been lost. But he was no covert warrior, had never killed anyone nor even fired a gun in anger. He was a planner who loved the complex manoeuvre that lured the enemy into a carefully laid trap.

Bob had come to intelligence with a visceral commitment to openness. He believed instinctively that too much was kept secret from the public, that lying had become part of the business and that the result had been a widespread distrust of the intelligence community. That was the logic of inexperience. Now, a few years in, his views had changed, not because he had changed his commitment to keeping the people informed but because that openness inevitably involved a compromise with the need for security. Too often he had seen operations placed in jeopardy and valuable intelligence wasted by leaks from people inside the system, fighting their own bureaucratic battles, or by speculation in the media that was sufficiently right to cause serious damage or even place lives at risk. Now, as a civilian, Bob still favoured a more open society but as an intelligence agent he recognized the need for secrecy. It was hardly surprising, then, that he had always envied the British their extraordinary secrecy. When Matt Shaw had been appointed there had been public testimony before Congress and the newspapers had laid his private and professional life bare. When Runner had replaced Duff, there had been no announcement, no appearances before MPs. Bob had seen the only article written about him some four months after he took office and it had been inaccurate in every single material fact. Such anonymity had its advantages. No photograph of Runner existed so he could travel in an unarmoured grey Ford Granada with an ancient government-issue chauffeur, who carried no firearm and would not know how to use it if he did.

However, those who did know him found that Runner had an outstanding brain and an encyclopaedic memory. His tantrums was legendary, his fury generally directed at a junior who could not defend an argument or whose knowledge of the facts was not as detailed as his own. But these tempers had reduced in recent years after a bout of illness brought about by a weakening heart. Pills and a daily stint on a bicycle at home had helped increase his fitness and relieved some of the tension. (Vanity prevented him from using the Service gym. A sedentary life and a dislike of sitting in the sun had made his skin uncommonly white and he was reluctant to expose himself to the ridicule of a shower.)

Runner gripped Bob in a brief handshake and moved him to the left towards the small crowd at the far end of the room.

'Bob, let me introduce you,' he said. 'You know Richard Caseby from SIS.' Prentice nodded at Caseby, the Controller of the Middle East Section. Gearheart had indeed come across Caseby before and had always cordially disliked him. He could understand Runner and respect his calculating brain but Caseby was a different matter. Looking at the two men now brought home the contrasting styles. Runner of medium height, large hooked nose, bushy white eyebrows and close cropped curly grey hair, dressed in an inexpensive and rumpled suit with plain cream shirt and inoffensive tie. Caseby, on the other hand, was the picture of patrician elegance: tall, slim with the dark brilliantined hair so popular among British officers in the Brigade of Guards. A well-cut dark chalk-stripe suit, a distinctive Harvie and Hudson striped shirt and garish yellow tie clearly underlined that here was an Englishman wearing the badges of the old school.

Whenever he met Caseby, Bob was reminded of a remark one of his instructors had made when he was studying for his degree at Georgetown: 'Beware the smiling Englishman. He is at his most friendly just as he slides the stiletto between your ribs.'

Caseby nodded and Runner moved on around the room introducing Gearheart to the remainder of the group, most of whom were familiar faces from other European countries. The single exception was Hirsh Kronstein whom Runner introduced as the representative from Mossad. The Israeli was wearing a creased light grey suit and in what was an obvious concession to the meeting had strung a tie around his neck but had failed to do up the top button of his green shirt. Always, Bob thought, the Israelis have to be different.

When last Bob had lunched here, the traditional, over-cooked fare of smoked salmon, steak and kidney pie and a memorably revolting steamed dessert had been served by an ancient wheezing retainer called Sam, amidst a cloud of stale cigarette smoke, the smell of which seemed to ooze from his every pore. Sam had gone, to be replaced by a young and attractive brunette, Joanna Holt, who spoke in the same accent as Caseby. Gearheart gathered her recruitment was an attempt to drag the food into the twentieth century along with the rest of the organization.

The men moved to the dining table at the other end of the room and sat down at the places identified with their names, Gearheart to Runner's right and Eamon Carron, the representative from Irish Special Branch, on his left.

After the spinach roulade had been served and a glass of white Burgundy poured, Joanna left the room for the kitchen about five feet away, closing the door behind her.

'Gentlemen, we have gathered here to discuss the progress of the hunt for the poisoners,' began Runner. 'Perhaps it might help if I begin with a brief summary to bring you all up to date.'

Runner explained that more than 173 people had now died from the poisoning.

'All Kola Co. stocks have now been withdrawn but even so the stock markets around the world, particularly in consumer products, have been badly hit. In New York the Dow has lost $100 billion so far and here in London the FT Index is down 150, wiping around £25 billion off shares. On top of recent price increases and the restlessness in the unions, my minister is not best pleased.

'But this issue is not all about money. If it were we might be able to handle it better. In the past when such attacks have received publicity we have had 400 copycat claims for every genuine attack. In the last two days there have been 2,000 calls to different police stations with claims varying from poisoning the milk to cyanide in the water.

'Even though nearly all of these have been hoaxes, every one of them has to be investigated and if this goes on for much longer the police will be overwhelmed.'

He paused and looked around the table, face grim.

'I assume you have all had the same kind of experience.' There were nods from all those present. 'I saw the Prime Minister yesterday and he too is concerned that unless we sort this out quickly public confidence is going to fall away.

'Now to the hunt itself. We have, of course, been in touch with the Israelis' – he gestured towards Hirsh – 'they claim to know nothing, but I'm not sure I believe them.' A small smile in Hirsh's direction took the personal sting out of the remark. 'Allowing this to continue can hardly be in their interests. The PFA demands are far too reasonable and the longer this goes on the more difficult it is going to be for our political masters to resist.

'But we still know nothing much about the PFA. We were speculating that it might be a front for Nidal but we can find no evidence for that at this stage.'

Gearheart leaned forward in his chair. 'Well, maybe I can move that along a little ways.'

He explained how the CIA had unearthed a possible link between the attacks and purchase of put options in Kola Co. shares.

'It may be that a man called George Bakr in the Arab Bank in Tunis is involved in some way. We are actively following both leads and we would be grateful for any help

222

you can provide . . .' There was a brief muttered undercurrent of interest from around the table.

Runner interrupted Gearheart. 'You may not have heard but, while you were in the air, your people have made some progress as well. It seems that we have managed to come up with an ID for the man who attacked you. Both prints and picture checked with us and with our Italian friends.' He gestured towards Paolo Franchetti of the SISDE. 'We tagged him at a meet before the Argov shooting here in 1982. He then resurfaced again in Rome in '85 just before the airport attack. We believe he is one of Nidal's men; one of the controllers who has never got his hands dirty until now.

'We are still working on a name but we are clear about the link to Nidal. I think we are also agreed here that the poisoning is just too complex and too sophisticated for Nidal. So we are still puzzled about just why you should have been attacked but unless the PFA are part of Nidal's operation it may be the two things are unconnected.'

He smiled briefly. 'However, all of us around this table learned long ago that coincidence is a convenient alibi when we lack intelligence. I am sure there's a link if we look hard enough.'

'It could be that Nidal heard I was involved in tracking the money,' said Bob. 'Perhaps he decided to take action before we made any progress.'

'But that's hardly likely, old boy,' drawled Richard Caseby. 'By your own account you didn't pick up the cash connection until the day of the attack. Nidal may be good but he's not good enough to get intelligence that fast and have a man in place to act on it. I think that's a red herring. You were attacked for some other reason – revenge, chance, whatever – and it was nothing to do with this.'

Runner contradicted his SIS colleague, traditional rivalries erupting once again. 'That may be, Richard. But the money sounds like a promising line of inquiry.' Turning to Bob, he went on, 'We'll obviously give you any help you need to track it down.'

There was a pause in the conversation as Joanna came in to clear away the plates and serve out the main course of quiche and salad. Once the door had closed behind her, Runner continued.

'We don't want to lose sight of the heart of this investigation. One thing that has concerned me from the start is just how so many terrorists have moved so freely around the world. They seem to have tapped a new source for papers which is not on any of our checklists. Have any of you any ideas?'

To the surprise of everyone present it was Eamon Carron from Irish Special Branch who spoke, in that soft brogue that sounds so attractive when happy and so mournful, even depressing, when sad. It was the latter current that swam through his words today.

'We have recently turned up some disturbing news at our end,' he began. 'I'm afraid one of our consular officials here in London has been selling blank passports on the black market.'

There was a stillness around the table as they waited for him to spell out the awful details.

'It seems that for the past two years he has been siphoning off passport blanks from the embassy safe,' he continued apologetically. 'He has disguised the loss by claiming that the blanks were either damaged on delivery or mistakes were made when they were being made up. Either way the records were changed to show that the blanks had been destroyed while he was actually selling them.'

The group around the table were too experienced to spend time in recrimination – they had all made mistakes. Instead the questions began immediately.

'If he's been selling them, who has been doing the buying?' asked Gearheart.

'We don't know, but we think it's the IRA. There is no way the Provos have the sophistication to do this current campaign so they must have passed them on.'

'Maybe, but certainly not to the Palestinians,' said Caseby. 'They hate each other after that business in the seventies.'

In October 1977, the Provisional IRA had negotiated a shipment of arms with PLO representatives in Cyprus. The arms had been packed in two crates labelled as machine parts destined for Dublin on board the freighter *Towerstream*. From the start the operation had been penetrated by British Intelligence and the container was opened when it was unloaded in Amsterdam. Five tons of arms and ammunition were discovered inside the shell of two electrical transformers which were addressed to the Progress Electric Company in Dublin. Irish police arrested Seamus McCallum who had set up the company and he was later jailed for ten years. The operation was a great success for the British but it blew apart the PLO's main arms smuggling route via Cyprus. At the time they decided that the IRA was simply too untrustworthy to do business with and all contacts were broken.

'If you're right, Richard, then we are looking at three different groups,' said Runner. 'The IRA buy the passports, sell them to another group who have got into bed with the PFA for this operation. They have had informal links with plenty of European groups in the past: ETA in Spain, the Red Brigades in Italy, the RAF in Germany, so maybe they've exchanged Irish passports for documents from the continent that they can use in their campaigns over there.

'So there are three lines we can follow. First, let's keep Gearheart on the trail of the money. From you, Eamon, we need the numbers of those passports just as soon as possible and finally we need to know which of the European groups are working with the Pals.'

The meeting broke up immediately after the coffee had been served. For others in the room there was renewed enthusiasm for the investigation, optimism that they were on the hunt and had seized the initiative at last. In Bob's case he simply wanted to avoid having to drink any of that horrible brown liquid the Brits were pleased to describe as coffee.

Before the meeting had broken up in Gower Street, Joanna had stored the food, put the plates in the dishwasher and left the building. Her timing was impeccable. As she stepped on to the pavement, a cab came around the corner with its orange 'For Hire' sign lit up. She hailed it and ordered the driver to take her to the Savoy.

Sitting back in the comfort of the cab as it moved down Gower Street, into Shaftesbury Avenue and then down Charing Cross Road towards Trafalgar Square, she began to anticipate the afternoon ahead of her. The prospect of seeing

Christian again after a three-week gap filled her with such excitement that she wanted to lean forward and shout into the cabbie's ear in a schoolgirl chant: 'I'm off to see my lover. I'm off to see my lover.'

As it was she sat back, a demure woman, perfectly dressed in her Harvey Nichols suit, with the Hermès scarf covering her hair and the knot tied in the centre of her chin, and imagined how his hands would explore her body. Anticipation made her nipples harden and she could feel a dampening between her legs.

She fully recognized that she was no beauty. Examining herself carefully in the mirror she would complain about her rounded hips and that her breasts failed the pencil test. But it was her face that was her greatest disappointment. A receding chin gave an impression of weakness and a chubbiness in the cheeks suggested that in a few years' time a weight problem would blossom into middle-aged fat. Her two greatest assets were her eyes – bright, almost luminescent blue – and cascading Titian hair. On good days she saw herself as a Rubens model and on bad days as an overweight and unattractive old maid.

She had had affairs in the past but her middle-class upbringing had produced that classic British woman who knows that sex should be fun but has no idea why it is not. The men she had gone out with had all groped her, fumbled her clothes off, stuck their thing inside her and then rolled over to start snoring. There had only been three, and she had wanted to kick each one in the ribs and demand 'Is that all?', but girls like her were not supposed to behave like that. She supposed that life would just continue until she found some suitable man to marry so that she could have a family and complete her life's role.

She knew she had a good brain and was impatient with many of her friends who seemed happy to talk only about horses, their house in the country and dinner parties. She had travelled for a year in China and for six months in Latin America, which had given her the social confidence to be an attractive dinner-party companion and acquire a wide circle of friends. Even so, she found most men boring and self-satisfied.

Christian was different.

She recalled their first meeting six months ago. She had just taken up her new post at the Security Service and she had been introduced to Christian at a party after the opening night of the *Mikado* performed by the English National Opera. The performance had been stunning, full of wit and originality, and she had felt stimulated. From the outset Christian overwhelmed her.

They had started talking and swiftly discovered a shared knowledge of South America. He was a Brazilian business-man with interests in timber – 'chopping down the rain forests', he had said with a laugh that revealed a perfect set of even white teeth – and had travelled extensively on the Continent. Usually when she mentioned that she cooked, the conversation swiftly moved on, but Christian wanted to know where she worked ('directors' lunches'), her favourite food ('Spanish') and whether she thought scrambled eggs cooked over a double boiler were better than those cooked in a normal pan. It had been very amusing but Joanna had been surprised when he had suggested they leave the party and head on for a late dinner.

He had chosen Kensington Place, a large, noisy glass-fronted café in West London. The restaurant had been lively, full of London's young, smart set all raising the decibel level to almost unbearable heights.

Over the goat's cheese mousse and a shared mushroom omelette, Joanna had breathed in Christian's sexuality. He was darkly tanned with strong wavy black hair, deep black eyes and a slim, graceful body. His voice had a slightly guttural accent which came out not Germanically unat-tractive but seductive. As they grappled with the second bottle of white Burgundy, Joanna found herself fantasizing about how Christian would look naked, what he would be like as a lover. It seemed almost inevitable then that he should ask her back to his room at the Savoy and that she should accept.

That first night he had treated her with humour, subtlety and respect. He had undressed her with a kiss for each button, a caress for each piece of clothing. He had touched her body with a gentleness that she had never experienced and reassured her with words of love and lust as her body was exposed to his smiling eyes. Her nervousness had fallen away and her passionate nature had been allowed full expression for the first time. It was her needs that mattered that night, her wishes that were important and her orgasms that came shudderingly one after another until that final delicious moment when he entered her and spurted his come inside her.

He showed such understanding that she felt able to tell him anything and everything. Each of his infrequent visits to London they spent together. The third time he had told her he loved her, that life was empty without her and she said she felt the same. He had said that he wanted to plan his future life with her and they had shared their ambitions of a family, a house outside Rio overlooking the sea, a cottage in the English countryside to escape the humidity of the Brazilian summer. They had no secrets and she had told him where she really worked and he had shown only polite interest.

She paid off the taxi and stepped into the Savoy's grand entrance. A few paces to the lift and then out at the fifth floor and along the red carpeted corridor to his suite. Heart thumping, she knocked on the door. He must have been standing just behind it because the door opened instantly and he was standing there naked, a single rose held out to her.

She fell into his arms, nuzzling her head into his chest. Kissing the top of her head, she could hear his throaty voice murmuring 'my love, my love' over and over again.

Joanna wanted his control, wanted him to lead the way. Sensing her needs, he pushed her away to allow his hands to move to her front and undo the buttons of her blouse. At each button he paused and allowed his mouth to move over her skin, the touch of his lips sending tiny shivers of anticipation down the length of her body to her groin.

He reserved special attention for her breasts, his tongue lingering around each nipple and then drawing first one and then the other between his lips. She could feel the nipples hard in his mouth and each nip of the teeth forced a groan from her. Faster now, his hands moved down her body, unzipping her skirt and drawing her pants down over her hips and then away.

He pushed her back against the wall and at the same time got down on his knees, his mouth moving down from her breasts, across her stomach to pause at the top of her triangle of dark red pubic hair. She put both hands behind her for support and urged him on. 'Please, your tongue, use your tongue.'

But he wanted to draw out the pleasure, crossing back and forth across the bridge that divided anticipation and reality, lust and frustration. His tongue moved away from her pubic mound, now glistening with the liquid oozing from her, and on down to her thighs. There his mouth moved across her legs drawing the soft down between his lips and tugging gently.

Involuntarily her legs parted, an open invitation to his mouth, his tongue, his hands. He moved forward and she felt the first delicious, delicate probe of his tongue between her lips. Gently at first and then with increasing urgency his tongue caressed the outer edges and then hardened to spear inside, reaching deeper to touch the soft and sensitive inner lining.

Joanna felt her knees begin to give way and she slid down the wall to the floor, his arms supporting her collapse. His mouth followed her, and as she eased on to her back he raised her legs over his shoulders, his tongue now sweeping across her buttocks, into the cleft to touch her anus and then on to the heart of her.

She felt so vulnerable; as if her whole body was open to Christian, a sacrifice to their love.

His hands now followed his tongue and she felt a finger slide into her vagina and then out and lower to push into her anus. The first time he had done this she had resisted, fought against the unnatural intrusion, but now each push of his finger was a sign of their intimacy, each moment of friction a heightening of excitement. As the movement of finger and tongue synchronized, she could feel the first spasms rippling across her stomach and down to her groin. The contractions grew closer until the pleasure became one single, overwhelming ball of fire as she came.

Christian allowed her no time to recover but lifted her up and carried her to the bedroom. As they walked she could feel the pressure of his erect penis pushing into her side, urgent and demanding.

He laid her gently on the bed and then rolled her over on to her stomach so that she was facing the tall mirror by the bed. The Savoy had become their hotel because the first time they had made love there in the daylight, she had been able to see their movements in the mirror. She had never seen herself in such a position before, never watched a man thrusting into her and she found the sight incredibly arousing.

Now she turned and saw Christian kneeling behind her, his prick sticking straight out from his lean body, seemingly too large for her ever to contain. Then he leaned forward, supporting himself on his arms while his penis moved between her buttocks. Her right hand snaked underneath her body to grasp his length and help slide it home. As his penis moved between her lips, her hand fell back so that her fingers were able to glide across the tip of her aroused clitoris.

She could see his muscles rippling with each thrust, the tautness in his thighs and stomach clearly visible and the brief glimpse of his prick as it moved out before beginning another downward movement.

As they became more excited, so his body collapsed on top of hers, the crushing weight of him exciting, comforting. Then his mouth moved next to her to whisper rough, harsh obscenities, words that until she met him she had seldom heard and would certainly never have used. Now, she found herself responding, urging him on to thrust harder, deeper, to spurt inside her, to fill her with his seed. Her cries excited him and she could feel his penis swelling, growing inside her and her fingers strummed across her clitoris, her excitement rising to meet him. She felt his penis push deep and watched as his head moved back, the muscles in his neck straining and she could feel his come pouring into her, deep inside her as his mouth opened wide to cry out his passion. The sight and sound of his orgasm pushed her over the edge and she came again in a shuddering, shouting climax.

It was in the moment after orgasm, that quiet time of gentleness and shared confidences that Christian came into his own.

As he moved off Joanna's body and his arm slid under her neck to draw her head into his still heaving chest, he began the gentle, loving questioning. He probed without pressure, sought answers freely given and stripped her mind of all the essentials that he wanted.

This time, she did not have much to give. A snippet of conversation there, an important meeting here. The best had evidently happened that day. A meeting of European and American terrorist experts to counter the contamination but no real idea of what they were planning to do. Christian was interested but not curious enough to arouse suspicion. As Joanna fell asleep in his arms she realized that he liked hearing about her work and she must try and bring him something that would really please him.

September 23

Tel Aviv

THE MOOD IN ISSER THE Big's office was sombre. He had called a special meeting of Va'adat, the Committee of the Heads of the Intelligence Services, for eleven o'clock that morning to discuss the terrorist attack. Like all these meetings, it was supposed to be an opportunity for the intelligence community to exchange views and information, but, in the informal way that Israelis have, Isser had been telephoned that morning by the Prime Minister who had invited himself to join them. So the meeting had begun with Isser sitting in his black high-backed Swedish chair facing a circle of eight people, including his Prime Minister.

The meeting had been called with one purpose only: to discuss progress on the PFA investigation. As with their European counterparts' meeting of the previous day, things had got off to an awkward start.

'You should all know that we in the Mossad have very little to tell you,' he began. 'We had no warning of the attack and have picked up very little intelligence since.' A lifetime of deception had given Sachar the ability to lie with great fluency. Even among his fellow travellers in the covert world, he showed no hesitation and none of them detected the deceit.

Sachar turned to his right. 'Most of you know Hirsh Kronstein. I asked him along today because he was at the meeting yesterday in London when the latest intelligence was shared between the Europeans, Americans and ourselves.'

Hirsh stood and, reading from a single sheet of notes, briefed the meeting. Unlike Sachar, he stuck to what he had been told and did not address what Mossad did or did not know prior to the attack. A professional, he realized that lies would not withstand the fierce scrutiny of this group, each man an experienced interrogator.

'In conclusion, gentlemen. We are clear that this attack is being carried out by the PFA led by Abu Hassan. The Arab Bank is implicated in the purchase of Kola Co. shares; one of their officials, George Bakr, may be involved. As usual Abu Nidal fits in the frame but we don't yet know precisely where.

'The meeting in London was told that they had identified the attacker of the American CIA agent in Washington. We have managed to find a name for him: Said Rosan, one of Nidal's most trusted disciples.

'That's on the plus side. On the debit, we still do not know enough about the PFA. We do not know Abu Hassan's real identity and nor do we know how the terrorists are managing to move around Europe with such ease.

'The second bit of information comes from the British who say that the terrorists may be travelling on stolen Irish passports. They hope to circulate the numbers in the next day or so. But that means that it is not the Arabs who are doing the attacking but some other group working with them. So one door has opened and another has shut – as usual.'

His résumé finished, Hirsh left the meeting so that the members of Va'adat could decide his country's policy of crisis management.

It was the Prime Minister who took the debate beyond the normal exchange of intelligence and into the real world of hard politics. For months he had held together a fragile coalition which was breaking apart on the back of American pressure for peace talks with the Palestinians. Coalition government had become an accepted fact of Israeli life but in a country where debate was the national pastime and depression a national condition, coalition government was killing political life. Even forming a government had been difficult – the Prime Minister had been forced to allow the ultra-right orthodox Jews two cabinet seats – and holding on to power meant constant compromise. Actually what it meant was stagnation because it was virtually impossible to get all the parties in the coalition to agree to anything, least of all anything to do with the Palestinians.

When he had taken up his post in the Knesset he had realized a lifetime ambition. He had advanced to the podium to make his first statement a strong, still vigorous man whose white hair was seen as a mark of distinction and whose only ambition was to bring peace to his troubled country. Today, his body seemed to have shrivelled within its shell. Spare flesh hung like the wattles of a cow over the neck of his short collar and the white hair no longer looked distinguished, only old. Increasingly he found his ambition had narrowed so that all he could focus on was his own survival and that of his government. Such a contraction in vision had been a bitter experience. Government had left him sour and the tension had tightened his mouth so that he looked as if he was permanently sucking on a lemon.

He had come to the meeting because he needed to tell these men that the political, rather than the military, pressures were becoming intolerable. These men and the organizations they served had saved Israel countless times and they were to be asked to do so once more.

'I'm afraid, gentlemen, that this time I need more, much more,' he began. 'I know we politicians always tell you that the situation is desperate, that we need answers yesterday, that the fate of the nation is at stake.' He raised his hand, finger stabbing the air for emphasis, head pushing forward like a snake about to strike. 'This time all of the above is true. From the moment this thing began my phone has not stopped ringing. I have had the American President, the British Prime Minister, the chairman of the Board of Deputies in Britain, the head of the B'nai Brith in the States, businessmen, political supporters, fund raisers, all of them on my back wanting to know what we are going to do. Each of them seems to believe we have a solution to their problems and to each of them I have had nothing to offer.

'You see, gentlemen, the terrorists have hit us where we have always been most vulnerable: in our wallets. Since this began Jewish businesses have had hundreds of millions wiped from their stock value, trade is suffering and moderate and militant are uniting –'

The head of Shin Bet interrupted. 'Are they saying we should just give up? Surrender to terrorists after all this time?'

The Prime Minister sighed, a deep, weary sound that, more than anything, told his audience how exhausted he was. 'It has not got that far yet but the signs are clear,' he replied. 'The questions I have had are all the same: What do we know? What are we doing? After the questions each conversation finishes with two statements. First: the demands seem surprisingly moderate, and second: this attack is costing Jewish business millions, maybe even billions. The implication is clear: either we sort this out or we deal. It's a stark choice and I am depending on you all to make sure we do the former and not the latter.'

There was a pause while the meeting digested this gloomy analysis. Then a tentative cough and Major-General Zvi Libak, the head of military intelligence, Agaf ha-Modiin, which is more commonly known as Aman, spoke up.

'We may have something that might be of help. We have been trawling the transcripts of the Golan intercepts to see if there is anything that we missed.'

The General was referring to the Golan Heights on Israel's north-east border with Syria, where there is the most concentrated collection of intelligence-gathering equipment anywhere in the world. Radar dishes pick up the movement of Syrian tanks and aircraft across the length of the country, microphones listen to conversations in Syrian camps on the other side of the border and electronic interception can pluck radio messages out of the air between Damascus and Tehran or between two army patrols speaking on walkie-talkies fifty miles away. Aside from giving the Israelis early warning of a Syrian attack, the ears on the Golan also spend a great deal of time listening to the different factions in Lebanon talking to each other.

The most important centre of Palestinian terrorist activity is the Beka'a Valley east of the Shouf Mountains. The valley is really a long depression about fifteen miles by four in which are smaller valleys, rocky outcrops, steep cliffs and, at its heart, hundreds of acres of fertile land watered by streams that flow off the nearby mountains. Here the farms grow hashish which is transported to the coast by different Palestinian groups. Here, too, most of the groups have their training camps. It is an inaccessible area and although the

Israelis periodically launch air strikes against specific targets, they have had little success discouraging the Palestinians from using the Beka'a as a base.

The fact that so many groups concentrate in one area makes it an intelligence priority for the Israelis. In any given month they record thousands of conversations and transcribe hundreds of tapes. Groups that are not a target, conversations that appear innocuous are swiftly passed over but never discarded, in case someone has made a mistake or a critical piece of information remains buried in the database. It was here in this vast trove of hundreds of millions of conversations about laundry, love and laxatives that General Libak's men had struck gold.

'We ran a search programme on the PFA and Abu Hassan and we have come up with four hits that look promising. The first message was intercepted two months ago and as they are low priority it was dumped into the pending file, which, as you know, means that it will be months before anyone will find the time to make anything of it. The same thing happened on two other occasions.' He paused as there was a stir around the table and held up a hand. 'Yes, I know. Someone screwed up. The second time the PFA came up it should have been flagged in the pending file but the operator didn't follow through. That's my fault and we have taken steps to make sure that it doesn't happen again.

'Hassan's name has only appeared once but from what the tapes say it seems they have established some kind of camp in the Beka'a. We have a single bearing but no cross so we haven't got the exact location pinned down.'

'If we locate the camp can we go in and take it out?' asked Sachar.

The question was a critical one. Although there was a widely held view (carefully nurtured by the Israelis themselves) that the Mossad had a long reach and would not hesitate to strike at targets of opportunity wherever they may be, behind the propaganda, caution was the guiding principle in all covert operations. Libak – who had run the intelligence assessments, organized the planning and then commanded the attack on Tunisia in 1988 to kill Abu Iyad –

had cut his teeth during the 1973 war as a paratroop captain and then in the 1982 Israeli invasion of Lebanon, emerging a wounded hero (though the shell fragment that shattered the ball joint of his left arm had struck him while he was giving a briefing three miles behind the front line). The memory of the dead and the cries of the injured at Beaufort had made him wary of the glib solution to complex problems by men who never had to see at first hand the results of their judgment. So he now began by explaining the complexities of the problem.

'You have to understand that the only way of going into a well-defended camp and taking them by surprise is by helicopter. That means we have to fly our noisy choppers up Lebanon along the Syrian border and then into the Beka'a. We have to do it at night, timing the mission to arrive at first light. We have to do the job and then get out the way we came with the Syrian Air Force on our backs and every Palestinian and Lebanese militia firing everything they have at us. It is likely we would take heavy casualties on a mission like that. If you ask if we can do it then the answer is yes. But success will not come cheap.'

In the way of all politicians who retain only what they want to hear, the Prime Minister embraced not the problems but the possibility of a solution.

'So. We have a target and we can mount an operation,' he said triumphantly. 'Zvi, I want you to run it. Pinpoint the camp and get our men organized to go in there and take it out. But remember, what we want is intelligence. Get Hassan if you can but at least get me somebody who knows about the poisoning campaign.'

Satisfied that he would now have something positive to pass on to his cabinet colleagues at their meeting later that day, the Prime Minister pushed himself up from the chair, turned and walked from the room, shutting the door softly behind him.

For the men who remained the problems were all too familiar. The political decision had been made. They had to execute the order and create a mission that could succeed at minimum cost. It was to be a tough assignment.

*

237

Tunis

Abu Hassan strode up the drive, the sand crunching under the soles of his shoes. In the short journey from his air-conditioned car, which he had left at the security gate, the heat of the North African night had brought beads of sweat to his forehead and he could feel the perspiration running down his ribs. As he walked, he took off his suit jacket and slung it over his shoulder, revealing the holster tucked into the small of his back.

As he reached the top step leading to the front door of the imposing white villa, a light came on above him. He glanced upwards and saw the single eye of a security camera. There was a pause and then the door opened. A servant, dressed in the red and gold brocade that was fashionable thirty years earlier, silently ushered him inside. With a movement of his palm the servant gestured Abu Hassan to follow him down the passage.

Pushing open the double doors at the end of the short corridor, the servant stood to one side as Abu Hassan walked past.

'Abu Hassan, my friend. Welcome. Welcome.' Yasser Arafat walked forward and embraced the terrorist leader with both arms, kissing the air next to both cheeks. 'Come in. Sit down.'

Arafat took one armchair and gestured Abu Hassan to another next to him, one of six in the large sitting room that looked as if they had come straight from Harrods. In fact, looking round the room, Abu Hassan reflected that the Chairman certainly did not suffer too much deprivation for the revolution. Beautiful Persian carpets on the floor – perhaps a donation from Saiqa's Majid Mohsin, Hassan reflected cynically – comfortable furniture including some respectable French antiques and what he recognized as several fine examples of landscapes and portraits by the Saudi artist Safeya Binzagr. Pride of place was given to a portrait of Arafat himself, pictured dressed in traditional Arab clothes and holding a small Palestinian child.

Rumour had it that whenever Arafat moved house, which he did frequently, a second executive jet followed him laden with the material possessions he had gathered over the years. Abu Hassan could now see how the rumour might well be true.

Abu Hassan could not help smiling at the contrast between the man he knew and the image he had made for himself. Arafat disliked children intensely, finding their insecurities and humour insufferable. Then again, the Arafat before him was hardly the Arab the public saw. He was dressed not in olive green fatigues but sand-coloured cotton slacks with a white tennis shirt open at the neck, the little green crocodile on the left breast betraying its fashionable origins.

'Before business, a drink perhaps?' Arafat asked.

'A Chivas on the rocks would be fine.'

A tinkle of a small gold bell on a sidetable and the order was passed to another servant who returned with a large cut-glass tumbler and a small bowl of Planters peanuts.

Abu Hassan took a sip of his drink, welcoming the cold of the ice against his lips and the warmth of the whisky. 'I got your fax yesterday and came as soon as I could,' he began. 'Now that I'm here, perhaps you could tell me the reason for the summons.'

Arafat, a man to whom every diplomatic nicety had become part of a daily discipline, frowned at the abrupt tone of the younger man.

'Since we met in Sana'a and Amman nearly three months ago, a great deal has happened and I want to hear from you just how you think the operation is going. I understand from Hussaini that all the purchases have been made and that we are already starting to reap the rewards. But money is only one part of the equation and it is the political end that I am worried about.'

'Chairman, you need have no worries. All is going precisely as I predicted and the result will be as we expect.'

The sight of the young man, sitting in his comfortable chair, drinking his whisky in his elegant suit and smart city manners infuriated the PLO leader. He banged his hand on the table making the nuts jump in their bowl and causing Abu Hassan's eyes to widen in surprise.

'You talk of "predictions" and "expectations" but you have no idea of what is really going on,' he shouted, the colour rising above the line of his grey beard. 'I have had every Arab leader on the phone in the past three days. All of them have been asking me what is going on. Of course, I deny everything but no one believes me. It's like the *Achille Lauro* all over again.'

'The Sauds and the Jordanians I can handle but it's the Europeans and the Americans that are the real problem. The governments won't sully their diplomatic hands by talking to me direct so I have had all the old men on the phone. The British got Ted Heath to call me – that honey-voiced old fart. He had the nerve to warn me that if this plan was anything to do with me then after it was all over there would be a reckoning. Hah! A reckoning! If we have a state they won't dare do anything and he will be one of the first to come and visit me in our new capital.

'Then yesterday Kissinger called. I had forgotten how horrible that German accent is.' Arafat grimaced at the memory. 'He had the same message but in rather more direct language. He asked me what I knew about the poisoning and I of course said I knew nothing. "I cannot control my people expressing their frustration at the action of the Zionists and their supporters in America and Europe," I told him.' Arafat's voice deepened and took on the guttural tones of a cartoon German character with a weak overlay of an American accent. '"You should know, Mr Chairman, that if my government finds that you had anything to do with this it will be the end of the PLO. This will not be like the *Achille Lauro*. There will be no diplomatic ass-covering. If the finger points at you or any of the people close to you then you and your organization are finished. There will be no contact, no meetings, no initiatives. Nothing. Remember Tripoli. Remember Kuwait. This is a new America. We always pay our debts."'

Arafat's voice reverted to its normal tone. 'The threats. The demands. They are coming from everywhere. Our friends, our enemies, they are all against us. Even if this works, I'm beginning to think the price we will have to pay may not be worth it.'

Abu Hassan had watched this performance with mounting revulsion. It was exactly this weakness, this need always to

240

compromise their principles that had led the PLO to achieve nothing while thousands of Palestinians died for the cause. Abu Hassan wanted to reach behind him, draw his pistol and place a bullet straight between those fat, weak lips. Instead, he took another sip of his whisky, a mouthful of nuts and between chews tried to reassure the Old Man.

'We always expected this kind of pressure. It's simply an indication of how successful the operation has been. We are hitting them where it hurts and they are wriggling, trying to find a way out that doesn't involve total retreat. Can you remember any other operation that has had this kind of response?'

A grudging 'No' from Arafat led him to press the point.

'Well, there you are. We've got them on the run. They have no idea who we are, where we are or how the poisoning has been done. It looks like we'll make all the money we wanted and, if the pressure keeps up, they'll have to call the conference for the fifth. If we show any weakness now then the whole operation will collapse and our last chance will have been lost for ever.'

Arafat sat back in his chair, hands steepled in front of his chin, thinking.

'You say that the Americans and the rest know nothing about you or your team. That may be but with the kind of pressure they are applying they are bound to discover something and it won't need to be much to give them the hope that a solution short of surrender is possible. We need to find a way to drive the politicians to the table in Geneva. As they put pressure on us so we must force their hand, herd them into the pen of our making so that they have to do what we want. The question is how?'

The younger man's aggressive instincts and acute understanding of Western psychology produced the answer. 'It's time to issue our second ultimatum. Remind the world that unless they accede to our demands by the fifth, another round of poisoning will begin. Make the threat, but leave the execution of it unspecified. It will create panic, the pressure on the governments in Europe and America from the public and business will be intolerable. They in turn will push the Israelis and we'll all meet in Geneva two weeks from now,' he finished triumphantly.

Arafat recognized in the younger man the vision and ruthlessness that he remembered from his early days in Kuwait and Egypt. He had fought hard to rise to lead the movement. Abu Hassan had a similar fire. Already Arafat's agile instinct for self-preservation had moved on to the future when the Palestinian state was a fact and Abu Hassan acknowledged as one of its architects.

September 24

Washington, DC

As of 0800 today, reported deaths from thallium poisoning reached 88 in the US and 189 worldwide. A further 22 are hospitalized in the US and 48 in Europe so the spread of the campaign appears to be slowing.

Analysis of poisoned Kola Co. cans shows that the terrorists are using syringes to inject the liquid thallium into the container. All the cans examined to date show that the seal around the ring pull on the top of the can has been pierced and superglue has been applied to the puncture to reseal the can. We are issuing an advisory to all consumers to inspect all soft-drinks cans carefully for tell-tale marks.

Alarm calls to different agencies reporting suspected poisoning have now passed 25,000 and several metropolitan police departments, notably in Los Angeles, New York and Chicago, are no longer able to investigate complaints.

In a further disturbing development, there have been three reported deaths from copycat poisoning, one a baby who died from eating ground glass inserted in bottled baby food.

The spread of the poisoning beyond Kola Co. is beginning to cause severe disruption in the food chain with families living off food stocks. Sales of all food have now fallen by 20 per cent and this decline is expected to continue until the crisis is over.

Bob had come to dread reading the opening SMART file, always a depressing litany carefully crafted by the FDA. The bland words were all the more damning for their anonymity. There was nobody to shout at or criticize; just a mute terminal spewing a constant stream of misery.

Flashboard had no good news either. The Israelis were saying that there might be some news 'in the near future'; the Irish passport numbers were now in the system; but there were no details about the terrorists who had clearly been in the United States and no news yet on George Bakr. However, the Arab Bank was now a clear link. His team had gathered information from London and Tokyo on a further fifty transactions and in each of them the Arab Bank was the source. That at least was a window to exploit.

Despite the glimpses of progress, there was now a palpable air of orchestrated panic in the corridors at Langley. In contrast to the calm order he had left two days ago, Bob could smell the sweat of long hours and adrenalin, see the drawn look of too much fluorescent lighting, machine coffee and cigarettes.

'We seem to have ratched up another few notches since yesterday,' he commented to Prentice, who was once again performing escort duty.

'Yeah, the DCI himself is driving this one. There was a meeting this morning in the Bowl and we were all given our marching orders.' Prentice was referring to the huge, modern auditorium tacked on to the main building which had been nicknamed, with stunning unoriginality, the Goldfish Bowl because of its glass roof and huge side windows.

'Another message has come in from our friend Abu Hassan,' Prentice added. 'This one says that unless we agree to the talks by the fifth, they are going, as promised, to start poisoning again. No details of where and when, just that it will happen.'

'How did we hear?' Bob asked.

'The usual. Through Reuters in Beirut and then out on the wires. Every paper will have it tomorrow morning. CNN have started their half-hour updates like they did in the Gulf crisis. They've even got a logo called The Poison Crisis complete with a syringe as a backdrop.'

'Oh, that's just great,' said Bob. 'With that kind of support, the Palestinians have got it made.'

'Yeah, the Dow opened an hour ago and immediately fell another fifty points. From what I hear the President's going nuts. Everyone's shouting at us and we're all running around trying to move the rock up the hill – without much success so far.'

*

244

At the end of a frustrating day, the limits of the technical intelligence were painfully apparent. Bob welcomed the opportunity to meet a real live source, hoping that people might help where machines could not. At six-thirty he left the huge car park at Langley and, taking the George Washington Parkway, headed down along the bank of the Potomac, crossing the river on the Theodore Roosevelt Bridge before cutting across to 19th Street.

The Palm is one of Washington's most famous restaurants. In the north-west part of the city, it is close to the White House and many government buildings. However, a fancy address cannot disguise the fact that the Palm is really just a jazzed-up café. Whirring fans and green-and-white checked tablecloths produce a down-home atmosphere to remind all the country boys made good of their roots.

The restaurant specializes in prices for steaks and lobster that would make any Midwestern farmer laugh at the weak joke: steaks at around twenty dollars and lobster at fifty, but the food is uniformly excellent and can be washed down with some of the more moderately priced wines.

Caricatures around the walls of congressmen, Presidents and senior government officials testify to the restaurant's enduring popularity. The reasons for its continued reputation as one of the places for Washington's power elite to be seen eating is in part based on convenience, in part on consistency and in part on the poor design that means the noise level is high, verging on the unbearable. In a city where gossip is currency and news is gold, quiet restaurants, where the next-door neighbour can overhear the conversation, are deadly. At the Palm, the next-door table has to shout to hear what others at the same table are saying and there is no chance at all of their conversation being heard by anyone else.

It was an appropriate venue for Ham, Helen and Bob to have dinner that evening. It was only a short cab ride from Bob's apartment to the restaurant and when he arrived, Ham and Helen were already seated beneath a cartoon of George Bush, entitled The New Elephant Boy, in which the President was sitting on top of an elephant, to commemorate the time he had just been made chairman of the Republican National Committee.

'Hamid, it's good of you to come down at such short notice,' said Bob, pulling out one of the wooden chairs and sitting down.

He glanced around, taking in the cartoon behind his head. It is the custom that people caricatured by the Palm's artists sign their likeness and George Bush had kept with tradition. Bob noticed that, unfortunately, Bush had allowed his fondness for appalling puns to get the better of him. He had written: 'The eyes of Texas are aPalm you.'

Bob had left Langley for this meeting with Hamid and Helen with two thoughts uppermost in his mind. He was determined to persuade Hamid to join the hunt and he was looking forward to seeing Helen, eager in a perverse way to see if there was still the undercurrent of tension between her and Hamid that he had detected when last they all met.

He had immediate confirmation of the latter as he entered the restaurant and caught sight of the two of them. From the flushed look on Helen's face and the familiar crossed arms he could see that they had been arguing and, as he moved towards the table, they both sat back in their chairs in an eloquent illustration of the gulf between them.

In deference to the antibiotics he ordered a fresh orange juice before addressing Hamid.

'As Helen may have told you, I'm involved in the hunt for the food poisoners. So far, as the world falls apart around us, we've been getting nowhere.'

Hamid took a sip of his drink and smiled engagingly. 'Helen told me you wanted to talk about the poisoning.' Bob nodded. 'I was horrified when the killing started. As you know, I have some sympathies for the Palestinian cause, but nothing can justify such indiscriminate slaughter. Obviously I'll do anything I can to help. But I'm not clear what any of this has to do with me.'

Bob then explained how investigators at the New York Stock Exchange had managed to piece together the deals that had been done in put options and to track them back to their source.

'We have gone back over the deals with the help of some of the overseas exchanges and, as far as we can tell, each of the purchases started with your bank.'

Ham leaned forward in his chair, a look of astonishment on his face. 'But that's crazy. I don't believe it. The Arab Bank is one of the most respectable institutions in the Middle East. They would never get involved in anything like this. Anyway, how can you be sure? You always told me that terrorists took all kinds of precautions to hide their trail, dummy companies, offshore accounts, that kind of thing.'

'Offshore is not as secure as it used to be since we started tracking drug money,' Bob explained. 'One or two people owe us favours and we managed to do a couple of under-the-counter deals that got us access to the right accounts.'

There was a natural break as the waiter came to take their order. They all settled on Caesar salad, fillet steaks, onion rings and fries, the house special. As the waiter reached into his apron for the appropriate cutlery, Bob reflected that Ham appeared genuinely shocked by the revelation that his employers were involved in the terrorist campaign. All to the good, he thought to himself. Maybe he'll be prepared to help.

'We have actually managed to narrow the search down even further and it is here that you come in. I'm afraid that the buy orders that we have tracked so far all came not just from your bank but from your branch in Tunis.'

'That's impossible,' Hamid cried, the denial both appalled and surprised.

Hamid's surprise was echoed by Helen, whose earlier apparent anger had given way to concern and a rush to the defence of the Bank she knew well. By implication she was also standing at the side of her husband, whose loyalties clearly lay with his employer.

'I can't believe that, Bob,' she exclaimed, her hand moving up to her throat to run the garnets of her necklace nervously through her fingers. 'Ham knows everything that happens in that bank and he would never tolerate such a thing. Anyway, the Arab Bank is one of the most conservative in the Middle East. There's no way that any terrorist would be stupid enough to risk pissing off potential supporters by using it. They'd be much more likely to use an American or European bank if they wanted a front.'

Bob put a hand up as if to ward off this verbal assault.

'Hold on a minute. I'm not attacking either of you. I'm just telling you what we think. At first we thought our information must be wrong as the Arab Bank seemed such an unlikely subject. Sure, they have Palestinian clients but they've always kept their hands clean of terrorist acts. But I can assure you there is no doubt at all that the Tunis branch of the Arab Bank is the one that's involved. Now you understand why I wanted to see you.'

The waiter arrived, pushing the trolley laden with lettuces and little bowls filled with the fixings for Caesar salad. The dish had become something of a ritual in Washington and the maître d' appeared to fill the enormous wooden bowl rapidly with the different ingredients. It was all designed to give the impression of individual service but like so much of Washington's high-priced expense-account eating, most of the ingredients came from bottles or cans. But then form was everything among a clientele who did not care what they were eating, only where they ate it and that someone else picked up the tab.

Hamid took a mouthful of Caesar salad and chewed rapidly. 'For anyone at my bank to have done what you say, it would have to be someone senior, with the authority to transfer large sums around the world without a bit of paper from head office.' He spoke as if thinking aloud. 'I have that power but I know it's not me. So who else does that leave? The most logical choice is my deputy, George Bakr. He has access to the accounts and acts with my authority so could easily have organized the cash transfers. There are a couple of other people who could do it but my money would be on Bakr. He has the clout and opportunity.'

Hamid paused and then struck his forehead with a clenched fist, as a thought struck him.

'Come to think of it, I mentioned Bakr to you a couple of weeks ago; that he was moving large sums around and being very secretive about it.' Bob nodded. He did not mention that he had already flagged Bakr as a possible target. The reaction was instinctive, the omission immediate, a measure of the gap that had grown between two old friends who were now divided by different goals and experience. Instead of honesty, Bob pressed Hamid for more details.

'Yes. But does he have the motive? Is he close to the PLO? Has he any terrorist connections? Has he been behaving oddly recently?'

Hamid reflected, seemingly running the image of his colleague through his memory, checking for abnormalities and inconsistencies. 'Well, maybe. We deal with Palestinians and some of us sympathize with their cause – not least because they are among our best customers – but political support and active terrorism are two very different things. I've never seriously discussed these issues with George but he has always seemed to me to be a quiet fellow, no particular quirks – '

Bob interrupted, impatient to get a feel for the man, an indication that his hunter's instinct was right. 'Describe him to me. His looks, his lifestyle. Where he comes from. Anything that will fill in the blanks.'

'He's in his early forties; from Jordan originally like many of us; was transferred to us from head office in Amman; trained as an accountant and then moved to the banking side; good brain; married a local girl two years ago and they have a young baby.'

Hamid stopped, struck by another thought as the image of the man floated before him.

'Now that I think about it, he does seem to have been working very long hours recently. He's always there before me in the morning and stays after I leave. There's been no particular crisis and I have always just assumed that he was a keen worker.'

The circumstantial details were enough for Bob.

'Well he's the best lead we've got so let's see if we can firm it up,' he announced, wanting action to harden instinct into certainty. 'Hamid, you're heading home tomorrow?' His friend nodded. 'Right, you see what you can find out at your end and I'll pass on what you've said to our people to see if they can find out any more details about him. This may be the one real break we've been waiting for. If we can just find one person who know's what going on then we can peel back the layers and get to the terrorists and to Abu Hassan.'

Hamid seemed readily to accept these instructions and agreed to find out what he could about Bakr. 'I am going back to Tunis with Helen but I'm only staying there for a short while before moving on to Jordan and then Saudi on bank business. But whatever happens I'll be back in Tunis in time for Abdullah's birthday on October 8. Meantime I'll see what I can get for you.'

It was Helen who broached the subject of Bob's security. 'Have they found out anything about the man who tried to kill you?' she asked. 'Was he part of this business or was he just some burglar?'

'So far all we know is that his name was Said Rosan and he was one of Abu Nidal's henchmen. As for why he picked on me, we have no idea. Maybe he thought I know something I don't. Maybe it was a warning to us all.' He shrugged. 'Maybe it was all just a terrible mistake. Anyway, the powers that be have decided it was a one-off hit and I'm a free agent again.'

As Helen and Hamid were taking the late shuttle back up to New York, the meal broke up shortly afterwards. The couple said their farewells to Bob on the sidewalk outside the restaurant.

As he turned into 16th Street to see the lights of the Jefferson ahead and the telephone he needed to pass on the details about Bakr, there were two images that he carried with him. The first was Helen smiling as she left his hospital room three days earlier and the second the look of anger he saw on her face as he walked into the Palm that evening. Both in their way were encouraging.

September 25

AS BOB WALKED DOWN THE beige-carpeted corridor of the third floor of the CIA headquarters he
could hear his phone ringing. Or rather he could hear
a noise somewhere between a warble and a bleep that told
him there was an incoming call. He hurried the last few
paces, unlocked his door and picked up the cream phone off
his desk.

'And about time, too,' the voice at the other end began.
'What's the matter with you guys down there? You only
work half days or something?'

'Hi, Frank. How are you?' Bob replied. 'What can I do for
you this morning?'

'Well, I have a little bit of news I thought you might be
interested in on the Kola Co. front.'

Bob moved round the desk, sat down in the swivel chair
and drew a yellow notepad towards him. 'I hope it's good
news. We could do with some in this part of town.'

'Well, not exactly. I have just heard from my opposite
number in London. Their exchange opened five hours ago and,
as soon as trading began, a number of brokers began selling put
options in our favourite company. It could be that our friends
are starting to unload. The market here won't open for another
fifteen minutes but I've put the word out that I want to know
the moment anyone offers puts in Kola Co. I've also told the
other US Exchanges and alerted Tokyo and Sydney so I should
be able to give you a fairly full report by close of play today.'

Bob did not know whether to be elated that something
tangible was happening at last or furious that the terrorists
appeared to be getting away with their plan.

'There's no way we can try and stop the money reaching the terrorists?' he asked Frank.

'Not at present. As long as the governments are not prepared to freeze all trade in Kola Co.'s stock then there isn't much we can do. The puts are sold, the deal is done and the money is transferred to the account holder. It's as simple as that. On most of these transactions the seller will have his cash within four or five days and in some cases even sooner if they say they're in a hurry.'

There was a small crack as Bob snapped the tip of his pencil on the notepad. 'Christ, this is so frustrating,' he exclaimed angrily. 'We're just letting these bastards get away with murdering people and making their fortune at the same time.'

'Hey, Bob, I feel for you. I really do,' Frank replied. 'Why don't you try and persuade those assholes in Washington that there's more to life than politics. These guys are going to make billions off this scam and that's going to pay for a lot more guns, bombs and poison, too, if that's what they want.'

There was a knock on the door and Jim Prentice put his head round. He saw that Bob was on the telephone and mouthed an exaggerated 'You're wanted'.

'Frank. Gotta go. I'll get back to you later.' Bob hung up the phone and looked questioningly at Jim.

'The DCI's called a meeting on the poisoning and, much as he hates to ask, you're wanted. Now.'

The two men took the elevator to the tenth floor, stepped out, turned left and headed for the Director's suite of offices. Two young men from the Agency's Office of Security stood outside the dark wood door. Bob knew that both men were armed and were in direct contact through lapel microphones and earpieces with another security man just inside the door. At the slightest hint of trouble they could raise the alarm and, if they failed, the video camera that watched his approach would pick up any hostile movement.

But they were expected and the door opened. Inside was a waiting room with two secretaries, one typing and the other looking up to greet the two men. With a smile she gestured them towards another door behind her left shoulder.

The DCI's office was magnificent; a vast room with enormous picture windows overlooking the sprawling Virginia countryside that was part of the CIA's empire. At the far end, facing away from the window, sat the DCI who rose to welcome them.

Clearly they were the last to arrive. Against one wall sat a rectangular conference table which was occupied by serious-looking men and women, some of whom Bob recognized from the TWIG meeting: 'Jaws' Dearth from State, Doug Frink from the Bureau, Rule from OCT and Sy Koch from NSA. The faces he didn't recognize, Bob assumed were from the Agency. This one was on the CIA's turf so they were certain to load any meeting in their favour.

There were no preliminary opening remarks, no introductions and certainly no get well wishes to Bob from the DCI.

'I've called this meeting so that we can all update ourselves on progress in the hunt for the poisoners,' said Matt Shaw. 'First, Jim, can you give us the results of the London meeting.'

The insult was clearly calculated and Bob felt himself flush with anger. But Prentice, a more experienced political game-player, simply picked up the ball without a flicker.

'All the players, including the Israelis, were there,' he said. 'As you will probably have already heard, the terrorists may be using stolen Irish passports. We got the numbers on those and they have been circulated. Also, Flashboard is running the details just in case it jogs anyone else's memory. That side of things is pretty much up to the Feebies now and I'm sure Doug has got it covered.'

Frink nodded. 'Sure. All our bureaux have been notified and all ports, ground, sea and air, are covered.'

'From State's point of view, we are catching all kinds of hell over this one,' said Dearth. 'The Israelis want us to tough it out but big business is giving us a real hard time. Whatever the damn Israelis want I can tell you that Wall Street is not taking kindly to being held to ransom by a bunch of terrorists fighting for a cause none of them understand and even less are interested in. All they care about is that this business is hitting the bottom line and they want us to solve the problem.'

'What are the Israelis saying about the Geneva conference?

253

Are they going to sit down with the Pals?' asked Prentice. 'If they leave it much longer, it will be too late to set it up and we'll be past the deadline.'

'Officially they are telling us that a conference is out of the question,' replied Dearth. 'But as usual, those guys have another agenda and, again as usual, they are only telling us the bits they want us to hear.

'We got an overnight signal from our ambassador in Tel Aviv saying that he had been summoned to see the Prime Minister last night and told that a conference was impossible, that the Israelis don't give in to terrorists. Blah, blah. But as he was leaving the Prime Minister said that they had one or two small leads that they were following up and that things might be a little clearer in a day or two. He refused to elaborate but we take that to mean they have got an operation going which they think will produce something.'

'What the hell does that mean?' Shaw exclaimed. 'Won't they tell us what they've got, what they are planning, anything?'

'No. You should know by now that the Israelis only tell us things when they want and not when we want. We'll just have to wait.'

'Waiting is not what this is about. The press are crying out for blood, Wall Street's going nuts and the President is on my back wanting action and we are sitting here waiting for the Israelis to do God knows what.' Shaw turned to Bob. 'Gearheart. You're the one who seems to have the ear of the President. What solutions do you have to offer?'

All eyes moved to Bob and he coughed nervously at the sudden attention.

'There are three things that have happened,' he said.

'First, we now know that all the put options seem to have been bought on the instructions of the Arab Bank in Tunis.

'Second, those put options are being sold even as we sit here and it looks as if the buyers will make hundreds of millions and probably billions of dollars on the deal.

'Third, one of the people behind the secret buying may be a gentleman called George Bakr, the Palestinian deputy manager of the Arab Bank in Tunis.'

The staccato delivery of this apparently hard intelligence

caught the meeting by surprise. There was a stunned silence, a few murmurs of surprise and then the barrage of questions began. Typically, it was the DCI who got in first.

'How did you get this information and how reliable is it?' he asked.

Bob explained the process of using favours owed to the DEA to prise open the offshore bank accounts, the contacts with the New York Stock Exchange and finally his relationship with Hamid which exposed the Bakr connection.

'While I can't say I approve of your methods, Bob, I have to commend your enterprise,' Shaw admitted grudgingly. 'This is the first decent intelligence we've had so let's make good use of it.'

He placed both hands on the table in front of him, elbows bent as if about to lever himself from his chair. In fact this was the posture that Shaw used to dominate a meeting when he was issuing instructions. First to Frink at the FBI to make sure that the passports were watched; next to Prentice to liaise with the DIA, FBI and his own people to pull together anything known about Bakr. The final question was to Koch at the NSA.

'What can we do to target the Bank and this guy Bakr? Do we have stuff out there that can listen in? Do we have overhead or anything else already in place?'

'I'll have to check on that but I doubt we'll need any satellites as the Brits have a station in Cyprus that can give us anything we need for this,' replied Koch.

'OK, fix it with the Brits and make sure they give it priority. We need information and we need it fast.'

The business of intelligence out of the way, Shaw the politician came to the fore once again. 'And I'll brief the President on this later this morning.'

Bonn

Abu Hassan had flown in that night and met Inge at the safe house. She had been shocked at the toll that the weeks had taken on the Palestinian. The dark eyes had been driven deeper into his head, his already lean body seemed to have shed pounds, drawing the already lean face into a series of deep valleys, each one a mark of tension and deprivation.

From the start, it had been clear that this meeting was not for pleasure. There was no pretence at the harsh affection they had shown each other at their last meeting. This was terrorism in the raw; survival the goal and people the tools used to achieve it. For Inge this arrangement was part of business and there was no time wasted in recalling happier days with a former lover.

'Your people have done a good job so far,' Abu Hassan began, cradling a cup of black coffee. 'No losses and we have sown the chaos I wanted.'

'We were very lucky,' admitted Inge. 'An operation on this scale in so many countries was almost certain to be detected. We had two advantages, the papers were very good and for once our security was also. They had no warning that the operation was going to happen and their defences were down.'

Abu Hassan reached to the side of his chair and lifted the black leather briefcase on to the table in front of him. 'I promised you money and here is the first instalment.' He turned the combination locks, flicked the catches and lifted the lid.

Inge leaned forward, her eyes taking in the banknotes that filled every corner of the case.

'There is $250,000 in cash here which I thought you might find useful for day-to-day expenses.' Inge nodded, her hands carefully stacking the wads of notes on the table. Abu Hassan reached to the inside pocket of his suit jacket. 'The balance is in the left luggage office at the railway station. This key has the number.'

'Is that cash as well?' Inge asked.

'No, it is a small bonus courtesy of our Syrian friends in the Beka'a valley. They agreed to pay you in heroin and it was brought in two days ago. That should allow you to make a good profit if you retail it carefully.'

This was indeed a bonus beyond anything she had expected. With careful marketing, the $4.75 million could be easily translated into $15 million and even with all the payoffs she would need to make, it would make the RAF perhaps the richest terrorist group in Europe and her team one of the most powerful.

Yet gratitude was swiftly tempered by the caution that had helped Inge survive for so long.

'You are very kind. But you and I both know that kindness usually costs something. Could it be that you want us to implement the next stage of your campaign that you so helpfully announced yesterday?'

Hassan chose to answer obliquely. 'Look, so far we have done well. The poison has worked, the governments are under great pressure. But they are all searching for a way out. As usual the politicians want to take the line of least resistance but they don't want to be seen to give in to terrorism. As we expected, the business community don't care a damn about principles, just the bottom line – and they are starting to hurt. But it's not enough. The pressure has got to force the hands of the Europeans and the Americans so they in turn will squeeze the Israelis. They must be forced to the table, squeezed by the rock of public opinion and the hard place of the fat cats with empty pockets.'

'I can see all that,' replied Inge. 'But you announced a new campaign before anything is in place. So, unlike last time, we have lost the advantage of surprise. All the counter-terrorist people will be on the alert and the chances of my teams getting in and out again look pretty small to me.'

'I accept that. But we had no choice. The pressure must be maintained. They have to feel that, if the deadline is allowed to pass, they are comprehensively in the shit. There was no time to set it all up in advance.'

While he had been speaking, Inge had been calculating, looking for an advantage to her. Clearly, Hassan had boxed himself in. Without her there could be no second stage and, with the announcement already made, he couldn't afford not to set it up just in case the conference didn't happen.

'If I do help – and I have to say that given the risks involved it has to be a big if – then what's in it for me?'

Hassan leaned forward, taking both her hands in his. As he did so his eyes caught the light from the table lamp so that he appeared inspirational, almost Messianic.

257

'I can offer you two things. First, in that safety deposit box' – he gestured to the key – 'you will find an example of the weapons I can offer. I can assure you they are better than anything else you have or are likely to get.

'Second, we are on the brink of a great triumph here. Imagine the prospect . . . ' The vision was so powerful that he stood up and began pacing back and forth in front of her, his physical presence looming over her. 'We may actually be about to found a Palestinian state after all these years of struggle. The conference is possible, really possible. I can smell the fear in the Americans. The Israelis must be shitting themselves. After all these years of squeezing my people they are finding out what it is like to be shafted by your friends and have nowhere to go.

'When we get the conference, the Israelis will have to concede and they will know that even before they get there. We get our state and then what? This won't be another Castro, another Cuba. This will be a prosperous, successful state. We will be able to draw on our talents from all over the world to build a new nation based not on oil but on business experience, on the reputation that we Palestinians have achieved all over the world.

'And I tell you now, we will not forget our friends. Those who helped make the state possible will get our support for their struggles – and not from meetings like this, huddled in dark corners, hiding from the world. We will support your revolution with all the power that our new nation can bring to bear. Your fight will be our fight, our victory will eventually be your victory.'

The rhetoric stirred Inge. In darker moments, she recognized the futility of the struggle. Too many of her friends had died, shot down before a largely indifferent public, or jailed to die a slower death, politically impotent and alone. The vision that Hassan conjured up might be fantasy, but revolution was all about realizing dreams.

'If we help, when do you need to start the next round?'

'Your people must be in place so that the moment the deadline has passed the next stage of poisoning can begin. And this time I want something that will be even more terrifying. A food that everyone eats but that is in hundreds, maybe thousands of different products. They will have to poison sugar.'

Inge recognized the devastating effect such an attack would have. She could imagine the chaos, the collapsing markets, the deaths, the panic. And she had the power to cause it all.

Her agreement seemed to release a great tension in Hassan and the exhaustion – which had been visible but controlled – surfaced. He asked for a bed and she was happy to provide her own, expecting their bargain to be sealed between the sheets. But their lovemaking was perfunctory, a failure. Without the urgency and adrenalin rush of a killing Inge found arousal increasingly rare, as if she needed death to give her life. He, too, had clearly been suffering from the pressure of the campaign. She had been prepared to give him the relief of her body but there had been no response. He had simply fallen asleep in her arms.

The morning provided her with the opportunity to get the insurance she wanted. While Hassan was taking a shower, she went over to the table where the briefcase was still sitting. She had carefully noted the combination code the previous evening and a turn of the dials opened the case. Quickly she flicked through the slots in the lid, looking for the travel documents she was sure Hassan had concealed there. Suddenly, her questing fingers felt the hard rib of a passport and, as she gripped it, she felt another. Pulling them out, she saw the green of a Syrian diplomatic passport and the red of Brazil. Flicking open the first she saw the name George Bakr, the second was held by Lami Garcia. Now, if anything should go wrong, she had something to trade.

September 26

Dan, Israel

WHEN THE PRIME MINISTER was giving his orders to General Libak, Benny Nathanson had just ordered his favourite dish of stir-fried shredded chicken with Chinese fried egg, noodles and stuffed mushrooms when his beeper began to pulse. It was programmed to emit a low beep that would gradually rise to a deafening crescendo in case he had put the device to one side while taking a shower or sleeping. Before he embarrassed the other diners at Ruth's Szechuan Restaurant (only Israel would have a Chinese cook called Ruth) he switched the bleeper off and leaned across to his wife Bula.

'The office calls. I'll just go and check in. I expect it will be the usual false alarm.'

Bula, who had become used to the infernal machine interrupting everything in their lives from love-making to dinner parties, merely grunted and forked another portion of chicken towards her mouth.

Benny got up from the table and found the vast figure of Ruth, grown fat on her own excellent cooking, perched on the end of the bar. She indicated the telephone behind her and Benny dialled the emergency number.

As soon as the receiver was picked up at the other end, he gave his name followed by his code number and the code for the day, 'Hakerem'. There was a brief pause while the operator checked the names with the numbers and the code and then the reply came back: 'Gospel Story'.

All Israeli military are trained to respond to such code words. With a standing armed force of only 142,000, the country depends on mobilizing 370,000 reserves within twenty-four hours if an attack is imminent. These reserves are called up by coded messages broadcast over the radio and television. For more specialist units there is a refined system where each unit has a number of specific code words that require certain responses. In Benny's case 'Gospel Story' was the call to arms, a demand for instant action.

He returned to the table and bent over to Bula. 'I'm afraid something has come up. I've got to go. I'll call you when I know what's happening.'

He kissed her cheek and headed for the door at a fast walk.

Thirty minutes later he had arrived at the underground headquarters of the Israeli army in the west section of Tel Aviv near Yarkon Park.

Nathanson was a lieutenant-colonel in the Israeli army, a member of the elite Sayeret special forces and commander of Unit 269, the secret group responsible for the most sensitive counter-terrorist missions.

Israeli special forces are divided into four Sayeret or reconnaissance squadrons. Sayeret Shaked (Almond) is deployed with the Southern Command and specializes in long-range desert warfare; Sayeret Haruv (Carob) belongs to Central Command and deals with terrorists infiltrating through the Jordan Valley and the hills of Judaea and Samaria; Sayeret Egoz (Walnut) works with the Northern Command and is trained for mountain warfare; and the most secret of the four, the Sayeret Matkal (Hebrew for General Headquarters), has a troubleshooting anti-terrorist brief which includes operating deep behind enemy lines.

Inside Sayeret Matkal Unit 269 is hidden. Their role is similar to the larger Sayeret except that they specialize in 'door blasting', the special operations: the rescue of hostages, an attack on a building or airfield, an assassination or a precision strike against a small but well-defended target. The men of Unit 269 are also trained in free-fall parachuting, diving, mountain-climbing and a variety of special weapons.

In an armed force that prizes courage and has made a cult out of heroism, the Sayeret squadrons have become a legend. In both 1967 and 1973, they played a key role in operating behind enemy lines and passing back vital intelligence.

261

It was Unit 269 that had carried out Operation Thunderball in July 1976, attacking Entebbe airport in Uganda after terrorists from the Popular Front for the Liberation of Palestine had hijacked an Air France jet with 12 crew and 246 passengers on board. In a stunning display of daring and skill, they surprised the terrorists and rescued the hostages. But since then there had been the debilitating experience of Operation Peace for Galilee, the unsuccessful Israeli invasion of Lebanon, and, more recently, the Intifada, which had slowly sapped the strength and morale of the military. At their headquarters outside Bet Mirsim deep in the Negev Desert, Unit 269 had been removed from Israel's day-to-day struggle for survival. On permanent standby, they kept themselves ready for the crisis that required their particular skills.

Benny's briefing from General Libak had lasted only a few minutes.

'We have some preliminary intelligence that suggests a PFA training camp may be up in the Beka'a. We think they are about here,' he explained, pointing with a silver stick at a spot somewhere north of Rachaya near the Syrian border. 'We want you to get together a team to take the camp out. But, and this is a big but, I need intelligence not bodies. Kill when you have to but make sure that when you leave you bring someone back for us to interrogate.'

'How long do I have?' Benny asked.

'For Entebbe you guys had a week. For this one you have three days.'

Before Benny could register a protest at the impossibility of such a timetable the General held up his hand.

'I know it's unreasonable but we are working to a very short fuse on this one. We have until October 5 to agree to the terrorist demands or another round of poisoning begins. So we must have information as soon as possible.'

He paused and then looked directly at Benny. 'That means there will be no time for a nice social chat. We need information and we need it now. So get what you can out in the field.'

Benny nodded his acceptance of the orders which he knew had been carefully phrased to make the goals clear but leave vague the methods by which he was to achieve them.

'If you fail, we will have no time to decide on another course of action.'

That had been three days ago. Three days in which Nathanson had gathered thirty-six men for the operation, shipped the equipment north to the airbase at Dan outside the settlement of Kiryat Shimona and devised an operational plan he believed would work.

This was to be his baptism as leader of 269. His arrival in the army had been something of an accident. He had been conscripted in 1976 and then took a degree in history at Tel Aviv University. He had specialized in Jewish history and written a thesis arguing the structure of Israeli society was inevitably going to lead to a new and more bloody Masada. He believed that the influx of North African Jews combined with the outflow of disenchanted European Jews was altering the balance of the once liberal state to create a more conservative and more militaristic society. It was inevitable, he felt, that there would be another conflict with the Arabs and that new weapons, either chemical or nuclear, would be used by both sides.

His solution was not to leave his country and head for America or Europe like so many of his contemporaries but to join the regular army. This had not been an act of passion but, like everything he did, a carefully thought-out response to a problem. He believed he had something to contribute to Israel, a country he loved and at times despaired of, and that contribution was best made inside the structure that would ensure his country's survival. The military could also, he told himself, be not just the instrument of the politicians but the control to curb their wilder ambitions.

He found he adapted readily to military life, enjoying the order and discipline and relishing the intellectual challenge of resolving complex tactical issues. At university he had found little satisfaction in athletics, his thin, wiry body making him defensive when surrounded by the more overtly aggressive Israeli men. But during military training he discovered in himself great strength, the stamina to run long distances and the endurance to survive. He was the perfect Sayeret recruit and he joined the Egoz squadron just in time for Operation Peace for Galilee. Eighty men from his squadron had attacked the PLO stronghold at Beaufort Castle just north of the Litani River.

This was an important base for the PLO who used the strategic position of the castle three and a half miles north of the Israeli border to direct artillery and rocket fire on to Israeli settlements.

In a fierce battle, the Israelis killed thirty-seven Palestinians and captured the castle. Out of his twelve-man team six had been killed and it was Benny's final assault on the bunker with a satchel charge that had cleared the way for the reserves to storm through the gates. His courage had been rewarded with a promotion and a transfer to 269 but that bloody battle had left its mark.

In all eight Sayeret were killed and twenty-one wounded – terrible casualties for such a highly trained unit. Benny had lost friends and he remembered with disgust the casual nature of the briefing he and his men had received, the expectation that at the first sign of battle the Palestinians would run. It had been a stupid and costly mistake which he was determined not to repeat.

Since 1982, the role of the Sayeret had changed. They were still responsible for reconnaissance, for gathering intelligence and for deep attack. But now much of the basic, high-risk intelligence gathering is done not by man but by a machine, in the shape of a remotely piloted vehicle or drone.

Nathanson had taken over a cavernous hangar at the airfield. Normally occupied by C-130 transport aircraft, one side now sheltered the unit's helicopters and the other was used for logistics support and briefing. At the front of the hangar was a single truck and it was here that Benny had spent much of the past three days.

The Israelis pioneered the use of RPVs and incorporated them into their battle tactics. The first drone had been developed by an American-born engineer called Alvin Ellis and three other men working in Ellis's Tel Aviv garage with balsa wood, modelling glue and tiny engines. In February 1974, Ellis demonstrated his invention, nicknamed Owl, in front of a sceptical military audience. He had arrived at the Kfar Sirkim military airbase outside Tel Aviv with his device strapped to the roof of his ancient blue Fiat. Tied underneath the model aircraft was a Sony video camera that had been modified to relay its picture direct to a television set on the ground. The aircraft took off and after a few anxious moments when the screen remained blank the camera broadcast an image of a cyclist pedalling along the airport road.

From this unpromising start emerged the Mastiff, a model aircraft into which is crammed a stunning range of equipment that allows the little aircraft to act as the Israeli army's eyes and ears. The Mastiff is just over three metres long with a wingspan of over four metres and is driven by a two-stroke twenty-two horsepower engine that can push it along at 180 kilometres an hour at 12,000 feet for more than seven hours.

Its fibreglass construction makes it invisible to radar and the height it travels makes it invisible to the naked eye. Flying over a specific area, the Mastiff can send back video pictures to its base or to relay screens at the front or at a military headquarters. It can listen to conversations on the ground, intercept coded communications, jam radars and even fool radars that it is a large fighter and so encourage enemy missile sites to expose themselves. It is the perfect battlefield weapon: all-seeing, all-knowing, virtually undetectable and, unlike its human counterparts, cheap and expendable.

For three days and nights the Mastiff had been catapulted from the hangar to climb north and east into Lebanon. The co-ordinates supplied by General Libak had been enough for the RPV operator to send the little aircraft into the area. Its high resolution camera had quickly detected the camp, the shadows cast by the tents clearly visible, the outdoor latrines a darker colour than the light sand surrounding the camp.

As the images had poured back Unit 269's planners had set to work. Using plywood and sand they had constructed a forty- by thirty-foot mock-up of the camp. The single track leading into the camp had formed the starting reference point and gradually every tent, every sentry and every machine-gun post had been marked. Every two hours, the men gathered round the structure and the intelligence briefer, a woman captain from Aman, had taken them round the course, pointing out new additions and going over the old information.

The camp was sited in a valley about half a mile wide with steep cliffs on three sides. The camp itself was just inside the neck of the valley and there appeared to be ranges and an assault course at the far end. During the night flights the Mastiff had used its infrared imaging system to reveal the patrol patterns and the location of any hidden traps betrayed by the tell-tale red spots of body heat.

They had carefully counted 105 men in the camp and twelve women, all of whom appeared to be combatants. This morning Benny had watched over the shoulder of the Mastiff operator as images floated on to the TV screen of a mid-morning parade developing in front of them. In what little time they had had to prepare a schedule of camp activity, this was unusual, and he watched with interest as a dust trail appeared in the top right-hand corner of the screen which quickly emerged as an open-topped jeep heading for the camp.

'Zoom in on the jeep,' Benny had instructed the operator.

A tiny movement of the small joystick in front of him controlled the angle of the camera and a roll of the ball under his left hand directed the lens. Out of the dust emerged the clear shape of a Toyota Land Cruiser with four men. Two in the back carried machine-guns and the passenger, his head swathed in a red-and-white checked keffiyeh, sat apparently unarmed, his hands folded in his lap.

The jeep drew up in a cloud of dust in front of the guard of honour and the man in the front seat got out to inspect them. After a ten-minute stroll up and down the line of fedayeen he ducked into the largest of the tents where he stayed until the afternoon. Then he had walked up the valley, surrounded by gesticulating aides, to watch the men and women go through the assault course.

Clearly the man was a leader – perhaps even the leader – of the group. Benny had rerun the video and taken a number of still shots of the man to distribute to his team. Although he had never taken his keffiyeh away from his face, that alone was a distinguishing feature and they had marked the tent where he had gone in the evening. Benny himself would lead his squad to that tent in the hope of capturing the man himself.

Benny had noticed with admiration that whoever had organized the camp was a professional. The machine-gun posts were sited to control the entrance to the camp with an effective crossfire; trenches had been dug near the tents that interlinked in a zig-zag pattern to retreat towards the far valley wall.

In the patrolling and the performance of the men over the assault course there had been no evidence of what the Israelis called 'the Abdul factor', that mixture of bravado and laziness that led to sand in gun barrels and guards asleep on duty. Instead this bunch seemed to be well trained and well prepared – a tough nut.

Three hours earlier the Mastiff had catapulted off on its final flight, heading away into the darkness, the diminishing putt-putt of its tiny engine belying the sophisticated nature of the technology it was carrying northwards.

Zero hour was at 0345. This allowed for thirty minutes flying just above the ground using every valley, building and wood for cover – known as nap-of-the-earth flying – to bring the team within sight of the target just as the first flush of dawn brought light to the valley.

Fifteen minutes earlier, four F-15 fighters had screamed down the runway heading into Lebanon. Their mission was to destroy the Syrian surface-to-air missile site at Rachaya which cut directly across the Unit's flight north. Benny knew that two F-15s would fly towards the SAMs and as they came within range they would release two gliders, known as Samsons, from rails underneath their wings. The Samsons, which looked like missiles, would fall away from the fighters and the force of the airflow push out huge wings to stabilize them as they flew towards their target. As the wings spread, so a Luneberg lens in the nose cone activates to emit a magnified radar signature identical to that of the F-15. To the radar operators at the SAM site it would appear as if they were under attack by four F-15s and they would activate their radars prior to releasing the missiles. Then the two other F-15s would strike, releasing volleys of missiles that would follow the signals given off by the ground-based radar.

Without the radars the SAMs were useless and by the time Benny and his men lifted off, he was confident they would offer no threat.

He always found the final briefing difficult. It is a moment when the nervous need a last word of encouragement and even the most experienced welcome some reassurance. He looked around the darkened hangar at his men. Their blackened faces and camouflage uniforms made their bodies appear hulking shadows; only the occasional shaft of moonlight glinting off a machine-gun or rocket-launcher hinting at their deadly purpose.

These men were all his friends. They had sweated together, cursed together, bruised together and some had even been wounded together. It had created a camaraderie that no one outside the military could ever understand. They were all men who had experienced the ultimate thrill, the total terror of facing death and surviving – just – until the next time. He knew that some of these men would not be coming back. He shook himself.

'OK guys. One last time.' He spoke softly, the words carrying easily across the vast space of the hangar. 'We go in fast and low. We look for officers and we try and take them alive. We need people to talk so watch your firing, watch each other and above all watch out for me.'

There was an appreciative murmur at the weak joke and the men stirred, the ritual of the commander's farewell exhortation over with, the need for action drawing them towards the waiting helicopters.

Attack helicopters are one of the most potent weapons in the modern armoury. The Israelis use a modified version of the Sikorsky UH-60A Black Hawk for special operations. They squatted like huge, dark, pregnant dragonflies on the tarmac outside the hangar. Even though the engines were turning the four carbon fibre forty-six-foot rotors, there was none of the piercing whine associated with helicopters, only the distinctive whup-whup to disturb the quiet night.

The Israelis had bought the helicopters from the Americans two years earlier, complete with some of the modifications designed for the US special forces. One of these was a sound-suppression system that cut flight noise by seventy-five per cent. The secret was in two enormous loudspeakers mounted on the air intakes above the main cabin. These speakers pumped out noise which exactly matched that produced by the helicopter's engines but precisely out of phase. The two noises cancelled each other out and made the sound undetectable to the human ear.

The teams had divided into three groups of twelve and Benny led his men into the first Black Hawk, ducking under the eight Hellfire air-to-ground missiles that hung from a stubby pylon by the waist door. His men filed quietly into the darkened cabin to take up their positions on the canvas seats lining the sides. There was no light to damage their night vision, no talking to disturb their concentration, to break into the last thoughts, that final prayer in every soldier's mind.

Five minutes later the first Black Hawk lifted into the sky and headed north skimming the hard brown earth at fifty feet. Benny was squashed into a jump seat behind the pilot and navigator, his view restricted by the television screen mounted on the fuselage slaved to the Mastiff operator's screen back in the hangar. He could thus keep the terrorist camp in sight right up until the moment of impact.

Benny always hated these night flights. Just before take-off the navigator had inserted a small cassette into the dashboard in front of him. This held the computer data that would produce the moving map display scrolling across the small television screen in front of him. Unlike modern fighter pilots, flying a helicopter is still a hands-on operation where the skill of the pilot determines the survival of himself and his passengers. Low flying at night is a terrifying, dangerous and exhilarating experience where the slightest mistake can mean crashing into an unexpected electricity line or a newly constructed building.

Like the pilot and navigator, Benny was wearing Cat's Eyes night-vision goggles that literally turned night into day. The goggles look rather like the special glasses that an optician uses to test eyesight and they amplify the available light so that every ground feature is clearly visible. The internal cockpit system had been modified so that to the naked eye the instruments appeared almost black but with the goggles they were clearly visible. Benny looked over the navigator's shoulder and watched as the Honeywell Moving Map Display System showed their position as they moved along the planned route, producing a three-dimensional hologram of the terrain.

After five minutes of lurching, swooping, climbing flight, Benny could feel his stomach beginning to rebel as the semicircular canals in his inner ear sent urgent distress signals around the body. He looked behind him and saw several of his men suffering. Two had already vomited.

Every soldier sees himself as a gladiator, a warrior fighting other warriors, man against man, until the right with the might survived. It is a romantic view of a bloody and violent business that brings sanity to a soldier's mad world. Benny, like the others in his unit, could not get used to the inhumanity of it all now, trusting to machines, sacrificing independence, initiative and control to a computer that was the final arbiter of life or death. It went against all his training which emphasized self-will and the endless struggle for survival. But he had had to learn to accept the role of the machine, if not really to trust it.

He turned back to the television screen and saw appear in front of him the blurred white shape of a cluster of bodies walking through the darkness of the camp. The group joined another source of heat, separated slightly and then the two white blobs merged. The single image then moved rapidly away to disappear north. Benny's mind swiftly matched the picture with the reverse image he had seen in full colour yesterday as the terrorist leader had arrived at the camp. They had missed him by a few minutes.

September 27

Beka'a Valley

ACHMED KHALAF HAD BEEN on duty since midnight
and the normal boring round of his patrol had been
relieved only by the departure twenty minutes earlier
of The Leader. He had listened eagerly when Abu Hassan
had spoken to them last night by the light of their fires.
Hassan had talked of their mission, the campaign that was
being waged against the Zionists in Europe and America
and how success was within their grasp. It had been stirring
and Achmed had cheered with the rest of the fedayeen.

'The Zionists are at bay and when a dog is cornered he
barks and then he bites,' Abu Hassan had warned. 'Their
politicians have been barking for several days but they have
not found someone to bite. They are getting desperate and
it may be that they will strike here at the heart of the Palestinian resistance. If they do, I know you will fight and
fight well.'

There had been an aggressive roar at this exhortation, the
fighters waving their AK-47s in the air.

'But remember, if they attack they do so not to kill us but
because they want information. This they must not have.
There is great dishonour in betrayal and I know none of you
would betray your brothers. But the Zionists have drugs and
will torture the information from you; it will be impossible
for even the bravest to resist.

'If there is a fight, brother must protect brother. Better to
die with honour in the field of battle than betray the revolution from a Zionist jail.'

They had returned to their blankets sobered by the harsh
warning.

271

For the first hour of his guard duty Achmed had paced with a spring in his stride, his weapon held in both hands across his chest, ready for instant action. But the effect of the speech had soon worn off, his rifle was now in its usual place on his shoulder, his pace had slowed to a shuffle and his mind wandered.

Another thirty minutes and he would be relieved, free to enjoy six hours of sleep and relaxation. It would be an opportunity, he thought, to make further progress with the delicious Miriam who had arrived at the camp two weeks earlier and had so far resisted all his advances.

Thoughts of how he might seduce her – it was always so much easier in thought than action – had been interrupted by the sound floating on the dawn air. Achmed moved his head from left to right and then turned his body, trying to pinpoint the sound which was growing louder and appeared one second to be coming up the valley and the next coming from the assault course behind him.

The view in front of him stretched for thirty miles across the Beka'a Valley and into Syria. Early morning haze narrowed his vision to a mile or two of flat light brown scrub. South, to his right and about 400 yards away, the wall of their valley merged with the flat lands of the Beka'a. Huge rocks had broken from the cliff and stunted olive trees clung for life in the shelter of the valley walls.

It began with a whisper, a soft sighing in the dawn. It was a sound so slight that it could almost have been the faint rustle of the wind through trees, except there were no trees in this part of the valley. Achmed Khalaf cocked his head and listened. The furrows on his forehead reflected the concentration of curiosity and not the wide-eyed anxiety of alarm.

Suddenly it seemed that one of the light brown, sandy rocks was moving, levitating out of the mist, advancing rapidly towards him. Now the sound had direction, focus. He watched, mouth opening with the beginnings of a shout of alarm as his brain registered the shape of helicopters flying just above the ground and heading straight towards him.

There was a flash from the side of the first helicopter and then another and another. He instinctively ducked but the rockets flashed over him, moving faster than he could turn

272

his head to follow their flight. He heard the explosions behind him and knew that the moment their instructors had warned them about, the moment they had trained for, had talked bravely about but had never really expected, had come. The Israelis had arrived.

A second ripple of fire came from the lead helicopter and then a third. The machine-gun posts at the entrance to the camp vanished in gouts of fire and sand.

Where there had been one shape there were now three, flying in line astern and then spreading out as if embracing the full dimensions of the camp. The first helicopter flew over Achmed, missing his head by ten feet, the downdraught of its massive propellers bowling him over, tossing him along the ground like a bush in a gale.

As the final helicopter passed him, he rose to his knees and watched as each of the helicopters came into the hover and then settled briefly on the ground. As soon as the skids touched, men began to pour out of the sides of the aircraft, scattering in the hunched, skittering run of the professional soldier. In a strange way, the movement reminded Achmed of times in his childhood when he had watched the fish settle their tails into the sandy bottoms of the river near his Jordan home to lay their eggs.

Yet these were no symbols of a new generation but deadly opponents here to wipe out him and his friends. Already the helicopters had lifted off and were circling above the camp. He could see continuous tongues of fire erupting from their bellies as the gunners used the waist-mounted heavy machine-guns to search out the enemy. It was a terrifying sight. With a ripping, tearing noise he saw one tongue reach down and lick at two of the tents. In an instant they disintegrated, torn to pieces by the heavy 7.62 mm bullets, pieces of cloth scattering in the air and great gouts of sand spurting up as the bullets beat their deadly tattoo on the earth.

There was sporadic firing now as the fedayeen reached their weapons and struggled to fight their way to the trenches at the rear of the camp. Achmed, too, realized that there lay sanctuary. In the trenches he could fight, even hide from the probing helicopters. Out in the open he could never escape, could already feel the horror of the first bullet hitting his exposed body.

He scuttled quickly towards the valley wall, still in shadow from the early morning sun rising behind. He moved along the wall, hurrying from shadow to shadow, clutching his AKM semi-automatic rifle to his chest as if it could shield him from the bullets flying across the valley.

Terror gave him speed and adrenalin surging through his blood gave him the energy to power over the ground unnoticed by the Israelis who were now scattered throughout the camp. Between the bursting grenades and the staccato machine-gun fire he could hear the shouts of rage or triumph from the invaders, echoed by the screams of fear and encouragement from his own side. Increasingly now, these normal sounds of battle were interrupted by the most common and haunting sound of conflict: the agonized screams of the wounded. Their cries spurred Achmed on until, at last, he saw the outline of the first trench. Without pause he leaped the last two yards and landed in the bottom of the trench, the shock of his jump forcing him to his knees. He welcomed the respite, his lungs drawing great gulps of air and his muscles beginning to spasm with the tension.

The operation had begun perfectly. As the helicopters had rounded the curve of the valley Benny could see that the camp was still asleep, their approach undetected. He blinked as a brief, bright flash followed by a burst light blinded his night-vision goggles when the first rocket went on its way.

Then it all happened very quickly. He felt the aircraft stop and then settle. His men were clustered around the open doors on either side of the fuselage, all of them eager to get their feet back on the ground and once again master their own fates.

Benny heard himself shouting 'Go, go, go,' and thumped the two men nearest him on the back. The extra encouragement was unnecessary. They had all trained for this mission hundreds of times, the sequence was pre-set and each man had the timings down to fractions of a second. Even so, they had all moved on to that higher plane where real battle takes over from exercise. In practice they had all moved through the drills calmly and efficiently. Now they charged from the aircraft with a battle cry designed to chill their enemy and encourage their friends.

Within sixty seconds Benny's men were advancing through the dust cloud created by the chopper's rotors, so thick that Benny could not even distinguish the features of the trooper next to him and there was no chance at all of seeing the enemy. But then the cloud thinned.

Fifty yards ahead he could see the first tent, a sleepy Palestinian standing in front of it clutching a rifle. Three weapons fired at once and the Palestinian was literally shredded where he stood, the bullets tearing his body apart, pieces of flesh, bone and brains spraying backwards in a bloody arc on to the canvas sides of the tent.

The deep bark of the unit's Galil rifles mixed with the chatter of their Uzi sub-machine-guns and the lighter cracks of the terrorists' Soviet rifles. The first few tents fell quickly, their occupants either shot as they emerged or killed with a single grenade as they huddled inside the spurious protection of the canvas.

Benny knew that the first thirty seconds were bound to be easy. After that resistance would stiffen as the terrorists recovered from their initial shock and their training and knowledge of the terrain came into play.

The air was now filled with the buzzing of low-flying bullets. A heavy machine-gun opened up from one of the trenches ahead, the green of its tracer still visible in the half-light as it dogged the line of advancing Israelis. A well-placed rocket grenade silenced the gun but not before two Israelis had fallen, one dead and the other with blood pouring in a crimson fountain from a torn thigh artery.

It seemed to Benny that around twenty-five of the Palestinians had fallen in the first seconds of the attack. The rest had retreated towards the trench system down the valley. With the protection of its walls, the fight was in danger of turning in the terrorists' favour.

'Sections three and four take the left, seven and eight the right and the rest clear the camp, check for survivors and hold,' Benny said into his throat mike. He received over his helmet headphones answering squawks from the section leaders.

The motto of the Israeli army's officer school is 'After Me' and Benny ran to take his place at the head of section three who were to be the first into the trenches.

275

There is a standard procedure for clearing trenches. The first man in the group throws a grenade around the first corner and immediately after the detonation the second man jumps the corner, gun blazing. The cycle is then repeated until the trench is cleared. The process works well provided that the trenches are not so long that the force on the grenade fails to clear the whole length or that there are no side slits concealing enemy unharmed by the grenade blast.

Benny pulled the pin on the first grenade, counted to two and lobbed it around the corner. Two seconds and an explosion rocked the trench, showering him and his men with sand, debris and a human hand. At a run the advance team swept round the corner, their Galils firing on automatic. Stepping over rubble and the remains of terrorists, Benny ran to the next corner and repeated the process.

It was at the third that he became over-confident. Over his radio he had heard the exultant sounds of victory in the voices of the team leaders. He knew that the battle was won but he wanted prisoners.

As he pulled the pin on the third grenade he was shouting into his throat mike: 'Take prisoners, take prisoners.' The grenade exploded and he leaped around the corner, too impatient to allow his men to pass. He felt a sting on his neck and then a blow on his arm that pushed the limb away and behind his body as if it had a momentum of its own. He heard a Galil fire next to him and watched as a terrorist tumbled out of the side entrance to the trench. His men continued firing, little puffs of sand and blood coming from the terrorist's dead body.

There was no pain but he could feel blood trickling down his neck and he saw that his right arm had been severed at the elbow. It was like looking at a wound on someone else. He felt detached from the reality of the horror. Then the shock hit and he found himself sitting on the ground, staring stupidly around him. Arms reached beneath his shoulders and hauled him to his feet.

The unit medic tied a tourniquet on his arm and tightened it, stanching the flow of blood that was staining the sand a deep, dark brown. Two minutes later Benny was back with the reserve units. The medic advanced towards him syringe in hand.

276

'No. No morphine,' he shouted. 'Bring me the prisoners.'

The men parted to let through two Palestinians, one woman and a man whose single red shoulder stripe suggested he might be an officer.

'You see that my career in the army is finished,' Benny said, thrusting the stump of his arm forward. 'What I want from you is information and I want it now. We have precisely four minutes before we have to leave here. If you tell us what we want then we leave without you and you live. If we don't get what we want then you are no use to us and you die where you stand.'

'You will get nothing from us, you Zionist pigs,' the officer said and then spat, the saliva landing on the front of Benny's camouflage jacket.

'There are two things we need to know,' Benny continued, as if the other man had not spoken. 'The first is the location of Abu Hassan's headquarters and the second is the identity of the terrorist gang doing the poisoning.'

Benny gestured to Ari, the blond giant of the unit, who stepped forward. It was a routine they had practised many times before. He began by kicking the man savagely in the balls. The terrorist lifted a foot off the ground with the force of the blow and then fell on to his knees retching, tears pouring down off the end of his nose to form a small damp patch in the sand. Ari lifted him up by the back of the neck so that his body was forced to straighten. Benny leaned forward and unzipped the man's trousers and pulled out his penis. There was a click and the man saw the shiny blade of a knife float before his horrified eyes.

'Now, my friend, you have felt the pain of a good kick in the balls. I'm sure you have also felt the pleasure that your cock can give you – perhaps even with this woman here.' He glanced at the girl standing next to him. 'As you can see, I have in my hand a knife. With this knife I am first going to cut off one ball. Now with one ball you can still make love and you can even have a family and grow old comforted by your children. But then I am going to cut off the other ball. Without that you become a eunuch, an effeminate, no longer the courageous leader of this band. You won't be able to have children and people will laugh at your squeaky voice and your mincing walk.

'Then if you still won't talk I'm going to take your prick and slice it off bit by bit. I'm going to cut it like a salami so that all that is left is a little stump. You'll never be able to fuck a girl again and you'll spend the rest of your life carrying a plastic bag around to pee into.'

The threats were delivered in a calm and matter-of-fact way that made them all the more frightening. Held upright by Ari, the Palestinian was unable to look down to see what was happening. He could only feel the huge ball of pain in his groin from the kick he had just received. Sweat, the sweat of terror, burst out on his forehead but he shook his head.

Benny nodded acceptance of his bravery. 'I understand how you feel, honestly I do. But really it is such a little thing that I ask and such a heavy price you will have to pay for not answering.

'So, the left ball first, I think. I am drawing the knife through the sack now. Can you feel it? It's slicing deep inside now.'

The man groaned, his agony clearly visible on his face.

'There we are,' said Benny, a note of triumph in his voice. He brought up in front of him a hand dripping with fresh blood. In the palm was lying a small football-shaped fleshy object.

The whites of the terrorist's eyes had doubled in size at the revolting sight before him. Already he felt half a man.

'Well, that's one down and two to go,' Benny said cheerfully. 'Are you ready?'

'No, no.' The words were dragged from the Palestinian. At this the woman started forward as if to drag him back from the precipice of betrayal. One of the men knocked her unconscious with a single blow from his rifle.

'OK, OK, I'll tell you whatever you want to know. Only don't hurt me. No more. No more.' With the dam of courage broken, the words came flooding out.

'That's very sensible. Now the two questions. Who is Abu Hassan and where is he based?'

'All I know is that Hassan is based in Tunisia, Tunis I think but I don't know where.' He screamed as Benny raised the bloody knife up to his face. 'No, I swear. I swear it's true. He never tells us where he's from or where he goes and I have never even seen him without his keffiyeh. But his guards were complaining about Tunisia, saying that the people are just peasants. They wanted to be back in Amman,' he added helpfully.

'And what about the poisoners?'

'I don't know. We asked him about the campaign and who was doing it but he refused to say. Only that the revolution has friends everywhere.'

'There must have been something,' Benny replied. 'What about those guards? Did they say they had been anywhere recently? Did they talk of other countries apart from Tunisia?'

The Israelis had missed Achmed. In his hurry to hide he had jumped not into the main line of trenches but into a single foxhole that had originally been built for a machine-gun post but, as the camp had expanded, had been abandoned.

Cut off from his comrades, Achmed had watched the destruction of the camp and the butchering of his friends. Now he had listened to the Zionists question the lieutenant and Miriam. He had heard the threats and seen the movement of the knife. Now he could hear that the lieutenant had broken under the torture and was telling the enemy all that he knew.

Achmed had waited and listened, wondering what he should do. If he kept quiet he might survive, the Zionists might get back into their helicopters and leave him alone. But then the final words of Abu Hassan began to run through his mind. Betrayal, he knew, was the ultimate ignominy and the lieutenant was about to destroy the one terrorist operation that could bring the Israelis to their knees.

He felt anger at the loss of his friends whose bodies he could see sprawled in the sand around him; he felt fury at the hated Zionists for destroying his world with a barbarity that he had heard about in camp lectures but had never before seen first hand; and he felt betrayed by a man whom he had once respected, an officer who had told him to have courage and to keep the faith. The emotions fused to give him a clear course of action. He did not see it as brave or even sensible. It just seemed the natural thing to do.

He slid the barrel of his AKM over the edge of the foxhole and brought the sights in line with the centre of the lieutenant's body. He gently took up the first pressure on the trigger and then squeezed. With a sound of ripping cloth the bullets leapt from the gun and sped across the short distance to the little crowd fifty yards away. He saw bits of flesh fly off the lieutenant, had a brief glimpse of the bloody mass that was once the face of the beautiful Miriam. Then his world compressed into a small moment of agony and he died.

As the first bullets struck the Palestinian, Benny flung himself forward to cover his body with his own and protect his most important asset. After the firing stopped he looked down at his prisoner and realized that his wounds were fatal. Blood was dribbling from the corner of his mouth, a sure sign of a punctured lung, and his breathing bubbled hoarsely.

Benny moved to one side and cradled the terrorist's neck on his knee, bending low over his ear. 'Tell me. Which terrorists? What country?'

There was a bubbled reply and a froth of blood spurted from his mouth. Benny shook his shoulders and repeated the question, desperate to hold on to him before he vanished into unconsciousness and death.

The lieutenant's lips moved, trying to mouth an answer. Benny placed his ear next to the man's lips and heard the single, gasped word 'Germany'.

Benny stood up and turned wearily to Ari. 'Well, we got what we wanted, let's go home.'

He reflected that the psychologists back at headquarters had been right. Interrogation works if the subject is made to believe the worst. A kick in the balls had focused the pain, a graphic description of what might happen had caught the imagination and a blood pack from the medic dripping over an army ration matzo ball had been enough to convince the Arab that he was being castrated.

September 28

Washington, DC

TERRORISM IS ALWAYS EASIER the second time around. But it is also much, much more dangerous. The first time the ground is fresh, the territory unknown and the target a potential death trap. The second time the ground is easier but the risks soar as the counter-terrorist forces always take precautions just in case.

Each attack is therefore a trade-off between the risk of capture because proper reconnaissance has been impossible and the risk of capture because the enemy is prepared. Most sensible terrorists today prefer to err on the side of caution, always believing that an assumption of excellence in the enemy is wise.

Hans and Brigitte Krocher were careful, which is why they had survived so long in the Red Army Faction. But this operation was different. They had had to carry out one task – the poisoning of Kola Co. drinks in America – and then return to do the same thing again, to poison any food made by the Kastel Sugar Co., one of America's largest companies with products ranging from granulated white sugar to pies, biscuits and sweets.

There had been a meeting two days before at the Bonn safe house where, once again, Inge had issued the orders. 'The last operation was a triumph,' she had told them. 'It was the most successful operation we had ever done and has created chaos in the centres of capitalism around the world.'

'Yeah, well, it may have been brilliant but nobody knows it was us so what's the point?' Hans had snapped.

Normally Inge would have slapped him down and

281

reasserted her authority. This time, she hid her anger and only smiled. Reaching behind her chair, she produced a brown cardboard box.

'You should look on this operation as a little investment. As the capitalists want dividends from their stocks so we want rewards for our work too. This is a sample of what we shall be getting.'

She held up a matt black rifle unlike anything any of them had seen before. It was around thirty inches long and had a solid stock and an inbuilt telescopic sight.

'This is the G11, a new rifle just on the market from our old enemies Heckler and Koch,' she explained. 'It is made entirely from carbon fibre, weighs in at just over eight pounds and can fire a fifteen-round clip at 2,000 rounds per minute in a three-shot burst.

'But the real beauty of this is the ammunition.' She held up a plastic tube not unlike a small packet of square sweets. 'This ammunition has no case. The bullet is inside surrounded by the propellant and encased in plastic. It's revolutionary. It works. It should be virtually undetectable to any modern security system. And we can have as many as we want.'

There was a buzz of excitement in the room as Inge passed the gun around. Few of them were particularly expert shots or even knew or understood guns. But they had the user's fascination with new equipment and suffered from the inferiority complex widespread among terrorists that it was only the government's firepower that prevented victory. 'If only we had the right equipment' was a constant refrain. (In fact victory or defeat had little to do with equipment and a great deal to do with poor training and security.) So the new weapon was greeted with great enthusiasm by the little group. Here, at last, was a weapon that might give them an edge in the war.

'How come we're getting this stuff?' Brigitte asked. 'I've read about this gun and it's not even in service with the German army yet.'

'All I can tell you is that the people we are working with on this operation have some friends in a large Middle Eastern country who have several hundred of these on trial. Some

282

have been "damaged" and are on their way to us. I can also tell you that we will be receiving both Semtex and detonators in the next two weeks along with some cash.

'So, I think this operation is worth it and I think we should carry out the next stage without delay.'

Inge had skilfully undermined the opposition she had expected from the group, justifiably sure that the bribe of guns, explosives and cash, the real currency of terrorism, would prove irresistible.

'I have received the message that we need to move to phase two,' she explained to her now silent audience. 'I want you to repeat your previous success. We have no indication that the authorities know anything of our involvement so you should have free runs. You will all need to leave tomorrow and begin planting the poison within four days so that it will take effect immediately after the deadline expires. For those of you who have to pass through border controls I have arranged new papers from the Ketel connection in Antwerp.'

There had been little discussion after that. Hans and Brigitte had taken their false papers and a bundle of US dollars and left the safe house. They booked on the Lufthansa flight to Paris the next morning and then picked up the direct overnight Air France flight to Washington, DC.

Hans had finely honed survival instincts. He had heard Inge's reassurances but was reluctant to take them at face value. He had seen the press, read of the most intense manhunt in international police history. There had been speculation in the media about the methods used to find the terrorists; the computers, the files, the men. He was sure that most of it was inaccurate but he was also sure that for every detail and every fact that the media got wrong there would be a hundred actions underway that they knew nothing about. There would be computer systems that could find facts and sift them in ways that he couldn't even imagine. What that added up to was trouble, so Hans had taken along a little insurance just in case.

The Washington airport at Dulles was as he had remembered it from his last trip. Transferred from aircraft to terminal in the ridiculous shuttle, he and Brigitte stood in line with their fellow passengers, slowly shuffling forward as the immigration officer worked at his usual leisurely pace.

When it was Hans' turn he strode confidently up to the desk. He knew that the Americans were trained to look for young single Arab men as the most likely terrorist suspect so he had dressed to appear as far removed from that image as possible. He was wearing a smart grey suit with a plain shirt and simple tie. He carried a briefcase and looked, he hoped, like a prosperous European businessman.

It seemed that American immigration officers were all poured out of the same mould. This one, too, was fat, his eyes myopic behind thick lenses. Hans felt his confidence rising.

'Are you here on business or pleasure, sir?' the officer, Juan Selgado, asked, voice bored with the routine. As he talked, his fingers were busily tapping Hans's details into the computer.

'Business.'

'And how long do you intend staying?'

'Oh, around a week or so. If I get my work done I hope my wife and I will have time for a little sightseeing.' Hans gestured towards Brigitte who was still waiting patiently in the queue.

While he answered, the computer digested the details of the doctored Irish passport. In five seconds, the data had been coded into a series of short blips, travelled 900 kilometres south to the Immigration and Naturalization Service headquarters in Tallahassee, Florida. There, four days earlier, details of all the stolen Irish passports had been entered. The computer had been instructed to check all passports automatically against this standard. Working in nanoseconds the computer sifted through the gates to check whether the passport was Irish and if so whether the numbers matched. Since the numbers had been entered, the computer had been interrogated 1,398,422 times with no result.

But this time the nationality and the numbers both matched. Three things then happened simultaneously. A signal was sent by computer to FBI headquarters in Washington; another signal was sent to the FBI office at Dulles airport; and the third signal flashed on the immigration officer's screen: 'Suspect wanted. Hold for questioning. AD', the initials suggesting he might be armed and dangerous.

Juan Selgado felt his blood pressure soar and his heart rush to keep pace. Struggling to keep the excitement from his face, he followed standard procedure perfectly. He pressed a concealed button with his knee. Fifteen feet away behind a long sheet of mirrored glass a red light began to flash over the number 4, indicating Selgado's station. The four officers inside put down their poker cards and moved to the window to examine the suspect.

Selgado looked up at Hans and smiled to expose a crooked line of nicotine-stained teeth.

'That seems fine, sir.' Hans watched as Selgado stamped the passport giving him a visa for a month and then stapled the bottom half of his white immigration card to the passport and handed it back.

With a reassuring glance backwards to Brigitte, Hans moved away from the desk. As he turned the corner four men came out of the glassed-in room and immediately separated, two following Hans and two heading for Brigitte.

When the end came Hans had always imagined a glorious battle, a firefight with the capitalist pigs that would go down in the revolutionary annals. It would be, he thought, like Butch Cassidy without the Sundance Kid. The pigs would fall before his guns until he was overwhelmed by sheer force of numbers. They might even name a day for him, celebrate his martyrdom with marches, the comrades carrying placards bearing his photograph and name.

In fact, he felt an arm and then a hand slide in on either side to reach up and grip his shoulders from behind. A gravelly voice – an impression of gum and cigarettes – in his ear murmuring: 'Would you step this way please, sir?' And that was it. No guns. No noise. No glory. Nothing.

He was lifted off the ground, turned in the direction of a blank door which opened as he approached. Before he even had time to shout a last slogan, to strike a final blow for the revolution, he was gone.

Brigitte did not suspect anything until two of the men who had come out of the room peeled off and headed straight for her. She looked around and their eyes met. She could see in them an intensity, a sense of purpose that acted like a signal. She turned away from Juan Selgado and stepped back from the booth. As she did so, she heard one of the approaching men cry out.

The shout was 'Halt, you're under arrest' but she didn't hear the words, could only grasp the threat they carried.

Pushing through the crowd of passengers standing behind her, she ran back the way they had walked a few minutes earlier. She stepped on to the ramp that led to the upper level and to the possibility of safety. As she did so, the next flight was disgorged at the top of the ramp and the passengers flooded out, eager to be first in the queue for processing.

The individual met the mass about halfway up the ramp. She was shouting now, screaming in German at the uncomprehending passengers. She could no longer see her goal, was enveloped in the bodies, the luggage and the legs. Stumbling, cursing, she pushed upwards, legs and elbows pumping trying to forge a path out, the illusion of freedom a few paces away giving her strength.

At last she was through, people scattering to either side. Ahead and to her left, she spotted a fire door, its single metal bar a lever that acted as a lock from the outside and a method of opening from the inside. She ran towards it, the cries of her pursuers drawing closer. A push and the door was open, an alarm bell now ringing nearby.

As she stepped through the door and on to the first step of the stairway, she felt a massive hand push her shoulder, propel her forward to the rail. At the same moment as she hit the metal barrier with her stomach and began the slow somersault over the rail to fall fifty feet to the ground below, she saw her chest explode in front of her. The bullet that had pushed her forward had entered her back and forced its way through skin, bone and tissue to burst out just above her right nipple. She would probably have died from the bullet wound but the fall removed any doubt by breaking her neck. She was dead before the first policeman reached her body.

Five hours later, Doug Frink was sitting in his fourth-floor office of the J. Edgar Hoover Building on E Street between Ninth and Tenth Streets in the north-west section of DC. He had heard of the airport arrests and had ordered the terrorist and his wife's luggage to be brought downtown, the former for interrogation, the latter for investigation. He had left the man to the experts, who understood pressure and mind manipulation, who might eventually be able to force the terrorist to talk. But Frink knew that it would take time – a commodity he just didn't have.

So far, he and his men had earned nothing but frustration. Two weeks of work had filled in some gaps. The hotel in Kansas City where the terrorists had stayed had been unearthed. The cars they had hired had been found and their credit card numbers run through the system. Everything had been forged and the trail was cold. His men had built up photofit pictures of the man and woman and these had been circulated around America and in Europe but there had been no comebacks – and nor would there be, he thought gloomily.

His telephone rang.

'Doug. Jim in the lab. I think you should come down.' Jim Lowenkron headed up the FBI's forensics division at headquarters. Relegated to the basement and sub-basement of the building they were, in fact, at the heart of the modern FBI. Forensics could take a mote of dust and by using electron microscopes produce enough evidence to convict a killer; they could match any handgun in the world to a bullet found at the scene of a crime; analyse any poison. They were the new eyes and ears of the detectives.

Three minutes later Frink was in the lab. On a bench along one wall lay the terrorists' pile of possessions. Frink always found this a depressing part of his business. The living carried with them lovers, family, friendships and idiosyncracies in the shape of pictures, letters, a rabbit's tail. In death, the things were just objects. Because they lacked an owner they seemed sad, even tawdry.

The clothes, passport, money and cards were not what had excited Lowenkron. Off to one side was the black leather briefcase that the terrorist had been carrying. Spread out on the bench was its contents: a copy of *France Soir*, a map of the United States, some keys, a Mont Blanc pen – the accoutrements of the innocent businessman he pretended to be. What caught Frink's eye was the suitcase itself.

'We emptied the case and then we weighed it,' explained Lowenkron. 'This brand should weigh four pounds precisely but this one weighed four pounds five ounces so we looked again. We cut away the lining in the top and found nothing. Then we cut the seams along the back and found that someone had very cleverly created a long thin pocket. In that pocket we found these.'

He moved to one side and indicated a small line of sachets and syringes.

'The syringes are industrial and have an exceptionally fine needle. We don't know what's in the packets yet but the colour and texture is right for thallium. So it looks like you've got your man.'

'God, that's just great,' Frink exclaimed, putting an affectionate arm around Lowenkron's shoulders.

'Ah, but that's not all. I've saved the best for last.' He moved back to the case and picked up a thin-bladed knife. 'After the poison we checked again and we found another ingenious little hiding place.'

He inserted the knife down the side of the case and levered gently. The whole bottom panel came up as one. Underneath was a light frame no more than two millimetres thick which had supported the panel. In the centre was a hollow where a green West German passport nestled.

Frink drew it out and opened it. The name on the cover was Anton Kleist, the picture that of the captured terrorist. 'At last, this may give us the lead we've been looking for,' he said, a note of excitement in his voice. 'I'll see what Minotaur has to say about this.'

A year earlier, a terrorist analyst at the Defense Intelligence Agency had finished a five-year project to establish a detailed computer database on terrorists. In the past individual countries had kept their own information and different agencies within the US had been similarly protective. The result was that not only was there no common data but there was little historic memory in the system. A visa might be rejected by the US embassy in Prague but granted by the embassy in Warsaw; a terrorist might attack using a particular type of detonator and then two years later the technology would move across borders but the details of how to counter the threat would not. The DIA man had put into the database 15,000 names of known and suspected terrorists, their descriptions, aliases, methods of operating and known associates.

Software was written so that names could be matched with methods, people with organizations and individuals with techniques. The whole system had then been made available to America's allies and gradually the flow of data into the central computer had grown from a trickle to a flood as each country had made their contribution.

Frink accessed Minotaur and five minutes of interrogation established that Anton Kleist was an alias used by a member of the Red Army Faction in Germany. The terrorist's real name was Hans Krocher, wife Brigitte. There was no address. Under the heading 'Known Associates', there was one name: Inge Becker.

September 29

Tunis

I T WAS A CHALLENGE THAT Abu Hassan could not ignore. The attempted killing of Robert Gearheart in Washington ten days earlier had been a direct attack on his own authority and as such had to be answered.

It had not been difficult to track down the source of the attack. The American papers had been full of the story, revealing first the details of the attack and the death of Gearheart's girlfriend and then a transcript of the note found on the assassin's body. Those reports had also said that the attack had been claimed in his name. Clearly, he was as much a victim as Gearheart and the challenge had to be answered. The next day, the *Washington Post* published speculation that the assassin was one of Nidal's men, a conclusion that Abu Hassan had already reached independently.

Two days earlier, he had summoned his lieutenants to a meeting to discuss retribution. The PFA were a disparate bunch recruited in part from other terrorist groups and in part from the eager pool of Palestinian youth anxious to fight for the cause, but the inner circle were all hard men who understood the business of terrorism and accepted its harsh realities. There was Jamil Shahada, an explosives expert who had come from the Arab Liberation Front; Muhammad al-Asafi, a planner and logistics man, was recruited from al-Da'wa; and Mahmud Ibrahim, a financial expert, came from the Palestinian Popular Struggle Front. Some came because of the money, but more often they transferred because Abu Hassan offered the promise of progress for the Palestinian cause.

Each of these men accepted that retaliation was essential.

As al-Asafi put it, with the logic of the planner: 'If we fail to do something Nidal will see it as a sign of weakness and strike again and then again. We must hit him now to show that we are not a beetle to be crushed underfoot but a scorpion with a deadly sting.'

They had debated the who and the how long into the night. It needed to be something painful enough to send an unequivocal message but not so damaging as to provoke further retaliation and a costly struggle between the two groups.

Eventually Mahmud Ibrahim came up with the answer. The world of terrorist financiers was a small one. Like international accountants, they tended to cross each other's paths in the subterranean highways of the false account, the dummy corporation and the laundering scams. Techniques were admired and copied, lessons learned and, occasionally, the gossip of the trade exchanged. It was Ibrahim who had first told Abu Hassan about Salah Hilmi, Nidal's chief bagman. Hilmi's ability to move money secretly around the world to finance terrorist acts were the envy of all; his pioneering work in the use of Cayman Island corporations as fronts for different operations had set a standard which many other groups now followed.

Like so many others in the terrorist network, Hilmi appeared to be somebody completely different. He owned and ran Sami Toys, a business specializing in the import and distribution of soft toys in East Africa. His headquarters was in Nairobi, a perfect international trading centre for currency and goods. The original seed money for his work had come from his mentor Abu Nidal at a time when he was fresh from Lebanon and fired with idealistic fervour.

'You must take this money, husband it and make it grow so that it can work for us all,' Nidal had told him. Hilmi had protested, arguing that he had joined his mentor to fight, not to be an accountant.

'We each must serve in the best way we can,' Nidal had replied. 'I am the public face of the revolution but you can be its private inspiration. Only you and I will know that without you, I am nothing.'

The flattery had got him started and then Hilmi found he

had what Nidal had recognized early on: a real talent for making money. Sami Toys proved a great success and those profits combined with a portion of Nidal's secret funds helped make him a very wealthy man. He was now a pillar of the Kenyan business community, a member of Rotary and a regular contributor to local charities. A small, round man, his happy smiling face and eyes peering over his half-spectacles featured often in the local press, opening a charity function or donating money to a good cause. He revelled in his double life, at once a pillar of the local community and the master financier of terrorist operations.

He had no idea that his fame had spread beyond his own organization. But over the years the defections and betrayals that occurred in all the Palestinian groups had affected Nidal as well. To that small and exclusive band of terrorist accountants, Hilmi was a legend.

The elegance of the Ibrahim solution appealed to Abu Hassan's refined sense of justice. Nidal had interfered with an operation that was going to secure the financial future of the Palestinian people. It was only fitting then that the price he should be made to pay would hit his pocket and hit it hard.

'We are agreed then? Hilmi is our man?' He looked around the little group. There were nods, smiles and no sounds of dissent. 'What we need now is the how. Something elegant, I think. A bit of subtlety to show that madman Nidal that we have the power but also have the reach to use it.'

Jamil Shahada was one of the best in the terrorist business. He did not concern himself with the plans, the logistics or the cash but only the weapons. He could recite the history of each major terrorist act in the past twenty years, the terrorists involved, their weapons and their training. More importantly, he had carefully studied how and why the counter-terrorist forces had succeeded in each case. He knew the strengths and weaknesses of the SAS and of Delta Force. He understood the capabilities of satellites and telephone taps.

'Why don't we follow the Israeli example?' he asked. 'They kill and put the blame on others. If we do something with their signature all over it, it will confuse the Americans and the Zionists. And *we* can quietly let Nidal know that it was the PFA and not the Mossad who did the job. That way, we confuse our enemies and teach Nidal a lesson.'

'What exactly do you have in mind?' Hassan asked.

The portable telephone is one of the great inventions of the latter part of this century. It is at once a powerful business tool and a symbol of success. To drug dealers and terrorists, the portable telephone is an opportunity to confuse listeners who want to find out when the next deal or bombing is about to happen. The portable telephone gives them a kind of spurious protection. With it and the handy bleeper, the dealer can call his contacts, set up the meetings and do his deals without any interference from people who may have listened to an ordinary telephone.

Of course, this protection is a fiction. But it is a fiction that every police force in the world has done everything possible to sustain. The fact is that calls made from portable telephones are routinely monitored by all the world's intelligence services and by most of the police forces. No tiresome warrants or permits are required as the law has not yet caught up with the new technology and law enforcement has not been slow to take advantage of the loophole. The result has been a wealth of intelligence, both criminal and terrorist, which is why no serving police or intelligence officer will ever say anything of importance on a portable telephone.

As a tool of business and a status symbol, Hilmi had installed a portable telephone in his Mercedes 380SE three years earlier. Now, as he walked down the four steps to the street running alongside the Norfolk Hotel in the centre of Nairobi, he could hear the phone burbling ten feet away. Hilmi picked up his pace, taking his keys out of his pocket and pressing the automatic door lock as he moved forward.

He opened the driver's door and eased himself behind the steering wheel, his left hand reaching for the telephone resting in its mount between the two front seats. Pressing the button marked RCV, Hilmi brought the phone up to his ear.

'Hilmi,' he answered in the business tone he had adopted for the telephone that resonated a couple of octaves below his normal rather high voice.

'Is that Salah Hilmi of Sami Toys?' the voice at the other end queried.

'Yes, yes, Hilmi here. Who's that?' he replied, an impatient tone creeping into his voice.

'This is Abu Hassan. You are the person I have chosen to carry a message to your master Abu Nidal.'

Those were the last words that Hilmi heard. The full portent of that last sentence had only just begun to register on his brain when a sharp, high-pitched tone echoed through his earpiece. There was a brief flicker of his wrist as Hilmi began to move the phone away from his head. Then the tone tripped the tiny micro detonator which in turn exploded the ounce of Semtex that had been carefully moulded inside the handset.

The explosion was small, not enough even to blow out the windscreen of the car. But it was enough to kill Salah Hilmi. The blast destroyed the left side of his head, splattering skull and the grey ooze that had once been his brain over the interior of the car. In a fraction of a second Hilmi was just a corpse whose heart continued to pump blood to a head that was no longer there.

Three thousand miles away Abu Hassan cradled his telephone. He was confident Abu Nidal would get the message.

Washington, DC

Deaths from thallium poisoning have now peaked at 103 in the US, 247 worldwide. That is still less than the 259 killed in Pan Am 103 over Lockerbie, Scotland in 1988. But the effects have been much worse than in any other terrorist incident.

Kola Co., the original target of the terrorist attacks, claims to have lost around $3 billion in sales. Other food manufacturers say that orders are down between 15–20 per cent. More importantly, the retail sector say their sales are down 30 per cent so the manufacturers have yet to feel the full effects. The retailers say they have had to destroy hundreds of millions of dollars of unsold stock.

In Europe there has been a similar response and stock markets worldwide have continued to slide as confidence fades.

294

Thallium itself is no longer considered an immediate problem. All
the likely contaminated products have now been withdrawn from sale.
But, as has happened in previous poisonings, the copycats have
taken over and there is now a poisoning epidemic across the nation.
There have been 35 reported deaths from poisonings unrelated to the
original terrorist attack. A further 250 people have been hospitalized.
The poisons used vary from rat poison to cyanide to ground glass
and the products contaminated include milk, baby food and meat.
One man has died from a heart attack after convincing himself
he had been poisoned after getting indigestion from too much fried
chicken.
The situation is likely to get worse until the terrorists have been
caught. While the crisis remains a focus of media attention, the
half-hourly television broadcasts and the daily headlines will
continue to encourage blackmailers and the mentally sick to exploit
the situation by carrying out their own poisoning.

Matt Shaw finished reading from the terminal on his desk
and turned to face the men seated in front of him.

'That, gentlemen, is a story of our failure. We've been
working on this for two weeks, the might of the American
intelligence community and what do we have?' His palm
slapped down on to the desktop. 'Absolutely fuck all. That's
what. And I've had enough. So you, gentlemen, are going to
tell me what we are going to do about it.'

The language and the anger were further signs to Bob of
the disintegration of the group in the face of the problem.
Shaw's round face had taken on a permanently flushed look,
clearly indicating raised blood pressure, which was confirmed
by his surreptitious swallowing of small white pills. Dearth,
who smoked quality Cuban cigars, had had to revert to
some vile-smelling cigarillos which offended everyone. But,
in the already tense atmosphere, no one remarked on the
discomfort caused by his unconcerned puffing. Even Prentice,
normally the fastidious company man, had been unable to
get home to his laundered shirts and looked as creased and
rumpled as Bob himself felt.

The meeting had been called that afternoon by Shaw with
the intention of pooling information to co-ordinate the hunt.
But as far as Bob could see the effect so far had been only to
undermine what little confidence remained.

'As a first step, can't we speak to the media and ask them to tone it down?' asked Dearth. 'At least that might take some of the heat off.'

'We've tried,' replied Shaw wearily. 'But this is the greatest story any of these people have ever covered. Competition is fantastic and they've all got their ratings at stake. They dress it up in high-flown phrases about "public interest" and "the need to know" but that's just the ritual noise they always make. The truth is we can do nothing to stop them and it's something we're just going to have to live with.'

Shaw popped another pill, and chased it down with a glass of iced water poured from a Thermos by his side.

'Where are we in the hunt for the terrorists?' He turned to his left. 'Doug?'

The FBI man stopped doodling with his pen and looked up. 'Well, as you know we got a couple of them on their way back into the country. One dead, one captured. We've run their prints through the system but nothing so far. The guy we've got isn't talking and if you want my honest opinion I don't think he will, at least not in the time we have available.

'But we did get a passport in the name of Anton Kleist and a quantity of thallium powder so we know these are the right people. We've passed the details to the Germans and I hope they will get on the job this time round.'

The bitterness in his voice came from the resentment widespread in the US intelligence community over the Pan Am bombing. The Germans had known about a plan to bomb an aircraft and even had an agent inside the terrorist gang, but, for internal political reasons, they had not informed the Americans and had allowed the bombing to happen.

'What about the Israelis?' Shaw asked.

'We're pushing them as hard as we can. You know they did an operation in the Beka'a a couple of days ago?' Shaw nodded. 'We haven't had a readout from that yet though I would have thought that if there was anything of real interest we would have heard by now. Time's getting too short now for us to do very much before the deadline. We'll have to pin our hopes on the Germans and the Israelis and hope they come up with something.'

'Christ Almighty,' Shaw exclaimed. 'This is not exactly the

time to rely on a wing and a prayer for answers. You guys don't seem to understand what's going on here. Each morning I see the President and he only has one question for me: "Have I any information about the poisoning?" Each morning I have to tell him: "Not yet, Mr President, but we're working on it." I hate those damn meetings in the Oval Office. They make me feel so fucking inadequate. At this morning's session he made it clear that, unless we produced something in the next five days, he planned to do a deal and he'll do whatever it takes to whip the Israelis into line.'

He turned towards Bob. 'What joy have you had? Where have you got with the Arab Bank?'

For a change, the question came not as an insult but as a genuine inquiry. Clearly the crisis was beginning to soften the DCI.

'We have confirmed that someone in the Arab Bank is behind the buying of options and it looks as if one of their officials, a George Bakr, is involved. I had hoped to have more information on that from my contact but nothing so far.'

'We've been looking at that line as well,' interrupted Prentice. 'We've sent some of our assets in Tunis out on to the street trying to track this guy down. He certainly works in the Bank and is in the right position to do what we think he's done. We've checked out his house and his wife is still there. She says he's been travelling a lot for the bank. Seems he comes and goes without telling her much. He was last in town just over a week ago and she doesn't know when he's going to be back.

'We've put the word out in Amman and we're tapping into the Pals to see if we can get anything. But right now we don't have enough to fill a single sheet. Time's simply too tight.'

Shaw could do little but urge them on. Bob found the exhortation hollow, as if they had all accepted the inevitable consequences of their failure. He took the elevator seven floors down to his office thinking over the discussion. The key seemed to be Bakr. He was annoyed to have been wrong-footed at the meeting, frustrated at not having heard from Hamid.

Back at his desk, he picked up the phone and dialled Tunis.

Tunis

The Koran says that a man can have up to four wives, a restrained form of polygamy that was justified on social and economic grounds. Frequent marriages helped inter-tribal bonding, gave some security for widows of soldiers killed in battle and ensured a large number of children which was essential given the high rate of infant mortality.

However, a hadith or story of the Prophet Mohammed tells of the problems that can result from trying to stick to the polygamy rule. A husband is dividing a bunch of grapes between his two wives but unfortunately there is an odd number of grapes. Instead of eating the last grape himself, the man cannot resist giving it to the wife he loves best. Islamic scholars have debated this story at great length and some have taken it to mean that the Prophet recognized that it is really impossible for a man to have more than one wife and to treat them equally, as he also demands. Therefore some scholars argue that polygamy should be outlawed. So far, only Tunisia has gone this far, which sets it apart from the rest of the Arab world. Hamid was fond of telling Helen this story as an illustration of how lucky she was to have ended up in the most liberal of all the Arab states.

Sitting in the garden of her villa, listening to the sea gently rolling against the sand in the distance, the tumble of the waterfall by her side, she could agree with her husband. It was only when she stepped outside the protective seclusion of her villa outside Tunis that the true nature of the Arab world bore down upon her.

When she had first arrived in the city she had been enchanted by the romance, the bright colours and the good humour. The setting, too, was perfect. They had a comfortable villa supplied by the Bank, complete with servants and a chauffeur; Tunis was set by the sea looking across the Mediterranean at Sicily and then Italy with the civilization of Rome only an hour and a half away by plane.

But the tourist in Helen was soon replaced by the reality of a resident. And the new reality coincided with the arrival of the Islamic revolution in liberal Tunisia. It swiftly became fashionable for women to wear the veil; even friends who had received a Western education covered their neck and head with the black shawl. It was as much a protest against the Western influence in Tunisian society – the cars, videos and televisions – that was undermining traditional life, as it was a visible expression of the Muslim faith. Helen was a very obvious manifestation of that corruption. Not only was she American but she had married an Arab and so the insult became personal.

She had complained to Hamid about the restrictions, expecting to be reassured by his anger. Instead he had been unsympathetic. 'You have to remember that these people have a culture that goes back a thousand years before yours even began.' Helen heard a bitter note creep into his usual calm voice. 'They have traditions and beliefs that have been upset by the arrival of the Westerners, particularly the Americans. The Yankee has come here, dollar bills in hand, convinced that their knowledge of a few decades gives them the right to impose their will on others. It is their arrogance that so upsets the people here.

'If Arabs come to your country you do not expect them to ride camels, wear funny clothes or to eat sheep's eyes. You want them to drive Chevrolets, wear Levis and eat hamburgers. Why should these people be any different?'

After that, she had been forced to wear the chador, the long black gown that covered her Western clothes, her head and neck. It had been a demeaning acceptance that her position as resident had turned to that of outcast.

Helen found it difficult to define when it had all begun to go wrong between them. There had been no sordid confrontation with a mistress, no betraying love letter or overheard conversation; there had been no destructive arguments where angry words become the inscription on the headstone marking the death of the relationship. Instead there had been a slow leak of air from the balloon of love until it collapsed on itself, leaving only two people with shared memories but no real future.

Helen's isolation had been exaggerated by the physical distance she felt from Hamid outside her own territory of the United States. The Arab world had quickly lost the romantic aura she had conjured up from the coffee bar conversations at university, the posters supporting the Palestinian resistance and the writings of Freya Stark and Wilfred Thesiger. They had all combined to produce an image of another age before the discovery of oil had destroyed the Arab traditions; a time when courtesy among the men was considered a virtue and the women were not servants but human beings who had an important role to play in family and state affairs.

Oil, the great seducer of the Arab world, had changed all that. Wealth beyond the imaginings of even the most fanciful Bedouin youth had propelled whole nations from a feudal system into the latter half of the twentieth century in one generation. Old customs had disappeared; the religious strictures, which for centuries had given life a purpose, were abandoned or so compromised by unprincipled mullahs that they no longer had any real meaning; and the worst excesses of the West were willingly embraced.

The women certainly benefited in a material sense with shopping trips to Bloomingdales and Harrods for the rich and fridges and cars for the poor. But the collapse in the social order meant the delicate balance between the women and the men, with each playing their part towards establishing a stable and prosperous whole, was destroyed, and the women suffered most. Now it was the men who made the money with which they could buy anything that the women normally helped supply, from food to clothes, sex and even childcare.

In such a changed society, chauvinism was rampant and women quickly became repressed and irrelevant. Helen found that Hamid's friends and colleagues saw her as simply an attractive adornment to wait on them, a demeaning role that could in some measure have been offset by contributing to Hamid's business life – but even this was denied her as he never discussed work.

Yet even this she could have tolerated. She finally knew that it was all over after the birth of her son. Hamid's insistence that he have an Arab name, speak Arabic, and shed all vestiges of his American heritage, showed Helen graphically that she and her young son were expected to become Arabs to survive. But it was a form of survival that Helen did not want, a loss of identity that she could not accept.

300

It was her naïvety and her apparent inability to do anything about it that she now found so frustrating. In the long, empty nights in Tunis she would sit on the balcony looking out over the sea and curse the innocence that had allowed her to sacrifice her youth and her ideals for a myth of freedom that simply did not exist. She would then berate herself for her passivity. A woman who once took decisions because she thought they were brave and different was now incapable of breaking out of this mould in the same way. 'Tomorrow,' she would promise herself. But when tomorrow came there were always reasons for putting off the difficult decisions.

She heard a soft footfall behind and turned to see Hamid's outline coming towards her. His hands came around her neck and began to massage her tense muscles. She allowed her head to fall back against him.

'You seem to have been upset recently, my love,' he began tentatively. 'Is it anything I have done? Is there anything I can do to help?'

The tenderness and the kindness of the questions undammed the well of unhappiness from deep inside her.

'Oh, it just all seems to be so different from what we had hoped,' she replied, angrily noting the catch in her voice, the constriction in her throat that marks the beginning of tears. 'It all seemed so hopeful when we began. You were going to take on the world. We were going to march forth bravely together, change things, affecting people's lives, making things better. It all seemed so possible then. Now here am I with nothing to do in a country where I am despised and which I am learning to hate with a husband I never see who does work he never shares with me.'

She turned in the seat to face him. 'I just don't see what any of this is for any more. My life is passing by and I have nothing to show for it except Abdullah and even his name is a constant reminder to me that he is Arab and not American.'

Hamid's hands had tightened as she was speaking. She could feel the fingers digging into her shoulders, a clear signal of the anger and tension in him. Yet there was no hint of this when he spoke.

'I know things have been difficult for you and I'm sorry.

301

First there was the move and then work seems to have taken over everything. I know that I have been neglecting you and I realize how hard things have been for you here.' He came around the chair and, taking both her hands in his, knelt before her. 'But I'll make you this promise: in a few weeks, things will be quieter at the Bank and I'll ask Amman for a transfer. Perhaps we'll be able to go back to the States – New York, Washington, or maybe catch some sun in LA. Would you like that?'

Just the suggestion made Helen realize just how much she needed the change. The prospect of a permanent return to a land she loved, friends she liked and a language she understood was overwhelming. She gripped Hamid's hands tightly. 'Yes, that would be wonderful, just wonderful. It's what I need, what we both need to find each other again.'

'Well, I'll see what I can arrange. I can't make any promises but I swear I'll try. And they owe me a few favours so maybe it will all work out.'

She stood up, took his hand and they moved together towards the house. Restored, Helen felt optimism replace her earlier despondency. Perhaps, after all, everything would work out. A sudden thought occurred to her. 'How have you been getting on in the hunt for the source of the poisoning money?' she asked.

'I've had a look through our records and there doesn't seem to be anything there. Certainly there's no trace of any orders being given for purchases on the scale mentioned by Bob.'

'What about George Bakr?' she pressed.

'Since I got back, he's been travelling doing stuff for the Bank. I've sent word that I want to see him when he returns but I can't do much more without alarming him. It's difficult to believe he's involved but he seems to be the only suspect they have right now.'

Helen was surprised at the lack of enthusiasm in Hamid's voice. It was almost as if he wasn't interested in the man or what he had been doing. 'But surely you have looked through his files, checked his diary to find any trace of what he was doing?'

'No.' The answer was abrupt, final.

'But why on earth not? This man may be responsible for the killing of more than two hundred innocent people; he is holding the world to ransom with tactics that should be despised by everyone. You are the one man who could do something. Bob almost gets himself killed hunting the madman behind this. You promised to help him and you've done nothing. I just don't understand!'

In talking, she had moved around in front of him and they had stopped, facing each other on the stone path. The moon was shining over Helen's left shoulder and she could see the anger on Hamid's face. It was rare that he showed such emotion and the sheer passion that flowed from him, the narrowed eyes, the hunched shoulders was both surprising and intimidating.

'You are talking of things you simply do not understand,' he replied.

'Don't patronize me,' she shouted, her voice rising. 'You may be able to stop these killings and you dare talk to me of *understanding*. It's you who doesn't understand. By doing nothing you may be condemning another hundred people to death.'

Hamid jerked his arm away from Helen's hand that had gripped him above the elbow.

'You know nothing' – his voice rose, beginning to choke with anger – 'you talk as if the choices are simple. They are not. Bob asks me as a friend to help him in his hunt for terrorists who are threatening his country. Yes, of course I should help him. But he wants me to betray my country.' He saw that Helen did not understand. 'Yes. *My country*. Palestine. The country of my birth. The country of my family. The country where my grandparents died. Every step I take to help Bob is a step on the road to becoming a traitor to my country.

'I am faced with doing something for a friend and betraying my country or doing nothing and remaining loyal to Palestine. I prefer to do nothing.'

He paused, gathering himself, and when he spoke again his voice was more measured, sad even.

'And anyway, what about you? I thought you were one of us, a supporter of the cause. Yet when Bob calls you jump,

303

betraying your ideals and betraying me.' He took her hands in his. 'Helen, this is a tough time and we are all having to make hard choices. I am asking you to trust me, to support me and my decisions. I promise you that what I am doing is right. Just this once, forget Bob, forget the morality of it all and try and understand.'

Helen pushed his hands away from her. 'But can't you see you are betraying everything you once believed in,' she cried. They were stabbing each other, knifing the words deep into their hearts, slicing through the cords of love that once bound them together, but Helen could not stop, could feel the conversation running out of control. She heard, too, the venom in her voice as she continued.

'You once told me that you were sickened by the weakness of politicians who do nothing while people die in wars and famine. You would be different, you said. You would change things, you said. You would never just accept the inevitable, you said. Now, when Bob and I call on you for help, you do nothing. *You* are betraying *me*, you are betraying Bob. You are a traitor to yourself. And you talk to me of loyalty . . .'

It was she that turned and rushed into the house with Hamid's last defence echoing in her ears.

'You know nothing.'

As she ran inside, her impotence and disappointment with her husband welled up and she could feel the sting of tears. She angrily brushed them away with her hand and moved towards the sanctuary of the sitting room at the end of the passage. As she reached the door, the telephone rang.

Washington, DC

'Hi. Helen. It's me, Bob.'

'Oh. Hi, Bob. How are you?'

Neither distance nor the distortions of a telephone line could disguise the distress in Helen's voice.

'What's the matter? You sound as if you've been crying.'

'It's nothing. Hamid and I have just been arguing.'

'Again?'

'Yeah. Well, this time it was serious. There seem to be so

many things we disagree about and so little we have in common. I get so frustrated I could scream.'

All the pain of the years of loneliness seemed to well out of her voice. Bob tried to bridge the distance between them and comfort her.

'I'm so sorry that life is so difficult for you. I just wish there was something I could do to help.'

'Oh, just hearing your voice is a reminder of a saner world out there somewhere,' she replied.

'Well, is there anything I can do? Do you want me to have a word with Hamid?'

'No, no,' she protested. 'That would be terrible. He would be appalled that I am talking to you about it at all. If you tried to interfere it would only make things worse. Anyway, it's partly about you that we were arguing. We were talking about the poisoning and I was asking him what he had done about tracking down Bakr. He says that he is away on Bank business and doesn't know when he'll be back.'

'Well that's hardly a crime. He may indeed be away and if he's doing what we think he's doing then he has every reason to be keeping a low profile.'

'No, you don't understand.' Helen's voice had dropped to that sibilant whisper that people always adopt when they don't want to be overheard without realizing that the voice actually carries much further. 'It's not just that Bakr's away, but Hamid has made no real attempt to find out how much he is involved. In fact, he seems to think that his duty is to the Palestinians and not to his friends or to anyone else trying to stop this awful terrorism.'

She paused as her voice caught again.

'I just can't understand him. He's one of us, not one of them. I can't believe that he wants him to succeed.'

Bob was torn between taking Helen's side against her husband and defending his friend. 'Perhaps he's just taking the line of least resistance. Or perhaps he really thinks that Bakr is innocent.'

'No.' Helen was quite firm. 'He has no doubt that Bakr is involved but he just doesn't want to find out more. I am sorry that we are letting you down. I feel that we're betraying you and I'm being betrayed by my own husband –'

'It's not exactly great for me either,' Bob interrupted. 'I've told the people here that Hamid has been very helpful and I was sure he would come up with some answers. Now I'm going to have to go back and tell them I've failed. Right now, I'm about their last hope. Maybe I should try and talk to him.'

'The way he is there's no point,' Helen replied. 'I think you'd both say things you'd regret and it would ruin any chance you might have of getting any help in the future.'

'OK. Well, see what you can do to change his mind. There's so little time left and anything either of you can do could be vital. Do what you can and I'll let you know if anything changes my end.'

Bob had wanted to be more reassuring, to tell her that everything was going to be fine once this temporary crisis was past. But he no longer believed in arguing the lie.

Zurich

Whenever Hirsh Kronstein wanted reassurance, he came to Zurich.

The antiseptic cleanliness was such a contrast to the lived-in mess of Jerusalem or Tel Aviv. The tight, pinched look of the Swiss, so prim, disapproving and humourless, contrasted with the cheerful, rude and excitable Israelis. Whatever its problems, Hirsh thought, at least Israel was alive. But he also knew that beneath the starched veneer, another Zurich lived. Behind the city's main railway station lies the red-roofed Swiss National Museum looking out over the university to the east and the Museum of Applied Arts to the west. Behind it lies a small park which twenty years ago used to be one of the city's most romantic spots with a network of paths for lovers to walk along during the long summer evenings. Today, the park is the headquarters for the city's enormous drug culture. More than one in ten of all Switzerland's population under twenty-one uses hard drugs and Zurich is the nation's drug capital. The park is where addicts barter for their next fix, men and women sell their bodies and the groans are no longer those of passion but of the dying or the ecstatic. It is a sad and tawdry reminder that behind even the purest heart can beat a soul of misery and degradation. So, whenever he came to the city, Hirsh would walk through this area of the lost and the damned.

Two days ago, the call had come from Essex – Ghassan Hussaini – through the usual cutout asking for a meeting. He had chosen Zurich for the rendezvous, believing the familiarity of the city would reassure the Palestinian. But he had also specified an open-air meeting behind the Museum in preference to another fancy hotel room. He calculated that the traitor would be unsettled by the misery of his surroundings and subconsciously bond closer to the Israeli, given his confident familiarity with the underworld.

There was a sharp chill in the air, the first hint of the harsh winter to come, and the two men had shivered in the wind, their breath frosting the air. Hirsh had got used to smelling the fear on Hussaini. But this time he looked tired, exhausted even. The normally urbane exterior was still in place but the little signs – the intermittent tic of the right eyelid, the clasping and unclasping of the hands – gave away how nervous he was.

'Everything that I feared has happened,' he had begun as they strolled, two middle-aged men heads bowed together deep in apparently friendly conversation. 'The Palestinian movement is back where it was in the 1970s. Everyone sees us as terrorists and all those years of diplomatic work have come to nothing.'

'But this terrorism has at least been effective,' Hirsh suggested tentatively.

'So far Abu Hassan has killed more than 200 people. The Jews say they won't deal so Hassan will have to kill again. In the meantime every country, but especially the United States, is putting such pressure on us you would not believe.' Hussaini almost cried with anguish. He drew a deep breath, exhaled in a long, white puff of misery and then continued in a calmer voice.

'You know that over the years we have built up close private contacts with the Americans.' Hirsh nodded. 'We saved Kissinger from assassination back in the seventies; we had meetings with Shultz and until now Chairman Arafat thinks we have the support of the policy-makers in the State Department. But this is ruining everything. We have been told that unless we stop this madness there will be no further contact, public or private. The Americans say they will stop all negotiations and the peace process will be abandoned.'

'What is the mood of the ruling council? Is it with you or with Hassan?' Hirsh asked.

'It's not that simple. Some of them believe that we are closer now than we have ever been to getting a Palestinian state, that the final act of terror will be enough to force the Israelis to talk. Then there are others like me who think that one small group cannot win against all the Western governments. And even if we do win and the Israelis talk, they can always go back on the deal claiming it was made under pressure.

'The different sides have talked but no one can agree what to do. The Chairman has met with Hassan. He would only tell me that he is confident of victory, whatever that means. Now the only man who knows where Abu Hassan is and what he is planning to do is Habash and he thinks everything is just fine so he's not saying a word. Hassan himself has gone to ground.'

'You know that we attacked a PFA camp in the Beka'a a couple of days ago?' Hirsh asked, turning the screw tighter.

'Yes, yes, I'd heard about it.'

'The Americans also caught a couple of terrorists trying to get into the US. They had more poison so it looks as if they are planning more attacks. It's now only a matter of time before this whole thing unravels. You should pass on what you know while you can. You wait much longer and the PLO may be history.'

Hussaini rubbed his leather-gloved hands together and broke away from Hirsh to pace a brief, nervous circle. The movement helped him make up his mind.

'I got a call three days ago from the Old Man. It was an instruction to buy stock –' He broke off. 'You know we've made billions out of the Kola Co. stock? My most brilliant operation and no one will ever know.'

It took all of Hirsh's self-restraint to hold back from puncturing the bubble of pride in his agent, disgusted that a man should take so much pleasure in capitalizing on the deaths of hundreds and the misery of thousands.

'About Arafat's instructions to buy more shares . . .' he prompted.

'Oh yes. I am busy buying stock in the Kastel Sugar Co. so that must be the next target.'

'What else? Where are you buying, where are the attacks going to happen? When?'

Hussaini recoiled from the Israeli agent, the umbilical cord of penitent and priest broken.

'We are buying everywhere we can find the shares. For the rest, you ask too much. I know nothing. I have told you everything. Now it's up to you to stop Hassan so that we can save what is left of the PLO.'

Tel Aviv

Hirsh had flown home and immediately set up a meeting with Sachar. Now, as he took the lift up to the Mossad chief's office, he rehearsed what he was going to say. He had determined to persuade his boss to tell the cabinet everything, to allow the politics to direct the fate of their country and give time for people to be warned about the second campaign.

Six weeks had passed since he had been embraced into the conspiracy of silence by his mentor. In that time he had watched his world collapse. Terrorists had brought off a brilliant crime that was forcing his country to its knees under the weight of international economic and political pressure. And above all he had the deaths on his conscience.

Each television picture of a grieving parent in London, Milan or New York had cut deep. Each tear had been a drop of acid on his heart, each cry of distress a reminder that he and he alone could have stopped it. They were the unwitting sacrifices on the altar of expediency. They were his compromises. With each death a little bit of his faith and optimism died too.

Since that first meeting with his nemesis, Isser Sachar, he had met with him as little as form and the working

309

relationship allowed. He was fearful of being drawn into another conspiracy of Sachar's devising. He had no wish to sell more of himself in a cause that had destroyed so much of his faith in his country and the man he most admired.

In a strange way Hirsh expected Sachar to have been changed by the past few weeks. He thought that, as he had burned inside, so Sachar too might have been branded by his experience. But it was the familiar chief who leaned over the desk to greet him.

'Hirsh. Great to see you. Take a seat and tell me about your trip.'

Hirsh spent ten minutes describing his meeting with Essex, the divisions in the Palestinian camp, the paucity of information and the nugget that Hussaini had finally delivered.

'This time, I think we must pass on the information so that it can be acted on,' Hirsh concluded firmly.

Sachar steepled his fingers on the desk in front of him and began to tap the tips impatiently together.

'Why?' The abruptness of the question threw Hirsh for a moment and his carefully rehearsed speech deserted him.

'Last time we did nothing we ended up with more than two hundred deaths on our conscience. Innocent women and children. I don't want to have to live with that again.'

'Hirsh, you knew that when you became part of Mossad you would have to make sacrifices, do things that other men would think dishonest, dishonourable or even disgraceful. All these things you have done in the service of your country. This poisoning is just another occasion when you have had to compromise those strong principles of yours for the greater good. Look at it realistically.'

He made a fist with his right hand and then began counting.

'One, the poisoning began and the PLO were immediately associated with terrorism once again. Two, without any prompting from us our politicians have refused to negotiate and are denying the terrorists their victory. Three, the Palestinian leadership is starting to divide and if this goes on much longer they'll start killing each other again, which can only be to our benefit. Not a bad score so far.'

'I can't believe you are saying this,' Hirsh said angrily.

310

'You talk of splitting the Palestinian movement. Well, what about Israel? We are alone in the world as we have never been before. There is not a single country that backs us and even our Jewish businessmen in New York and London have turned against us. We are responsible for killing people and you talk of the Palestinians being exposed as terrorists. What does this make us, for God's sake? We are no better than they. This whole business makes me sick. Where is Israel, the bastion of morality? What would the people think if they knew what we had done?'

As he spoke, Hirsh watched the scar on Sachar's face swell and pulse. It was puffed out, angry and purple, as if it had an independent existence on the side of his head. It was a revolting indication of the passion he had aroused in the Mossad leader.

'You talk of morality of the people,' Sachar began, emotion making his voice a sibilant whisper, 'and you understand nothing. In 1948 this country was a place where everything was possible. It was sanctuary for a persecuted race; it was a liberal haven in a region of barbarians; it was home to the finest architects, scientists, doctors in the world. It was a country to believe in.

'Then we had the wars with the Arabs. We survived those because we are strong and when faced with a clear enemy we know how to fight. But terrorism changed all that. It has been death by a thousand cuts. Each time they attacked and killed one of us we took action but it didn't stop the attacks. What it did do was convince us that nowhere was safe and that the enemy was everywhere, and we have developed a siege mentality. We know that we have no real friends, that in the end we have to rely only on Israel and – perhaps – on the Jews outside Israel.

'Today we have terrorism. We have the Intifada. We have Arabs all around us with chemical weapons, ballistic missiles, nuclear weapons, just waiting for the opportunity to use those weapons to destroy us and further their own ambitions.'

He sighed, the deep sigh of a disillusioned man who has seen a dream destroyed.

'There have never been times like these and extraordinary times require extraordinary measures. If we allow

311

the terrorists to win this then Israel is finished. The peace process will gain such momentum that we will be swept along by the Americans and the Russians falling over themselves to do deals and Israel will be sacrificed at the altar of political expediency.'

He leaned forward in his chair and fixed Hirsh with a fierce stare.

'I will not allow that to happen. So what if two hundred people die? So what if five hundred people die? These are just specks of sand blowing across the face of Israel's history. The important thing – the only thing – is that Israel survives.

'Look, Hirsh, you're seeing this in the worst way.' Sachar had adopted a more reasonable tone. 'We know the Germans are hunting the people from the Red Army Faction, the Americans have captured one of them and we have some time to go before the deadline. I am sure that something will give so we don't have to make any decisions right now. Give it time and things may yet be all right.'

Hirsh listened as his relationship with a man he had once admired and loved fell apart. For each argument that Sachar advanced Hirsh could only see the dead bodies and the weeping families. It was too easy to justify death as an excuse for life.

Hirsh had welcomed the patronage of this man. He had seen a father figure who encouraged him, praised him and by implication promised him a glittering if secret career. Now he realized that the old man had been passing on not just his experience of the intelligence world but also his perceptions of the world at large. It was a perception that had been moulded by years of fighting in the underworld. He had made compromises. He had lost his wife to a terrorist bomb. He had watched his nation change. At every step idealism and principle had been replaced with bitterness and the harsh reality of *realpolitik*.

Hirsh had been sucked into the old man's perception of reality; forced to accept his advice, his ideas and his way of doing things. Yet Hirsh still retained the idealism about his country that had caused him to emigrate from South Africa all those years ago. Now, faced with a conflict between duty as defined by an individual and duty to his country, he knew

312

what he should do. But telling the cabinet what he knew would mean the end of Sachar's career and inevitably word of the earlier deception would leak out. In the past few years there had been the scandal of the Vanunu affair, the murder by Shin Bet of Palestinians held in custody, the wholesale faking of evidence against suspected terrorists and a series of scandals related to attempts to suppress the Intifada. If Israelis were to learn that news of the planned poisonings had been suppressed by the Mossad there would be outrage. Outside Israel's borders it would be used as further evidence that Israel was a rogue nation in the international community whose policies, goals and methods were unacceptable to the civilized world.

If he talked, his mentor and his country would pay a high price. If he remained silent, the problem might be resolved. Silence was the easy option.

October 1

I N CONTRAST TO TEN DAYS ago, Director's Buns was a more positive affair. Now there was hope, a feeling that tangible progress was being made. It was not so much that any of those sitting around the table could see the end in sight or even knew what that end might be, rather that the enemy had made mistakes and had thus taken on human form. It was no longer some inanimate, all-seeing, unblinking machine that they were fighting, but flesh and blood like themselves. That helped them break through the confidence barrier and allowed them all to think that answers could – no, would – be found.

Around the table were the two deputies and three directors responsible for counter-terrorism, counter-espionage and counter-subversion. They were all men except for Sue Steele, who was only the second woman to be appointed a director of the Service. It was her department, counter-terrorism, that had been leading the hunt for the terrorists.

She was a tall, big-boned woman with a surprisingly quiet voice and a slight, almost undefined lisp that some men found very appealing. In the tough and masculine world in which she had competed and won, she had sacrificed femininity for function. She wore the conventional Jaeger clothes, the blouse with the old-fashioned Victorian cameo pinned above her left breast. But somewhere the clothes had failed to make a match with the body. A gaudy fake sapphire ring spoiled the under-statement of the brooch, while a cheap page-boy cut made her look unkempt and the Rothman's King Sizes that had badly stained her teeth polluted the atmosphere around her.

However, this was no Amazon fighting her way to the top.

She was happily married to Professor Hugh Steele, one of the world's leading authorities on the storks and spoonbills of Asia. More importantly she had an outstanding brain, fast and analytical, and her views were widely respected inside Gower Street and internationally. Now fifty-three, there were those who believed she would be the first woman Director-General of the Service.

There were no preliminary drinks as this was a working lunch without guests to impress. After Joanna had served the salmon mousse and the hot French bread she retired to the kitchen behind Sue's left shoulder.

'Perhaps you would like to bring us up to date with the hunt for the terrorists,' Runner suggested, looking at Sue.

She paused to put her cigarette out. 'We have made a lot of progress since last we all met. Three days ago the Americans managed to capture one of the terrorists coming through Washington and kill another.' She made a face that suggested pain. 'They were using the passports that our Irish friends forgot to tell us about.'

'Well, at least they told us and it was of some help. Be grateful for every little bit of help we get from the Republic.' Runner gestured with a fork laden with mousse. 'Go on.'

'The Americans also think they may have tracked down the source for the funds to a branch of the Arab Bank in Tunis. GCHQ have been talking to the NSA to co-ordinate that so we should get some information in the next few days.

'But for the moment all roads seem to lead to Germany. The Israelis attacked a PFA camp in the Beka'a five days ago. It was a pretty bloody business but they managed to extract from one of the terrorists that the poisoners were coming from Germany. At the same time the American database coughed up the name of Inge Becker in connection with the two who were stopped in Washington. Becker is one of the leaders of the RAF but even the Wiesbaden computers can't tell the Germans where she is.'

The first course over, Sue reached for her cigarettes, lit one and drew the first mouthful of smoke deep into her lungs. She continued speaking as the smoke came from her mouth and nostril in little puffs as if each word was also a coded message to an Indian reading her smoke signals from some hidden part of the room.

'But they may have made some progress there, too. The Bundeskriminalamt have got a flat staked out in Bonn that they think is part of an RAF cell. The murder of their Deputy Justice Minister a few weeks ago had all the hallmarks of a Becker killing and the BKA hope she may still be in the area. If they're right then the terrorists could be in for a surprise.'

As she finished speaking, a hand came round her left shoulder to remove the plate, and Joanna quietly circled the table, clearing away the first course. In a few moments the salad, coronation chicken and rice was on the table and she had quietly retreated to the sanctuary of the kitchen. As she stacked the plates into the dishwasher she idly turned over in her mind what she had heard. Perhaps this time Christian would be interested in what she had to offer. The thought of him caused a smile of anticipation to hover on her face.

Joanna made the taxi wait outside Bloom's in New Bond Street while she ran inside. She was determined to buy Christian a memento of their meeting today which he could take with him to Brazil. She settled on a Victorian gold pendant in the image of a tiny Buddha. She inscribed the card: 'Wisdom for the wise. Love for the lover – Joanna', and had the assistant wrap it in a small box.

The cab cut down Bruton Street, to Berkeley Street and then Piccadilly, dropping her off on the corner. She crossed the street, entering the red and gold foyer of the Ritz by the main entrance, the change from their usual rendezvous suggested by her lover. Her heels clicking on the marble floor, she turned right for the lifts and was taken quickly up to the fourth floor.

Christian had called the day before to say that he would be passing through London 'only for the day, I'm afraid' and would she like to get together? She had been almost disgusted at her eagerness to see this man again. Instinct and logic told her that, if she was honest with herself, there was no future in any of this. A man who comes into town from God knows where to romance her and then fly off again to God knows where for God knows how long was hardly a relationship in which to have any faith. But she felt helpless, unable to sacrifice the few golden moments to a common sense that argued for distance when her heart longed for his touch and the sight of those white teeth showing in a smile of welcome. Her subconscious was still sufficiently awake to warn her that every opportunity had to be taken while it was offered. She knew, really, that one day he would leave, promising to call, and then the phone would never ring. But she knew she would always be able to treasure the memory of those stolen hours when she had been fulfilled.

In the taxi she had slipped off her bra and stuffed it inside her handbag, relishing the feel of her nipples moving against her blouse, anticipating the touch of his hands against her body. She wanted the urgency, the demands of his body upon hers. She supposed this must be like a drug addiction; a demand that had to be satisfied which was never satisfied enough.

When the door opened, it was just as she had expected. The heart-stopping smile, the embrace, his mouth on hers, his strong hands drawing her to him. At the moment of his touch she could feel the soft pain that branched out from her groin, swelling out and up her body in anticipation.

Yet this time it was different. He drew back from her, holding her with both arms, locking her blue eyes with his.

'Jo. How is it memory never does you justice? You look wonderful. I am filled with love for you here' – he drew one hand off her shoulder and placed it on his heart – 'and here' – he gestured to his crotch. 'But I only got in a few minutes ago. I ordered tea for us both and thought you could play mother while we talk. I'll take a shower and then we can spend the rest of the day together.'

What she wanted was to say 'No' and drag him to bed. What she said was 'That sounds fine' and drew him across to the sofa where they sat down.

Afternoon tea had helped make the Ritz famous and the two silver trays were piled high with scones, Devon double cream, homemade jam, cakes, biscuits and two pots of tea, one Lapsang Souchong, the other Darjeeling. While Joanna poured the tea, Christian began his gentle probing.

She wanted to please him and had come prepared. The casual questions about her work gradually became focused on the hunt for the poisoners. She passed on the little she had learned: the German connection, the fact that one of the people had been identified as a woman, Inge Becker, and that an apartment was under observation.

Christian seemed pleased, satisfied even, and she was happy that this time she had managed to win his approval.

After the tea, Christian had undressed and gone into the bathroom to take a shower. This was the opportunity she had been waiting for. She reached into her purse and pulled out the small box with the gold pendant and got up from the sofa as she heard the shower start to run. Looking for somewhere where he wouldn't find it immediately, she lifted up his suit jacket from the back of the chair and reached into the inside pocket. Her hand touched a thin book. Curiosity about her lover, his other life, spurred her on and she lifted it out. She turned over the green passport and examined the gold writing on the front. The gold Arabic letters were a surprise and incomprehensible but the English translation underneath made no sense at all. Why would Christian, a Brazilian, be carrying a passport from the 'Syrian Arab Republic'?

With a growing feeling of despair, she opened the front cover and saw Christian's face, uncharacteristically serious. But underneath was not his name but that of George Bakr.

The realization came in a rush, or rather a series of flashes brought before her horrified gaze: the mystery of his background, the evasions, the questions about her work. She had been used – abused. God, what a foul, awful, bloody cliché.

'Joanna.' The word lashed across the room and she dropped the passport in fright. It fell, to land at her feet in full view of Christian, his guilty secret and her lost innocence, clearly visible.

'I'm sorry that you had to see that. So sorry that you couldn't stay sweet, stupid Joanna.'

She had no time to protest, just a brief glimpse of the towel falling away from his body and then he was moving, fast, so fast across the room. God, there was no time, no last plea, no nothing.

His hand whipped out, seeming almost to hover in front of her face and then two fingers sprang forward, curling at their tips, reaching deep inside her head to pluck out pain that she could never have imagined.

Blinded, she began to draw breath for the first scream of agony and then the other hand struck, shattering her Adam's apple, choking off all sound apart from the last, awful sucking gasp as she tried, and failed, to drag oxygen into her starving lungs.

She fell to the floor, legs jerking spasmodically as the body fought in vain for survival. And then she died.

In her final agony Joanna was spared a last glimpse of Christian the killer, taking with her to the grave the memory of Christian the lover. Now, he was all cool calculation. In a few swift movements he had packed his bag and was ready to move. He did not dust the room to remove fingerprints, or seriously attempt to disguise his presence from the police who would inevitably start hunting the murderer within a few hours. He recognized that the sands were running out. Within days he would either be triumphant or have lost. Either way a murder mattered little.

On his way to the door, he picked up the telephone and dialled the number of another PFA agent in Tunis. It was time to pass on Joanna's legacy.

Cyprus

For the spy business, the Cray supercomputer has been one of the great inventions of the late twentieth century. The company was founded by Seymour Cray in April 1972 and it was three years before the first computer was ordered by the National Center for Atmospheric Research. The Lawrence Livermore Laboratory in California bought one to model nuclear bomb design. Within two years, the reputation of the Cray had spread through the intelligence community and Cray-1s were installed at the National Security Agency and the Government Communications Headquarters (GCHQ) in Cheltenham and the Atomic Weapons Research Establishment at Aldermaston.

What makes the Cray unique is its processing power. Alone among the modern computers Crays can work at a fantastic speed – around three billion calculations a second – and do so in very little space. The longer the distance each electronic pulse has to travel, the longer it takes to compute. Cray managed to make his machines fast by designing them small.

The Cray YMP-8 series currently in service with both US and British intelligence takes up no more room than a large circular seat. Indeed the Cray comes with a padded top so that weary operators can take a rest on its comfortable surface.

The Cray is so fast that it can produce a three-dimensional image of the inside of a heart to help surgeons or produce not only an exact imitation of John Wayne in full colour but mimic his voice so precisely that even the Duke himself would not know the difference. Such skills encouraged film-maker George Lucas to buy a Cray so that he could, in theory, make a movie using famous stars whose image and voice could be entirely created by the Cray.

But the computer's benign skills are insignificant compared with its capabilities in the intelligence field. Its capacity to process large amounts of information in a very short time makes it the perfect tool. Radars and satellites sweep up millions of pieces of information from telephone calls, telexes, faxes and simple conversations. All these have to be sifted, graded and then priorities given to the different information.

In the Second World War such processing was done by people. This was possible because the volume of data being gathered was not that large and the complexity of codes not beyond the ability of man to crack. The information revolution has meant that no group of individuals would physically be able to read and understand all the data that is now swept up by the different listening devices. It remains a labour-intensive business – NSA and GCHQ are the largest intelligence agencies in America and Britain – but computers now bear the brunt of the work.

The Cray is the perfect replacement for the man with earphones faithfully taking down the dots and dashes of Morse as they come crackling through the air waves. Today, the trail begins not with a tapping key but with radar dishes and satellites and ends with the awesome number-crunching capabilities of the Cray on the ground floor of the GCHQ headquarters.

The moment Christian picked up his telephone in his room

in the Ritz, dialled 9 and then 010–216 for Tunisia and the figure 1 for Tunis, he had begun the process that alerts the passive monitoring systems.

Inside a small barbed wire fence on a small hill at Ayios Nikolaos near Limassol in Cyprus is the base of the Mediterranean Field Intercept Station of GCHQ. Mostly staffed by 150 men from the Army's 9th Signal Regiment, it also has a complement of civilians from GCHQ and a handful from the NSA, as the base is also known as UKM 257, a code that shows it is part of a worldwide UK–USA eavesdropping network. It squats like an enormous toad in the middle of the Mediterranean, the computer its tongue flicking out to pluck from the ether the more tempting flies of information buzzing by for the toad's body to digest.

The NSA's contribution to the hunt for the poisoners and their paymasters had been to programme the computers with a number of new words such as 'poison' and 'Arab Bank' so that if any messages were picked up with those words in them, the computers would assign the message a priority status and flash it immediately to an analyst's screen. This process, known as 'entering the hit word in the dictionary', is effective but still tends to produce an enormous volume of material relating to perfectly innocent matters. Even to read this takes more time than the listening posts can spare.

The preferred option is to target specific countries and then, if possible, narrow the search down not just to a city but to specific telephone numbers. In the case of the Arab Bank it had been a simple matter to look up the number in the Tunis telephone book and programme it into the computers. For the last three days, every single telephone call made to the Bank from overseas had been intercepted.

That evening the computer suddenly detected the pre-programmed pulses of the Tunis code followed by the number of the Arab Bank. Two things then happened. The databank absorbed the information but a relay diverted the call, changing the language from electronic pulses first to the spoken Arabic and then translating it into written English which was flashed on to the screen of one of the eight operators sitting in the analysis centre of the base.

The cursor on the screen produced the message in a series of short bursts as the system downloaded each segment of translated text.

There were no pleasantries, both the caller and the listener knowing each other well enough to need no introduction.

The German operation is compromised, the message began. *The house is being watched and a raid is planned. You must warn our people. The second stage must go ahead as planned. We are within sight of victory. I will be coming home tonight.*

It was short and clear. As the call ended, the Cyprus monitor began a series of commands that would send a copy of the message to GCHQ in Cheltenham. He then drew a recording of the original Arabic from the database and that too was sent on its way, this time to the NSA at Fort Meade in Maryland where it could be further examined.

Three minutes later, the telephone in the Arab Bank dialled a German number. This time the caller had taken the precaution of scrambling the call using a Cairntech Cypherphone DPX, a machine with sixteen million different ways of disguising a voice. In theory this should have made the call incomprehensible by reducing the speech into a series of jumbled electronic pulses. But, unknown to the users, there is a standing legal requirement for all manufacturers of scramblers in the industrialized countries to supply a sample of their product to their intelligence agencies. So, a scrambler that makes conventional eavesdropping difficult for the industrial spy is no problem at all for the supercomputers. Unscrambling a ciphered conversation is a simple matter of programming the scrambling machine's characteristics into the computer and then trying each one of the keys. With a Cray, even having to try all the combinations, it takes only minutes for the supposedly indecipherable message to come out *en clair*.

At the same time as Inge Becker picked up the telephone in Bonn, the Cyprus base had registered the outgoing call from Tunis, and started recording. As the words made the thousand-mile journey between Tunis and Bonn via a satellite hovering 25,000 miles in space, a deciphered, translated version of the conversation was on the screen.

The police have found the Bonn house and a raid is imminent. Warn your people. What effect will this have on stage two?

We have lost the American team. The European units are intact, the Bonn number replied. *It may be too late for America. But even if I can't reach the others we should be able to set up another team. That may take too long but I can do some of the work myself.*

Good. The Israelis are not going to meet the first deadline so we must begin the next stage immediately. They almost cracked and it only needs one final push.

The cursor paused as the Bonn number considered the problem.

Don't worry. We have done so much. I am not going to fail now.

Good. But take care. They are close, very close.

The cursor paused, blinking at the end of the message. But there was nothing more.

October 2

I T WAS UNFORTUNATE THAT Gabriele had chosen to reply to Frau Ludgera Herrmann's advertisement three days earlier. The Bonn housewife had advertised a second floor flat for rent at 135 Friedrichstrasse in the suburb of Ippendorf. She already rented the two floors above while she herself lived in the basement.

Frau Herrmann resented the fact that she had to rent out any part of her home and as she got older she particularly resented the fact that younger people with a seemingly inexhaustible supply of money were able to afford her prices.

Fifteen years ago she had been proud of her husband, her children and her status in the community. Then her husband died – pushed into an early grave by her dominating ambition and a surfeit of her perfect bratwurst – and Frau Herrmann was left alone. The carefully laid pension plans matured too early to be of any use and her children had fled the nest to fend for themselves. She was forced to swallow her pride and take in lodgers.

As the years passed she had become convinced that her social standing had declined in direct proportion to the number of lodgers she had housed. Paradoxically, she felt that to maintain her position she had to affect ever grander airs so that neighbours felt despised and tenants barely tolerated.

But she was, after all, a German and still loved order and respected authority. She believed in checking up on all her tenants, took no one on trust and reported every car crash, every suspicious person loitering on the street. It was, she repeatedly told the long-suffering local police, the least she

324

could do as a good citizen. The police thought she was a tiresome and interfering old busybody.

Gabriele was always on the hunt for new safe houses and 135 Friedrichstrasse was the third apartment she had visited that day. She wore what she thought of as her house-hunting uniform: two-piece grey suit, plain cream blouse and flat black shoes. She was, she explained to Frau Herrmann, secretary to the new sales director for Shell in Europe. He was a bachelor and had just been posted to Bonn from Paris. He would be travelling a great deal so there would be no trouble and would like to settle all his bills in cash, three months in advance.

The tempting offer to swindle the government out of tax by accepting a cash rent was carefully calculated to sway even the most righteous of landlords. But staring at the perfectly formed little blonde girl chattering away in front of her, Frau Herrmann felt all the resentment against the unfairness of her life and the wealth of people younger than her own children well up inside her. Her naturally suspicious nature translated a cash offer from a swindle into something criminal. The bitter old woman even turned Gabriele's beauty against her.

She is clearly a whore, Frau Herrmann said to herself. Only whores can afford to pay cash and I'm not having a brothel in my house.

She asked the unsuspecting Gabriele for references and the forged letters written on stolen Shell paper were handed over.

'Well, Fräulein, that seems to be perfectly in order,' she told Gabriele. 'If you would like to come back tomorrow you can sign the documents and move in next month.'

As soon as Gabriele had left, Frau Herrmann was on the phone to Shell. Yes, they did have a Werner Lotze working for them but no she could not speak to him as he had just been transferred to New York. Filled with the excitement of vindicated suspicion, Frau Herrmann then phoned the Ippendorf police station. She could hear the weary sigh at the other end when she announced herself but ploughed on regardless. Bored inattention was replaced by welcome enthusiasm once the good Frau had explained that the references were forged and the woman wanted to pay in cash. Fortunately, the call was taken by the desk sergeant and not by the duty constable who was on another line. The sergeant made a careful note and passed a copy of the message along to the BKA.

The Federal Crime Investigation Office (Bundeskriminalamt or BKA) based at Wiesbaden had been formed in 1951 to co-ordinate police efforts between the Federal and State authorities. In 1972, after terrorism had reached Germany, the BKA was authorized to gather together all the available information on terrorist activity. A large computer system called INPOL and nicknamed the Kommissar was built to house the data. Millions of bits of information on terrorists and their modus operandi were entered into the database.

It was an ambitious programme that proved too big for the policemen handling it. So, in 1975, the BKA established a new terrorist department that used a special computer system called PIOS for Persons, Institutions, Targets and Aims, and Movable Things. The touch of a key would summon up an astonishingly detailed profile. Everything from childhood pictures and the names of friends at school and university to dental records, fingerprints and if a suspect always phoned his mother on her birthday.

Over time, the computer proved to be a goldmine, producing patterns or narrowing a search in a way that would have been impossible using ordinary detective work, as in June 1979, when the Red Army Faction was believed to be keeping a number of safe houses in the Frankfurt area. Most Germans pay their electricity bills by Post Office or bank transfer and most Germans are registered with a residents' registration office. To narrow the search, the police obtained the electricity account records for the Frankfurt area and eliminated everyone who had not paid in cash. The police then ran that list of 18,000 names against other lists of known property owners, automobile owners and the list at the residents' registration office. In the end there were only two men left who paid their electricity bills in cash and were not registered. One was a drug dealer and the other was Rolf Heissler, a wanted Red Army Faction terrorist.

In Wiesbaden, the information from Frau Herrmann was logged in the Kommissar and then relayed back to Bonn to the BKA team responsible for hunting the killers of the Deputy Justice Minister, Hans-Joachim Wirtz.

In six weeks of hunting, the BKA had not discovered very much. They knew how he had been killed, the weapons that had been used; they had tyre prints from the motorbike; they even had samples from the seat that told them the type of leather that had been worn by the terrorists riding the bike. The word on the street was that it was a Becker operation: it certainly had all her hallmarks of ruthlessness combined with split-second timing. But they did not know the terrorists' identities and had no idea where they lived. Informants had given them the location of two safe houses which had been kept under surveillance but no one had shown up.

Frau Herrmann's description matched another given by the owner of one of the other safe houses. The Kommissar also revealed that a blonde girl fitting Gabriele's description was a known associate of Inge Becker. There was no ID but it was enough. So, when Gabriele had turned up to sign the agreement the next day, men and women from the BKA on foot and in cars and vans had been around the building. She had been followed first to an address that appeared to be her home and then to another building in Bad Godesberg.

A team from the BKA had then moved into the area, questioned the neighbours and found the owner of the building. They learned that the blonde had rented the flat for her businessman boss two months before but that the boss rarely, if ever, appeared. It wasn't much, but it was enough to get the beginnings of a pattern and for the BKA men that was more than enough.

Directly opposite the flat, the BKA had established a surveillance team in the sitting room of an elderly couple who had willingly promised silence and an unaltered routine in exchange for the thrill of being at the centre of such action. Now the room was filled with the paraphernalia of observation: binoculars, night-vision equipment, cameras and a telephone that was tapped directly into the line opposite.

In charge of the observers was Sergeant Erich Sternebeck, a man of apparently infinite patience and the limited imagination essential for a good Watcher. Ten years earlier he would have been chafing for action, furious that he had been given this bum job of surveillance, the task passed to the deadbeats. That was before The Shooting.

He had transferred to the BKA from the regular police as a way of moving more rapidly up the career ladder. He and his partner had been on a routine job following a known drug dealer through the Hamburg docks to what they thought would be a rendezvous with his overseas supplier. The dealer had turned a corner and then, as the two policemen approached it, he had leapt out, the gun in his hand firing short, sharp barks. Erich had seen his partner's face disappear in a mass of blood and brains before he was knocked to the ground by a series of hammer blows.

He had spent six weeks in hospital and emerged to learn that the dealer had been caught and had willingly confessed to the shootings, claiming he thought the two men were gunmen from a rival gang. He had pleaded self-defence at his trial and got five years. It was then that Erich Sternebeck lost his ambition and decided on the quiet life.

The years spent behind the camera and the binoculars, the hours spent transcribing notes dictated into a Dictaphone had taken their toll. Sergeant Erich Sternebeck was fat. Not just overweight but truly fat, with a huge stomach and deep rolls of flesh hanging over his collar. But this was Germany and, unlike the rest of the Western World, size was still considered a sign of good health among the working classes. Erich was secretly rather proud of his considerable girth.

The previous day he had watched while the blonde had appeared laden down with bottles and packages of food. Sternebeck had reported the event into his tape recorder. 'Subject arrived at 1750 hours carrying four brown paper bags. It was possible to observe the tops of bottles and what appeared to be packets of nuts and chips. My opinion: she is laying in the food and drink for a meeting.'

He turned his cheek away from the binoculars and took an enormous bite out of a knackwurst, then fixed his eyes back to the lens and chewed happily, a small dribble of juice from the sausage slowly making its way down his chin, to pause briefly and then drop to the floor.

He paused in his chewing, belched a deep, rumbling noise

and turned to his partner. 'She should be coming along sometime soon.'

As usual, the sergeant's instincts were to prove correct. The radio on the table beside him crackled into life to warn him that the blonde was approaching the building. As before, she let herself in and the team could watch her progress through the building and then into the apartment as she turned on the lights to guide her way.

Forty-five minutes later a man walked along the street, up the steps to the house and pressed the bell. Ten minutes after he had gone inside, a couple appeared.

Sergeant Sternebeck lifted the telephone receiver. As soon as the operator answered, he spoke urgently: 'Get me GSG9 at Hangelar.'

Hangelar

The lieutenant on duty that evening was Carl Raspe. The call came direct to the mess where he was sitting in front of a single bar electric fire reading a copy of *Stern* and wondering how much longer he would have to wait before he could retire to bed with a clear conscience. The alarm is not a bell but a low warbling sound that begins in the radio room at the end of the long, cream corridor of the main building and then spreads down passages and into rooms so that its ululations reach everyone.

Raspe flung the magazine to one side and pushed himself up from his chair. Running down the passage to the operations room, he was joined by other members of the ready unit who appeared from rooms, the sergeants' mess and the lavatories.

Twenty seconds later the eleven men were seated in the operations room. In front of them one of the intelligence officers from the headquarters unit took the short briefing.

'The message comes from the Bonn police,' he began. 'A group of RAF terrorists are meeting in a safe house in Bonn. The police have it under surveillance and the meeting is getting under way right now. Identity of the group is not known but they may have been responsible for the Wirtz killing.

'Your mission is to take out the safe house and capture the terrorists if possible.'

'What if that isn't possible?' asked Raspe.

'Then you are authorized to use whatever force is necessary to secure the building.'

There were a few covert glances among the men in the room. The message was clear to each of them. If there was a fight they could shoot and when trained men shoot they shoot to kill.

There was another short pause as the briefer worked the slide projector and the dark, glowering features of a passport photograph of Inge Becker appeared on the screen.

'This woman is Inge Becker and we believe that she may be in charge of this team. Remember this face. If she's there we want her alive. The Americans picked up two of her people trying to get into the States and we know she is involved with the thallium poisoning. So, we want her. The rest of her mob are just blunt instruments but she has the brains so try not to shoot them out.'

Some light chuckles greeted the weak humour.

'The only other ID we have is this woman.' A colour photo of Gabriele came on the screen which had been taken earlier that day by the surveillance team. There were a few appreciative whistles from the audience.

'She's in the apartment now but we think she's a fixer not a gunman. We would like her too as she may know where the other safe houses are.

'OK, men. That's it from me. You'll find the cops are waiting for you and they'll be able to give you the current status. Good luck.'

There was no pause for gossip. The men had trained for this moment and their reactions were almost subconscious, each man knowing his job, the equipment he needed and the role he would have to play over the next few hours. They moved down the passage to the equipment store. Each man had his own cubicle which contained his personal equipment. Much of it was standard: the green Bristol body-armour vest that covered neck and groin, a 9 mm pistol, a .44 magnum pistol, a Heckler and Koch MP5 sub-machine-gun, pump-action shotguns and small torpedo-shaped grenades. These were a derivative of the 'flash-bang' grenades that GSG9 had borrowed from the SAS for the Mogadishu operation. Each grenade consists of thousands of particles of magnesium and fulminate of mercury. When thrown the mercury detonates with an ear-splitting bang and the magnesium lights up, giving off the equivalent of 50,000 watts. Such a combination of light and noise is sufficient to deafen and blind anyone within range for a critical seven seconds.

One man from each unit carried a long green box. These were the marksmen and their job would be to stand aside from the actual attack to provide covering fire for the teams. The boxes contained a Heckler and Koch PSG1 7.62 mm rifle and an Eltro nightscope and laser sight.

Each man donned a black fireproof overall, the body armour and then a heavy webbing belt laden with pistols, ammunition, grenades and first-aid pouch. The final piece of equipment was a specially converted motorcyclist's crash helmet. Painted black, the helmet contained effective mufflers to minimize the impact of the stun grenades and a microphone and earpieces so that each member of the team could keep in constant contact with each other.

The teams moved out to the four black Mercedes-Benz 280SE. These cars looked identical to those driven by thousands of German businessmen. In fact, they had been specially converted to suit the needs of GSG9. Each door contained a recessed clip rack that held a H and K MP5 sub-machine-gun. In addition small gun ports were drilled in each door so that the guns could be pushed through the thin aluminium skin and fired without exposing the men inside the car. Three different radio systems allowed the men to keep in touch with each other, headquarters and the police.

As Carl Raspe settled into the passenger seat of the lead vehicle, he dialled up the police frequency and was patched through to Erich Sternebeck who was still peering through his binoculars at the apartment opposite him.

'This is Lieutenant Raspe of GSG9,' he began. 'We are just heading for you and should be with you in twenty minutes. Over.'

Even from this distance, Raspe could hear the undercurrent of excitement in Sternebeck's voice. The lugubrious sergeant had apparently been shaken out of his normal leth-argic state.

'We now have four people inside. One woman and three men.' There was a pause. 'Wait a minute, there's another couple coming down the street. It looks like they are heading for the apartment too. Yes, they've just turned in. That makes six.'

'OK, keep counting. We'll be with you in a few minutes. Out.'

Raspe could feel the knots starting in his stomach, an indication of the tension building inside. This would be his first 'active' mission; the first time he would actually be required to fire his weapons in anger. He had trained for just this kind of operation but at the same time his training always stressed the value of reconnaissance and planning. There would be no time for that on this operation. They would have to rely on instinct, skill and surprise to make up for the gaps.

Twenty years earlier when Palestinians had attacked Israeli athletes at the Munich Olympics they found a Germany completely unprepared. The terrorists demanded the release of 234 prisoners held in Israel and members of the Red Army Faction held in West Germany and an aircraft to fly them and their comrades to Cairo in exchange for the release of nine Israelis. After seventeen hours of talks, the terrorists and their hostages were flown by helicopter from Munich to Fürstenfeldbruck military airport where they had been told they would board a Boeing 727 and fly to Cairo. In fact, as the terrorists left the helicopters at Fürstenfeldbruck, snipers hidden on the roof of the terminal building opened fire. Two terrorists were killed and others wounded, along with two of the helicopter crew. Two of the snipers, even though they had terrorists in their sights, lost their nerve and failed to fire; the light was poor anyway and the distances too long for accuracy.

The remaining terrorists had time to reboard the helicop-ters, and when the Germans followed up their abortive sniper attack by launching a direct assault using troops and armoured cars, the Palestinians killed five of the bound and gagged hostages in one helicopter and then blew it up. As the firefight continued, the second helicopter with another four Israeli hostages on board also exploded. Although five of the terrorists were killed and three arrested, nine Israelis died and the entire rescue operation had been fatally bungled.

Out of the ignominy and carnage was born the Grenzschutzgruppe 9 or GSG9, a 210-strong division of the West German Federal Border Guard, whose primary mission is countering terrorism. They have their own separate compound inside the one-mile-square Federal Border Guard base at Hangelar, about thirty minutes from Bonn.

Behind wire fences and a battery of surveillance cameras, the men live in seclusion in a five-storey light-brown building and train in a number of low modern buildings that form a square in the centre of which is a grass-covered parade ground acting as both an outdoor unarmed combat practice ground and a helicopter pad. Inside the mess conditions are spartan and the food arguably the most disgusting of any special forces' mess in the Western world. Certainly when visitors from the SAS or Delta Force pass through every reasonable excuse is made to eat at a nearby Gasthaus instead.

The structure of GSG9 is based around the five-man cell consisting of a master sergeant leader, a marksman, explosives expert, pointman and coverman. Each of these jobs is interchangeable between individuals, depending on the mission. The primary role of the unit is hostage rescue from buildings or aircraft but they are also trained in reconnaissance.

Five years after their formation, the West German government were given a second opportunity to show their mettle against Palestinian terrorists. This time, in a brief firefight in the desert at Mogadishu in Somalia, there was no mistake. The unit successfully stormed a hijacked Lufthansa jet, killing three of the four terrorists on board and freeing all the passengers alive.

Since the collapse of the Baader-Meinhof gang and the decline in Palestinian terrorism, GSG9 had found itself with time on its hands, but however quiet it is the unit keeps two five-man teams on permanent standby, commanded by a lieutenant, to deal with kidnaps, hostage-taking or a cry for help from any of the police forces or German diplomats around the world.

Raspe had joined GSG9 from the regular Border Guard two years earlier. Still only twenty-four, he had worked his way through the rigours of the unit's five-month selection course and had then been put in charge of two five-man units. He had joined the Border Guard in the first place because his father, a policeman in the small town of Dannenberg on the West German plain not far from the border with East Germany, had unintentionally brought him up with a mission in life. Their house was in sight of the border, that barrier of mines, machine-guns and barbed wire that separated German from German, communist from capitalist, East from West. To the young Carl, his father had been a hero, one of the few standing guard to protect the citizens of Dannenberg from the ravening hordes of the East. His father had the respect of the community and Carl benefited from that respect at school. He learned from his father the threat posed by the East; the tanks, artillery and helicopters that were poised just over the horizon waiting to strike. Above all, he learned that protecting the Fatherland was an honourable job.

Rather than joining the police like his father, Carl decided to join the Border Guard, the body responsible for patrolling the barrier with East Germany and giving the nation early warning of any hostile action. When he had joined, he had relished the prospect of an exciting career, but almost as soon as he had signed up the wall started to crumble and even the minefields and machine-guns began to disappear. He couldn't complain about the peace, of course, but now it all seemed so boring. So he had applied to GSG9, a group which he reckoned would still have a role whatever happened in East or West. It wasn't the money – the basic pay was the same – or the glamour, but more that he felt he could make a useful contribution that would mean something in these newly peaceful times.

The training had been tough but he found that he relished the physical and mental challenge as well as the camaraderie of being part of a small group of highly motivated people. He found, too, that he had quickly developed new skills of which he had become inordinately proud. In the Border Guard his battalion of 600 men fired between 120,000 and 200,000 rounds a year. The 210 men of GSG9 fired more than a million rounds a year. In the combat shooting range in the basement of the main building in Hangelar, Carl had practised until he had been able to beat the one second standard for turning, drawing and firing his pistol at a target twenty-five metres away.

He had learned to trust his men with his life and he had total confidence that they shared that trust. Looking now to his right, in the dashboard light he could pick out the calm features of the unit's master sergeant, Thomas Seidler, a veteran of six years' service with the unit who was his right hand, the man who quietly guided him when he was in doubt and who covered his back when he was in danger.

The Mercedes cars drew up in the street running parallel with Friedrichstrasse directly behind the observation post.

'Cars two, three and four remain here. Thomas and I will go inside and talk to the cops.'

The two men went down the side of the house facing them, through the garden, over the garden wall at the rear, through the next garden and then into the house and up to the third floor where Raspe introduced himself and Seidler to Erich Sternebeck.

'There are now eight of them in there,' the sergeant began as Raspe bent to look through the binoculars. 'We have the blonde whose picture you have seen, two other women and five men. We snapped each of them as they came along the street which should help you when you go in.'

Sternebeck fanned out pictures of the terrorists and handed them to Raspe. Gone were the days when pictures had to be sent to the printers for developing. Instead the BKA used a new Polaroid camera developed by Pentax that could take and instantly develop pictures shot with a telephoto lens.

'We've lost sight of them since it got dark, about thirty minutes ago. Our thermal imager is pretty useless through these kinds of buildings and we only see them when they go past the window.'

As Sternebeck was speaking, Sergeant Seidler opened a fat black briefcase and produced a small machine that looked

335

identical to a video camera with the exception of an enlarged lens and a rectangular tube along the top. It was the latest thermal imager from Marconi Command and Control Systems in Britain. GSG9 had been shown its capabilities two months earlier during a joint night exercise with the SAS and, using their contacts at Hereford, had managed to borrow a machine for evaluation.

There was a low hum as Seidler turned the machine on and then handed it to Raspe. He brought the imager up to his eye and looked through the lens. Immediately the black of the night was transformed into a shadowy green-hued day. The buildings, cars and even windows and the curtains covering them were clearly visible as the imager intensified the available light by 50,000 times. As Carl panned along the street, a series of ghostly white shapes appeared inside the green picture. These were the hot spots found by the infrared detection system. The imager was so sensitive that police used it to fly over a field where they suspected a body might be buried. The heat given off by a decomposing corpse immediately registered as a white spot in a sea of green.

Now, Raspe saw cars whose engines had been used recently, a street lamp, a dog pausing by a lamppost and its urine a ghostly, hot, white stream. Moving the imager on to its target, he could see the safe house on the first floor. As one of the terrorists moved across the window, Carl could clearly see the upright human shape. Through the thick walls of the building other images were less distinct although he could count eight heat sources in the room opposite him.

He turned back to Sternebeck. 'Have we got the plans of the flat?'

'We've spoken to the owner and gone through the flats above and below so we think we have a pretty accurate description.' Sternebeck handed over a drawing of the flat which had been pieced together that day. After ten minutes of further discussion, the two GSG9 men left to return to their car.

By the time they had rejoined the main force, the other members of the unit had prepared for the assault and were ready to go. Laid out on the pavement was a bewildering array of equipment from ladders to ropes to stretchers and bottles for emergency drips.

On the hurried walk through the gardens, Carl had been running through an assault sequence in his mind. When he reached his men, he had the tactical orders ready. Squatting in the headlights of one of the cars and surrounded by his standing men, Carl began the briefing.

'Right. We have eight terrorists in a first-floor flat. There are no civilians involved so anyone you see is hostile.'

There was an almost audible relaxation of the tension among the men. No hostages increased the odds of each man's survival and reduced the chances of the terrorists coming out alive. No hostages meant a clear line of fire; fewer complications.

'The flat's on one floor. Main door is wood with two locks. We'll use the pumps for that. Windows are wood frame so, Eddie, I want you to make up two shaped charges.' He had turned to the explosives expert who nodded and bent to his task while still listening to the briefing.

'The flat has five rooms: two bedrooms, sitting room, kitchen and bathroom. Right now all the terrorists are in the sitting room but I've left the imager with the cops and they'll keep us posted on any movement there.

'We'll play it like this: two teams each with four men, I'll take the lead and Thomas the other. The lead team will go through the door and the rest will take out the sitting-room windows. We should be able to get to the first floor with the ladders so there's no need to rappel off the roof. The two snipers are to cover us from across the road. I want the apartment swept clean and I want someone alive if possible, preferably the blonde. Any questions?'

It had been a short briefing but it had been enough. Each of the men had trained for this moment, had practised house assaults until they could do it – literally – with their eyes shut. The routines were familiar, the instincts sharp; a final synchronization of watches and they moved off.

It took fifteen minutes for Raspe and his three men to work round in the shadows of each building until they were outside the door of number 135. An alerted Frau Herrmann was waiting, hands shaking and jowls quivering with excitement, to let them into the building. The second unit had been following in Raspe's wake carrying a rubber-tipped lightweight aluminium ladder, uniquely designed in a T-shape. The stem of the T rested on the ground and all four men were able to climb the ladder and pause on the cross of the T waiting for the signal. Two of them carried a rectangular-shaped charge made to fit around the edge of the window. A single movement to raise the charge over the sill, pull the spring release and two seconds later the charge would blow, lifting the whole window out of the frame and into the room.

Raspe paused outside the door to the flat. He spoke directly to Sergeant Sternebeck through the throat microphone. 'Any movement your end?'

'No. Nothing. The terrorists are still in the sitting room.'

Raspe heard a bell ringing in the background. 'Wait a minute. Their phone is ringing.' There was a pause as Sternebeck listened while the tape played over the conversation. When he came back on thirty seconds later, there was a new urgency, even panic in his normally calm voice.

'They've been warned. They're on to us. The call told them to get out as a raid is planned.'

Raspe cut the sergeant off and flicked his wrist switch to move back to the tactical channel connecting him with his men.

'We're blown. Expect trouble. Attack counting from five. Mark. Five. Four. Three. Two. One.'

It had been Gabriele who had taken the call inside the flat. She had recognized Inge's urgent voice at the other end of the phone. Hanging up, she had turned back into the room.

'That was Inge. She says we have been discovered and that they may be about to attack us. She's been trying to get hold of me for twenty-four hours but she missed the drop. She says we should get out now.'

The meeting had begun in an atmosphere of quiet confidence. The team had been successful and had done their work throughout Europe and returned apparently undetected. The failure of the American unit was unfortunate but had not compromised the operation as far as they could tell, and the US operation had always been a higher risk. The loss of Hans and Brigitte bothered these terrorist veterans not at all. Now the group were ready to go out again on what had so far proved to be their most spectacular mission ever.

As Gabriele was relaying the message to the group she felt her confidence melt away. Her heart began to race and she wanted to be sick. She had talked with her comrades about the glory of death and they had all joked about how they would confront it and welcome the martyrdom it offered. But Gabriele had never actually shot anyone, never even been under fire herself. She had secretly rather despised the macho action men seeking glory, seeing herself as the cerebral figure, preparing the ground on which they all walked. Without her, she had often thought, they would all have been dead or in jail a long time ago. But now she was being forced to confront the fearful reality of the destiny she had chosen.

Ali the Turkish immigrant was the first to react. He tossed aside his glass of red wine and in two strides had reached a large wooden chest. He flung open the lid and began throwing out Uzi sub-machine-guns, Beretta automatics and even a stubby Ingram MAC10. There was a snicking of safety catches, a metallic clacking as magazines were checked. Before anyone had time to take up defensive positions or to check windows and doors the attack began.

The two shaped charges burst simultaneously, spraying glass and wood into the room. The concussion in the confined space had all the effect of a stun grenade. Gabriele watched as a number of horrifying black shapes appeared at the shattered windows. She had not even heard the blasts of the shotgun at the front door. When she turned seeking an escape, she saw another black-clad figure burst through the door in a rolling somersault, like some vast inflated deadly rubber ball. Then the firing began.

It was Ali whose reactions were fastest. He still held the Ingram in his hands and as the first of the invaders at the window brought his Heckler and Koch up to the aim, he unleashed a stream of 9 mm bullets in the direction of the window. The first bullets were aimed low and struck the first GSG9 man through the window in the legs. The force of the bullets pushed the man back against the window and then, as the recoil from the gun forced the barrel upwards, the bullets climbed up the man's body. His bullet-proof vest took the impact but the bullets' force drove him backwards over the windowsill to somersault to the street below.

As Ali frantically tried to change the clip on the Ingram, the second GSG9 man opened fire. The bullets were clinically and surgically delivered, the first burst stitching a four-shot tattoo left to right across Ali's chest. As he was lifted into the air, a second batch of four blew his head apart like a ripe melon. The stump of his body came to rest against the far wall, his heart still pumping a spray of arterial blood from his headless corpse.

There was firing all around now and the room was filling with smoke and the gagging smell of intestines and blood as both sides attempted to destroy each other. There was no thought now of prisoners or mercy. This was kill or be killed.

Gabriele wanted to surrender. She had no weapon, no way of defending herself even if she had wished to. Miraculously she had survived the first few seconds unscathed. She was standing in the middle of the room, mouth open in a soundless scream, ears still blocked after the first concussion from the explosives. The action – like a bloody full-colour silent movie – the flames sprouting from the barrels of guns, the horror of friends destroyed, the screams and the curses all took place in this soundless world. She even knew that she was crying, could feel the sobs of terror, but could only imagine the noise she was making. Certainly there was no sign that anyone was listening. She was impotent, carried along by a tide of death.

Seeking an escape, a friendly face, anything to draw her away from this, she turned to face Norbert, the carpenter who like her helped the group find safe houses. He had a Beretta 9 mm sub-machine-gun in his hands and was firing towards the door. His lips were drawn back in a snarl that exposed his tobacco-stained teeth. His hunched shoulders, the stuttering gun, the fierce eyes all spelled defiance. Somewhere this quiet man had found a courage under fire he never imagined he possessed. But it was an empty gesture. His comrades were either dead, dying or too busy with their own final acts of defiance to notice.

340

Gabriele saw Norbert stagger as if blasted by a massive wind. Then bits of clothing started to fly from his body. Blood and bone sped across the room to slither down the far wall as he was literally torn apart by the force of the bullets hitting him from all sides of the room.

As he was flung backwards, the Beretta flew from his hands towards Gabriele. Her reactions were instinctive and a terrible mistake.

Carl Raspe was inside the room and moving towards the single remaining figure of the blonde who was his target. But she had the Beretta in her hands, appeared to be bringing it up to fire. Then a tiny red dot appeared in the centre of her face just above the bridge of her nose. Carl knew the dot was the laser sight trained on the woman. Where the dot was now a bullet would surely follow.

As Carl shaped the single shouted 'No' he saw the whole front of her face implode under the impact of a 7.62 mm bullet fired by the sniper across the road who had not hesitated to protect his commander.

October 4

' **I** DON'T WANT TO HEAR any of that "won't co-operate"
shit. I'm not interested in principles or moral positions or
any of that crap.'

The words were barked across the room, each phrase punctuated by the sound of Shaw's fist thudding on his desk top.

The violence of the outburst quietened the room, the occupants looking at feet, corners, the view, their notepads,
anything to cover their embarrassment and ensure that the
violence was not redirected towards them. Everyone in the
room knew that time had run out. There was nothing anyone
could do to stop the terrorists launching the next stage of
their campaign. What was supposed to be a meeting to plan
the way ahead had swiftly degenerated with the DCI flushing
with anger at the news that Hamid had so far failed to help
find Bakr.

It had started reasonably enough with Shaw asking for an
update on the financial position.

'I did some final tallying last night. The figures are
probably incomplete but I think we are talking a ballpark
sum of around $11 billion. If it's any consolation, we have
all been witnessing the biggest scam in the history of the
world.

'They have the money now but if they don't satisfy their
political aims and if the operation begins to fall apart then
we'll probably get a good bit of that money back. We've
already been in touch with the various governments concerned and they have promised to do what they can to open
up the companies and banks when this is all over. Even if the
money has been moved, we'll be able to track it. The key is

capturing Hassan and stopping the poisoning. Once the black-mail is over we can move in and get the money. No government is going to want to be seen to benefit from this business so we have plenty of leverage.'

Shaw listened to Bob's explanation with growing anger. He had watched his career disintegrating over the last few weeks and he was now desperate to salvage something from the wreckage. Salvation was represented not by a mopping up operation in the future but a triumph now.

His fist banged on the table. 'Ah, for God's sake, Gearheart, that's all just bullshit,' he yelled, voice rising to match his anger. 'You've found some bank accounts. Fine. You get the cash back later. Fine. It'll all be all right when it's over. Fine. But,' sarcasm now underlining the rage, 'that's not going to be worth a row of beans. We don't have the terrorists, we don't have this bastard Hassan and we are on the brink of another poisoning. What are we going to do about that? You can be damn sure that unless we do something we're all going to be hung out to dry. And that means all of us in this room so we'd better think of something. And fast.'

Bob felt his stomach knot with tension as an already exhausted nervous system tried to cope with the latest escalation. He also felt himself flush, part with anger and part with the humiliation of being verbally abused.

'You promised me that your man Hamid would deliver –' Bob began to protest at this distortion. 'Don't argue,' Shaw shouted him down. 'Twenty-four hours from ground zero and what do we have? Nothing. Zip. Ab-so-lut-ely fuck all. And all because your friend, your tame Palestinian, gets an attack of morality. A Pal with a conscience, for Christ's sake. I knew I should never have let you back in here. You're nothing but a liability and your judgment's lousy.' He leaned forward, fixing Bob in an angry and spiteful gaze. 'And I can assure you, Gearheart, that when all this is over, you'll be going right back where you came from. And if I have anything to do with it, you'll start where you belong, at the bottom.'

Insulted beyond endurance, Bob found himself standing, shouting back at the red, overweight face below.

'Every single lead you've got in this lousy investigation

has come from me. The money, the bank, Bakr, everything. So don't look to me to be your fall guy. When the Hill starts asking the questions I'm going to be there to give them the answers that you won't want to hear. It's your ignorance and stupidity that has failed us here. It was you that failed to exploit the financial database I set up. If you had done, then we would have moved this show along far faster. Instead, I had to start from scratch with you fighting me every step of the way.

'Sure, Hamid hasn't delivered. Sure, that's a disappointment. But at least he has some principles worth believing in. All you care about is your back and your political future.'

He leaned forward, hands resting on the table, his face close to the DCI's. 'When this is all over you won't have a future because you're the one that's going to be hung out to dry. So don't threaten me.'

Bob felt a hand pulling at his left arm and turned to see Prentice trying to draw him back into his chair. The contact broken, Bob subsided into silence.

It was Frank Dearth from State, ever the diplomat, who broke the tension. This was a different Dearth from two weeks ago. Then he had been aggressive, full of fight and eager for action. But the frustrations of the hunt had drained him, flattened his voice, and he spoke with a resignation that accurately reflected all their feelings.

'It's too early for this kind of talk. We're still hunting the poisoners and so far we haven't done a very good job. So in the time left to us, let's see if we can do a little better.

'For those of you who don't already know it, I'm afraid I have more bad news. You all know about the German raid on the Bonn apartment two days ago. Eight terrorists were killed in the shootout and we had hoped that had taken care of the European end of the operation. But now the Germans think that while the group were responsible for the poisoning their leader was warned off. She was Inge Becker, the same woman whose name was linked to the two terrorists we got at Dulles. So we're on the right track but have reached a dead end.'

He paused, looked around at the tired faces, sighed, and continued.

'There's no sign that the Israelis are going to move so that option is closed as well. There will be no conference tomorrow. They seem to have been counting on the Germans to pull something off and now that they have failed they have no room left to manoeuvre. As far as I can see, there is nothing to stop the next round of killing. After that God knows. The market is going to crash, the President will want my head as a first offering to Congressional wolves and I dare say you guys will be next on the list.'

'What about Bakr?' Shaw asked.

'We're pretty sure he's the right man,' said Doug Frink from the Bureau. 'The links in the chain that we've got so far work like this.' He began ticking off his fingers. 'We've got the Arab Bank link. We've got Tunisia from the Israelis so that checks. We've got a detailed description from our people in Tunis. Then two days ago the Brits lost one of their people, low level I gather. She was killed in the Ritz by a man travelling on a Brazilian passport and his description matches that of Bakr.'

'Another fucking Brit leak,' muttered Shaw.

'What we don't have is Bakr's location right now and without that we're just pissing in the wind.'

A small smile appeared on Shaw's face. 'OK. Well why don't we give wonderboy here another chance.' He flapped a hand in Bob's direction. 'Get on a plane and go see your friend in Tunis. Tell him we need his help. Tell him we'll make him a hero. Tell him he has a chance to save the world. Tell him any damn thing you like, only get from him where this guy Bakr is and how we can get hold of him.'

Bob knew Hamid well enough to realize that the mission was probably doomed. But here was a chance to get out of the stifling atmosphere of Washington. And who knows? It might work. 'OK. I'll give it a go. When do you want me to leave?'

'Right now. This minute. Yesterday in fact. Get going.'

As Bob got up to leave, Sy Koch of the NSA intervened. 'Matt, I think you should know —'

The DCI did not let him finish. 'Give it a rest, Sy. Whatever you've got to say can wait until Gearheart has gone. We've wasted enough time.'

As soon as Bob had left the room, Koch spoke up again. 'I think you might want to call Gearheart back when you hear what I have to say,' he began. That the normally reticent man from the NSA should volunteer anything was a surprise, the fact that he might have an answer to part of their quest was an extraordinary development. Koch actually enjoyed his moment in the light. He waited, savouring the seconds, and then took off his spectacles and began to polish the lenses, peering around, his eyes blinking rapidly like a mole seeing the first light of day.

'As you know, for many years criminals have been identified by the fingerprints. Each fingerprint is unique and a whole science has built up in this area. In the past ten years we have learned that the human voice is the same as a fingerprint. It identifies an individual in just the same way and each voice has certain unique speech patterns of tone and resonance.'

He stopped and reached down underneath the table. Bringing his briefcase up, he opened it and took out a dozen colour prints which he handed around.

'It was the Germans who did the pioneering work in this field. In their fight against the Baader-Meinhof, they had literally millions of taps and they found they were unable to make full use of them. They developed a machine called a Spektro Analysator which looked at a number of characteristics in a voice to see if matches could be made between one tap and another.

'The card you have in front of you is taken from a case around five years ago. A member of the RAF kidnapped a Hanover businessman and tried to ransom him. When the terrorist called in with the ransom demand he disguised his voice. But the man had a slight lisp. When the police ran the recording through their machine, it saw through the disguise and quickly detected the lisp. A look at his file, a raid on his likely hideout and bingo, they had their man.'

Shaw looked down at the card in his hand. It was divided in two horizontally. The top half showed a jagged green line running steeply up and down peaks and troughs measuring a period of 880 microseconds. The bottom half showed a waterfall effect of blues and greens with the lisp clearly identifiable as a yellow and red shape in the middle. It certainly didn't look like any voice he had ever heard.

'Using computers we have managed to isolate more than 5,000 individual speech characteristics. We have written the software and we are now able to use computers automatically to match one voice with another. The Agency now has a bank of around 250,000 voices: drug runners, people whose phones we have tapped, suspected terrorists, politicians. Anyone who we think might be of future interest is in the bank.'

The impatient Dearth interrupted. 'What's all this have to do with us, Sy?'

Koch would not be hurried. 'Two years ago, after the murder of François Raffet in Paris by the PFA, the Israelis picked up a call between France and Lebanon which they believe was the hit squad reporting back to Hassan. They gave us a tape of that call and we put it in the databank.

'Then three days ago the Brits picked up a call from London to Tunis, probably from Bakr after he'd murdered that girl. That call was the tip-off that the Germans had found the RAF safe house in Bonn. The Brits picked up another call which we think was to Inge Becker, the leader of the RAF cell doing the poisoning. That's why she slipped the net when the Germans raided the house.

'We've got the tapes and on a first run it looks like we may have a match for the tape the Israelis made two years ago. These voice matches are tricky and take a bit of time, particularly as the conversations were all very short. But we should be certain in another twenty-four hours.

'We also know that Bakr is on his way home. If we make a match, great. If not, we can get the listeners to feed the voice print into the system so that it will automatically flag any other call made from the area by the same voice. That way, we can find Hassan and get his location in real time. Then, if our guys are in position, we can go in and get him. I think we should call Gearheart back and wait until we have the intelligence.'

Dearth added another note of caution. 'We can't go sending our people in without speaking to the Tunisians and they may veto the whole idea.'

'That's a really dumb idea,' said an angry but newly determined Shaw. 'The Tunisians most probably won't do what we ask. Second, even if they did, they would probably tip the Bank off. Third, by the time they got their act together our man would have flown the coop. If we are going to do anything we better do it ourselves.

'Sy, you keep working on the voice match. We'll still send Gearheart. We can always update him when he's in place and anyway he might come up with something.' He turned to Prentice. 'Have a word with the guys downstairs and give him something that will keep us in touch with him. I'll see the President and see if he'll agree to our sending some people over there.' He rubbed his hands together, a smile indicating how his mood had swung from despair to cautious optimism. 'Gentlemen, we're on the road at last. Mr Abu Hassan had better watch his ass.'

October 5

Paris

MONIQUE YFF WAS ONE OF the lucky few to
whom sugar meant pure energy and not fat. Despite
an unfashionably large consumption of the little
white crystals she had maintained her slim figure and her
youthful eighteen-year-old enthusiasm kept the horrors of
cholesterol and hard arteries in a safe and far distant future.

Monique was reading French literature at the Sorbonne,
specializing in the works of Voltaire. She shared an apartment with four other students in the Latin Quarter off the
Boulevard Saint Michel or Boul' Mich' as it is called, in the
area of Paris known as the Montagne Sainte Geneviève. This
is one of the most attractive parts of Paris, filled with pavement cafés, publishing houses and bookshops for the learned
and the students. In the backstreets, night clubs, "cellars",
exotic restaurants and cinemas showing avant-garde films
abound to reinforce the city's image as the cultural and
Bohemian capital of Europe.

For Monique, Paris had always been home. She had
been born and brought up within sight of La Cité, the
architectural and cultural heart of the city. From her bedroom window in Saint Severin, she could see the towering
mass of Notre Dame Cathedral to the right and the
majesty of the Palais de Justice to her left. Her father, too,
was a Parisian, her mother from Neuchâtel in Switzerland.
From an early age she had been imbued with a sense of
the culture and history of France and in particular of
Paris.

It was hardly surprising then that she chose the Sorbonne as a university and Voltaire, the writer who perhaps

349

epitomizes the glories of eighteenth-century France, as a subject of special interest.

During the summer months, Monique used to walk from her apartment to the Sorbonne, a journey of some fifteen minutes, stopping on her way at the Café Benoît on the Rue Victor Cousin. It was a small café with tables covered in red-and-white-checked cloths on the pavement. For that part of town, prices were reasonable and she generally met other students so a coffee became a morning gossip and a joke or two before the start of lectures.

This morning she joined a table where four other students were already sitting. It was Monique's misfortune that she was the first to want sugar with her coffee. It was also her bad luck that she wanted three heaped teaspoons rather than one. The bag of sugar from which the bowl had been filled had been purchased the previous day at a nearby supermarket. The bowl at Monique's table was the first to be filled and the concentration of poison was therefore very high.

The strong, dark Colombian coffee completely masked the taste of the poison and when Monique picked up her satchel and walked with the others towards the Sorbonne she had no idea that the deadly substance was already eating away her insides.

As she passed inside the gates to the university and into the main courtyard, the first spasm hit her. It was not too painful, just the beginnings of indigestion perhaps. Monique frowned briefly and walked on. As she moved under the arches towards her lecture hall, she looked up to admire the magnificent decorative panels by Weerts illustrating the traditional Lendit Fair. As her head moved back towards the horizontal, she suddenly retched, first a deep, dry heave and then again, this time spewing a fountain of dark liquid on to the wide concrete steps in front of her.

There was a momentary feeling of embarrassment as she took in the sideways glances and the concealed smiles of the students walking by her. Then another spasm hit and then another and another. She fell to her knees as the pain began, first in her stomach and then spreading seemingly to embrace every pore of her body. She heard a scream and realized it was herself crying out in her agony.

There were no sniggers from the students now. A crowd gathered around Monique as she lay alternately spasming and screaming. One moment she was still, the next jerking on the concrete like a marionette manipulated by some sadistic puppet master.

The deterioration was terrifyingly fast. In five minutes, Monique had changed from being a tall, vivacious and attractive student to a tortured, semi-conscious animal. The ground round her was a snail's trail of mucous and bile which had been dragged from her protesting body. Now, each heave produced only a cry of anguish and a tiny spume of phlegm. Then, as her body decayed in front of the horrified students, each heave produced first tiny flecks of blood and as the rupture spread the flecks became spots and the spots a reddish brown stain spreading around her body.

The wail of a siren broke through the attention of the crowd. But now the spasms were settling down to tiny twitches as Monique's body was drained of life. Then, with a final, tiny, mewling cry like that of a new-born kitten, she died.

The poisoning had begun again.

London

Curiously, the panic began not in Paris but in London. Like so many stock-market disasters, it began with a rumour that in a few electronic messages and telephone calls had become hard fact exaggerated many times.

The rumoured death of President Reagan in 1988 had sent a frisson through the world's financial markets. Rupert Murdoch's heart attack had sent News Group shares tumbling in March 1990 until the man himself appeared fit and well on US television to deny the tale. This time, the word was out that the poisoners had struck again.

It was, of course, inevitable that someone would whisper that word. The day of the deadline had been reached and no concessions had been made. The markets had climbed back from their low points of six weeks earlier. But it had been a nervous journey, a tentative few steps up and then one or

351

two back as market-makers and analysts waited to see what the politicians would do. Now that they had done nothing, there was a recognition that more serious trouble was on the way. No one knew what the next target might be but everyone realized that the price they would have to pay would be high.

London is exactly in the middle of the world's stock exchange clock. As the London market begins trading at nine a.m., Tokyo, Hong Kong and Sydney have shut down for the day and the US exchanges have yet to open. So that morning, London was dictating the trading terms for the next twenty-four hours.

The day opened calmly enough with the Financial Times 100 index hovering around the 2,100 mark where it had been for the past two weeks. In front of the dealers, the computer screens showed their usual mix of reds and blues, the reds indicating falling prices and the blues stocks that are on their way up.

Later, no one would claim responsibility for the start of the fall. But around ten o'clock the word swept through the market. While the detail differed – with one call, soft drinks had been hit again, with another message, it was frozen chickens – the central theme was common to all: the poisoning had started again.

The reaction of the market was almost instantaneous. Screens changed from blue to red as the market-makers anticipated the sell orders which followed shortly afterwards. By lunchtime, the FT index was down 200 points to fall below the 2,000 mark for the first time since the October 1987 crash. Seventy-five billion dollars had been wiped off the value of shares and more than 600 million shares had been traded, more than twice the number that would usually change hands in a whole day.

Then, rumour turned to fact. With perfect timing designed to hit the *Today* show and *Good Morning America*, the two prime time early morning news shows broadcast before Wall Street opens, the terrorists issued their statement.

The Israelis failed to meet our deadline and to discuss our reasonable demands. We know that many governments want an agreement between the Palestinians and the Israelis and we would ask the people of the world to stand alongside us in our legitimate demand for a home.

It is with great regret we have to announce that we have poisoned another batch of food. We have poisoned sugar in a number of different forms in a number of different countries. We know that some people will die and we are sorry that this has proved necessary.

However, our demands are reasonable and the leaders of the Palestinian people are reasonable men. It is the Israelis and their ally the United States who are stopping peace.

Our demands remain the same. Unless they are met within fifteen days, we will poison again.

This time, the generalized nature of the threat accelerated the panic. In the minds of the public and governments alike every sugar product from a packet of raw cane sugar to artificial sweetener to any product with sugar in it could be affected.

The New York exchange opened thirty minutes after CNN had broadcast the latest statement. The start of trading on the Big Board of major companies is signalled by the ringing of a bell. That morning, when its ringing echoed through the building, disaster was already echoing its tones. Before trading even began the index had been marked down 125 points, after one hour it was down 240 and by the end of the day the Dow had fallen 550 points, a record that cut 28 per cent off the value of shares. Understandably, sugar companies had suffered the worst. Kastel's stock, for example, had fallen from $134 at the start of trading to just $64 by the close of business.

Once New York had finished it was the turn of the Far East. There, too, the pattern was the same. A wave of panic selling slashed values as the money men saw in the weakness and indecision of their political masters the prospect of financial ruin.

October 7

Tel Aviv

THE DAYS HAD GROWN INTO a continuous nightmare for Hirsh Kronstein. He had lived with his conscience for seven weeks. Each day the killings had tormented him. Each night he had relived the television pictures of the innocent participants who died in a war they knew little about and cared nothing for.

He had come to see his mentor Sachar in a new light. Sachar was no longer the wise counsellor, the father figure who had adopted him, a stranger in a new land. Hirsh had finally come to understand that he was the personification of everything he had left his own country to escape. A man obsessed with the rectitude of his cause, who justified all excess by arguing it was 'for the greater good'. Such arguments implied a compromise of principle. But Hirsh had seen the results of those compromises. He had killed believing that Sachar's judge and jury was enough. He had schemed and dissembled thinking that small sacrifices were necessary to win the bigger games made possible by the small deceptions.

This time had been different. He knew when the information had come to him from that first meeting in Paris with Hussaini that the political leadership should have been given what few details they had. But Sachar had persuaded him otherwise. Then Sachar had persuaded him that the military option would do the job, that the Palestinians were hopelessly compromised, that they could never succeed.

He now saw Sachar as a man obsessed, so enmeshed in the game of intelligence that he was unable to distinguish between the national interest and his own fascination with intrigue. He had sucked Hirsh into his scheme, underlining his arguments with the subtle complexities produced by their long-standing relationship. Hirsh felt used by the old man, manipulated into accepting a position he now knew was indefensible. He had agreed a moral compromise that had led to him betraying his country and himself.

He had heard from journalist friends that the Beka'a raid was common currency and he knew that it was only a matter of time before the news that Israel had known about the terror campaign leaked out too.

The media in Israel is a strange paradox. It is at once courageous and craven, questioning and supine. Like the country itself, the media is ambivalent about its role in the world. Used to living in a country at war with its neighbours and with itself, journalists have made some difficult compromises that were at first resisted but are now simply accepted as being part of the job. At the start of the terrorist campaign three weeks earlier, the Prime Minister had summoned the editors of all the national newspapers and the directors of the television and radio stations to ask for restrained reporting during this national emergency. At the beginning, the media had responded to the request and had been largely uncritical of the government. Then, too, there had seemed to be little other than the facts to report.

However, Israel is a country that both thrives on crisis and has an almost pathological national absorption with the political future of the country; the role of the military, the Palestinian question; indeed anything that can become a centre of conversation. Running through this persistent need for self-examination is an underlying pessimism fuelled by the paranoia lurking just beneath the Jewish consciousness.

It was hardly surprising then that as the crisis dragged on, the media began to question the role of the politicians, the intelligence community, the military and Israel's allies abroad. In doing this, newspapers, radio stations and television were only reflecting the debate that was going on among the liberal intelligentsia that makes up the opinion-forming elite in Israel.

That debate might not have been too significant except for one important loophole in Israel's censorship laws. This clause says that provided information has already appeared in the foreign press then the Israeli media is free to publish or broadcast it as well. In the past this had been a useful way for frustrated journalists to get their stories published. But in the case of the poisoning, which saw an unparalleled degree of criticism aimed at Israel from abroad, the effect had been devastating. Day after day the Israeli media had reported the criticism of Israel's intransigence. The Israelis saw for the first time that their worst fears were being confirmed. The country was cut off from world public opinion amid talk of the United States flexing the aid muscle, unwelcome debates in the United Nations and a growing feeling that it was Israel and not the Palestinians which was the cause of the crisis.

Then the next round of poisoning began. A mounting death toll and a growing financial crisis had allied the traditional critics of Israel with their more moderate supporters. All argued for compromise. Within Israel the criticisms of the politicians became more shrill, the calls for a deal more numerous. Once the public knew that the military option had been tried and had failed to resolve the crisis, the clamour for peace would be impossible to resist.

Once the dam had been breached, Hirsh was certain that the role of Mossad in keeping news of the planned poisoning campaign secret would leak, too. Then not only the Mossad but the State of Israel would be at the mercy of its many enemies. Better, then, that Israel once again took charge of its own fate and began to make decisions based on all the available information and not simply on the parts that Sachar chose to pass to his political masters.

Hirsh had called the Prime Minister's office that morning and spoken to his personal adviser on counter-terrorism, an old friend. An appointment had been arranged for later that morning in the Minister's office.

Now, as he walked down the plain corridor, pausing outside the simple light wood door, Hirsh felt the slight weakness in his legs indicating his nervousness. He moved into the ante room and to his surprise saw Isser Sachar sitting there.

The two men eyed each other. Hirsh saw that Sachar had aged since their last meeting a week earlier. At last he seemed burdened by the responsibilities of the decisions he had taken, his flesh had drawn in around his face. His eyes, always dark and impenetrable, had sunk deeper into his skull so that they were hidden pools, deep and unfathomable. As the flesh had fallen away so his scar, the terrorist's mark that always reminded Hirsh of Sachar's heritage, had become more prominent. It now lay like a brand across the old man's face.

Sachar seemed to sense the betrayal. He nodded at his protégé, a brief smile flickering at the corner of his mouth. No word passed between them but Hirsh, caught in the act of destroying the career of his mentor and friend, flushed guiltily as he walked past. He felt no satisfaction, not even a shedding of the guilt as he walked into the Prime Minister's office. He felt instead the shame of having betrayed his country and a terrible sadness that the man he had once loved should have seen the betrayal of their friendship.

In only three weeks, the Prime Minister's frustration had turned to fear. Since the beginning of the crisis he had fended off all the pressures from the hawks and doves in his fragile coalition and defended himself and his country against the critics from abroad, both Jews and goyim. But in the last few days his nerve had begun to fail him and a deep underlying pessimism that had seemed to colour so many of his thoughts in recent years began to dominate his thinking.

As the military failed him and the politicians squabbled endlessly with each other, he searched for a solution, yet at every turn his way seemed to be blocked. The terrorism had not been stopped but had got worse. The markets around the world had collapsed to levels that would have been unthinkable six months ago. Above all, there had been a propaganda and political onslaught against Israel the like of which he had not seen during his whole life of public service.

Then with the new round of poisoning he knew that this time the Palestinians were going to triumph. As the markets started to react, his ambassadors had begun to telephone and he knew that he was counting the days, perhaps even the hours remaining of his political life. Each ambassador spoke in the couched and guarded terms of international diplomacy. There was no sharp report as the bullet left the gun but the effect was just as deadly. The message was stark: either Israel compromised, they said, or she was doomed. This was not a war that Israel could win with military might or political guile, they argued. This was a time to accept reality, they suggested.

Then Hirsh Kronstein had appeared with the dreadful news of Sachar's stupidity. Even in that black moment of despair he understood what the old man had been trying to do for his country. He understood that Sachar had passed his prime and was operating not in the real world of the 1990s but in the half-remembered world of yesterday when Israel was the lion among sheep struggling to survive. Of course, his old friend would have to go and the reasons for his departure would leak. Better then to be honest about the problem so that everyone could search for a common answer.

The Americans would be horrified but he suspected that those stiff-necked Yalies in the State Department would be secretly rubbing their hands at Israel's embarrassment. Those schmucks have been looking for a way to force us to deal with the Palestinians and now we have handed it to them, he muttered to himself. There would be no need for the Americans to remind him of their failure. They would simply have to hint gently at the way the intelligence had been ignored and he would have little choice but to do what they wanted. There would be no moral high ground here, no reminders of the holocaust to play on the American public's feelings. They would pay dearly for Sachar's mistake.

The Prime Minister had survived so long in Israeli politics in part because of his intuitive understanding of the people, but also because he had the courage to face up to the tough decisions, to meet the challenges head on.

He drew a deep breath and reached out for the telephone. He was sad to note the tremor in his hand, the sign that now, when he needed it most, his body was betraying him. He began to dial the President of the United States.

*

Washington

The President was staring out of the Oval Office windows behind his desk. The view was stunning, taking in the Ellipse and the magnificent Washington Monument in the distance. It was perhaps the finest view in the city and one the President never tired of, despite the slight greenish tint to the vista produced by the two-inch-thick bullet-proof glass shielding him from potential snipers.

The trilling of the telephone brought him back to his desk. He lifted the telephone, cradling it between shoulder and cheek. When the operator told him that the Prime Minister of Israel was on the line, he took the call with a feeling of dread. He had never understood the Israelis. His firmly middle-class privileged East coast upbringing had produced a culture gap that made the insecurities, paranoia and routine rudeness of the Israelis incomprehensible. This crisis had done nothing to bridge the gulf. His attempts at persuasion had been met with thinly veiled insults and the mobilization of the Jewish lobby. He had not enjoyed any part of the relationship and secretly despised the Israelis as an untrustworthy bunch of bigots, a prejudice that had been reinforced by the new alliances forged with the Arabs after the Gulf war.

'Good morning, Mr President. I am sorry to disturb you this morning at what I am sure must be a difficult time.'

The formality of these conversations always seemed faintly ridiculous to Bush. Everyone talked as if the world from God on down was recording every nuance, dot and comma for history, which was probably exactly what was happening.

'I am calling with a message that is painful both for me and for my country.'

'Mr Prime Minister, we have known each other long enough and our countries have been allies for too many years for there to be any message that could cause pain between us. What is the trouble?'

'I have to tell you that there has been an error by our intelligence services. It appears that we had some information about this terrorist campaign before it began. If that information had been made available, it is possible that the affected countries could have taken action. It also appears that we

359

had information about the second stage of poisoning. That intelligence, too, was not made available.

'I heard about these lapses this morning and, of course, I have punished those responsible. As soon as I knew the extent of the damage, I telephoned you. I have learned that the new attacks are all aimed at products produced by the Kastel Sugar Co. I hope this information will be of help to you in controlling the damage.'

It was a small attempt to salvage something from the wreckage. But there was to be no forgiveness.

'If the State of Israel bears even partial responsibility for the appalling tragedies that have taken place in the past few weeks, there will be a heavy price to pay. Have you seen the latest television pictures of the dead and the dying, the panic in the world's financial capitals? When the world learns of your part in this, there will be outrage, an outrage which I share.'

The Israeli tried to interrupt. 'Mr President, I –'

'I do not feel any purpose will be served by discussing this further now. I need time to consider our position. I will get back to you later this morning.'

President Bush hung up the phone, took off his spectacles and rubbed his eyes. Sitting back in the chair his unfocused glance took in the bronze Remington sculpture of a cowboy astride a horse rearing before a rattlesnake. Just exactly how I feel, he thought.

The office intercom beeped to announce that the DCI had arrived for his morning appointment. The President moved out from his desk to greet Shaw as he came into the Oval Office through the door to his left. 'Good to see you, Matt. Come in.' He ushered the DCI towards one of the two chairs next to the fireplace at the far end of the room. The two men were overlooked by a stern George Washington, whose portrait hangs above the fireplace.

'Matt, I've just been speaking to the Israeli Prime Minister who tells me that their intelligence people screwed this one up. They had advance warning of the poisoning and for some unknown reason kept it to themselves.'

'Christ Almighty,' Shaw exclaimed. 'That's going to raise all kinds of hell when it gets out!'

'Well, we have to pre-empt that by taking some action.'
The President began ticking off his fingers. 'First, I'm going to
get those Israelis to Geneva. They've given us just the lever we
need and I'm not going to stand by while we get crucified for
their stupidity. Enough Americans have died already.

'Second, the Israelis say that the terrorists have targeted
products from the Kastel Sugar Co. this time round so we
can at least limit the panic.'

'But that means everything from raw sugar to pies to soft
drinks to baked beans,' Shaw protested. 'Just about everything uses sugar and how in hell are the public going to
distinguish between Kastel sugar and sugar from other companies? We're going to be telling the world to stop eating
sugar. It's impossible . . . Those bastards,' he added bitterly.

'Look, Matt, I know it's going to be tough but at least we
know the parameters of the problem and the FDA will have
something to get hold of. Anyway, we'll get people on to
that problem right after this.

'Third, we need to do something about Mr Abu Hassan. I
want that guy caught.'

Shaw judged his moment perfectly.

'Well, Mr President, we have some good news on that
front. It looks like we've pinned his location down to Tunis
and we think he's there now. I've sent in one of our men,
Bob Gearheart, the man who did such good work on the
finances of the operation.' The President nodded. 'He may
have a line into the terrorists. I would also like your authority
to send in ISA to back him up and to get Delta out there so
that we can take action if necessary.'

The President sat back in his chair, considering the implications of Shaw's request. Action in Tunis would annoy the
Tunisians but they could be sweetened with a few fighters or
some tanks. He'd call in the Congressional leaders and let
them know something was in the wind; nothing too specific
but enough to make them feel involved. If it worked, it
would be a triumph for his Presidency. If it failed, well, if it
failed he would at least have tried. The decision made, he
looked up at the DCI and met his questioning gaze.

'Do it.'

*

Fort Bragg

Major General Carl Stiner mounted the podium and faced the men of Delta Force seated below him. Stiner is the head of the Special Operations Command which has overall control of all US special forces in the army, navy and air force.

He had flown in that morning from his headquarters at McDill air force base near Tampa in Florida so that he could personally brief the men. Fort Bragg is a sprawling army base on the outskirts of Fayetteville in North Carolina. The town itself, a single dust-blown street offering massage parlours, tattooists, used cars and numerous seedy bars may be paradise to off-duty soldiers but it is in stark contrast to the base itself four miles further down the road.

Normally home to the 82nd Airborne, Bragg's heart is the Stockade, which is the headquarters of Delta Force. Protected by a high wire fence, security cameras and microwave detection devices, security is absolute. In fact Delta take these matters so seriously that the men are no longer allowed to park outside the buildings as overflying Soviet satellites might be able to gauge the level of activity by the number of cars in the car park.

The Stockade is where Delta men eat, work and sleep. It is a totally secure environment with a large grey windowless concrete building in its centre. On the roof of the building is a fifty-foot-high white communications bubble that allows Delta soldiers to communicate with headquarters by tiny hand-held radios from anywhere in the world. Inside the Stockade are live firing ranges, special rooms where the men can practise hostage rescue, an intelligence centre and communications room. But Stiner had passed all those to go to the briefing room where he now faced his audience of eighty men.

Stiner was a familiar figure at Fort Bragg and to the Delta veterans who had actually seen action in the past decade. It was he who had commanded the special forces when they intercepted the terrorists who had hijacked the cruise liner *Achille Lauro* in October 1985, and four years later he was in command of Joint Task Force South for the December 20, 1989 invasion of Panama. Both those operations had left Stiner with an abiding distrust of his political masters and little confidence in much of the equipment issued to his men, but he had learned lessons as well and he had determined that this one was to be kept as simple as possible, using only battle-proven equipment.

Now he stood before his men, a tall, tough veteran. His audience were mostly dressed in jeans and T-shirts, an informality common to all elite forces and a sign that they had been summoned at short notice to this briefing. Stiner was dressed in the light brown summer uniform of the US army, the rows of medals over his left breast evidence of his combat record, his short-cropped grey hair a sign of his special forces background and his flat stomach and broad shoulders a clear indication that this was no unfit deskbound general. A hush fell on the auditorium as he began to speak.

'This, men, is the one you have all been waiting for. This is The Big One.' There were a few chuckles in the audience. Stiner held up a large, calloused hand. 'No. I know you hear that each time you head out of here and I know that nine times out of ten you come back frustrated. But this time will be different. It's different because of the urgency. It's different because of the target and it's different because I'm here telling you it's different.'

A few real smiles appeared now, a recognition that the General had managed to get past some of the cynicism.

'You have all heard of the poisonings being carried out by the terrorist organization known as the Palestine Fighting Arm led by Abu Hassan. We have been trying to find Hassan for some weeks and we now have a lead on his location. We believe he is in Tunis and we also believe we will have him identified within the next forty-eight hours. As soon as he is identified your mission will be to go in and get him. We want Hassan back here for trial. But, more important than that, we want to know where the people actually doing the poisoning are. We believe only Hassan can tell us that.

'So, I want you to go in, get him out alive and get the information we need. This mission has been personally sanctioned by the President and I know he joins me in wishing you God speed and good luck.' Stiner gestured towards the front row. 'Now I'll hand you over to your mission commander, Colonel Andrew Duncan.'

Stiner stepped aside and moved to the front row as his position at the podium was taken by Andy Duncan, the commander of the Delta team and the man who would actually lead the men on the mission. Duncan was a veteran of Delta and one of the few in the team who had actually been under fire.

A graduate in psychology from Texas A & M, Duncan had initially joined the Rangers, but found they were simply a vast bureaucracy hooked on endless cycles of mind-numbing exercises of routines that had been established many years before. Seeking to test both his physical and mental capabilities, Duncan joined Delta, who were recruiting new blood in the aftermath of the 1980 Desert One disaster when they failed to rescue the American hostages in Tehran.

Shortly after qualifying, Duncan had taken part in Operation Urgent Fury, the 1983 invasion of Grenada designed to overthrow the government of Bernard Coard and restore democracy to the island. As part of the invasion force, a team from Delta had flown to Barbados on board C-5 transports. There they had reassembled their Black Hawk helicopters for an assault on Richmond Hill prison where a number of political prisoners were being held.

The men were due to assault the prison at dawn but in fact arrived five hours late and Duncan had watched as first one helicopter had been shot down by the alert Grenadian defence force and his own had crashed after running out of fuel. While the invasion force landed to the south, the Delta team had spent the day being fired at by Coard supporters until they were rescued. It had been an ignominious experience for Duncan and his men.

Since then, he had spent a year with the British SAS learning their techniques. That had been a salutary experience. Charlie Beckwith, Delta's first commander, had returned from his visit to the British at Hereford believing that muscle and technique combined to make a good special forces soldier. The result had been a unit of huge men all with eighteen-inch necks, massive chests and tiny waists who could all do 500 push ups before breakfast while whistling Hail to The Chief. They could also do many tasks brilliantly in practice because they had a rule book and a manual for every single eventuality. But Duncan learned from the SAS that Beckwith had completely misunderstood the nature of the British elite force. Certainly they were strong but the emphasis was not on muscle but endurance. And there was a great deal of technique but the training stressed that in real life manuals are hopeless because if plans can go wrong they do. Therefore the SAS taught their recruits to think and placed great value on individual initiative. How you get to a solution does not matter, they argued, as long as the answer solves the problem.

Duncan had tried to instil some of this radicalism back at Bragg and had largely failed. There was still a commitment to technology and technique because – as he had been told repeatedly – that was the American way of doing things.

Even with this frustration, Duncan had stayed with Delta as a home of excellence in a military that had little regard for individual achievement. Increasingly, too, he had seen that units like Delta would be used more and more as terrorism and the drugs business replaced the Soviet threat as a major Pentagon preoccupation. There could be opportunities in the future that he could exploit and this mission was one of them.

'Men, General Stiner has outlined for you the purpose of our mission. I will now tell you how we will achieve those goals.'

He pressed a button on the lectern and the first slide appeared on the six- by eight-foot screen that dominated the front of the room.

'For those of you who don't know where we're going this is Tunisia, a country on the north coast of Africa. It's about forty-five minutes flying time from the Nato base at Sigonella in Sicily which some of you may remember from the *Achille Lauro* mission.

'This time we will have the co-operation of the Italians so we should be left alone. Two hours ago we flew a Condor from the base and we should be able to provide you with an aerial shot of the target area in a moment.'

The Condor is the world's biggest unmanned aircraft with a wingspan of more than 200 feet, bigger than a 747 Jumbo jet. It was built by Boeing and flies at more than 65,000 feet with an endurance of several days using two six-cylinder

365

turbocharged piston engines which each produce 175 horse-power. The aircraft had first flown in 1988 and since then had apparently languished at Boeing headquarters in Seattle. In fact, the Special Operations Command had ordered two aircraft at $40 million each using secret 'black' funds.

In the past, special operations had faltered through lack of advance intelligence. The average flying time from the US to the Middle East is eight hours and Delta had been concerned about receiving accurate intelligence, a critical factor in any mission so that when the men actually go in to rescue the hostage he is in the building and the room where he was when the mission began.

The US government had approached a number of countries including Britain, France and West Germany to get agreement to position an advance force in Europe so that they would be available to gather intelligence in time of crisis. All the countries had refused and so Condor had come into service.

With its ability to fly over a target for several days, its intelligence-gathering was constant and timely. Sideways-looking radars could keep a target permanently in sight and cameras could photograph any target asked for by the aircraft's operators either at a nearby base or even back in America. In this instance the Condor's computers had been programmed to fly over Tunis and the surrounding coastline picking up intelligence on military bases, radar sites and airfields. As soon as the specific target could be identified, the Condor would narrow its flying cycle to relay back more detailed information.

Now Duncan pressed another button and a razor-sharp full-colour picture appeared on the screen showing a black Tarmac road unfolding below.

'That should be the coast road between La Goulette and Tunis,' Duncan explained. 'This is coming to us courtesy of a Keyhole satellite and then a Fort Meade relay. What you are seeing now is actually what the aircraft is seeing as it flies along.'

Duncan leaned to one side and spoke into a microphone attached to the desk. The picture on the screen changed instantly as the cameras closed in on the image 65,000 feet below. Evidently Duncan had told the operator to guide the cameras forward and then freeze-frame on an identifiable target as the screen was suddenly filled with a red-and-white road sign which read: 'Tunis 5 km'.

'The Condor should stay up there for the duration of this mission and the information will be fed to us as we move into position.'

Duncan pressed the button once more and the screen went blank.

'OK, gentlemen, enough of the film show. To business. The mission profile is clear. We stage in C-5s to Sigonella and then wait for the signal to go. We hope to receive a clear message within the next seventy-two hours. Current thinking is we'll use the Night Stalkers to take us in and we'll extract the same way taking Mr Hassan with us.'

There was a quiet buzz at this news. Duncan had just told the men that this would not be a sea landing, something which most disliked because of the unpredictable nature of the sea and the uncomfortable boats they had to use. Instead, they would be going by helicopter flown by men from Task Force 160, a 75-helicopter unit based at Fort Campbell in southwestern Kentucky. TF 160's motto is 'Death Waits in The Dark', a reminder to all who fly with them that their speciality is night flying. Indeed, TF 160 are probably the finest exponents in the world of the rarefied skill of flying at between fifteen and fifty feet over long distances at night skimming hedges, pylons and buildings. Delta Force had a healthy respect for the pilots of TF 160, a recognition of their courage and skill.

'We have a team from the Intelligence Support Activity on their way in right now and they should be feeding us some good intelligence by the time we get to Sigonella. You'll get a detailed briefing on landing.' He looked at his watch. 'Departure in one hour, ETA Sigonella 0630 local. Let's move it.'

October 8

THE INTELLIGENCE SUPPORT ACTIVITY were waiting for Bob when he stepped out of the terminal at Tunis airport and stood searching for a taxi.

The three men and a woman had arrived four hours earlier aboard a Gulfstream executive jet from Wiesbaden in Germany via Muscat in Oman. They had chosen the most obvious of covers to enable them to pass through customs and immigration with their luggage. The leader of the group was Sheik Mohammed bin Abdul Aziz who was travelling on a green Saudi Arabian diplomatic passport. He spoke fluent Arabic and answered the few questions from the immigration officer in the high Arabic of a member of the Saudi royal family. His three companions were described as 'bodyguards' (the men) and 'companion' (the blousy blonde woman). It was the perfect disguise, a scene so familiar to the officials at the airport that they passed through the checks without any difficulty.

Their luggage – there was of course a great deal of it – took up one taxi as the Sheik and his party piled into another. They checked into their hotel and then set about their real job. The blonde wig came off to reveal short cropped dark hair, the sheik shed his flowing, gold-edged white robe and changed into less obvious slacks, cream shirt and dark jacket. Unpacked, the cases revealed a bewildering array of equipment: cameras, listening devices, radios and four Glock 9 mm automatic pistols. Made entirely of plastic, these guns cannot be detected by any scanner.

The briefing given to the ISA team had been simple. They had each been handed a photograph of Bob and had been told to pick him up on entry into the country and feed all intelligence on the people he met and the places he stayed back to Washington.

By the time Bob arrived they were ready to do their job. Their brief was to follow him, protect him if necessary, and relay back any information that might be of assistance to the Delta team waiting at Sigonella. It was a fairly simple task for which the small team had been well trained. Tunis was a welcome assignment compared with others they had to do recently including the monitoring of drug barons in Colombia, two separate missions to try and spot a house in Beirut where the hostages were being held and the Panama operation where Noriega's goons had almost found them lurking in the shrubbery outside the Presidential palace.

Bob was a clear and obvious target and easy to follow. The taxi drove east from the airport, skirting the main city until it turned off the highway towards the sea and the prosperous outer suburbs of the capital. The ISA team were following in a Volkswagen camping van they had hired earlier from the local Hertz, ostensibly to go touring.

The taxi stopped in front of a large white stucco villa with high walls topped with glass and razor wire. As Bob paid off the taxi, the whine of a camera motordrive began inside the van as the woman photographer began recording his arrival at his destination.

Bob moved towards the locked iron gates and paused as if searching for a way in. He then moved to one side and spoke into a metal grille set in the left-hand wall. Whatever he said must have satisfied the hidden guard as the gates swung open and he disappeared inside.

For the Watchers the task now took on a familiar form. This routine was not the same as that familiar to the fiction writers. There was no huddling on street corners, notebook in hand surreptitiously to record every movement before searching for the loose change and a public call box. The world of surveillance has moved light years ahead of that tired image. Today, the ISA team relied on technology to make their job much easier and infinitely safer.

The telephone wires that arced away from the villa would be tapped so that all conversations would be heard by them and relayed by satellite first to Washington and then back over a different, secure, link to Delta at Sigonella. By means of a small dish, video pictures of the building and anyone coming in or out would be relayed back to base. At Fort Bragg, a computer known as SPY had been designed for precisely this situation. The computer has a comprehensive database that includes such essential information as the thicknesses of doors in key buildings that are potential targets and whether they open in or out, the design of all aircraft in commercial service and detailed designs of US embassies. And SPY also contains templates for the design of several thousand buildings around the world. Although each country has a different building style, certain basic parameters are common to all countries – bathrooms are frequently above kitchens, for example. This has allowed a database to be constructed that can take account of every variable in house design.

If the basic design is not in the database, details such as the construction of outside walls, the number of windows and the location of bathrooms can be manually entered into the system. The computer can then design the interior of the building setting a probability factor for accuracy which increase as more information is added. Each Delta unit takes a SPY terminal with them on their mission and can access the database so that a three-dimensional image of their likely target can be produced in the field.

As the gates closed behind Bob and he disappeared into the grounds of the villa, the sound of his walking up the gravel drive came clearly to the listeners outside. The noise was being relayed to them by the green Ball Pentel pen given to Bob before he left Langley. Perfect as a writing instrument, Bob had been told this was his court of last resort. A push of the blue button at the top would activate a homing signal. What he had not been told was that the pen was also a voice-activated microphone.

Although a stranger in a foreign land, arriving at the villa had been like coming home. Helen had greeted Bob with a warmth and an enthusiasm he had not seen in her for many years. The crisis and Bob's suffering had brought out the generous side of Helen's nature and, at the same time, this new intimacy had allowed Helen to confide her troubles to him. This alliance of circumstance and confidences had breached the barriers to produce a new intimacy.

Bob had been surprised to see the security surrounding the villa. The gates were enormous and clearly guarded by someone unseen who could vet arrivals via a hidden camera. Then, too, he had noticed a number of armed guards patrolling the grounds armed with sub-machine-guns and rifles. But security problems faded when Helen, alerted by the guards, came to the door to greet him. She was wearing jeans and a cream silk shirt, the combination a firm statement of her origins.

'Bob, how wonderful you're here at last.' She greeted him with a laugh revealing her firm white teeth. They embraced in that particular American way, arms around each other, her face to his chest; two old friends very pleased to see each other.

'God, it's good to see you,' Bob exclaimed to the top of her head. She responded with a squeeze from both arms before releasing him and stepping back.

'It's so wonderful that you've come to my home at last. It's just a pity that the circumstances aren't a little happier. Come in out of the sun and I'll show you around.'

As Bob moved through the carved oak front door, there was a patter of bare feet on the marble floor and around the corner ran his godson Abdullah. The boy stopped at the sight of the stranger and then ran to his mother clinging on to the back of her legs and peering out nervously at the tall white man.

He was a good-looking little boy, more Arab than American but with none of the fat that spoils the looks of so many Middle Eastern children. Instead he was slim and graceful with deep, dark eyes, a dark honey complexion and a mop of short, curly black hair. It was a year since Bob had seen him and during that time he had changed dramatically from a little boy taking the first tentative steps of childhood to a formed tiny adult. He was dressed in the flowing thaub of the Arab male, though this was more to do with the hot climate than any protest against his origins. He was too young to make such political statements but was happy to side with his father's preference for Arab dress against Helen's wish for the jeans and T-shirt of the American child.

Bob moved towards him, hand outstretched. Encouraged by his mother, he stepped gingerly forward and they shook hands briefly and formally.

'Hi, Abdullah. Remember me? I'm Bob. We last met when you came to New York and we went for an ice cream in Central Park after the visit to the zoo.' A tentative smile crossed the boy's face at the reminder. Bob reached into his shoulder bag and produced a box wrapped in brightly coloured paper decorated with pictures of clowns. 'I brought you a present from America.'

The boy thanked him and then tore off the wrapping to find a Transformer, a toy that looks like one object but then can change shape to become another, in this case a gorilla that transformed into a futuristic fighter complete with pilot and navigator.

Abdullah ran from the hallway towards the garden to play with his new toy and Bob and Helen followed at a more leisurely pace. Helen tucked her arm inside Bob's.

'I know you've come all this way to see Hamid but I'm afraid he's not going to be here until tonight,' she explained. 'Another business trip.'

Bob laughed lightly. 'Well, that suits me just fine. You can show me the sights. We can swim in the sea, stroll arm in arm along the sand and solve the problems of the world on our own.'

Helen smiled. 'Sure, Bob,' she replied sarcastically. 'We'll forget why you're really here and just pretend the real world doesn't exist. That's going to be a lot more difficult than you think.'

They had reached the patio of the house and the bench where a few nights earlier Helen had sat listening to the sound of the garden waterfall and reflecting on the past and her future. Since that awful evening when Hamid had dismissed her worries about their relationship and what she saw as his duty to fight terrorism, the gulf between them seemed to have become almost unbridgeable. Helen had withdrawn from Hamid and he from her.

The pressure of work at the Bank appeared to be sapping her husband's strength. He looked worn and had grown increasingly impatient with her attempts at casual conversation. Frequently, he had replied to her simple questions as if they were interrogations from an enemy rather than inquiries from a lover and wife. She could sense the tension in him and worried that he was actually going to raise a hand against her or throw something. The stress was clearly too much but he would not discuss it and there was nothing she could do to help.

Now, as she sat on the bench in the garden, looking out at the sea in the distance and watching the sun begin its gentle slide down towards the horizon, she could not help but contrast the two men in her life. The one calm, friendly and warm, the other distant, anxious and seemingly dismissive of her concern. It was quite apparent to Helen that Bob wanted to resume the relationship that had ended all those years ago when they were both so much younger. What was less clear was whether he was serious. Did he really care or was this just the thrill of the chase?

As if reading her thoughts, Bob took her hand in his and raised it to his lips, kissing each of her knuckles gently with his lips. He looked up to meet her questioning gaze.

'You know, Helen, I have been thinking a lot about us in the past few weeks. I suppose losing Mary has made me think about my life, where I'm going and why. I've come to the conclusion that all of it has been fairly pointless up to now.'

Helen began to protest.

'No, hear me out. I understand better the limited value of success at work, something you always talked about. I now know that success in that area can be dependent on the whim of some guy who sees me as a disposable asset. I'm just one of many working for a huge organization that can hire or fire me at will. I believe in what I do but belief is no longer enough. What is missing in my life is a woman to love and a family to care for. I'm just like everybody else, I guess. I want to have a reason for doing what I do. I want to be able to believe not in some abstract theory about countering terrorism abroad or in my country, however worthy that may be. Instead I want to believe in people.'

He paused, as if testing the weight of his words, balancing their import for offence and their tone for sincerity. He nodded, satisfied that what he had said sounded more honest than pompous.

'I've thought a lot about those days at Harvard when we both seemed to be made for each other. I've never really understood why it went wrong. You had windmills to attack and I hadn't found the confidence to fight my own corner. Hamid seemed romantic and to offer you a way of expressing yourself, of throwing off the conventions that family and friends had imposed on you.' He sighed deeply. 'God, those were great days. They were times when we believed everything was possible; when we believed in ourselves and each other. Life seemed to have a real purpose.

'In the past few weeks, I have rediscovered that purpose. I have watched you and Hamid and I can see how unhappy you are. Every time I see you distressed I want to do something to make you happy again. Every time I see you sad I want to cry, too. It's clear to me that my love for you never died, that time hasn't really healed the wounds. The more I see you the more I want you.'

He drew a deep breath.

'What I'm saying is that I would like us to have a second chance. I didn't fight hard enough to keep your love once before and I am not going to make the same mistake again. I know we could be happy together. We could live in Washington, bring up Abdullah in the States and maybe we could even have some children of our own. I know that's what I want and I know that would be right for us both.'

The speech over, Bob turned away from Helen and stared out towards the setting sun. He was frightened to face the answer he thought he had seen in Helen's eyes.

She took his hands in both of hers and spoke softly.

'I know just what you mean about those Harvard days. I look back on our time together and sometimes I think how mad I was to give up our love. But Hamid seemed to offer so much and, you're right, I was seduced by the idea of the grand gesture and the romance of it all.

'I know there are problems with my life here. I'm an American in a world of Arabs. I'm married to a man who is more Arab than American, who may wear Brooks Brothers suits in New York but really despises the trappings of the Western world. He is happier in Arab dress among his Arab friends being waited on by me dressed in Arab clothes. But he is still my husband and he is still Abdullah's father. We talked a few days ago about our problems and he said that in the next few weeks we may be able to move to the States. If that happened everything might be all right.

'You see, Bob, I have one real problem. I may have made a mistake with you one time, I don't want to make the same mistake again. So, you say you love me and maybe I love you too, but I'm married to my husband and I will not betray him and our child. I'm sure you can see that I shouldn't run away just because you have come riding over the hill on your white charger. I was weak and frivolous with our relationship and I won't do the same thing again.'

Bob had created and then embellished a fantasy of this conversation. Helen would have broken down, confessed her unhappiness and her recognition that salvation lay with him. Yet he knew such a happy outcome was unlikely, so Helen's reply was not unexpected. He felt a mixture of relief and discomfort. If Helen had agreed to abandon Hamid, Bob suddenly realized he would have had to confront the loss of his friend. Now he did not have to face the trade between the reality of true friendship and the possibility of future love.

Their conversation was – perhaps fortunately – interrupted by the arrival of one of the white-jacketed servants carrying a tray of drinks which he put on the table in front of them. As he bent over, Bob noticed the distinctive bulge of a concealed pistol tucked into the back of his trousers. As the man walked away, Bob asked Helen why it was necessary to have so many guards at the house.

'Hamid says that with so many of the PLO based in Tunis, there is always the danger of attack from one of the factions wanting to get access to cash belonging to another,' replied Helen. 'He says they might think he had access to that kind of money. And there have been a lot of robberies in houses along the coast so Hamid makes sure there are enough people around to look after us.'

'How many people do you have?' Bob asked curiously.

'There are around fifteen servants, most of whom double up as guards, so we are pretty well protected.'

Helen poured each of them a freshly squeezed lime juice and added a generous measure of gin. Taking their glasses, they walked to the end of the patio, to the railings that marked the border of the house with the scrub and sand that led down to the beach three hundred yards away.

Sigonella

For Andy Duncan, the past twenty-four hours had merged into one long blur of action. The flight from Fort Bragg had gone smoothly enough, the huge C-5 Galaxy transports taking him and his men in one hop to land at Sigonella on schedule. That had been the easy bit although even then there had been no opportunity to rest. The C-5s used by Delta were specially converted so that detailed intelligence could be fed continuously to the aircraft in flight. As a result, Duncan had been passed a stream of messages, photographs and intercepts all of which had been discussed with his intelligence officers in an attempt to thrash out an attack plan.

At the start of the journey, the conversations had been very general in nature: the terrain of Tunisia; the structure of the country's armed forces; the radars they would be facing and what counter measures were available; the best disposition of the men to mount an effective assault on a building from the air and the sea. But these had all been abstractions, the kind of planning that always happens among men who have no real objective but need to feel busy, to be seen to be doing something. The theory runs that it helps to reassure the men but the fact is it helps to reassure the officers who are generally more terrified than any of the other ranks and are grateful to have something to do.

By the time Duncan and his men arrived at Sigonella, the whole vast machinery that accompanies a US special forces mission had moved into gear. Ahead of the C-5 carrying Duncan and his Delta team was another loaded down with planning and logistics specialists from the Special Operations

Command. Duncan was impressed. On every other mission he had been on, the support guys had either arrived too late or never arrived at all. This time they seemed to have got their act together.

Then there was a whole support network from the 1st Special Operations Wing at Hurlburt Field, Florida, who had arrived laden down with spare rotors, fuel pumps, filters and engines to cater for what they hoped would be every eventuality. No one wanted to repeat the humiliating débâcle at Desert One in 1980 when two out of eight helicopters had broken down on the way to the first rendezvous.

Two other C-5s had landed with four Sikorsky MH-53J Pave Low III helicopters and two Bell OH-58D AHIP helicopters in their cavernous holds. The Pave Lows are the latest helicopters to have emerged from the investment in special forces equipment made during the Reagan years. Pilots are expected to fly these helicopters at no more than 100 feet carrying eleven fully armed soldiers. The pilot operates entirely from instruments depending on an infrared system that projects an image of what lies directly ahead; a vertical radar display that shows what may lie above the aircraft's altitude; and a moving map display that is slaved to the central navigation system and scrolls forward as the aircraft heads towards its destination. While the pilot monitors the cockpit displays, the co-pilot relies on night-vision goggles and his eyes to peer ahead and give warning of any hazards the computers might have missed.

The OH-58D is designed to give fire support to the transport helicopters. It looks tiny but packs a formidable punch, including twelve 2.75 inch rockets and a 12.7 mm machine-gun. All the weapons can be aimed using a sighting system fitted on to a mast above the aircraft's rotor.

As Duncan had walked out through the enormous uptilted nose of his Galaxy he had heard the distinctive low whistle of the AC-130H Spectre gunship coming in to land. These aircraft would provide the real muscle if this operation ever came to a serious shooting match. The latest gunship, like its predecessors, is built on the fuselage of the ancient transport workhorse, the C-130 Hercules. But there the resemblance ends. The front end of the all-black aircraft has a round pod giving it the appearance of a bad-tempered dolphin. The new nose houses a number of different radars to allow the aircraft to fly in all weathers and see clearly in night or day. Other pods dotted around the fuselage enable the plane to jam any known radar system and to guide its formidable array of weapons to their target.

Each of the Spectres is armed with two 20 mm Vulcan cannons mounted just behind the flight deck, a 40 mm Bofors cannon mounted amidships, and a 105 mm howitzer mounted near the rear ramp. The Vulcans can fire 5,000 rounds per minute while the Bofors can deliver about 100 rounds a minute. However, the figures are theory rather than practice as firing such a volume not only depletes the ammunition stocks but sends the aircraft skittering sideways across the sky making accurate fire very difficult.

As Duncan stepped out on to the Tarmac, the helicopter pulled up a few feet away and he could see the distinctive Spectre motif painted on the side just below the cockpit, a green half-moon background with a white skeletal head and bony arms embracing a Vulcan cannon that was spewing yellow flame. Behind the head flowed blue flames. It is a frightening image that reflects the picture the Spectre crews have of themselves. They refer to the aircraft as 'The Devil in Disguise'.

By the time the second Spectre had landed to complete the mission inventory, more than 400 men were on the ground at Sigonella. The equipment was secured in a large corrugated hangar at the end of Runway Bravo. Once the helicopters were safely hidden inside the hangar away from the prying eyes of overflying satellites, the C-5 took off for Ramstein in Germany.

Delta took over a corner of the hangar and set about the task of preparing a detailed mission profile so that when they left Sicily each man would know his exact role in the operation; each helicopter would have a flight plan accurate to the nearest metre; and each Spectre gunship would have a list of targets in order of priority.

It never ceased to amaze Duncan just how much intelligence was available once the questions were asked of all the resources available to the United States. From the National

Reconnaissance Office came satellite photographs of Tunisia and Tunis so detailed it was possible to read the road signs. From the CIA came intelligence on what the President of Tunisia's itinerary was for the next week, the composition of his cabinet and a country profile including the prospects of a coup within the next twelve months (forty per cent). The DIA delivered a detailed profile of the armed forces, including the breakdown of different units, their training and firepower. The NSA sanitized its intercepts but still managed to appear knowledgeable about all aspects of the country including the location and status of all Palestinians living in Tunisia, the conversations leaders of the PLO had had within the past week both inside the country and with allies abroad.

Stunning as much of this information was, most of it was useless. The sheer volume of the information – hundreds of thousands of words and hundreds of photographs – was beyond the ability of the intelligence cell to absorb, let alone incorporate into a plan.

What Duncan wanted was the location of the target and real-time intelligence telling him when the target would be on site. That had begun to appear shortly after they left Bragg. In a conversation with Stiner at Bragg, Duncan had learned that Hassan was expected to be in Tunis at 1930 local on the night of October 8th. The Condor had been programmed to overfly the target and for the past six hours had been relaying full-colour video pictures of the target and the surrounding area.

In the short time available, the Delta intelligence cell had constructed a rough outline of the target zone and Duncan had been able to plan the assault. He had settled on an airborne attack using the Pave Lows to deliver his men to within a few hundred yards of the target. The OH-58Ds would provide covering fire and the Spectres would control any threat posed by an army base situated five miles west of the target.

Now the plans had been finalized and the intelligence was clear, the men had been given their tasks and the final briefing was Duncan's responsibility. He stood up on a makeshift wooden podium in front of his men and their pilots.

His men were dressed in their all-black, fireproof coveralls, webbing harnesses festooned with grenades, ammunition, radios and first-aid packs. Each man carried his personal weapon, a sidearm and another piece of equipment. For some it was a sniper rifle, for others a mortar tube or a heavy machine-gun. The faces were blackened so all Duncan could see as he surveyed his troops was the bulky shapes of his men and the occasional glitter of the white of an eye reflected in the glow from the aircraft standing behind.

'The latest from the Condor and the men on the ground is that it is all systems go,' he said above the noise of last-minute preparations aboard the aircraft which echoed around the vast hangar. 'We are now at zero minus fifteen and ETA is 1930. Our mission is to capture Hassan and get him back for interrogation. Time is short so there will be no time for Mr Nice Guy. We'll need what he has and we'll need it fast.

'Thirty minutes ago I received a message from the President which I would like to share with you.' He unfolded a yellow signals form. 'It reads: "The men of Delta Force are recognized as the finest troops in the United States military. I am trusting you with this mission knowing that you can succeed where others might not. My thoughts are with each one of you this night. God speed."'

Duncan paused and then came to attention. 'Gentlemen. "The Star Spangled Banner".' His right hand snapped up to his forehead in a parade ground salute as the first words of America's national anthem echoed around the hangar.

When Charlie Beckwith had sent his men to rescue the hostages held in Iran, he had made them sing the national anthem in a hangar just like this outside Cairo. After the mission failed, that ceremony had been ridiculed, as had the performance of Delta itself. But for the men the ceremony had not been ridiculous at all but a simple affirmation of faith and pride in the country they served. It had swiftly become a tradition in Delta that, before any operation, the men would sing 'The Star Spangled Banner'. It was now not just a gesture of affirmation but a message to all those outside the elite that Delta didn't care what anyone else thought.

So now as night fell on Sigonella, work stopped in the hangar as mechanics, intelligence analysts, pilots and aircrew came to attention and picked up the refrain.

380

Washington, DC

It was still only early afternoon in Washington. Just after lunch the President had got the call he had been hoping for from Dick Cheney, his Defense Secretary. He had left the White House and made the fifteen-minute journey to the River entrance of the Pentagon. There he had been met by Cheney and Colin Powell. The two men, accompanied by the ever-present Secret Service agents, walked past the security checks, the bomb detectors and the door behind which twelve heavily armed Marines were permanently waiting to pounce on a potential adversary.

Thirty paces ahead of the small party, underneath the spreading wings of a bald eagle, was the sign 'Joint Chiefs of Staff'. This is the heart of the American war machine, the place where the wars are planned, the men dispatched and the battles fought. Bush passed through the glass doors, past another security check, along a passage and then through two huge plain steel doors, the hiss of air as they opened plainly indicating a pressurized area.

Down a short flight of stairs, another passage, another security check and then the President stepped into the National Military Command Center, known affectionately to the men who work there as the Hole.

It is in fact several holes, one piled on top of another, going seven floors underground, each of them built to withstand a nuclear explosion.

Underneath the Center itself, where the President took one of the large padded chairs in the front row of the auditorium, is a communications centre, intelligence unit and a number of war-fighting centres for the different branches of the services.

Facing the President were four enormous screens, each measuring fifteen feet by twelve. On the left-hand screen was a locator map of North Africa; the next one showed the scene from inside the hangar at Sigonella; the third the view from the Condor flying over the area and the final frame had an outside view of the target taken by the ISA team.

In front of the President and his team were telephones on small stands and single microphones on flexible metal stems.

A touch of a button links any of the men with the communications room below. From there calls can be patched anywhere in the world where there is a telephone or a radio. Simultaneously the President could have a conference call with Delta in Sigonella, ISA in Tunis, Stiner in Fort Bragg and the Israeli Prime Minister in Tel Aviv. This was American technology at its most awesome.

All the pictures were coming over live in full colour so the President was able to see the events he had set in motion unfolding before him.

This, he thought, is the real responsibility of command. No other general in history has sent his men out and been able to watch their triumphs or their failures as they happen.

The final chorus of 'The Star Spangled Banner' faded away and the men of Delta Force moved off to their allotted positions.

Bush turned to Powell. 'Can I speak to the officer in charge of those men?'

'Certainly, Mr President.' Powell leaned forward and pressed a switch on the microphone in front of him. He talked softly for a moment and sat back. Two minutes later the picture of Andrew Duncan appeared on the left-hand screen.

Powell turned to the President. 'His name is Colonel Andrew Duncan. He's with Delta and you're patched through his helmet communications so he can hear you fine.'

'Colonel Duncan, this is President Bush. I wanted to tell you, son, that you and your men are America's finest. The mission you have agreed to do will be both difficult and dangerous. I am confident that you will be successful.'

'You can rely on the men from Delta, Mr President.' Duncan brought his hand up in a perfect drill salute and turned away.

The President sat back, ready to watch the show.

Tunis

Hamid had arrived. He had rushed into the house, the speed of his walk making his Arab dress stream out behind him. A quick embrace for Helen and double handshake for Bob and he was gone again to shower and change. In the brief time he had been in the room, the house had seemed charged with his energy. Bob noticed that the lassitude that seemed to have haunted him in the past few weeks had been replaced by a renewed enthusiasm for life that contrasted starkly with the repressed and withdrawn personality Bob had become used to.

Helen had also noticed the difference. 'This trip must have been a triumph,' she remarked to Bob as they strolled out on to the patio. 'I've never seen him so full of energy.'

For the first hour of dinner the conversation focused on the little boy, his every wish granted until his stomach began to rebel against the assault. He quietened down then and sat at the table playing with his toys, transforming Bob's gift from gorilla to a space-age fighter ace battling to save the world.

The conversation turned once more to the purpose of Bob's visit. 'Hamid, you may have guessed why I've come over from DC,' he began tentatively.

'I assume that you want some information, old friend,' Hamid replied. There was an undercurrent to his voice, a hint of something that Bob could not quite place. Resentment perhaps? Dislike, even? Certainly, Bob saw a cold half-smile flit across Hamid's face. 'After all, that's usually why you get in touch so I suppose this trip is no different.'

'That's a little unfair, Hamid. Sure, we've talked a lot in the past few weeks but you have to admit the circumstances have been a little unusual. If friends can't help out in time of trouble then who can?'

Without pausing to hear an answer to this rhetorical question, Bob pressed on.

'Hamid, I know that Helen has already spoken to you about helping us in the hunt for the terrorists and I can quite understand the difficult position you are in. But let me try and persuade you.

'When I left Washington the deaths from these poison attacks had passed the 250 mark. Losses in the international markets had topped $50 billion. Businesses are going bankrupt all around the world and if this continues thousands of jobs are going to be at risk and maybe hundreds more lives.'

Hamid grunted dismissively and Bob hurried on.

'Well, you might not care very much about that. But what about the Palestinians? They're your people and you keep telling us how much you care about them. Well, they have been exposed as a bunch of murdering terrorists and the chances of them getting their precious homeland are less now than they have ever been, thanks to Abu Hassan, terrorist at large and enemy of the Palestinians.

'We know that his main contact is in your Bank right here and that you could help us with information that could lead us to him. I am asking you for help. I am asking you as one civilized human being to another for your help in stopping the killing. And I am asking you as a friend.'

Hamid, apparently unmoved by the arguments and the plea, reached across the table to pick a cigar from the mahogany humidor. Carefully cutting the end, he lit it with a match and blew a thin plume of blue smoke towards the fan whirring in the ceiling. When he spoke, he did so softly, reflectively, almost as if he were speaking to himself.

'You talk of friendship, of civilization and loyalty and yet you really know nothing of these things. You argue about deaths and terrorism and jobs and business losses and in the same breath you talk about the Palestinians. You clearly know nothing of this either. I am a Palestinian and I have walked through the refugee camps and down Wall Street and I understand both worlds. So, let me share a little of my knowledge with you.'

He looked directly at Bob, his eyes appearing to take on new life as they met those of his old friend, a passion briefly glimpsed as if Hamid had drawn back a curtain only to close it again swiftly. Hamid's voice rose as a new heart entered his voice.

'You talk of 250 deaths. Well, I can talk of 2,000 in the Intifada alone and countless thousands more who have died not just in war but from starvation, from torture in Israeli jails, from wars between Arab and Jew. You talk of money lost and businesses bankrupt. Well, I can tell you of a nation that was once the business heart of the Middle East, of a

Palestinian nation that was to the Arabs what the Jews once were to the Europeans. Now they have lost it all.'

Hamid produced a deep, forced laugh with every tone dripping sarcasm.

'And you talk to me about the Palestinians and Abu Hassan.' His fist crashed on the table, startling Helen and Bob and making Abdullah drop his toy with a clatter on the floor. 'You say that the Palestinians have been exposed as terrorists. You say that they have no chance of getting a homeland. You say that Abu Hassan is no friend of the Palestinians. You say all these things and you know nothing.

'I say that the Palestinians have become terrorists because the role was forced upon them. I say that Abu Hassan has saved the Palestinian nation from a future of misery, despair and oppression at the hands of the Zionists.'

Bob tried to interrupt, to contradict the lies, but Hamid was not to be stopped.

'Ha. You are going to say that this is just rubbish, the dreams of a man who has been deceived by his own people.'

Hamid paused, with a flourish dabbed some ash from his cigar on to the plate in front of him, leaned back and embraced both Bob and Helen in an expansive, confident smile.

'You see I know that today the Israelis gave in. They have announced that tomorrow they will sit down in Geneva with Arafat and the Americans. They have said they are prepared to negotiate a deal. And not just any deal but a deal along the lines demanded by Abu Hassan.

'Today is a great victory for Abu Hassan and the Palestinians. And you ask me to betray my people and their saviour in our moment of triumph?

'Never. Never. This day above all days I am proud to be a Palestinian.'

Twelve miles down the road, Yasser Arafat was packing. Four hours earlier he had received a call from the American State Department informing him that the Geneva peace conference was on and his lifetime's work was going to be realized.

As he opened his wardrobe cupboard, he cast a critical eye

over the fifteen green and khaki uniforms that hung there. He pursed his large lips, hand flicking the hangers along the rack. Military or Arab? he wondered. As always he chose the compromise of military uniform to symbolize the armed struggle and the checkered head scarf of the Palestinian. He could see it all now, the conference, the media, the magnanimous victory speech, the triumphant return. It was a wonderful vision, one that he had hardly dared allow himself to dream in recent years and it was all coming true.

He wanted to shout, dance, do something to show his exuberance, his joy. Instead, as he carefully folded his uniform into his bag, zipped it shut and headed for the door, gripping his Samsonite case in one hand, Adidas sports bag in the other, a favourite song from his student days sprang from his subconscious.

In the days of exile in Cairo, he had been an avid fan of the cinema. He was forced to watch the dull revolutionary films from the Eastern bloc but for preference he chose American movies, sneaking out to catch the latest Disney. When *The Wizard of Oz* came to town he had naturally queued to see it expecting another lightweight fantasy. Instead he had found an allegory directed at him. He was Dorothy walking down the Yellowbrick Road to the Oz of Palestine. His faithful followers helped him along the way until in the end he would confront the Wizard of Israel. Again and again he would return to the cinema mouthing the words of the song and clapping his hands as Dorothy discovered that the Wizard was human after all.

So now, as he walked off to the meeting that would change his world, he found himself singing in his off-key guttural English: 'Oh, we're off to see the Wizard, the wonderful Wizard of Oz. We're off to see the Wizard . . .'

Through his night-vision goggles in the lead Pave Low helicopter, the sea below appeared as a green shimmering mass. Duncan could see ahead of them the occasional flicker of light as the goggles picked up the bright beam of a car's headlights moving along the coast road. They were now fifteen miles from the coast skimming fifty feet above the sea. Looking to left and right Duncan could see Tigers 2 and

3, the other Pave Lows with his Delta Force on board. A fourth Pave Low was tucked behind them, ready to provide cover in case of accident.

Behind and slightly above them the two Bell OH-58Ds flew in a tight formation ready to sprint ahead or dart up to provide covering fire for the force.

'Tiger 1, this is Leopard 1.' Duncan heard the voice of the commander of the lead Spectre gunship in his earphones. 'Breaking right. Now. Good luck. Out.'

The pilot of Tiger 1 pressed his on/off switch twice to acknowledge the message without breaking radio silence.

Duncan looked ahead and saw the lighter image of the surf and the beach and then the darker shape of the ground behind. The co-pilot tapped his arm and indicated a line of instruments in front of him. He saw a flashing green cursor appear in the centre of one of the television screens. The navigator rolled a ball on the dashboard in his hand and the cross hairs on the television screen moved to cover the flashing cursor. The navigator spoke into his microphone.

'Looks like those boys from the ISA have done their stuff.'

Duncan knew that ISA had promised them a laser beam to guide them the last few miles to target and the cursor showed that the aircraft had picked up the signal. The navigator had slaved the computer to the laser beam and unless the pilot overrode the technology, the helicopter would simply ride the beam down to the target.

Duncan removed his earphones and backed down to the cabin. He held up five fingers to indicate to the ten men hunched in the main cabin that the countdown had begun. The men nearest the two sliding doors unlocked the safety catches and slid the doors open. Immediately the cabin was filled with the roaring wind generated by the forward movement of the helicopter. There was a brief stomach-lurching dip and the helicopter rushed towards the sea before the pilot corrected for the change in drag and brought it back to an even keel.

Duncan was counting the seconds away in his head. As he reached three minutes, he held his hand up again, this time to show only two fingers. His men stood up and began to shuffle towards the doors. The normally slim Delta troopers were made obscenely fat by the weight and bulk of their equipment. Pouches were filled with ammunition, grenades and emergency medical supplies. Each man had two knives, one strapped low down on the left thigh and the other strapped hilt down across the chest. A pistol at the belt and for most the security of another, smaller, gun at the ankle as a court of last resort. But the real firepower was strapped across each man's chest. For the first four men on either side of the lead helicopters this was the Heckler and Koch MP5. This time the normally stubby weapon had been extended and expanded by the fitting of a bulbous silencer. If the first team in had to kill, they wanted to do it quietly.

Each man wore a complicated harness that strapped across shoulders, chest and thighs. A rope ran through a central clip and was knotted to a rail just above the door.

As Duncan took in his men, checking each of them to make sure that nothing had been forgotten, no pocket left unbuttoned, he thought they looked like members of some bizarre cult of fetishists or invaders from some subterranean world. Their gas masks had huge swollen eyepieces giving the impression of a person used only to seeing in the dark while the ropes, pouches and guns looked frightening, as indeed they were supposed to.

As the men moved to the doorway the pitch of the aircraft changed and the forward movement slowed. Four men on each side moved out on to the landing skids as the pitch of the helicopter blades changed again and the aircraft steadied into a hover.

Washington, DC

Six thousand miles away, President George Bush had watched the image on the second screen change from the hangar at Sigonella to the cabin of the helicopter. Then by some sleight of technology he had been in the cockpit with Duncan following every stomach-churning swoop and turn of the aircraft on its course to target.

All the communications between the different groups,

Delta and Sigonella, the ISA team and the JCS staff, were being relayed through speakers in the Command Center so sound effects supported the moving image.

The scene was somehow made all the more disturbing by the contrast of the imagery. To the left remained the static map of the region; to the right the Condor's bird's eye view and then the image from the ISA team. Bush felt his brain struggle to absorb the barrage of information as the operation accelerated towards the confrontation he had set in motion.

'Quite a change from my flying days,' Bush muttered to Cheney. Then, as the helicopter hit an updraft and his stomach swept upwards in sympathy, he continued, 'I think I preferred carrier landings with the Navy than sitting watching this.'

As the helicopters came in towards the coast, and there was a reference point other than the black of the sea, the operation seemed to speed up, accelerating towards a conclusion. As the helicopters moved over the target, the President's eyes switched to the Condor's screen. He could see the dark shapes of the helicopters in line astern, the flashes of their exhausts clearly visible on the infrared image. Then the picture changed again and he could see the hot shapes of bodies moving down and away from the choppers. His hands gripped the padded edge of his chair, the knuckles whitening. The die was cast.

Tunis

To recover from Hamid's onslaught, Bob had taken a sip of the lime juice in front of him. Before he had time to reply, Hamid continued in a milder tone.

'You came to ask me about George Bakr. I know you think I've been unhelpful but that's not really true as you will now see.'

There was a brief movement of his hand underneath the table and Bob heard a bell ring somewhere outside. A moment later the door opened and a tall, slim man walked confidently into the room. He came round the table and stood next to Hamid.

'May I introduce George Bakr.' Hamid gestured to the newcomer. 'You wanted to ask him some questions. Well, here he is. Ask away.'

Before Bob had a chance to speak to the man whom he had been hunting for so long, the door burst open and one of the servants rushed into the room. There was a rapid gabble of Arabic and Hamid looked startled, leapt from his chair and strode quickly to the window. He looked intently through the glass for a few moments, head cocked to one side, and then turned back into the room. There was a further burst of Arabic and the servant ran out, his hand reaching back and behind underneath his jacket to draw his pistol.

Bob could hear confused shouting outside as the servant transmitted the message he had received from Hamid.

'What's going on? Is there some kind of trouble?' Helen asked.

'You could say that,' Hamid replied. 'I think we might be under attack. I have just seen what looks to me to be a helicopter fly past the window and the servant tells me that our friends at the air force base down the road have telephoned to say that they have picked up some unusual signals on their radar.'

Hamid sounded almost fatalistic, as if the news was not unexpected.

As the helicopter hovered, its nose inclined slightly upward, the first of the Delta men kicked a coil of rope out of the aircraft and jumped out of the cabin. In five seconds all eight of the first wave had followed and ten seconds after that Duncan himself was on the ground.

His men had been told there would be between fifteen and twenty guards armed with automatic weapons and there might be some guard dogs. But wherever the guards were they must have been taken completely by surprise as there had been no shooting.

Then ahead, at the corner of the house, his night goggles picked up the ghostly white shape of a man emerging in a crouch from the protection of the building. He was followed by two more in quick succession. Duncan swiftly moved his weapon forward, instinct driving the reaction as the goggles relayed the threatening movements ahead of him. Even as he brought his Heckler and Koch round to fire, his military mind noted that the men ahead were running in that quick, jerking, crablike style of trained infantrymen the world over.

He heard a succession of light coughs, as if a well-trained butler were trying to attract the attention of his sleeping master, and the first of the men in front of him jerked wildly and then fell over backwards. His goggles could even pick up the spray of hot blood which appeared as a green splash across and to the side of the body as the arteries pumped out the man's life.

The enemy were shooting back now. He could hear the sharp crack of automatic pistols and the deeper bark of heavier machine-guns. Over the tactical radio net he could hear the sounds of war: the grunting, gasping noises of men under stress drawing breath; the occasional cry of excitement or pain as a target was hit or an enemy bullet struck home.

Duncan knew that victory for his men was only a matter of time. They had the advantage of surprise and darkness. In addition, the silencers on their guns suppressed the muzzle flash so the enemy could see nothing, only hear the whipcrack of the bullets as they passed nearby. Without any flash to guide them, the enemy was shooting blind while Delta could both see the shooters and detect the flash of the guns being fired which showed as a succession of bright green flashes of light through the goggles.

Suddenly Duncan felt a blow to his side and was pushed back towards the ground. I'm hit. I'm hit, was his first panicked thought and his hand had even started to reach behind for his medical pack when he felt the tugging and heard the snarl. Then the shock and the pain hit his right forearm as the dog bit deep.

Training did not include lessons in fighting well-trained guard dogs but the atavistic killer instinct normally dormant in man was bubbling just below the surface that night. Duncan's left hand reached for his chest and pulled the hunting knife from its clip sheath. He stabbed right and felt the blade bounce off the dog's skull. He stabbed again and again, plunging the eight inches of blade deep into the animal's flesh and then twisting the blade before pulling it out to stab again. It was a brutal and bloody business that could have only one end. With a final paroxysm, the dog bit down hard and deep on Duncan's arm drawing a cry of agony from his lips before its jaws slackened and it fell back to the ground dead.

The fight seemed to have gone on for minutes but had in fact lasted only fifteen seconds. As Duncan came back up on to one knee he saw that all three of the men who had emerged from the building were now dead and his unit had headed towards the house. He stood up and ran towards the building.

At the first sound of automatic rifle fire, Bob saw Bakr move away from Hamid and head for the door. As he came past, the weeks of tension and frustration exploded. The memory of the dead and the dying, his own personal humiliation at the hands of Matt Shaw, Helen's misery and Hamid's betrayal welled up in a subconscious focus of hatred. Bob pushed his chair back and reached for the terrorist, determined to prevent him escaping. His hand grabbed the sleeve of the suit jacket and the movement was enough to disturb Bakr's forward motion. The two men tumbled back against the table knocking glass, plates and cutlery to the floor.

Bakr reacted with the instincts of the trained killer, turning quickly, his left hand coming up and then down in a savage chopping motion. Bob felt agonizing pain flare up his arm as the shock moved out from his wrist. His fingers spasmed, opening and freeing the jacket, allowing Bakr to power towards the door. Right arm trailing, Bob moved after him. Two fast strides and he was behind the terrorist just as Bakr reached out for the door. Bob punched forward, driving his shoulder into the back of the fleeing man who fell forward carried by his own momentum. Bakr's shoulder hit the door first and then his head cracked into the wood. He reeled back, leaving a smear of blood from a broken nose tarnishing the highly polished surface.

Bob could hear Helen screaming as he fell backwards pushed over by Bakr. Bob hit the ground with the weight of his opponent crushing out his breath in a huge 'woof' of expelled air, winded.

Effective hand-to-hand combat depends on training, reach and calm under stress. The advantage, then, always lies in the fitter and better trained man. But once distance is compressed and panic sets in, training counts for naught and amateur and professional fight on nearly equal terms.

So it was with Bob and Bakr. The terrorist's early advantage had been lost once the two men fell to the floor, the one winded and the other stunned and bleeding from his contact with the door.

Both men knew this was a fight to the finish which only one could survive. For a few seconds, both sought advantage, pushing, punching, thrusting and heaving like two children struggling for supremacy in a playground tussle. Then Bakr drove a fist into Bob's kidneys and the blinding pain forced Bob back, hands slack, chest heaving.

Bakr used the opportunity well. His hand reached up to the back of his neck and in one smooth movement pulled a long, thin-bladed knife from the sheath concealed underneath his jacket. There was no hesitation now, just the certainty of victory. Bob could see the eyes focus and compress as Bakr prepared for the final, deadly thrust. Frantically, Bob's fingers scrabbled along the carpet, searching for something, anything with which to defend himself. He felt something. No time now to question, to think. His fingers closed and his hand jerked off the floor, all his strength powering towards the grimacing head above him.

The fork hit Bakr in the centre of the cheek, the force of the movement sufficient to push it deep inside. Bakr's mouth opened to emit a shocked cry of pain and Bob could see the tines of the fork which had gone straight through the cheek and now filled his mouth.

Bakr swayed. Bob twisted the fork, desperately struggling to maintain the initiative, but he had used his opportunity and it was not enough. Bakr, his mouth now a horrible, bloody grimace, drew back the knife, almost slowly now, confident that Bob had nothing left. Bob felt the first prick of the blade at his throat, the first push of the incision that would cut his throat.

A shot rang out and Bob saw Bakr's head explode. His face disintegrated, blood, mucus and brains sprayed out, pouring over Bob's face. The body was pushed forward, the bloody head coming to rest alongside Bob's. Revolted, chest heaving, he pushed the corpse to one side, sat up and vomited, the tension and revulsion spewing out of him.

Still panting he looked up and met the horrified gaze of Helen, with Abdullah's tiny head huddled into her shoulder. His eyes shifted and he saw Hamid looking down at him, a small pistol still smoking in his hand.

'Christ, Hamid. Thanks.' The gratitude came out in short gasps as he struggled to regain his breath.

Hamid said nothing as he sat, his head cocked on one side listening to the firing outside, a small smile flickering across his face.

Bob could hear the bullets hitting the building, the screams of agony and then, after a final burst of firing, silence. Bob pushed himself painfully up from the floor. As his head appeared above the level of the table he could see that Hamid had laid his pistol down and was now toying with a cigar, a half-full glass of lime juice at his right hand.

'For Christ's sake, Hamid, what the hell is going on here?' Bob shouted. 'The world is blowing itself to pieces out there and in here, and you're sitting there as if there's just been a small interruption to the dinner party!'

'Well, in a manner of speaking that's right,' Hamid replied, the small smile once again in evidence. 'I assume that the people outside are either Americans or Israelis. But whoever they are, they are too late. They may win this piffling little battle but I have won the war.'

Just then, Bob heard the door crash open. He turned to see a figure dressed all in black roll through the door to be followed by another coming from the opposite direction. Both men came up on one knee, their guns searching the room, seeking a target. Finding none, Bob heard a muffled voice from inside one of the masks and through the door walked another man. Bob saw that his right hand was dripping blood steadily on to the marble floor.

'Good evening, lady and gentlemen. My name is Andrew Duncan, Colonel, US Army. I'm sorry to interrupt the party.'

'Just what the hell is going on here?' Bob stood up, outrage giving his voice a harshness that was part anger, part relief.

'Ah, you must be Bob Gearheart,' said Duncan. 'I was told you would be here. I'm sorry for the inconvenience.'

'Well, you're too late. The man you want is lying there.' Bob gestured towards George Bakr.

'That guy is George Bakr, right?'

'Yeah, that's right,' Bob replied.

'Good. That's what I thought. Then we're in great shape. The man we really came to see is your host. You know him as Hamid Nazari but I know him as Abu Hassan.'

There was a moment while neither Helen nor Bob fully understood what Duncan had said. Then, when comprehension broke through, they both started shouting at once, instinct rebelling against what they had been told, the room filling with their denials on behalf of Hamid Nazari, the man they had known for so long as friend and lover and, more recently, as saviour.

Duncan raised a bloody hand. 'Now wait a minute, folks. Let me just explain one or two things to you so that you'll come quietly and then we've gotta go.

'First off the conversation you had with Mr Nazari when he arrived here was picked up and relayed through the computers back in Washington. They already had matched his voice from a conversation he had with Bakr several days ago and with his friends in Germany. Our guys outside covering you relayed the last lot and that was the final confirmation we needed that Mr Nazari here is really Abu Hassan.

'You've been kind enough to transmit to us all the conversations that have been going on in here since you arrived.' Duncan reached over and plucked the green Pentel pen that Matt Shaw had given Bob back in Washington for use as an emergency signal. 'This little beauty is a pretty good microphone that our guys outside picked up so we knew just where you and your friends were from the second you touched down in Tunisia.

'Finally, take a look at your good friend Mr Nazari. He ain't denying he's Abu Hassan. In fact, if you ask me, he's rather pleased with the idea.'

Bob turned to look at Hamid and, sure enough, he was

still sitting at the head of the table, a satisfied smile playing around his mouth. He spoke in answer to Bob's accusing look.

'Well, Bob, it seems that my secret is out. I am Abu Hassan, the man who designed the greatest and most successful campaign ever waged by the Palestinian movement. The victory we talked about earlier is my victory. I have won the war for the Palestinians.'

The words knifed through Helen. Her loyalty to her husband, her sublimation of self in her support for him and for her son, her determination to stand by him in defiance of her own feelings all exploded in her mind. With a cry she rushed at Hamid, her only thought to destroy the man who had betrayed her and destroyed so many other innocent lives. But one of the Delta men stepped forward and held her in one huge arm. She struggled briefly and then collapsed against him, her body racked by sobs.

'But why, Hamid?' she cried.

Bob echoed her. 'Yeah, for God's sake why? You've betrayed your wife, your friends, your family and the country that adopted you. You're nothing but a terrorist, a murderer of innocent women and children. Christ, you even organized the killing of my girlfriend and nearly killed me. And why kill Bakr? Why not let him kill me?'

Hamid stirred and in one savage downward stab stubbed his cigar out on the plate.

'First, Bob, that attack on you was nothing to do with me. There were some among us who did not want to see our plan work and you were a convenient target.' He laughed. 'Anyway, you were far too valuable to me alive. Every question you asked told me how far the investigation had got. Every answer I gave led you in the wrong direction.

'Bakr was a fake from the start. Once I'd set the hare running you all followed it faithfully. You Americans always believe the obvious. Bakr and I both travelled on passports in his name so if you tracked my movements you would think it was him. You saw what you wanted to see and you never thought to look in my direction.'

He glanced at his former comrade.

'Poor George. He never really understood his role either.

It would have been a pity if you had not lived to understand. George would have died anyway. Better that you survived. I am not a total savage, you see. There are still some loyalties.

'But you are standing there thinking how can my good friend Hamid, my old buddy, my Harvard friend have turned out like this. Well, let me take you back to a time you've probably forgotten and an event you almost certainly never heard about: 1982, the Israelis had invaded Lebanon and were laying siege to Beirut. One morning they sent one of their fighters over Beirut to take out an ammunition dump. Instead they hit an air-raid shelter and killed thirty innocent civilians, men, women and children. That was terrorism.

'In the rubble they found the bodies of my grandmother and grandfather. He was a doctor in one of the camps. He had done nothing but protect the innocent and heal the infirm and they killed him. That was terrorism. From that day I decided to fight the war my way, using my skills and my brain. I was patient and I planned it all carefully to exploit the greed and weaknesses of the capitalist economies. It was a brilliant plan and it worked.'

He turned towards Duncan.

'And now I suppose my new American friends will want to take me away.'

'You got it, buddy,' said Duncan, turning towards one of his men to order him forward to handcuff Hamid.

'I'm afraid, Colonel, you don't quite understand the situation. I will be a hero to my people for getting them the homeland they have struggled for for so long. But if you take me in I will be just another person in your jails. On the other hand, if I die here, I will be a martyr, perhaps the biggest martyr the Palestinians have ever had.'

As he was speaking two things happened in quick succession. Abdullah had understood little of the conversation. But with a child's instincts he knew that something was terribly wrong, that the room was full of fear and hatred. He understood that these dark, frightening men were a threat to his father and perhaps to him. He broke away from Helen and ran to Hamid, wanting, perhaps, to help him as he had been helped so often in the past.

Abdullah moved across the room. As Hamid finished

speaking, he reached below the table to his ankle. There his hand found his second weapon, the tiny SIG-Sauer P230 automatic pistol in its leather ankle holster. As he drew the gun and his hand moved to pull it above the table, he caught sight of Abdullah running towards him. A half-thought shout, a hesitation and there was a soft double click as the Heckler and Koch of the guard at the door fired twice.

The first round missed and, as the second round left the barrel, Abdullah stepped directly into the line of fire. The bullet entered Abdullah's back just below the right rib line and exited out of the front of his stomach in a spray of blood. The child was picked up by the bullet and propelled past Hamid to slam face first into the wall at the back of the room. His small body crumpled to the floor without a sound.

A terrible cry of anguish burst from Helen and, with the strength born of a mother's terror for her child, she wrenched herself free of the Delta soldier's restraining arms and ran the few steps to collapse by the pitiful little bundle that had once been her life's hope. Unthinking of the blood and the broken body, Helen raised Abdullah's head to cradle him in her lap, a low, keening sound coming from her lips.

Distracted by the sight of his son, Hamid missed his opportunity and felt a crushing weight on his arm and the agony as the tendons tore. Then his elbow joint popped as the second Delta guard wrenched his arm up and back. The pain was so great that Hamid simply dropped the weapon. With a muttered 'Thanks a lot' the soldier returned to his position by the door.

Duncan was speaking urgently into his microphone and in seconds a soldier burst through the door, medical kit in hand. He squatted by Abdullah and Helen. A cursory examination of the wound with one hand while the other felt with sensitive fingers for a pulse in the neck allowed the soldier to make a preliminary assessment.

'His pulse is still strong and the bullet seems to have passed through without hitting the kidney or the lung. We need to get him out of here right now.'

Duncan took charge. 'OK guys, you heard the man. Down to the beach and let's get out of here. That means you too, Gearheart,' he added, pushing Bob towards the door.

Bob watched Hamid as he rose to his feet, that annoying little smile of triumph still hovering round his mouth.

'There's nothing for you now, Hamid. You've been caught and you'll tell us all we want to know about your operation.'

Bob could not keep the note of satisfaction out of his voice. The thought that Hamid would be humiliated as he had been by his friend produced a small knot of gratification in his stomach.

'No, Bob, I'm afraid it won't work like that. Your people will ask me some questions. I'll refuse to answer them and by the time they manage to persuade me – if they do – the Israelis will have given away everything we want.'

Duncan came up behind Hamid. 'That's where you're wrong, my friend. This time we don't piss around. You kill women and children and you expect us to play by some kind of game with civilized rules? Well, I'm afraid the President changed the rules for this one. My orders are to get the information we want out of you by the time we get back to Sigonella and I'm going to do just that. How I do it is up to me.'

Bob was disgusted to realize that the prospect of Hamid suffering did not revolt him as it would have done ten minutes earlier. Instead, he was silently cheering the American officer on, glad that justice would be done.

They hurried in a tight group out of the house, across the patio where only that afternoon Bob and Helen had spent such a quiet time, then down the steps and on to the beach where four helicopters squatted like huge and pregnant dragonflies, rotors gently turning.

As he stepped on to the sand Bob saw off to his left an arc of light streak across the sky followed by the blossoming of a red firestorm on the ground.

'That will be our guardians taking care of us,' he heard Duncan say in his ear. 'Those are Spectre gunships keeping the Tunisians off our backs while we head home.'

In fifty yards they had reached the first of the helicopters. At Duncan's urging Helen and Bob followed the medic abroad with Abdullah. As son as they were inside, the door slid shut and the aircraft lifted vertically and then leaned sharply to the right and turned away over the sea. Bob joined Helen on the floor by Abdullah as the medics began the task of fixing the drips and feeding the blood back into his shattered body.

Bob's hand moved around Helen's waist and she leaned her head back against his shoulder. It was a gentle gesture of comfort to them both in their shared moment of despair.

Behind them Hamid was lifted into the second helicopter and pushed down into one of the canvas seats lining the cabin wall. He was strapped in and even as the aircraft lifted off, he saw one of the men filling a syringe by his side.

He began to struggle but was held fast in his seat. 'What are you doing? You can't touch me. Leave me alone.' Each entreaty sounded more desperate in his ears and he realized that courage is hard to find when all hope is lost. Even his triumph that had sustained him earlier had faded now that he was faced with the bleak reality of his future. He looked desperately around the cabin and saw nothing but implacable purpose.

'This needle contains a little concoction made up by the interrogation experts,' explained Duncan. 'You've probably heard of sodium pentothal. Well that was nineteenth century and this is twenty-first. You won't feel much and you won't be able to resist answering our questions.

'We only have one question for you right now and that is the location of Inge Becker. If we find her we stop these attacks and that's what I'm here for.'

Hamid laughed sarcastically. 'But you're too late. The conference starts tomorrow and you can do nothing to stop it.'

'Maybe you're right. I'm no politician and maybe if they all sit down together they will talk instead of shooting each other. But my job is to stop terrorists like you and your friend Becker. I leave the bullshit to the politicians.'

Fear made Hamid strain against his bonds to move his body the few inches possible away from the advancing needle. He felt his sleeve being rolled up and watched with morbid fascination as the needle slipped beneath his skin and the liquid began to squirt into his veins. Curious, he thought, how it had all started with a needle. But he would tell them nothing, nothing. Even as the reassuring thought passed through his brain, he knew with certainty that this, too, was another lie and the betrayals were not yet over.